THE KING JAMES MEN

SAMANTHA GROSSER

SAM GROSSER
BOOKS

D147O488

THE KING JAMES MEN

Copyright © 2010 Samantha Grosser
All rights reserved.
First published in 2018, Sydney, Australia

ISBN: 978-0-6483052-2-4

Samantha Grosser asserts the right to be identified as the author of this Work. No part of this publication may be reproduced, copied, scanned, stored in a retrieval system, recorded, or transmitted, in any form or by any means, without the prior written permission of the author.

Cover design by Luke Harris at Working Type Studio

Translation it is that openeth the window, to let in the light; that breaketh the shell, that we may eat the kernel; that putteth aside the curtain, that we may look into the most Holy place; that removeth the cover of the well, that we may come by the water.

From the Translators' Preface to the Reader
King James Bible, 1611

NOTE ON QUOTATIONS FROM THE BIBLE

The quotations in the chapter headings are taken from the
1611 King James Version.

Unless otherwise stated, quotations within the text are from the
Geneva Bible, which was the most-used translation of the time.

A list of quotations may be found at the back of the book.

CHAPTER 1

OCTOBER 1604

*A*nd *then shall many be offended, and shall betray one another, and shall hate one another.*
(*Matthew 24:10*)

BISHOP BANCROFT SAID, 'And so our great task is nearly at hand.'

'Indeed, My Lord.' The Reverend Richard Clarke was outwardly composed, sitting quietly and observing the Bishop as he stood behind the great oak desk in the presence chamber, legs planted solidly onto the oriental rug, shoulders back in the belligerent stance of the short-statured man. They had met once before, Richard recalled, many years ago, barely exchanging a word at a dinner at Cambridge. But he doubted Bancroft would remember: he had been beneath the great man's notice then, a humble fellow with nothing to offer in the other man's sure and zealous journey up the episcopal mountain path. Any day now, it was common knowledge, Bancroft would be formally elected Archbishop of Canterbury, head of the English Church, second only to the king.

The Bishop leaned across and poured wine for his guest. Richard nodded his thanks. He was unused to rubbing shoulders with such power and Bancroft was a man who tended to inspire humility: there was a hardness in the lined sad face, a ruthlessness known well to Puritans and Papists alike. In Elizabeth's reign there had been many who met their end because of Bancroft. Richard sipped his wine from the fine Italian glass. It was sweet and cool and he wished the Bishop would sit. Instead Bancroft smiled. 'You have the living at Minster-in-Thanet, do you not?'

'Yes, My Lord.'

'It is a poor living, I believe?'

'My needs are modest,' he replied. 'I want for nothing.'

Bancroft nodded, apparently pleased with his answer. 'But still, you must expect to be recompensed for your labours on the Bible Translation. You will find life in Westminster somewhat more expensive than you are used to in Kent.'

Richard said nothing, uncertain what was coming. The Bishop settled himself finally behind the desk and made a steeple of his fingers, eyes narrowed above them, apparently considering. Richard gently twisted the stem of the glass between his fingers and waited.

'There is a post at Canterbury, Doctor Clarke, that would do you very well. Nothing too onerous, it would take little of your time from the Translation.' The Bishop paused, enjoying his guest's unease. 'One of the six preachers. We are currently five and in need of a sixth. The post is yours, Doctor Clarke, if you would care to accept it.'

Richard was silent. He had almost given up hope of any preferment, accepting it as punishment for mistaken loyalties in the past. But now he had a place in the Westminster Company of the king's translators and a post at Canterbury. He was drinking wine at the Archbishop's palace at Lambeth, where Bancroft was already

Primate in everything but name. Perhaps his years in the wilderness were over. Perhaps he had been forgiven at last. A small flame of hope lit inside him.

'Doctor Clarke?' Bancroft prompted.

He brought his mind back to focus on the Bishop. 'I am honoured, My Lord. Truly.'

'Then the post is yours. It is small reward for the work you are about to undertake, but ...' He opened out his hands in a gesture of conciliation.

'I am well pleased with it, My Lord. It is far more than I expected.'

Bancroft nodded and there was a moment of silent goodwill. The unease had left him, replaced by a sense of hope of better things to come. He smiled at the Bishop but received no smile in return.

'Where do you intend to lodge while you are here, Doctor Clarke?' Bancroft asked. The Bishop's native Lancashire accent was still pronounced, Richard noticed. His own northern accent he had discarded long ago.

'I've taken a room in a house by the river,' he replied. A draughty chamber, and damp, with mice that kept him awake at night.

'I see.' Bancroft sighed. 'You used to have friends in Westminster, did you not? The Kemp family?'

He looked up sharply. A wariness prickled over his skin, all pleasure in the meeting draining at the mention of a name he had kept at a distance these last seven years, a name that still roused a multitude of emotions.

He said, 'It has been many years since I last saw the Kemps, My Lord.'

The Bishop observed him, feelings well hidden behind the

weather-beaten face, and Richard could make no guess at the thoughts behind it.

'The older Master Kemp still keeps a house here, I believe,' Bancroft said.

'I'm afraid I wouldn't know,' he replied. 'As I said, it has been many years.' In his mind he saw the image of it, well known and familiar. Time was when it had almost been a second home.

'The house is still there. And the family.'

Richard swallowed, aware of a threat in the sumptuous room. A weak morning light filtered through the stained-glass windows, the figures of St Jerome and St Gregory casting coloured shards across the floor. He set his expression with care to hide his disquiet, and his eyes came to rest on a mediaeval tapestry on the wall at Bancroft's back. A forest scene, a huntress with a bow, a stag in flight. Exquisite, but pagan. It was a strange choice of hanging for an Archbishop's chamber.

'Are you aware,' the Bishop was saying, 'of Ben Kemp's whereabouts these days?' There was an edge in the question that ushered in a coldness despite the heat from the fire. Richard suppressed a shiver and closed his thoughts against the memories that threatened.

'Last I heard, My Lord,' he said carefully, 'Kemp was working for his father trading in the East, in Aleppo ... silk mostly. I believe they are part of a company that has business in the Levant – a grant from the old queen or some such.'

'Yes. The Levant Company. His father sent him away out of trouble for a while.' The Bishop leaned forward in his chair, hands resting on the carved edges of the armrests as though he were readying himself to spring. 'Tell me about your friendship with Kemp, Doctor Clarke. Tell me what you know of him.'

Richard moistened his lip with the tip of his tongue and let his eyes drift towards the fire. It was burning low and smouldering and the room felt warm. He did not know how to answer.

'We were friends at Cambridge,' he offered. 'We shared a room.' It had been a cold room, he recalled, that never saw the sun nor a fire, and Ben's young body had been hard and warm next to his in the narrow bed they had shared. He kept his eyes on the fire.

'What of his beliefs?'

He stared down into his wine. There was only a mouthful left and he wished there was more. He drank it, framing his answer in the pause.

'His beliefs were ... Puritan, My Lord.'

'Tell me.'

Tension spiralled into fear. What were the Bishop's intentions? Why was he asking? Why now? He had had three years of Ben in irons at the Fleet to ask such things. Silently he prayed. *The Lord is my strength and my shield. Mine heart trusted in Him and was helped.* The familiar words soothed him. He remembered the new post at Canterbury, the Translation. He had nothing to fear, he told himself, but still his mouth was dry.

'He believed that wearing a surplice has no basis in Scripture,' he said, though that had been the least of Ben's complaints against the Church. 'He questioned whether we should kneel at prayer. There are many in the Church who believe such things.'

'Yes,' Bancroft hissed. 'Puritans. I am aware of it. But that is not all he believed, is it?'

'No,' Richard agreed. 'That is not all.'

'I'll tell you what he believed since you seem so reluctant to do so. He believed in a Church without bishops, without priests, without ritual. He believed in a Church with no king at its head.'

Richard was silent, watching, still unsure where all of this was leading.

'Did you share those beliefs, Doctor Clarke?' the Bishop demanded. 'You were his friend.'

'No, My Lord. Never. I was his friend, but I never shared his beliefs.' It was the truth. They had argued over it constantly, hours and hours quoting Scripture at each other, going in circles, never changing.

'Yet you visited him in gaol. Why?'

He thought, because someone had to tell him that his wife and child were dead. Because, for all my many weaknesses, I was his friend. He said, 'I hoped to bring him back into the Church. I hoped to persuade him to recant.'

'I visited him also you know, and with the same purpose. Many times. It appears that both of us failed.'

'I don't understand, My Lord.'

'Kemp has been back in England for several weeks. It seems the change in monarch brought out both Papists and Puritans, hoping for change. You did not know?' Bancroft seemed surprised.

'I did not know,' Richard confirmed, eyes still lowered to the empty glass he was twirling in his fingers. He was aware of Bancroft's scrutiny, the sharp shrewd eyes appraising before finally the Bishop smiled and sat back in his chair. But his hands still gripped the ends of the armrests, knucklebones showing white through the reddened skin.

'I am not convinced your friend's views have changed in his years away. A man like that doesn't alter his beliefs.'

'I would not know, My Lord,' he answered, though he guessed the Bishop was right. It was hard to imagine Ben might ever change.

There was a pause and in the heartbeat before Bancroft spoke again, Richard finally understood what was coming. He held his breath.

'I want you to lodge with the Kemps during your work here,'

the Bishop said. 'I want you to keep an eye on Master Benjamin Kemp. And I want you to keep me well informed.'

'But ...'

'His family will know what he is doing. His family will know where he is, who he consorts with, what views he holds. I am sure of it.' The Bishop paused a moment to let his words have their effect. 'I want to know where he is. I want to know what he is doing. And I want to know where he worships and who he worships with.'

Dread seeped through his blood, weight in his gut. He had not thought to cross Ben Kemp's path again, nor to rekindle the conflict that Ben trailed in his wake.

'You are asking me to spy, My Lord?' His voice was scarcely more than a whisper but it made no difference; the Bishop's ears were keen.

'The king is anxious for unity,' Bancroft said. 'Only the true Church can give us that. The Church to which you belong, Doctor Clarke. The Church in which you are ordained. And we will have one Church, one doctrine, one creed. These Separatists would rip the very fabric that binds Church and state together.' He paused to draw breath. He was preaching now and all Richard could do was listen. 'Shall every man worship according to his humour? Shall any man in the street be permitted to preach? That is what your friend Ben Kemp would have. And we cannot allow it. There must be order in the Church. These illegal congregations who refuse to kneel, who would deny the king his position under God, they are traitors. They would have a king with no power to rule and a Church that is divided, leaderless, a people with no guidance to bring them to God.' He lowered his gaze to light on Richard. 'Is that what you want, Doctor Clarke?'

'No, of course not.'

'Then what is your hesitation?'

He said nothing. There was no point. Bancroft would never understand the pain Ben Kemp had inflicted, the wounds he still carried. Fury threatened, prickling under his skin: fury with Ben for returning, fury at what he was being asked to do. He placed the wine glass on the desk.

'You think such work is beneath you?' The Bishop inclined his head, apparently re-evaluating the worth of the man before him.

'No. Not at all. It is just ...'

'Yes?'

He could not think how to begin to explain. He said, 'I would be a guest in their home ...'

'And it offends your sense of honour?'

'A little.'

'And your sense of honour is more important than your loyalty to the king? To the Church?'

'No, My Lord.' What else could he say?

'Good. Then we are of one accord.' The Bishop rose from the depths of his chair with a surprising lightness and Richard recalled the rumour that Bancroft still wrestled now and then. He suppressed a shudder at the thought of it: Bancroft's grip would be like a fighting dog's jaws. Standing up, he allowed himself to be shown to the door, which the Bishop held for him with a gracious smile. It seemed he was in favour again, an obedient servant.

'Of course,' Bancroft said in the doorway, 'it goes without saying that this goes no further than this room.'

'Of course, My Lord. It goes without saying.' He bowed his goodbye and was gone, hurrying away before the older man could press him any further. He wanted to be away, feeling tainted by the atmosphere of a room where he imagined other more violent cruelties had been hatched and demanded, other men more brutally persuaded into acts against their conscience.

In his distraction he mistook the way out, taking a wrong turn from the presence chamber that took him almost to the Lollards' Tower. He paused before it, eyes drawn upward towards the prison at the top, looming five floors above him, and instinctively he shivered. Then, regaining his bearings, he found his way back to the courtyard, relieved to see the long ivy-covered wall that bordered the Thames and the fig tree standing sentinel outside the great hall. The gate leading out stood open beneath the ancient stone archway, red brick towers rising up on either side, another prison contained within their walls. The porter in his lodge bid him a cheerful good day as he passed and he replied with a distracted nod of acknowledgement. Outside the palace, the autumn breeze was still gusting off the river, showering him with the last of the season's leaves from the elms that lined the bank.

At the landing stage, a party of lawyers in dark finery had just arrived, their boat shifting and tossing on the choppy water. As they clambered ashore, one of them slipped and dropped his papers. There was a shout as the wind caught the sheets, scattering them across the steps, and the lawyers raced after them, stooping to catch them as they fell. The boatman watched, laughing. Finally, when they had rescued what documents they could, they brushed themselves down with hurried movements, resumed their dignity, and strode towards the gate.

Richard Clarke watched them go from the shelter of the trees and when they had moved away, he hurried down the steps and hailed the boatman who had brought them. The wherry rocked under his feet as he stepped into it and he sat down heavily – he had never felt safe on the river. Only once they were mid-stream on the way back to Westminster did it occur to him to think that it was not only for his skill in Hebrew that he was chosen for the task of the Translation.

CHAPTER 2

F *or it was not an enemie that reproached me, then I could haue borne it, neither was it hee that hated me, that did magnifie himselfe against me, then I would haue hid my selfe from him.*

But it was thou, a man, mine equal, my guide, and mine acquaintance.

Wee took sweet counsell together, and walked vnto the house of God in companie.

(Psalms 55:12–14)

THE RIDE SOUTH was hard in the autumn rain, the roads flooded and thick with mud, almost impassable in places. Twice the horse slipped under him, unable to keep her footing in the quagmire, and both times Ben Kemp found himself face down in the mud, blood running down his cheek unnoticed amid the rain and the dirt. His clothes clung to him wetly, the linen soft and cold against his back, wool breeches chafing on his thighs.

He thought of the warm hearth back at the manor house in Scrooby and wondered what had possessed him to agree to go. The mare struggled to her feet, a reproachful look in her eyes, head low. She was enjoying the ride no more than he was. The thought made him smile. 'Come on, Bessie girl,' he soothed, rubbing her ears. She bumped her head against him. 'Let's get it over with.'

His father's summons had come just a few days since, unwelcome and unexpected: Ben had thought his father preferred to keep him at a distance, safely far away. He had been half tempted to ignore it, unwilling to leave Scrooby even for a short time, but he knew his father would only write again. And again. His father was nothing if not tenacious. So he had asked for advice from the others, the small community of righteous men whose life he had shared since his return from the East. It was a simple life, but godly, far removed from the iniquities of London, and he had found some contentment at last amongst them.

Though there had been nothing explicit, nothing hostile in the neat and precisely chosen words, his father's letter still threatened this peace. On the surface it seemed no more than an affectionate letter from father to son, requesting he return home for a visit for important matters to discuss. But Ben's instinct was doubtful, the habit of a life often lived in danger, and he had been reluctant to accept. It was William Brewster who persuaded him, as they broke bread together in the hall after morning worship, souls cleansed and aching with the joy of God's love. The new loaf had been warm and fragrant in his fingers, and Ben listened with attention to their leader's counsel as other members of the household took their places at the table. Behind him the kettle hissed and sang in the hearth.

'You are his son and heir,' the older man said, 'so perhaps it is a matter of inheritance, a settling of property. Or perhaps he wishes to consult you on matters that relate to your sister.'

'My father has never consulted me on anything,' Ben answered. Long-held resentments flickered, but he had learned through many years to keep a check on them, forcing them back to the corners of his heart where he kept them, out of sight and tightly fettered. 'He has never considered my opinion worth a fig.'

'Still,' Brewster said, 'he must have his reasons, and he is your father. In all good conscience I think you cannot refuse.'

Ben nodded, and said nothing, resigning himself to the journey. Then he had scrawled a hasty note of acceptance to be sent when the next post rider came through, and made his preparations to leave.

~

IT WAS ALMOST night when he reached London, dark falling early with the rain. Figures hurried through the downpour, cloaks drawn close about them, heads down and faces hidden. But there was no one loitering: traders had shut up shop, and the housewives were keeping dry in the warmth inside. Lanterns swung from their hooks beside each door, flames glittering uneasily against the storm, and the mare skidded and slipped on mud that was rutted and treacherous underfoot.

He turned the corner into Thieving Lane. Three-storey merchants' houses loomed up on either side of the narrow street, red brick and timber leaning out across the road. At his father's house he stopped and cast a glance up across its front, blinking at the rain in his face. Cold water trickled from his hair down his spine and he shivered. The latticed windows winked blankly into the evening, curtains drawn tight behind them, and on the house next door the shop sign groaned as it swung on its rusting hooks. It was the house of his childhood, tall and solid, a fit house for a prosperous merchant, and it had not changed in the intervening years. He sighed, aware of the familiar weight of reluctance in his gut. A memory touched his thoughts, himself as a boy stealing fruit from the young trees in the orchard, and his father's hand against his leg in punishment. The recollection lit no sense of nostalgia: he was still wayward in his parents' eyes, though his father could no longer raise his hand to force obedience. He wished he had not come.

Sliding from the saddle, he closed his eyes, a moment of silent prayer for courage. *Blessed are ye if you suffer for righteousness' sake.* Then he lifted his fist to the door and hammered. Inside a dog barked, the familiar voice of the old greyhound that had once belonged to him. He heard her claws against the wood before a woman's voice ordered the dog away and the door swung open.

A girl he had never seen before stood in the doorway peering out into the rain. She was plain and mousy, and her hesitation annoyed him. He had ridden too far and too long to be kept waiting now on his father's doorstep in the rain. After a moment, she sensed the impatience and stepped hurriedly back to let him in. A tree of candles on a hallstand at the base of the stairs flared and quivered with the draught from the door, throwing ghoulish shadows across the walls. He stepped inside, his cloak dripping onto the polished boards of the entranceway, and looked around him. The loose rushes that had covered the floor in his childhood had been replaced with woven mats, but the same faint fresh herb scent still hung in the air, doing battle with the smell of damp and wet wool and horse that clung to his clothes. All of it was so familiar but he did not feel at home.

'My horse,' he said, and at a word from the girl a boy he had not noticed slipped out past him and into the street. The greyhound nudged at his hand with her nose for his attention, and he rubbed her ears.

The girl said, 'You must be Ben.'

'Yes. And you are?'

'Your cousin Alice.'

'Well, Cousin Alice, I need hot water and dry linen. And quickly.'

She half curtsied and hurried away towards the kitchen, leaving him to drip in his cloak in the cold hallway. Ben watched her go, swung himself out of his cloak and let it fall across the banister, then strode towards the warmth of the main hall that was the heart of the house. It was here that the family gathered, the only room where a fire always burned. Low flames glimmered now in the hearth, and more candles flickered in their clusters on the cupboard, casting shifting shadows across the Turkey rugs that covered the floor. It was cheerful and welcoming, but he far preferred the simple austerity of the manor house in Scrooby.

RICHARD REMAINED by the fireside as the others got up to greet the traveller. He had no wish to intrude on a family reunion, he told himself, but in truth it was more that he was dreading the meeting, fearful his old friend would see straight through him and discern his purpose. His heartbeat quickened as the door swung back abruptly, juddering with the force, and Ben Kemp paced into the room with his eyes on the fire. Squatting at the hearth, his friend snatched up the poker, stirring life and more warmth back into the dwindling flames. Then he caught sight of Richard from the edge of his eye and hastened to his feet. The two men faced each other across the fireplace, and Richard saw the doubt in the other man's face.

'It's good to see you again, Ben. You've barely changed,' he said. It was the truth. The lean face with its angled cheekbones had weathered a little from the Eastern sun, and more flashes of grey flecked the dark mop of hair and short-cut beard, but the eyes held the same bright passion and he still moved with the quick, spare movements of a cat.

There was a moment's hesitation before Ben replied. 'It's good to be home,' he said. Then he turned to his sister. 'Do we have warmed wine?'

His sister moved closer, an angry hand gripping her narrow waist. 'Hello, Ellyn,' she said. 'It's lovely to see you. How are you? I'm fine, thank you, Ben. How are you? Well, a bit wet obviously and in the foulest of tempers ...'

Ben laughed, his humour restored in an instant. 'Forgive me, Nell. It was a hard road and I've forgotten my manners.' He stepped towards her and bent to kiss her cheek.

Richard observed them, brother and sister, more than ten years between them but as alike as two berries. Olive skin, near-black hair, dark eyes that so often glittered in temper, the same restlessness. Ben took his arm from her waist and she wiped the rain from her face with impatient fingers.

'How are you, Nell?'

'I am well. It is truly good to have you home.'

He squeezed her hand and cast his eyes around the room, searching for an instant for the other sister, Sarah, the fair one, before he remembered she had gone, taken by the plague in his years away. He slid his eyes towards the fire.

'I miss her too,' Ellyn said.

A servant at the door broke the silence. 'There is hot water now, Master Kemp. It has been taken to your chamber.'

'Good.' He turned to his family. 'Give me a few minutes.' Then he strode out behind the servant, boots slopping on the floor and a trail of drops behind him.

'As you see,' Thomas Kemp said, turning to Richard when the door had closed, 'my son is little changed.'

'Barely at all.' Richard smiled, though he had hoped to find him otherwise. He had prayed many times that time and age and exile would have mellowed him, but he had known Ben's beliefs would never change: they were in the fibres of his soul, inextricable. The family resumed their places at the hearth while they waited for Ben to return, and the rain lashed at the windows in sudden squalls.

'It's a filthy evening,' Richard said, and the others nodded their agreement. The easy conversation of before had been disturbed by Ben's arrival, and they were silent now, waiting. Ellyn sat on the cushions before the hearth with the greyhound's head across her lap, but the dog paid her no heed. Her eyes were on the door, ears lifted, waiting for her master's step on the stair.

'She's a little large for a lapdog,' Richard said, and Ellyn smiled.

'She misses Ben. I'm not much of a substitute I'm afraid.'

'She seems content enough.'

'Perhaps. But one can seem content and still be missing someone absent, don't you think?'

'Of course.' We do it all the time, he thought, putting on a mask to hide our sorrows and our fears, showing the world a brave face. Who can ever know what griefs a man is nursing underneath, what private pain? He thought of his father, dead these fourteen years, and not a day going by he had no thought of him.

Ben rejoined them, dry and warm now as he took the vacant stool at the hearth. The fire had been tended and was burning higher, comforting against the wildness of the night. Ellyn rose and fetched spiced wine for her brother, and the greyhound shifted position to lay her head across her master's knee. Ben smoothed the soft fur and the dog closed her eyes in pleasure.

'What happened to your cheek?' Emma Kemp noticed the cut across her son's face and leaned forward, reaching out her hand to check. 'It's nasty.'

Ben lifted his head away from her touch. 'It's nothing. Don't fuss.'

She lowered her arm. 'You always were such a hard one,' she said softly. 'Even as a small boy, you would never allow anyone to comfort you.' She turned her head to address their guest. 'I used to watch him fighting back the tears even when I knew he must be hurting. But he never came to me for comfort, never let me hold him.'

Ben gave her a smile. 'Forgive me. I'm sure I was a most ungrateful child.'

'A mother just wants to protect her children however old they get.' Her eyes rested on the gash across Ben's cheek but she kept her hands tightly clasped together in her lap. Richard saw the struggle and pitied her.

'Did you used to let your mother comfort you, Richard?' she asked, forcing her gaze away from the damaged face of her son.

'I can't recall,' he said. 'Perhaps. But it's been many years since I saw my mother.'

Too many, he thought, the farm a distant, indistinct memory, his family strangers to him now. He had never once regretted leaving.

'Where is it you're from?' Ellyn asked.

'You wouldn't know of it.' He smiled. 'It's a tiny village in the north.'

'It's almost in Scotland,' Ben said. 'Richard is actually half-Scottish.'

Richard met his friend's eye, a moment of the old understanding between them, and struggled not to laugh.

'Are you really?' Ellyn sat up with sudden animation.

'I am not half-Scottish.'

'He's lying,' Ben persisted. 'He's ashamed.'

'Why would he be ashamed of being half-Scottish when our king is wholly so?'

'I am not half-Scottish.'

Ellyn lifted her chin, unsure who to believe until finally she caught her brother's eye. Scowling, she shifted her body to turn her back on Ben and give her attention to Richard. Ben smiled and returned to fussing over the dog.

'Have you been there, though, to Scotland?'

'No. I left the north for Cambridge when I was still a boy.'

Ellyn was disappointed.

'You would like to go there?'

'I would like to go somewhere,' she answered. 'Ben is lucky to have seen so many places.'

Her brother said, 'You live in the greatest city in the world, little sister, and I would as lief have never left these shores.'

'Tell me again about Aleppo,' she pleaded. 'About the sunlight and the heat and the smells of the food ...'

'Another time, perhaps,' he said, then lifted his eyes towards Richard. 'So, how goes the great Translation?'

'We've barely begun yet. We're still gathering our sources, reading, thinking, debating. It's no light task ahead of us.'

'It is a mighty task indeed,' Ben agreed. 'But I can think of no one better suited for it. How many in your company?'

'We are ten, and led by Lancelot Andrewes.'

He saw his friend tense at the name. Ben had met Andrewes many years ago: they had argued Scripture in a cold cell at the Fleet.

Ellyn said, 'Why do we need another Bible translation? What's wrong with the Geneva?'

There was a pause, all of them looking to Ben for an answer, but he said nothing, his gaze steadfast on the eyes of the greyhound, his fingers working the soft fur of her neck. Richard stepped into the silence.

'There's nothing wrong with the Geneva. For its time it was the best of the translations. But it pleases the king to have a new one made in his name, and scholarship improves all the time.'

'And of course,' Ben added, without lifting his gaze, 'there's the small matter of the marginal notes.'

'Yes.' Thomas Kemp joined the conversation for the first time. 'Of course the marginal notes in the Geneva are not to the king's liking. He finds them partial and untrue, traitorous even.'

'So he will have a Bible written in a way that pleases him better.' The bitterness in Ben's voice was unmistakable.

'The Translation will be true,' Richard said quickly, 'only there will be no notes.'

'But we need notes,' Ellyn said. 'How else can we understand?'

'Exactly,' Ben agreed. 'You will need to have the Scripture explained for you in church by some kind of cleric who will inter-pret it according to the king's bidding.' He lifted his eyes towards Richard with ill-disguised contempt. 'Heaven help us, must we even have our Bible written by the king now? Is it not enough he places himself at the head of the Church?'

'The new translation will be pure, I promise you.' Richard's own temper was rising, his professional pride at stake. How dare Ben make such assumptions? He sat up straighter in his chair, muscles tensing.

'Pure?' Ben scoffed. 'With Bancroft at the helm? I think not.'

'That is enough!' Ben's mother stood up abruptly, skirts rustling, and placed herself between them. Ben kept his eyes averted, staring down at the dog.

'Richard is our guest,' she said, 'and he has ever been a good friend to you, to us all. Now he works in good conscience to open more light upon the Scriptures. If it pleases the king to have no notes, then it is hardly Richard's fault. I will not have you insult our guest. Now apologise.'

Beyond her skirts Richard could see the working of Ben's jaw, anger held in check by sheer force of will. He was sorry for the argument but unsurprised. They had only ever argued, their friendship forged through debate: only their love of God bound them together, brothers in the way of Christ.

'I am not a child,' Ben breathed.

'Then do not behave like one,' she retorted, still standing over them, her hands twisting together in anxious movements. Richard wondered when she had changed to become so nervous. It was not how he remembered her. Thomas Kemp sat back in his chair, hands folded across his stomach, watching.

'I'm sorry, Mother,' Ben said softly. Then he turned his head towards Richard. Emma Kemp stepped away. 'Forgive me, Richard. My anger is not with you, as I hope you know.'

'I know,' Richard replied, accepting the apology, but in the warm room a chill settled over him. Any last hopes he had cherished for Ben had died with the argument. Seven years in the East had wrought no change in Ben's beliefs. He would never now recant – Bancroft had been right.

In the silence Ben moved forward to the fire and threw on more wood, poking at the embers so that the old logs fell through, throwing sparks into the room. Richard watched them scatter and fade as his friend stepped back to retake his seat. No one spoke, an awkwardness between them all until Ben took it on himself to dispel it. He turned to his sister, forcing a brightness to his speech.

'So, little sister,' he said. 'I hear you have a suitor at last.'

'I've had a good many suitors, thank you very much. You make it sound as though no one's ever shown an interest before.'

'But this one, our father wrote me, might actually come to something.'

'Our father's opinion is premature. We have not met.'

Ben smiled. 'Be careful, Nell, lest you become an old maid.'

'I would rather be an old maid than an unhappy wife.'

'You cannot put off marriage for ever.'

'You married for love. Or have you forgotten?'

The good humour slipped from Ben's face, and when he spoke his voice barely rose above the crack and roar of the fire. 'I haven't forgotten.'

Thomas Kemp said, 'His name is Hugh Merton. He is a spice merchant and his father keeps a house just a few streets away.'

Ben nodded, managed a smile. 'So you will be able to come and go here as you like,' he said, chucking his sister's chin with a none-too-gentle finger. She snatched her head away from his touch, just as Ben had jerked away from his mother. They were too alike, Richard thought, and watching them was painful.

'He seems a likeable fellow,' Thomas Kemp went on. 'I've known his father many years. They are a good sort of family, and I believe he will make a good husband for Ellyn.'

'He sounds like a good match, Nell. I may yet have nephews and nieces to spoil.'

Another silence fell, the other sister's children come and gone in the years of Ben's absence so that he did not feel their loss as keenly as the others. Every so often a spatter of rain fell through the chimney, causing the fire to hiss, and, outside, the Abbey bell rang the lateness of the hour. Its chime just reached them above the pounding of the rain against the road.

CHAPTER 3

OCTOBER 1604

A friend *loueth at all times, and a brother is borne for aduersitie.*
(Proverbs 17:17)

BEN WAS ALREADY at breakfast in the dining room when Ellyn came down the next day. He had been up since before the dawn, using the quiet of the early hours to pray undisturbed by the chatter of the house. His morning prayers had been for patience to get him through these days in London away from the true congregation, the people who knew his heart, and where he had no need to pretend. The worship had brought him joy and he was peaceful now in the silent dining chamber, his soul at one with Christ, the words of prayer still fresh in his thoughts. Remembering Brewster's counsel, he resolved to use soft words.

The old greyhound lay at his feet, gazing up at him with dark adoring eyes. Reaching down to touch her head, he toyed with the idea of taking her back to the Midlands. She would like it there, freedom to roam, rabbits to chase. But she was too old now for the journey, her muzzle turning grey and stiffness in her joints. She had been just a pup when she came to him, a first gift from his wife right at the beginning, when love was still just a possibility between them.

Ellyn took a seat across from him at the table, her back to the window, and he watched as she picked at her bread, lifting crumbs and morsels of ham to her lips but barely eating a mouthful. She had changed little since the days of her childhood, and he waited awhile, knowing she had something she wanted to say. Eventually, though, his patience wore out. 'What?' he demanded.

'Is that how they converse in the Midlands?' she flung back. 'In one-word sentences? You must have your work cut out as a tutor.'

He almost smiled. He had forgotten her acid tongue. He asked again. 'Was there something you wanted to say to me?'

'I was wondering how long you are going to be with us. Now I'm not so sure I care.'

'Why do you want to know?'

She sighed. 'Because you are my brother and though it pains me to admit it, I have missed your company these many years.'

He gave her a wry look. 'I pity the man that marries you,' he said.

The archness left her eyes, all the humour snuffed out in an instant. She sat back, sullen, her head turned away.

'I'm sorry, Nell. I was teasing. I had forgotten.' About the marriage negotiations, he meant, the deal that was almost done.

She shrugged and pushed her food away from her. She had eaten none of it. 'It's not your fault,' she said. 'And I suppose it had to happen sooner or later. I can't put it off for ever, however much I would like to.'

'It's God's will that we marry,' he said gently. 'What future is there otherwise?'

'But you married for love.'

'I did. And if I had not, she might still be alive.' He stabbed at a final hunk of cheese with the point of his knife and it crumbled with the force. He picked up a piece, lifted it halfway to his mouth before he lost interest and let it drop back to the trencher.

'You still miss her, even after all these years?'

He nodded, though the word *miss* barely began to describe the ache he still felt when he thought of her, his Cecily. He still saw her sometimes, in the face of another woman in the street, a certain way of movement, a look. Or he saw her in the corner of his vision when the light was dim, how she was the day he saw her last, the day she had begged him not to go, when she was big with child and pleading. He had relived that moment many times. He should have listened, should have trusted her instinct.

'You should marry again,' Ellyn was saying. 'You're still not bad-looking. I'm sure there must be some poor girl that would have you.'

'Have you anyone in mind?' He remembered the girl Alice from last night and how she had watched him, and wondered if his sister was plotting. But she shrugged.

'A man should have a wife and children. Or else who will carry on the name of Kemp?'

She was right of course. He was a disappointment to his father on more than one account. 'Perhaps I will,' he lied. 'And surprise you all.'

The door swung open with a creak and Alice appeared, sleep still around her eyes. She was very plain, with her large-boned features and short-sightedness, and as the thought went through his mind, she saw him, stopped abruptly and looked away, confused.

'Alice?' Ellyn said. 'Did you want something?'

The girl remained just inside the door, undecided.

'Come,' Ben said kindly. 'Have some breakfast.'

'I was looking for Doctor Clarke,' she replied then. 'Have you seen him?'

'I don't think he's down from his chamber yet,' Ellyn said.

'Thank you.' The girl turned and her skirts swished out around her as she fled the room.

'Well' – Ellyn smiled – 'I think Alice would have you if you asked her.'

He shook his head. 'Where did she come from?'

'She's some kind of cousin.'

'And what kind of cousin would that be?'

His sister shrugged. The complexities of family relationships held no interest for her. 'A stepchild of Aunt Grace I think.'

'Aunt Grace has married again? How many times is that?'

'This one is number four, and he has made a fortune in spices.'

Aunt Grace, their father's older sister, as successful in the acquisition of wealth as her brother, her trade the only one that was open to her: her hand in marriage.

'What does she do to them?'

'It's probably better not to ask.'

He smiled. 'So ... tell me about Alice.'

She considered for a moment. 'Aunt Grace's new husband's daughter wanted out of the way. Father said she could come here. He thought she would be good company for me after Sarah ... died.'

Ben nodded. It was the first direct mention of their sister, the sweet one among them, the peacemaker. 'And is she? Good company I mean.'

'Mostly, though she doesn't say a lot.' She thought for a moment. 'She hasn't become the sister I'd hoped, but perhaps she will in time. Perhaps she is still missing her family. I don't know.' She shrugged. Then she said, 'And it would seem she's scared half to death of you.'

'Why would she be scared of me?' He was surprised.

Ellyn laughed. 'Remember how you were last night? Drenched and muddy from the road, blood on your face like some mad spirit from the storm?'

He recalled. 'I was not in the best of tempers. It was a hard ride.'

'And of course if she likes you and she's shy, then that would make her afraid of you too.'

He turned to look at the door where she had stood as if to recollect her better.

'So be kind to her, big brother, please?'

He swung back to face her, temper roused by the insinuation he would be anything else. What was it about his sister that brought him so quickly to anger?

'What do you take me for?'

'I just want you to be kind to her.'

He said nothing and stabbed at his cheese again, more carefully this time, lifting a piece to his lips on the point of the knife. Ellyn broke her bread and began to eat. The door creaked again and Richard appeared.

'Whatever is wrong with Alice?' he enquired. 'She looks as though she'd seen a ghost.'

'Ben frightened her.'

Richard laughed. 'You aren't still scaring women, are you, Ben? I would have thought you'd grown out of that by now.'

Ellyn shot him a look of contempt she more usually reserved for her brother. Ben lifted his eyebrows at Richard, who looked bewildered.

'Men!' Ellyn spat, getting up from the table, smoothing her skirts. 'The world would be a better place without them.'

'You love us really,' Ben chided, but the look she gave him over her shoulder as she strode from the room said otherwise.

Richard watched her go, dismayed. 'What did I say?'

'She thinks me unkind and your comment confirmed her belief.'

'I am sorry, Ben. I didn't realise. It was something of nothing, just something to say.'

'You have no need to worry. Worry when she and I stop fighting. Then you will know something is truly wrong.'

Richard took the seat at the table that Ellyn had left, broke his bread and began to eat, small mouthfuls of mutton and cheese, washed down with ale. They sat in silence. The ease of the old friendship had left them, too many years gone by. Ben put down his knife and sat back to watch the other man eating, observing the new lines on the pale baby face, the jowls growing heavier and grey flecks in the thinning hair, but the same blue eyes with their air of innocence. He could think of nothing to say, and it made him sad.

At Cambridge they had loved each other, sharing a friendship that buffered them against the cold severity of university life. They had been little more than boys at first, striving to find their way in a world that was harsh and strange. He could still remember his relief when he realised that the boy who would share his room and his bed and his life was a boy who was, above everything, kind, even when he did not deserve such kindness. For Ben had been adrift when he arrived at Cambridge, searching for something he could not have named, and the fire of his unchannelled desires often led him into trouble. It was Richard, with his kindness and his steadfast faith and a love that never wavered, that had won his soul for God. No man could do more for another. But in spite of all they'd been to each other once, they were as strangers now, and the realisation grieved him: such a friend had surely been a gift from God.

Richard sensed the scrutiny and looked up. He said, too

quickly, 'I am grateful to your father for having me here. It has been most helpful.'

'My father is a generous man,' Ben replied. 'And he feels beholden to you – all that you did for me ... before, when I was in prison. No father could hope for a better friend for his son. But ...' He stopped, hesitating to broach the doubts that had begun to form, suspicions he was reluctant to consider.

'But?' Richard prompted.

'But,' Ben echoed, 'I am surprised you would choose to come here now, when loving me has cost you so dear in the past.'

Richard gave an equivocal tilt of his head, as if to say it surprised him too. Then he said, 'Many years have passed since we parted.'

'Do you see any change?'

Richard smiled. 'A few more lines. A grey hair or two.'

'That's not what I meant.'

'I know. But what would you have me say?'

Ben nodded, their differences well known and intractable: there was no need to speak of them. He said, 'But I had thought you preferred to keep a distance between us these days.'

'Your father offered,' Richard said. 'I paid him a visit when I first came to Westminster and we talked together as though no time had passed at all. He told me of your work for the Company in Aleppo, and his belief he might have made a merchant of you after all. How could I refuse?'

Ben was silent. Richard had always been loved by his father, an ease of conversation between them that Ben had never enjoyed. And he could understand the appeal of lodging here: a comfortable house and good company, a stone's throw from the Abbey. But Richard knew well the costs of keeping close to a Separatist – he had paid for the friendship many times over. Left out in the cold, his loyalty questioned, his ambitions thwarted in spite of his talent. Now, at last, he was a king's translator, a preacher at Canterbury, the taint apparently lifted at last. So why would he risk it all again?

'Does Bancroft know of your choice of lodging?' he asked.

'I've made no secret of it.'

He said nothing, considering. They had parted on uneasy terms seven years ago, love strained by the chasm that divided them, neither prepared to bend towards the other. But Richard had never given up trying, always hoping he might yet bring Ben round. Did he still imagine he could persuade him to recant? It was hard to say.

He watched Richard for a moment more before he slid back the stool from the table with a harsh grating on the floorboards that made the other man wince. Then he got up and walked away, leaving Richard to finish his breakfast alone.

LATER, outside in the long, narrow garden that stretched behind the house, Ben sought out the weak autumn sun to sit and read. In the aftermath of the rain a pale warmth dappled the grass, the trees stripped bare now and the ground strewn with the unraked leaves. High clouds scudded overhead in a clean blue sky, and the raindrops that still clung to twigs and grass glistened brightly.

He made for the pond, knowing from long ago where to find the warmest spot, but when he got there he found the seat already taken. He swallowed a sigh of irritation, and Alice looked up in alarm as his shadow fell across her page. Remembering his sister's warning, he stepped back a pace: he had no wish to frighten her further.

'It's a lovely spot,' he offered. 'I used to read here often as a boy.'

'I will go,' she answered quickly, closing her book in preparation to leave. 'You have prior claim.'

'No, not at all. You were here first and you're reading your Bible. Don't let me interrupt you. There's room on the bench for us both.'

She gave him a small smile and shifted along, tense and reluctant, and he thought he should have let her go when she offered. He sat down, a person's body width between them, his own Bible unopened in his hand. The silence grew uncomfortable.

He said, 'Who taught you to read?'

'My mother.' She answered eagerly, smiling as she remembered. The thought made her prettier, smoothing out the furrow on her brow.

'You must miss her.'

'Very much. She taught us all to read from the Scriptures, my brothers and I, and the servants' children. It was a godly household. My mother's great-grandfather burned as a Lollard.'

The Lollards had been the first to read an English Bible – translated by their founder, John Wycliffe – and they paid dearly for their beliefs.

'I am sorry to hear that.'

'My mother told me they used to keep pages of Wycliffe's translation hidden in the roof. It must have been terrifying.'

'Yes, it must.' For Cecily too, he thought, when he had his pages of Henry Barrow's writings hidden in the walls, and Barrow about to hang. He should have paid more attention to her fear. He should have understood.

'Ellyn said that you taught her to read,' Alice said.

'I taught both my sisters, but Ellyn was the keen one.'

'I never met Sarah.'

'You would have liked her. She was the kind one among us.'

'Ellyn is kind.'

He smiled. 'All the time?'

She nodded and turned her face away from his look, a self-conscious flush blotching her neck.

'Your loyalty does you credit,' he said, 'but I know my sister well.'

She said nothing, her head still averted. One hand smoothed the battered leather cover of her Bible, over and over. Like his own it was well used, a Geneva, the version the king hated most. Poor girl. She had little choice but to be loyal to Ellyn – who else had she got? At least until her father found her a husband and shipped her off elsewhere. Still, if Aunt Grace was involved it would be a good match: that woman had never done anything except for advantage.

In the silence he opened up his Bible. It fell open at Psalms where the pages had worn thin from constant handling. He ran his eye across the page, the words well known, so long his source of sustenance, and began reading silently.

Judge me, O God, and defend my cause against the unmerciful people: deliver me from the deceitful and wicked man. For Thou art the God of my strength: why hast Thou put me away? Why go I so mourning, when the enemy oppresseth me?

He lifted his eyes from the page, aware of Alice beside him, watching him, her Bible still unopened on her lap. He turned towards her. 'You should read also,' he said. 'You will be glad of it.'

She nodded, her cheeks reddening again, then fumbled with the book, flicking through the pages, unable to find what she wanted, or unable to decide.

Ben held out his hand. 'Here, let me.'

She passed him the Bible with a tentative hand and he took it from her gently. The leather was warm and supple from her touch. He turned the pages, found the place and handed it back to her, his finger marking the passage.

'You might find this helps you.'

She took it from him with an uncertain smile, her finger touching his as she sought to keep the passage marked. Then she held it close before her face, so that she might read the words more clearly.

'Read it,' he encouraged.

'*Let your conversation be without covetousness, and be content with those things that ye have,*' she began in a low voice, hesitating, as if unsure if she were doing right. '*For He hath said, I will not fail thee, neither forsake thee ...*'

She stopped and lowered the Bible to her lap. 'Thank you,' she murmured. But she did not turn again towards him and the blotchy blush across her cheeks remained.

CHAPTER 4

LATE OCTOBER 1604

O bey them that haue the rule over you, and submit your selues: for they watch for your soules, as they that must giue account, that they may doe it with ioy, and not with griefe: for that is vnprofitable for you.
(*Hebrews 13:17*)

RICHARD DINED WITH LANCELOT ANDREWES, the head of the Translator's company, Dean of Westminster, generous, passionate, brilliant. They ate venison and trout in the Dean's rooms at the Abbey and, looking round him, Richard judged that the Church had served the other man well. There was no Puritan plainness here: Turkey rugs covered the floors, soft underfoot, and Flemish tapestries hung along the walls, the Exodus depicted exquisitely in fine coloured wool and silk. He took his place on a chair upholstered in velvet, and the dark oak arms were smooth against his hands.

The Dean himself was expansive, the delicate silk of his robes shimmering as it caught in the light of the candles. He spoke often with his hands, sculpting shapes in the air before him as he talked. Before long, Richard thought, those elegant fingers would bear an episcopal ring. It would suit him. Richard sipped his claret. He was at ease with Andrewes: they shared a love of ancient language, the same Old Testament paths treading in Hebrew through their thoughts. He was glad to be in Andrewes's company for the Translation, and eager to begin.

'I am told that your mastery of Hebrew is second to none, Doctor Clarke,' the Dean said, finishing the trout and wiping his fingers on a napkin. The candles guttered with the movement of the fabric of his sleeves, and the thin face lengthened and darkened with the changing shadow.

'It suffices,' Richard answered. 'One can always improve.'

'In scholarship as in life.'

Richard smiled. 'Of course. But Thomson is also brilliant.'

'Indeed, he is. Regrettably, however, he is a drunk and a lecher and consequently somewhat less reliable than he might be. But he is loyal to the Church and rather entertaining company: I pray for him constantly. You are friends?'

'We know each other from Cambridge, though not well.' He preferred to avoid Thomson's excesses when he could; such debauchery seemed to him somehow less excusable in a man of intelligence than someone of lesser gifts – it angered him to see such a rare gift from God so dishonoured.

'You do not like him?' Andrewes read between the lines.

Richard tilted his head, preferring to give no answer.

'We are all of us sinners, Doctor Clarke. He needs our prayers and not our judgement.'

'I know.' He smiled in acknowledgement of the gentle rebuke.

'Being a good Christian is no easy matter. But God knows the conflict within us and forgives us.'

Richard took another mouthful of the excellent claret.

'You are staying with the Kemp family during your time in Westminster, I believe?' Andrewes said.

He shifted in his chair, straightening, clearing his mind to be wary. He had not expected to talk of Ben Kemp with Andrewes: he had thought such matters lay solely with Bancroft. A puff of resentment billowed inside him that Ben's return to England could taint even this.

'Yes,' he replied. 'It is very convenient. Only a few streets away. Originally, I took a room by the river, but it was damp and unwholesome ...'

Whereas his room at Thieving Lane was warm and quiet and comfortable, he thought, its narrow window overlooking orchards and the Tyburn as it flowed on its way to meet the Thames. Dressing this morning, he had seen a pair of swans, graceful and serene against the current.

'And how are the Kemps?' Andrewes asked. 'I hear that trade is going nicely. Master Kemp has invested in the Levant Company, has he not?'

Richard was impressed. No one could accuse the Dean of not being well informed. 'They are well.'

'And the younger Master Kemp is still working for his father?'

'He has been in the East these last seven years. He is only recently returned.'

Andrewes lifted his glass and sipped at his wine, observing his guest with shrewd deep-set eyes. Richard shifted again under the scrutiny, a vague and ill-defined sense of guilt threading through him.

'I met Ben Kemp, many years ago,' the Dean said. 'Did you know?'

He knew it well: Ben's version of the meeting was still clear in his memory, questions in a prison cell. It was hard to match the image with the gentle man before him, but he had never once known Ben to lie. Instinct kept him silent.

'I thought he looked like a Spaniard.'

'Yes,' Richard agreed. 'His sister too,' steering the topic away. 'Though I don't know where it comes from. The other sister was as fair as day.'

'Indeed?' Then, 'I understand Bishop Bancroft has asked you to keep an eye on the business of the younger Master Kemp.'

Carefully, he set his expression to neutral. 'Yes. That is so.'

'I don't imagine this is easy for you, Doctor Clarke.'

A moment's hesitation before he said, 'We were like brothers once, Mister Dean.' Ben had always been so full of vigour, so full of passion. Even in the days before he turned to God he possessed such an ardour for life, and his fire had been hard to resist. In the cold austerity of their Cambridge college their bond had given him warmth, a human touch that sustained him when it sometimes seemed the love of God was not enough. He turned his mind from the memory.

'And like most brothers, I assume you had your disagreements?'

'We ...'

'Of course you did.' The Dean cut across him, then paused, wiping his fingers and sitting back in his chair so that his face moved out of the candle's reach and his voice came out of the shadow.

'You have been a good friend to Kemp in the past and at no small cost to yourself.'

Tainted by association, his own loyalties questioned, overlooked for preferments: he still wondered at his own persistence, his willingness to pay that cost, the price his love for Ben demanded. But love was the greatest commandment, and he could not have turned his back.

'You must bear him great love,' Andrewes continued. 'Kemp is a fortunate man indeed to have such a friend.'

'It was many years ago.' He doubted he would be so eager now.

Andrewes moved forward once more into the light. 'But you must make a decision now where your loyalty lies. If – and notice I use the word *if* – *if* Ben Kemp still has Separatist sympathies and *if* his sojourn in the East has done nothing to cure the errors in his thinking, then he represents a threat to the unity of the realm. It is really very simple. God's Church in England under the king demands conformity. The Separatists refuse to bend to authority, threatening the hierarchy of tradition and custom that has kept our nation ordered and quiet these many years. Separatism is a path that can only lead to schism and controversy.'

'I only ever sought to save Ben from himself. My loyalty to the Church has never wavered.'

Andrewes observed him for a moment. 'I had hoped as much, though I'm sure you're aware others have thought otherwise. I see very little of the Puritan in you, Doctor Clarke.' He smiled. 'So, no secret sympathy for Separatists?'

'Only pity for their misguidedness.'

'They choose a hard road,' Andrewes agreed. 'And it leads them nowhere. We must continue to pray they will find their way back to the Church's fold.'

Richard nodded. 'I do.' Constantly, he thought. Ben in his error and his grief and his exile was always in his prayers, though scant hope remained he would ever return to the Church.

'But the Church,' the Dean continued, 'and the king are asking something more from you now. It is one thing to offer comfort to a friend in extremity but it is altogether something different to—'

'I understand, Mister Dean,' Richard interrupted. 'And I will do my duty to the Church. I will do what needs to be done.'

But all the same, he thought, he did not want to hear the word.

~

It was late when he left the deanery. There was a new chill in the air, the beginnings of winter, that made him draw his cloak tighter round him and quicken his step. But inside him there was a deeper chill that came from the cold of his decision. He had wondered many times when his faith would be tested as Ben's had been, and now it seemed the time approached.

In his presence, the Dean's thinking was hard to resist: Ben's way of worship was wrong, against the Church, against the king, against God. Like a wayward child, Ben Kemp must be stopped and brought to see the error of his ways, punished for his disobedience. The Separatists would rend the fabric of the English Church – how many souls would be lost without it? All the Dean had said, he agreed with. But now, walking back across Broad Sanctuary beneath a clear sky and the panoply of God's stars, Richard recalled the stench of the cell at the Fleet and the chains that had scarred Ben's wrists, and a small voice inside cried out against bringing his friend again to that. Friendship was a gift from Heaven, sacred and precious. Could it truly be God's will to lift a hand against his fellow?

A memory of Ben at Cambridge cut across his thoughts – the wiry young boy he had met on his first day there, the two of them thrown together as bedmates in the tiny cell of their room, neither knowing what to make of the other, both suspicious and eager and wary. Farm boy and rich city merchant's son: it was an odd combination. But for all Ben's knowing London ways and the easily accepted privilege of wealth, he had never once looked down on Richard's poverty or social awkwardness, nor the naiveté of his country boyhood. He had accepted him as fellow without question, respected his intellect, and threatened violence to those other boys who showed less courtesy. It was a union

Richard had never known could exist between two people – there had been no pretence between them, no artifice borne of fear of the other man's rejection. They had been truly themselves with each other, and it was the only time in his life he had not felt as though everything that mattered were taking place on the other side of a window he could only look through. With Ben, all the life that counted was right there between them in the fierceness of the friendship that they shared. Even before Ben found God, when he was wild and still searching, their bond had been true.

He strode hurriedly now to shake off the memory, wary of the Westminster night. The hanging lanterns he passed seemed barely to disturb the moonless dark, and other men hurried on their way through the darkness bearing torches. A pair of prostitutes huddled in a doorway called out to him and he lowered his head, kept walking. At the end of Broad Sanctuary he came to the archway that led to King Street and walked through. Despite the cold, the street was busy – torches bobbed along its length and he could hear men's voices drifting from the taverns, the shrill shriek of a woman's laugh. On the other side of the arch he turned immediately left into Thieving Lane, where the houses closed in on either side of him, looming dark, and the sky narrowed overhead to a thin strip between them. He shivered: he had felt safer in the open space of the Sanctuary. Something in a doorway stirred at his feet. He jumped, startled, and strained to make out the shape for a moment until he saw the form of a beggar, sleeping huddled in the cold. Surely, he thought, there must be a more sheltered spot somewhere, a better place to spend the night. His conscience troubled, he took a coin from his purse and squatted down.

'Here,' he said. 'Take this. Find somewhere warmer to rest yourself.'

There was no reply but a cold and bony hand reached out and

snatched the coin. Richard stood up and backed away, then turned his footsteps towards the Kemp house.

There was still light behind the curtains when he arrived; he guessed the men must still be up. Eager for the warmth of the fire, he went straight to the hall, but his arrival stopped the conversation dead. His first thought was to wonder if he had been its subject.

'Richard.' Thomas Kemp recovered his composure in an instant. 'Come join us at the hearth.'

'Thank you.' He smiled and looked to Ben to greet him, but the other man simply turned his head away. Richard took the cup of wine the older Kemp offered him and drew a stool in closer to the fire.

'The nights grow cold,' he said, clasping the cup in his palms. There was still just enough heat in the wine to warm his hands.

Ben got up abruptly and squatted to tend the fire, throwing on new wood and forcing more heat from the smouldering embers.

Richard addressed Thomas Kemp. 'How was the day?'

Kemp settled back in the high-backed chair and replied with the even-tempered courtesy that was habitual. 'Not bad, thank you, Richard. One of our ships came in from the East today so there is much to be done.'

'Business is good, then?'

'God be praised.'

Ben was still silent, squatting at the hearth, poking at the fire with savage thrusts.

'We were just discussing it,' Kemp continued. 'I'm thinking of sending Ben back to the Levant. It's good to have him there – I sleep easier at nights.'

Richard realised what he had interrupted and took a mouthful of wine. The fire was roaring now, new wood catching with a snap of sparks, and his limbs began to lose their chill. The warm wine and the heat threatened him with drowsiness and he sat up straighter, blinking the sleepiness away. Then he looked across at Ben, who still crouched by the fire.

'When would you sail?' It seemed a gift from God that Ben could leave again so soon, and that he, Richard, might be spared his awful task.

Ben said nothing and Thomas Kemp answered. 'Early in the new year. There's much to prepare.' He paused. 'And of course, I have yet to persuade him to go.' He regarded his guest above Ben's head, and in the changing light of the fire Richard noticed for the first time the lines in the older man's face, tiredness etched into the skin. He wore the mask of equanimity well, but underneath it the cares of his family were wearing him down.

'I see.'

Ben stood up, quick and loose-limbed. Richard had always envied him his physical grace, the ease with which his body moved. Even now, though he was close to forty, his movements still were effortless, and Richard found it hard to tear his gaze away. The other man bent to drop the poker back in its place, then squatted again, this time to fondle the ears of the greyhound that was stretched out across the hearth. He spoke without lifting his eyes from his hands. 'What of my post in the Midlands?' he said. 'What of the children I teach?'

'They can find another tutor. There is time enough.'

'I do not wish to go.' He stood up – the boyish restlessness he had never outgrown. Only at prayer was he still.

'I need you to go. You are my son.'

'I was there seven years. It is enough.'

'You have nothing to keep you here, Benjamin. No wife, no children. There is no reason for you not to go but bloody-mindedness.'

Scowling, Ben leaned his palms against the chimney breast,

kicking at the hearthstones with his boot, staring down into the flames.

'You would be doing me a great service.'

'That is not why you want me to go.'

'Hush, Ben.' The warning in his father's voice was gentle, but still it was enough to swing Ben round to face their guest. There was neither love nor friendship in his glance. Richard looked away.

The older man spoke softly. 'You are my only son. Who will take over the Company if not you?'

'I am no merchant,' Ben replied. 'Three years in Amsterdam, seven in Aleppo. We both know I'm not cut from merchant's cloth.'

'Yet you have done me faithful service and I trust you.'

'I do not want to go.'

'You are afraid of the dangers?'

'I'm not afraid.' The response was quick and hurt and angry.

Richard wondered if it would provoke the change of mind it had aimed for. He had never known Ben to be afraid of anything. He said, 'It's late. I think I'll go to my bed. You've matters to discuss that are not my business to hear.'

Their silence confirmed the thought. He moved to the door, opened it, hesitated, turned back. Ben watched him, waiting.

'For what it's worth, Ben,' he said, 'I think you should do as your father bids you. I think you should return to the East.' It was as much of a warning as he dared to give, a last chance to turn them both to a different path.

Ben lifted his chin, wary, but all he said was 'Goodnight.'

'Goodnight,' his friend replied, and as soon as he had closed the door behind him he heard the argument resume, their voices low and rumbling through the walls as he slowly climbed the narrow stairs to bed.

CHAPTER 5

LATE OCTOBER 1604

*T*hinke *not that I am come to send peace on earth: I came not to send peace, but a sword.*

For I am come to set a man at variance against his father, & the daughter against her mother, and the daughter in law against her mother in law.

And a mans foes shalbe they of his owne household.

He that loueth father or mother more then me, is not worthy of me: and he that loueth sonne or daughter more then me, is not worthy of me.

And he that taketh not his crosse, and followeth after me, is not worthy of me.

(Matthew 10:34–38)

SUNDAY MORNING and the household at Thieving Lane prepared itself for church.

'You will come?' Thomas Kemp addressed his son across the table at breakfast.

Ben kept his eyes on his food, heartbeat rising for the old confrontation. It had always been like this. 'I will not.'

He heard his father's sharp intake of breath, irritation barely suppressed. 'For your mother, Benjamin. It would do you no harm to think of your mother once in a while.'

Breathing deeply, he forced himself to be calm, but his fingers curled and uncurled, over and over, and his jaw was set tight. It was cruel of his father to use his mother against him.

'It is not a true church,' he said.

'It is a true enough church for your family and for your king.'

'It is a false ministry.' He spoke quietly, keeping his temper in check. 'And I cannot take the Host from such a man.'

'Would God have you dishonour your father and mother?'

He said nothing, mouth clamped shut against the words of anger, fists clenched and white-knuckled, containing the resentment. *A soft answer putteth away wrath,* he counselled himself. *But grievous words stir up anger.*

'Then you may take the Lord's Supper back in the Midlands,' his father breathed, 'where you can do what you like with the Host. A bare table, a basket, passing it hand to hand. I don't care how you worship when you are elsewhere. Not any more. But here, in my house, you will honour your father and mother, and you will come to church.'

Ben lifted his hands to his face, wrestling with his conscience. He wanted to please his father, to earn the old man's approval for once, but St Margaret's was anathema to him. How could he worship alongside the sinners that filled the English Church? Their very presence defiled it. It was no gathering of the faithful, but a base set of rituals devoid of spiritual meaning, and governed by men who served the king over God. It was not for such things that Christ gave His life: He had died that we might follow Him, in purity, in poverty, humble, obedient to His Word. Only to His

Word. And only in His Word lay salvation. The English Church was not the church that Christ commanded, sanctified by God with each man a fruitful branch and God's grace freely given, recognising no king, no priest, no prophet, no lord but Christ. To go would be a betrayal of all he believed.

He shook his head. 'I cannot,' he whispered.

'You did it for Cecily.' Ellyn looked up from her ale.

Ben shot her a look of hatred. 'Only for our marriage,' he breathed, and it had hurt him to do it. He had been abject before God, desolate with his own unworthiness, and he had spent countless hours afterwards in prayers of repentance, confessing the sin of his desire, his need to do whatever it took to marry her.

'But still ...' His sister shrugged, meaning to say that if he had done it once he could do it again.

He swallowed. Footsteps and voices sounded beyond the door of the dining chamber, his mother and Alice and Richard hurrying down to breakfast. His father leaned across the table towards him and spoke softly. 'Do it for your mother, Ben. The God of our church would forgive you that.'

He was silent, staring at his uneaten bread, unseeing. It was tempting, a chance to please his parents; he had never sought to bring them pain. But he belonged firstly to God and there could be no compromise. 'I cannot,' he murmured.

His father slammed a hand to the table in frustration and Emma Kemp's laughter in the doorway stopped abruptly. She surveyed the scene for a moment with a nervous frown, hands twisting together in front of her skirts. The motion was becoming habitual.

'Is anything wrong?' she asked, with a determined lightness in her tone.

Ellyn flicked a glance to her brother. 'Ben is feeling unwell,' she said. 'He's going to rest while we're at church.'

He looked up quickly, grateful but surprised. It had always been Sarah who had tried to make peace: Ellyn's temper was as hot as his own. Briefly he met his sister's look, and the glance he received in return clearly said that he owed her.

There was a moment's silence before Emma Kemp chose to believe what was easier to hear. 'Nothing serious I hope, Ben?'

'Just a headache,' he replied, stepping out from his place at the table. 'I slept badly.'

'Then you should rest.' She smiled as he moved towards her and touched her fingers to his arm as he passed.

'I'll be fine,' he said, gently, squeezing her fingers with his own in a rare moment of affection. Then he turned away and left them all behind him.

RICHARD WALKED next to Ellyn as the household moved in slow procession through the Westminster streets. A chill wind was blowing from the north between the houses, and the sky hung low above them, clouds bulging deep slate grey with the promise of more rain. Underfoot the road was rutted and slick with mud, and they picked their way over it with care. He drew his cloak tighter round him, wishing they could walk more swiftly to let the movement warm them. Thieving Lane was quiet, few people in the streets – even the prostitutes and thieves took themselves to church on Sunday – but a lone child scurried past them chasing a reluctant hen.

Ellyn barely came to his shoulder, but she had the same lithe grace as her brother. He stole glances at her as they walked side by side, aware of her for the first time as a woman. He had only ever thought of her as a child before and the sudden realisation sent a flush across his skin. She turned to him and smiled and, confused, he looked away. Then, to cover it he said, 'I'm sorry your brother is unwell.' It was all he could think of to say and even as the words came out he knew it was foolish: Ben had never given in to a headache in his life.

She turned her head towards him again and this time her face wore the same look of contempt he had seen so many times on her brother. 'There's nothing wrong with him. Surely you realise that?'

'I hoped ...' He trailed off. There was no way to explain to her what he had hoped.

'As did we all,' she replied.

He said nothing, wondering how much she knew, if her family had tried to shield her from the truth of her brother's past. She had been little more than a child when Ben was in prison, and she had grown up in his years away. But somehow they had stayed close to each other – of all his family it was Ellyn that Ben had always loved the best.

'The years in the East did nothing to change him,' she said. 'Though I'm not sure why anyone thought they would. But my mother has become delicate since Sarah's death, and so we like to pretend that things are otherwise.'

'I understand,' he answered. 'We shan't talk of it again.'

She smiled in agreement. 'It is better, I think. And safer.'

He said nothing, disturbed by her trust in him. It was not only Ben he had been asked to betray.

Crossing Broad Sanctuary, they came to the parish church of St Margaret's that stood next to the Abbey, familiar to him from the times he had stayed with Ben when they were boys, and then in later years when he had visited Ben in prison. It was a fair building, larger than his parish church in Kent, stone walls shining pale against the darkened sky. The Kemp children had all been baptised within its walls; Ben, under protest, had solemnised his marriage vows here, and the churchyard held the graves of Cecily and her child.

Inside, out of reach of the wind, rows of columns rose up strong and graceful, and great trees of candles flickered warmth in defiance of the winter morning. They took their places, the benches filling quickly, the hubbub good-humoured and expectant. Richard gazed up at the stained-glass image of Christ above the altar. Even with a weak sun behind it the colours glowed deep and luminous, lapis lazuli blue and Tudor rose red, Christ vivid in his Passion.

He let himself sink into the image, the scene of that first Good Friday when all had seemed lost, the horror of Christ's death amid the jeering crowd. Opening his heart, Richard found himself amongst the throng, the Eastern sun hot against his back and head, a cough in his throat to clear the dust. Around him hung the sour stench of unwashed humanity, men calling out in their anger and grief and lust for violence, and over their shouts rang the high ululations of women as they keened and wailed their sorrow. And above it all, the dying body of our Saviour hung from the cross.

The pale skin of His torso glistened with its sheen of sweat, and the mangled flesh of His palms and feet was bloody where the nails had ripped through tendon and bone, the weals vivid where the ropes had worn at his wrists. Blood trickled from the crown of thorns, mingling with the tears that Christ was weeping for the world. Even in the throes of his own violent death, He wept for all mankind. Close to his side the spear tip glinted, and Richard's breath stopped in anticipation of the wound, Christ crying out in his agony. Tears welled and he blinked them back. Then he sank to his knees, trembling, and closed his eyes, the image burning sharp behind them, his words of fervent prayer unheard by any save God.

You gave your life for me, my Lord, poor sinner that I am. You died to save me, to bring me home. You suffered agonies that I might

*live through all eternity with God. Teach me to serve Thee better.
Let me be with Thee always ...*

The hubbub round him quieted, the vicar waiting in the pulpit for hush. Slowly, Richard became aware of the growing silence, and he opened his eyes as he let himself be drawn back to the day, the outside world lightly meeting the joy in his soul. He got up from his knees and retook his place on the bench beside Ellyn, gazing around him at the crowd with new understanding. It was for this that the English Church existed, he thought, a place to bring each soul to this love and this grace. It was imperfect perhaps, and flawed, vessels of wood and earth amongst the vessels of gold and silver, but how should it be otherwise? Who but God could tell one from the other?

A peace settled over him, a sense of certainty. Here within the sanctity of the Church he understood the need to protect it and keep it whole. Ben and his kind would break it down and rend it at the seams. Then who would bring all these good people to God? Such destruction could not be allowed to happen. As the minister began to speak, Richard felt his burden lighten. It was God's will that he should fight for the Church. Ben had set himself against it, and there could be no other way.

∽

THE WELCOME SUPPER took place at the deanery, the first official meeting of the First Westminster Company. Richard was nervous, aware of the weight of the task ahead of them, the Scripture placed in their hands for generations to come. They would be building on the work of those who had gone before, taking the best of each, and revising: each man bringing a new expertise, a new understanding to render the Hebrew ever more perfectly in English.

When he stepped from the door of the Kemps' into the lane, he was aware of the quickness of his heartbeat and the dryness of his mouth – a heady mix of nerves and excitement, the joy of God's work in his blood. The day was just starting to darken, the autumn chill beginning to bite with the disappearance of the sun, and all along the street the merchants' wives were overseeing the lighting of the lanterns that hung outside their doors, exchanging news and gossip with each other, their chatter lively as they called from one side of the narrow lane to the other. Apprentices and journeymen passed between them, heading home at the end of the working day, adding occasional male banter to the mix. The night was clear, but above the busy streets of Westminster the stars were all but invisible, obscured by smoke from a multitude of chimneys, and the lights that were slowly mastering the night. A half-moon gleamed wanly, looking down on the earth without interest.

Richard turned left out of the door and drew his cloak tighter round him, then bent his steps towards the Abbey. It was a short walk along Thieving Lane, so called for the pickings it once gave to those who claimed sanctuary, untouchable by the law in the precincts of the Abbey. The custom was less observed these days than in the past, but still he kept his wits about him – Westminster streets after dark offered little safety. One of the neighbours, a middle-aged widow standing on her doorstep with a broom, hallooed him with a merry little wave, and he nodded in response, hurrying on, embarrassed by the attention. He heard her cackling at his back as he turned the corner – apparently she had achieved the reaction she wanted.

At the end of the lane he turned through the arch that led to Broad Sanctuary where the houses gave way to the open space before the Abbey. It was still peopled with traders and locals, small braziers giving off light and heat, the hubbub of the city even after dark. The busyness disquieted him; he was still unused to such crowds, and he quickened his steps towards the Abbey, eager for the quiet and scholarly conversation he hoped to fir deanery.

He was not disappointed. The tranquillity of the Jerusalem Chamber soothed him as soon as he entered, and he stood just inside the door for a moment, allowing his eyes to drink in the mediaeval splendour. Cedar panels lined the walls – later he would learn the timber had come all the way from Lebanon – and a fire was roaring in a fireplace as big as he had ever seen. Vast tapestries reached almost to the ceiling, scenes from the story of Abraham and Sarah. He could think of no finer surroundings for the work of the Translation.

He was one of the first to arrive and Lancelot Andrewes greeted him warmly in Latin, a language both men spoke as easily as English. He took a seat at the great oak table that occupied the centre of the floor and accepted the cup of spiced wine he was offered. Nerves gave way to excitement and anticipation, the great work almost begun. The others drifted in one by one. Some of them he knew from his days in Cambridge, scholars and clergymen all, and introductions were made for the others. He was pleased to be in this company: he had long held Andrewes in awe, for his learning, for his knowledge, for the piety of his faith. Casting his gaze around the table, he catalogued the other scholars in his mind: John Overall, Dean of St Paul's; John Layfield, fellow of Trinity College, Cambridge, and one-time chaplain to the Earl of Cumberland, with whom he had sailed to the New World; Richard Thomson, brilliant, corpulent, arrogant, drunk; Hadrian Saravia, half-Flemish, half-Spanish, prebendary of Westminster; William Bedwell, Arabic scholar and mathematician. With the possible exception of Thomson, Richard was proud to be among such company.

When all of them were settled, Andrewes spoke to welcome them. Even though his voice was soft his words never faltered, and each man at the table paid him rapt attention. He went through the rules one by one as they were set out by Bancroft and the king, giving them the details of the days that would make up their lives for the next coming years. Each man would work alone each day, amending, translating, revising the week's allotted chapters as he saw best. Then one day each week, yet to be decided, the Company would meet again at the deanery to discuss and compare, and find the best of what had been done. Andrewes, as leader, would have the last word, but it was hoped they could reach consensus amongst themselves, sifting truth from untruth, marrying the Hebrew and English to reflect God's perfection. And so, week by week, little by little, the ten men that sat around this table would work through the first twelve books of the Old Testament, from Genesis through to Kings II.

When the business of the evening was concluded, a banquet was served. The large table was laden with platters of all manner of meat and fish: ducklings piquant with spices; Scottish salmon poached in ale; beef served in the style of the Levant, stuffed with oranges and dates and spiced with nutmeg. The aroma was beguiling, and for ever afterwards the catch of such a scent would reawake for Richard the excitement of that evening, the feeling that at last he had succeeded – his knowledge recognised and valued, and no more lingering doubts about his loyalty. He had earned his place among them, finally accepted, respected. Sitting between Andrewes and Layfield, he listened, rapt, to Layfield's stories of the New World – a new Eden. It was the most perfect of any day he could remember.

❧

A few days later was All Hallows' Eve and the city was bright with bonfires to celebrate, preparing for the Feast of All Souls the next day, when the lives of the saints would be remembered. It was not yet five o'clock when Richard strolled from the Abbey on his way back to Thieving Lane, but the day was already darkening, the air brisk and cold. Torches had been lit in their sconces, and the streets around the Abbey were thronged with people in festive spirit and children playing. A crowd of labourers was clustered round a cart that was selling ale, and a baker's boy with a basket of fresh-baked pies was working his way among them; Richard caught the scent on his way past and remembered he was hungry. He huddled deeper inside his cloak, one hand keeping safe the small purse of coins, the fabric rough against the dryness of his hands and the slight weight of it pleasing in his palm.

He stopped now beside a small fire to watch three young children ducking apples in a bucket, their faces wet and glowing in the firelight, oblivious to the cold. A sharp memory of the farmhouse of his childhood sheared across his thoughts, the fire bright and warm in the hearth, the bowl of apples on the table, his sisters waiting, chattering with excitement. He could see their faces even now with perfect, vivid clarity, flushed and happy, and water spraying from the tips of their hair. Searching the image, he looked for his mother. She was there, looking on, tendrils of hair come loose from the worn linen cap, but the details of her face were lost to him. Only his father was absent, still working, long days of labour stretching from darkness to darkness for most of the year. There had been little time for frivolity – even for the children, apple bobbing was a rare treat. Grateful for his escape from such a life, he winked at one of the boys who had turned to observe him with the open-faced scrutiny of the very young. The child continued to stare, blankly, so Richard turned away with a smile and walked on.

The Kemps' windows were brightly lit when he got there, welcoming him in from the biting dusk of the street. From inside the house looking out, night seemed already fallen, and he was glad to be indoors in the warm. Ellyn ran down the hall to meet him.

'We're building a bonfire in the garden. Come and see!' She was breathless, her cheeks brushed with pink, though whether it was from excitement or the heat of the fire he could not say.

He smiled, her mood infectious, building on the delight he had seen in the street. Emma Kemp appeared, brushing stray strands of hair back under her cap. 'He has just stepped through the door,' she chided. 'Let him rest a moment and warm himself before you start to bother him.'

'I don't mind,' he replied. 'There are bonfires all the way from the Abbey. It's very festive.'

'You see?' Emma Kemp turned to her daughter. 'He's already seen a hundred bonfires. He doesn't need to see any more.'

Ellyn's look threatened sullenness.

'I will come,' he said. 'I like bonfires.'

'As you like,' Emma Kemp answered. Her efforts wasted, she turned away, and as she disappeared along the hallway he felt ungrateful: she had only been trying to be kind. He stood with Ellyn for a moment watching her go, her skirts sweeping over the woven mats with a whisper as she passed. Then they followed her, through the house and out to the garden behind, threading their way past the kitchen garden with its high protective wall and on to the bare patch beyond the trees where a fire was burning brightly. Sparks flew up as new wood caught and popped, flames leaping up with a whoosh.

Ben was squatting close beside it, poking at the base with a stick to arrange the pyre and spread the flame more evenly. He looked up at their approach, nodded a greeting, then returned to his task. Ellyn drew closer to the fire beside him and hugged her shawl around her shoulders. Beyond the flames Alice was busy with one of the servant's children, keeping him away from the fire.

Satisfied with the fire at last, Ben stood up in one languid movement, throwing the brand he was holding onto the pyre. Richard remembered unfolding his own stiff limbs in the Abbey library earlier that day and felt the usual prick of envy. It was hard to imagine Ben with an aching back, the feline grace diminished, and all the certainty of that moment in church on Sunday left him, brought up short by the reality of Ben in all his errant human beauty.

'It's a good fire,' he said.

His friend was silent, still staring into the flames. Richard followed the gaze. The new timber cracked and ignited, flaring before it settled, and he found himself thinking of William Tyndale, dying in the fire for Englishing the Bible, the same work that he was doing now. Would he do it still, he wondered, if he had to live in hiding for it, an exile always fearful for his life, dependent on the charity of strangers? Would he have the courage of his faith to keep on going? No, he thought. Probably not. He would be too afraid of the fire. He stepped back a pace from the heat, his face beginning to scorch, and the movement drew Ben's attention.

'Too hot for you?'

Richard started, the question too close to his private thoughts. 'A little.'

'It would be a painful death,' Ben said.

'Yes,' he agreed. 'I have thought so myself.'

Ellyn moved between them. 'Stop being so morbid. No one dies at the stake any more.' A pause. 'Do they?'

The two men exchanged a glance, but Richard could not read the light in Ben's expression.

'Not many,' Ben said.

The fire began to die, the wood dry and light and burning hard. They moved closer to its fading warmth, stretching out their hands towards it. Ben turned to his sister.

'Go inside now. It's cold.' He raised his voice to Alice on the far side of the fire. 'You too, Alice. Take young George in. It's late and wintry for him to still be outside.'

Ellyn regarded her brother with a long cool look. 'And you?'

'We'll see the fire safely out first.'

Her gaze shifted to include them both and Richard turned his face away from the hostility.

'Come, Alice,' she said, turning abruptly from the fire, skirts swirling out behind her. 'We are no longer wanted.'

The women disappeared with the child through the bushes in the darkness, sure-footed, the way well known. Richard stretched out his hands once more to the hypnotic shifting light of the flames, and as the heat ebbed he felt the coldness of the night at his back. He could sense Ben's scrutiny, and doubt touched him once again.

Richard said, 'Have you thought more about your father's offer? To go back to the East?'

'I've thought,' Ben replied, turning his eyes back towards the dying pyre. 'But what does it matter to you?'

'I am your friend and I would see you safe.'

Ben withdrew his gaze from the flames and regarded him once more, appraising. Richard averted his face, uneasy under the other man's judgement. The pause lengthened. Then finally Ben spoke again.

'Why did you come here?' he asked. 'Why would you choose to stay in this house after all that has happened?'

Richard inclined his head. 'It is very convenient. Just a short walk to the Abbey ...'

'But still ...'

'You wish me to leave?'

Ben hesitated. 'We are both of us safer apart.'

'Then go to the East.'

'You need me that far away?'

'It's a long way from Bancroft.'

Ben half smiled his agreement across the last of the flickering light, embers sparking at their feet. Then he said, 'It's a long way from everything.'

Richard said nothing, and felt the weight of his task harden in his gut. He had hoped he might be spared the need for betrayal after all, Thomas Kemp's wish to send his son away again an answer to his prayers. But Ben's mind was made up and he would not go.

The two men remained at the fading fire, watching the smouldering embers catch light and die. Only when the last of the sparks had dwindled into darkness did they turn away from the ashes and walk back towards the house through the cold winter night.

Richard worked in the library at the Abbey, leaving the house before first light for the short walk through the predawn streets. Torches burned low on the buildings, and he could see the shadows of others moving in the greying light. The business of the day started early in London, the streets already lively. Artisans and apprentices had begun their day; braziers were lit in the streets, groups standing round them, talking. A washerwoman bumped his arm with her basket, and two young gentlemen wove an uncertain path towards the river on their way home from a night of debauchery.

He paid them no heed, his thoughts already turning on the words of the Translation as he reached the Abbey door, the great Gothic towers looming dark above him. Inside, candles flickered in the draughts, shadows spinning across the marble columns. He crossed the nave and drew his cloak tighter about him – it was colder in the shelter of the walls than in the soft damp of the winter morning – then bent his steps towards the East Cloister and the sanctuary of the library.

Inside was silent, the old, heavy door at the base of the steps shutting off the hubbub from the cloister, and he set out his papers on the long table in the centre of the room, the bookshelves with their heavy tomes lining the walls around him. The fire had not yet been lit but candles burned along the length of the table and a couple of torches flickered on the wall at his back. Wandering along the shelves, he lifted down the Bibles one at a time, heavy and awkward, and took his time to arrange them to his liking on the table. Then he laid out his own precious Hebrew grammars and his lexicon and set himself to work.

He worked for an hour before matins, oblivious to his fingers growing cold, hunched over the desk, books spread before him and the pages shifting in the candlelight as the sky lightened slowly unseen behind the walls. But he was no longer there in the Abbey, his soul, his mind, wandering instead through the pages of the Garden of Eden, God's voice in his heart and a light within to guide him through the sacred words. All around him was forgotten. Ben, Bancroft, Ellyn – none of them existed: there was only the search for the truth of the words.

He turned first to Tyndale's translation. It was beautiful in its language, the man's feel for the Hebrew sublime in its expression, and the lightness of his English a faultless touch.

And the woman sayd unto the serpent of the frute of the trees in the garden we may eate but of the frute of the tree yt is in the myddes of the garden (sayd God) se that ye eate not and se that ye touch it not: lest ye dye.

Then sayd the serpent unto the woman: tush ye shall not dye.

Next he turned to the Bishops' Bible, the version they were to alter as little as the truth of the original permitted:

> *And the woman sayde unto the serpent: We eate of ye fruite of the trees of the garden. But as for the fruite of the tree which is in the myddes of the garden, God hath sayde, ye shall not eate of it, neither shal ye touche of it, lest peradventure ye dye.*
>
> *And the serpent sayde unto the woman: ye shall not dye the death.*

Then he surveyed his own attempt to marry what was best in both against the sacred truth of the Hebrew.

> *And the woman said unto the serpent, We may eat of the fruit of the trees in the garden. But of the fruit of the tree which is in the midst of the garden, God hath said, Ye shall not eat of it, neither shall ye touch it, lest ye die. And the serpent said unto the woman, Ye shall not surely die.*

The verse was a straightforward one: a few changes to word order, the addition of verbs that English requires to make sense. Only the Hebrew double use of the verb *to die* in the serpent's sweet talk posed a challenge. Tyndale had solved it beautifully with *tush*, catching the serpent's mocking tone with the speech of the common man. But still, it was an addition to the text and could not remain, though it saddened him to lose it. He had always loved the serpent's *tush*: it brought the scene alive for him in English, the serpent's character contained within that gentle chiding, clever and persuasive.

It was how the Devil worked, he supposed, with charm and guile, leading us along the road to Hell unaware and willing, enchanted, believing in his wiles. Most of us would turn from evil if we saw it as it really was – such trickery was Satan's way to lure us from the path of righteousness without us really knowing.

An image of Bancroft trod across his thoughts, drinking cool sweet wine in fine Venetian glass, and he shook his head at himself for making such a link. But the thought remained, a memory of the deal that was struck at Lambeth – Ben's head in return for a place on the Translation.

Tush, he reproached himself, using the serpent's word. It was God's work he was about, not the Devil's: the English Church, God's Church, under threat from Separatists who would see it smashed to rubble. Then how could he doubt the rightness of his path? But still the image lingered, an apple in Bancroft's hand; and somewhere in the background of his thoughts the voice that feared for his eternal soul asked again, What if I am wrong?

The toll of the bell for matins called him back to the world of the Abbey. He blinked, gazing round him as though he had woken from a dream and was surprised to find himself awake. The library walls with their burden of books, the high-beamed ceiling, the chill of the as yet unheated chamber slowly permeated his reality, and he laid down his quill with reluctance. He was happier in the world of the Word.

Flexing his stiffened fingers, he stood up, straightening his back with a grimace. When had study become so hard on his body? he wondered. It seemed no time at all since he could work all day without respite, then get up and walk with no stiffness. He was getting old, he reflected, and the letters were becoming harder to decipher.

He finished stretching and tidied the pile of papers, moving the Bibles into neatness with gentle, reverent fingers. Hurrying out and down the stairs, he ducked his head through the low door that led out into the cloister, before he turned into the tiny ancient chapel of St Faith's for morning prayers.

~

'BEN HAS LEFT?'

'Indeed he has,' Thomas Kemp replied, stretching out his legs before the hearth at the end of the day. The women of the house had already retired for the night and he was enjoying the precious moments of peace before bed. 'He left before dawn this morning, before even I was out of bed. His sister is furious that he didn't wait to say goodbye.'

Richard smiled and helped himself to wine before settling into the empty chair by the hearth. He was tired after a long day at the library but pleasantly so, and the room was warm against the night outside. The old greyhound lay spread out at their feet, uninterested in the two men who weren't her master. It was a good house, he thought, and Ben should be thankful to come from such a family.

'Though of course it wasn't his sister he wanted to avoid.' Thomas Kemp took a satisfying mouthful of wine and sank a little lower into the chair.

'How so?' he asked, thinking it might have been himself Kemp meant, that Ben suspected the truth.

'He was avoiding me.'

Richard was silent, relieved. But he knew all the same that Ben had been doubtful, a natural misgiving that Richard had renewed the contact between them when it had seemed he was at last free of taint. He, Richard, had expected no less – a life lived in danger breeds suspicion in us all.

'Aren't you going to ask me why?' Kemp said.

He smiled. 'Why?'

'Because I want him to go back to Aleppo and he wants to stay here.'

'He was never one to listen to reason.'

'Now there's an understatement if ever I heard one. Even as a child he was the same – a passion in his heart he would follow no matter what. In all my years I've never met anyone, boy or man, with more determination to follow his own will. I suppose it should be no surprise the way he turned out.'

'Perhaps not.' He remembered Ben at Cambridge, arguments between them even then as Ben discovered his new-found faith and sought for his salvation in the teachings of reformers.

'Has he talked to you?' Kemp asked. 'Has he told you anything about the people in Nottingham? What he's doing there?'

'He hasn't said a word. I think perhaps he no longer ... regards me as a friend.'

'Nonsense. You've been a truer friend to him than he has ever had any right to expect. I'm aware that it has cost you, Richard. His mother and I appreciate every moment that you've spent with him. I know it can't have been easy.'

Richard shrugged. 'I was his friend.' But no more, he thought, and unworthy of the older man's praise.

'I had hoped,' Kemp began, 'that the years in the East might soften his views a little, that he might come back less ... fervent in his beliefs, but I'm not sure he's changed at all.'

'So you think he is ...?' He was reluctant to say the words and put a name to Ben's crimes, as though to do so would make it true. But the meaning was clear enough to Kemp. They had spent many evenings like this when Ben was in prison, talking about his beliefs.

'Yes,' Kemp answered. 'I fear I do. Why else would he choose to live so far from London? Why else would he be so determined to stay in England?'

'A woman perhaps?'

The older man smiled. 'Now there's a possibility I hadn't thought of. In the midst of all the danger of his religion it's easy to forget he also has an eye for the ladies.'

'Or used to anyway,' Richard qualified. He had spent too many hours with Ben after Cecily's death to believe his friend would easily love again. But it was ten years since then, and seven years in the East must surely change a man somehow.

'Perhaps,' he said, 'he might consent to go to Europe to live. The Levant is a long way from England and it's not a Christian place. But he'd still have friends in Holland, would he not? And he could worship there unhindered.'

Kemp nodded and his mouthful of wine went down the wrong way, leaving him coughing and spluttering. Richard half rose to help but Kemp waved him away with his hand and the younger man sank back in his chair, playing gently with the empty glass in his fingers while he waited.

When Ben's father had recovered he spoke again, his voice hoarse, his eyes still watering. 'I blame myself, you know. I should never have allowed him to go to Cambridge. That's where it started. When he met that Francis Johnson ...'

'You couldn't have known where it would lead,' Richard said. 'And to be fair it has never been only learned men who dissent. Tradesmen, artisans, merchants ...'

'You know this?'

'The London congregation was composed of such. I imagine things are little changed.'

'He'll end up in prison again. Or worse.'

Richard was silent: it seemed Thomas Kemp knew more than he was saying, for all his assurances about Ben's friendship. A log cracked and fell in the grate and the flames licked at it, cold blue before settling back to orange and warmth.

'What did I do wrong with him, Richard?' Kemp asked. 'What did I do to make him so uncompromising?'

'It was nothing you did. Ben has always been his own man.'

'Why can he not just accept what cannot be changed like the rest of us? Why can he not accept the Church as it is?'

'But you don't know for sure that he's still ...' He stopped, searching for an apposite term. '... living dangerously?'

Kemp hesitated. 'I know my son,' he said finally. 'That's all I'm saying. I know my own son.'

Richard's stomach turned. So Bancroft's suspicions were founded on truth: Ben was still living outside the law, risking prison and death for his faith. An image of Bancroft rubbing his wrestler's hands together in glee at the news flickered behind his eyes. He lifted the wine glass to his lips and drank off the last few drops. Then he rose and went to the cupboard and poured himself some more.

CHAPTER 6

NOVEMBER 1604

Beloued, let vs loue one another; for loue is of God: and euery one that loueth, is borne of God and knoweth God. Hee that loueth not, knoweth not God: for God is loue.
(*1 John 4:7–8*)

BEN HAD LEFT in the early-morning dark, startling the sleepy lad who rose hurriedly at the unexpected sound of hooves. By sunrise he was out of London and on the Great North Road, a mist rising from grass that was heavy white with dew beside the road, the track firm with cold beneath the horse's feet. Farm carts, loaded with the foodstuffs that kept the capital fed, forced him often off the road, but he made good time even so and the chill air was fresh in his face and hard in his lungs after the unclean atmosphere of London.

A shepherd's whistle, carrying sweet and clear through the winter morning, disturbed his thoughts, and he lifted his head to see. Across the field a shepherd was working his flock, two dogs responding in perfect harmony to divide the sheep into separate groups. Ben slowed the mare to an amble and watched for a moment, enjoying the skill of the shepherd, the agility of the dogs, and the sight brought to mind again the ageing greyhound he had left at Thieving Lane. He still wished he could have brought her with him. Turning his eyes away from the shepherd and back to the road, he nudged the horse forward into a trot. But thoughts of the greyhound had stirred other memories, drawing his mind back to those first days with Cecily, when she had given him the pup and named her Hope, and his life had seemed to hold such promise.

With nothing else to distract him and a long ride ahead he let the recollection come. He could still recall each moment perfectly, every detail vivid in his memory, the images visited over and over through the years since her death. The thought of those early days still made him smile, the delight of anticipation, the apprehension his feelings would not be returned. Before it all went wrong and the innocence was lost. Youthful desire, he knew now, but the force of the love he had for her could wake him from his sleep even still, calling out her name to the empty dark.

Ben had not long returned from his three years in Holland when they met at the door of her father's house near the Strand. He was working for his father and he hated it. 'You must start at the bottom,' his father had said, 'so you know every detail of the company,' but it was an ill-tasting pill for a man of Ben's age and education to be sent out delivering documents.

In his anger at the meanness of the task he had stridden all the way from Westminster, growing hot in the weak April sun, his shirt clinging wetly to his back as he wound through the busy narrow streets. He found the house with ease – even in strange cities he had never lost his way – and he hammered at the new oak door, unimpressed by its quality or the elegant stonework surrounding it. He wanted only to deliver the papers and be gone, his pride still smarting at the menial work. It was not what he imagined when he came home from Holland.

When there was no answer to his knock he lifted his fist again, only barely quelling the urge to turn and walk away. Eventually the door swung open and a servant dressed in rich grey livery looked him up and down.

'Yes?'

'I am here to see your master,' he snapped. 'My name is Benjamin Kemp.'

The servant stepped back with practised courtesy and Ben followed him into the sudden cool of the house, where he was told to wait in the entrance hall while the servant disappeared with unhurried unconcern. With nothing else to do he filled the impatient moments gazing round him. The hall was vast. New and ostentatious, it was lit by a morning sun that fell golden through a high arched window at the bend in the stairs. Herbs among the rushes at his feet gave off a heady scent, thyme and something sweeter he could not put a name to. The hall at Thieving Lane seemed dark and narrow in comparison.

A door slammed at the back of the house and a child's voice wailing in protest was cut short by a woman's command. A movement on the staircase above him turned his attention upward as a female form took shape against the brilliance of the window behind her. He watched the shape descend but the face was hidden, eyes lowered as she stepped carefully down the stairs, skirts trailing lightly one step behind her. At the bottom she stopped, lifted her eyes, and noticed him. A stern narrow face with hooded eyes opened into a smile that transformed her into the most captivating woman Ben had ever seen. Green eyes challenged him, and there was laughter in their depths that unsettled him.

'Good morning,' she said.

'Good morning.' He bowed lightly, and all the irritation of the morning slid away. 'Ben Kemp at your service.'

She touched a hand to her hair, flicking back an auburn strand behind her shoulder. She was almost as tall as him, he noticed, their eyes nearly level, and her skin was apple blossom pale.

'I have papers for Master Lowe.'

'I am Cecily Lowe. Master Lowe is my father,' she told him. 'Come, I'll take you to him.'

She turned and led him towards the back of the house, and all he could think of as he walked along one step behind her was the smile she had given him, and a strange sense that this moment would change him for ever. They came to a door too soon and she showed him into a chamber with windows that looked over the gardens. They stood looking out for a moment, watching the gardeners work, trimming and planting, the garden still new, still taking shape.

'It is a new house,' Cecily said. 'As you can see.'

He nodded but he had no interest in the newness of the house. She smiled and slid her gaze away from him.

'I will tell my father you are here, Benjamin Kemp. Please make yourself comfortable.'

'Thank you,' he said.

Then with a whisper of silks she was gone, and the room had seemed empty without her.

In Scrooby they had missed him. The children flew out of the door when they saw him and Love jumped into his arms, almost knocking him flat. Ben laughed, swinging her round, her small arms clinging to him with surprising fierceness. He greeted them all, squatting down to meet them one by one, delighted by their

delight in seeing him again. Then he bid them quieten down
before their father heard the commotion. They fell silent straight
away, a habit of obedience, and their mother appeared behind
them.

'Ben.' She smiled, her own pleasure in his return plain to see.

'Mistress Brewster.'

They embraced, a warmth and acceptance between them he
had never known with his own mother.

'How was the road?'

'Very cold.'

After four days of hard riding the view of the manor house
across the fields had been a welcome sight – the thought of the
hearth in the mediaeval hall had often warmed him on his journey.
Kings and cardinals both had enjoyed the warmth of the hall's
great fireplace in years gone by, and though the manor still
belonged to the diocese of York, Brewster remained a faithful
bailiff and postmaster, as his father had been before him, for who
would suspect such a respectable man of worshipping outside
the law?

Ben rubbed his hands together, stamping his numbed feet
against the frozen dirt as Mistress Brewster beckoned him in,
giving the children orders to take his things and the horse, to fetch
him food and ale.

'Be good to Bessie,' he said to Jonathan, handing him the reins.
'We rode hard.' He ran an appreciative hand down the mare's dark
neck. It was slick with her sweat and she butted her head against
his shoulder for more attention. He smiled and rubbed his fingers
in her forelock before the boy led her away toward the stables.

Inside, he stood before the hearth in the old timbered hall,
still the heart of the house, and let the warmth suffuse him,
toes painful as they thawed. Then he sat at the table as the
children brought him bread and cheese and ale. He had eaten

nothing since morning and the loaf was still warm from the oven. It steamed as he broke it, and filled him with its wholesome scent. It was good to be home. The children stood silently, watching him eat until Jonathan returned from taking care of the horse and their mother sent them back to their chores.

'You can talk to Master Kemp later. Let him recover from the journey first of all.'

He saw their disappointment, their eagerness to hear about the world of London, so he gave them a wink as they filed out into the passage. Jonathan nodded his understanding, a flicker of a smile touching his lips.

Mistress Brewster sat across from Ben, and with the firelight flickering behind her in the gloom of the hall it was hard to see the details of her face, but he knew them well enough. Though she seemed older than her years, there was a kindness etched into the lines, and in her eyes often lurked the same fear he used to see in Cecily. Reformers may no longer burn, he thought, but they paid dearly for their faith just the same and often it was hardest on the women.

'What news?' he asked, finishing his meal. 'What have I missed?'

'Sir William is recently returned from Court,' she told him. 'The gardener's wife at Gainsborough Hall is a regular source of news, though she could talk less than she does and it would be blessing.'

Ben smiled. He had met the gardener's wife. 'What other news did she have?'

'It seems Sir William is making enemies. He tore down some stalls in Gainsborough Market and allowed outsiders in to undercut the locals. And when the townsfolk protested he brought in his henchmen. Simon Parfitt still bears the bruises.'

'Why would he do such a thing?' If the blacksmith had bruises the fight must truly have been brutal: he was a giant of a man.

'Who can know? But he remains good to us, Ben. His house is ever open for our meetings.'

'He'd do better to draw less attention to himself.' To us, he meant, who depend on him.

'My husband says we should have meetings here. There is space enough and for many it would be closer. It's more isolated too and safer for it.'

'And if sixty people tramp the ten miles from Gainsborough he thinks it won't be noticed?'

Mistress Brewster rose and fetched more ale. This time she poured a cup for herself.

'He plans to split the congregation. With so many it gets more dangerous ...'

He nodded his agreement. Brewster had led them well so far, but now the king was stepping up the hunt, his fear of nonconformists spurred on by Bancroft's zeal. Between them they would rid the world of any man who disagreed. He drained his ale. Scripture placed no king but Christ at the head of the Church, and there were no archbishops in the Bible.

He had thawed now, sleepiness from the ride and warmth and ale creeping over his limbs. The house was quiet, the children busy, and from somewhere beyond the window he could hear the irregular tap of a hammer.

'Where is everyone?' he asked.

'The Williams' – she always referred to her husband and his ward this way – 'are in the village, sorting out some dispute about a pig that escaped and did some damage. You'd think the people could agree amongst themselves, wouldn't you, rather than getting the bailiff involved. As if he doesn't have enough to do.'

Ben nodded and smiled his agreement as expected, but he

thought it was good that Brewster was out doing his job, being seen as upholder of the law. It gained him respect amongst the locals and allayed suspicion, though he suspected that many of the people hereabouts were still practising the old religion anyway. Seventy years ago, Lincolnshire had been the seedbed for the northern rising against the old King Henry, when more than forty thousand men had protested the dissolution of their monasteries. It had ended in deaths, of course, as most rebellions do. Had they really thought King Henry would care about the protests of a rabble from the north? That he would dump his pretty new Protestant bride and reinstate the Papist one? They had been fools: kings are not so easily swayed from their purpose.

And now there was new rebellion growing here against a different king, but this one was hidden and secret, at least for now. He hoped their revolt might end better than the last one.

'And Reverend Clyfton is outside building a new coop for the hens,' Mistress Brewster told him. He laughed his surprise. 'He offered. He likes to work with the hands God gave him, he says, and be out of doors. So I let him get on with it. And if I get more eggs as a result then so much the better.'

Richard Clyfton, the Puritan rector at Babworth, a seven-mile tramp across the fields come Sunday, enjoyed the company at Scrooby amongst these men he helped to inspire.

'I'll go and see if I can help.' He got up from the table, shaking off the tiredness with the movement, restless energy returning, and went out through the passageway and into the yard beyond. The open meadows stretched flat towards the village beyond the manor's moat, and the sky above glowed a dull, even grey, the sun dying behind it unseen. It was hard to tell how much daylight might be left.

Clyfton heard the door swing shut and looked up from his work. Standing up straight, he stretched his back. 'Ben,' he greeted him. 'It's good to see you safely back.' Then he said, 'I've become unused to hard work. I must be getting old.' He held up blistered palms to examine.

'Mistress Brewster will have a salve for that,' Ben said. 'Here, let me.' He took the hammer from Clyfton and squatted down to examine the half-built coop. He could turn his hand to most things if he had a mind to: the voyage to the East had taught him much. He lifted up pieces of wood in turn, trying to place them until Clyfton bent to help him, to explain. Once Ben had understood, the two men worked side by side, not talking but easy in each other's company, content in their work, breaking sweat in the chill afternoon.

The child Love brought ale for them and they stopped to rest, sitting down on the cold earth, observing their handiwork. It was bigger than the coop his mother kept at Thieving Lane, more solid, and he thought they'd made a good job of it. Love stood beside him and regarded it too. With him sitting on the ground her head was a little above him and he had to squint to look up at her, outlined against the clouds. She was very like her mother with her flaxen hair and her eyebrows drawn down as though she had the worries of the world to think about. But she laughed a lot less than her mother: he had never met a more serious child.

He said, 'So, Love. Do you think the hens will like their new home?'

She turned grave grey eyes towards him. 'I think so. I think I would like to live there if I were a hen. It looks like it would be cosy.'

'You think you could lay a lot of eggs there?'

Her look turned contemptuous: her childish imagination would only go so far, and Ben had to fight to hide his smile. There was a brief silence while she ignored his question. Then she said,

'Excuse me, Master Kemp. Mother has asked me to gather some herbs for supper.'

He nodded his assent and she stepped away from him across the yard, skirts flapping against the short and serious stride until she disappeared behind the wall that kept the kitchen garden sheltered.

'Well, that's *you* told.' Clyfton laughed.

He smiled and shook his head, drained his mug of ale. 'Shall we?'

The other man nodded and placed his mug close by Ben's, out of the way of their work, and they went back to their hammering, fitting the last slats easily in place. By the time it was finished the last light was leaving the sky: the fields beyond the yard had been swallowed by the encroaching gloom, and they could see the flicker of candles through the windows to the hall. The warmth was inviting, and with a smile to each other of a job well done they packed up their tools, took up their jackets from the ground where they had left them and went inside to meet the rich aroma of roasting chicken.

~

WILLIAM BREWSTER SAT at the table with a sigh. He was a slight man, neat and particular, a sense of order about him that was reassuring. His greying beard was tidily trimmed, his hands well kept and clean. Ben observed his own hands in comparison. They were large and red now from the cold and manual work, and they had never been the hands of a scholar, like Richard's, soft and pale.

Silence sat at the table with the master's arrival, all of them waiting on him.

'Say grace for us, Ben,' Brewster invited.

They bent their heads.

'Dear Lord, we thank Thee for the gifts Thou hast given us, for food and warmth, for health and safety, for friends. Protect us, Lord, from Thine enemies and increase our love through time and eternity. Amen.'

Peace filled the room, a sense of rightness and belonging. He had missed this joy in London: the evasions and the arguments had worn at his thoughts, and his father's constant disappointment left a weight in his breast. Here was freedom to be who he was. Here he could meet whatever fate God had planned in good heart and with friends. Why could they not be left alone for this?

'How was Westminster?' Brewster asked.

Ben hurriedly swallowed his mouthful of meat: Brewster's fastidiousness always made him feel uncouth. He wiped his mouth with the back of his hand and ran his tongue across his teeth before he spoke.

'My father wants to me to go back to the East, to work for him and be part of the Company again. He's afraid for me here.'

'What does he know?' Brewster's question was casual but Ben could sense Mistress Brewster's sudden attention, intent and waiting.

'Nothing,' Ben answered. 'Except enough about me to know I haven't changed.'

'And he knows where you are?'

'Aye. But no more than that I am tutor to a family here. He didn't ask more. He would prefer not to know.' But his father's shrewdness would have told him everything: Ben's choice of living, his refusal to go East.

'Who can blame him for that?' Brewster said. 'But you are his only son. I don't doubt he would still do what he can to protect you.'

'Of course. He loves me still in spite of everything.' Though even as he said it he wondered if were true. Perhaps even a father's love can wane if it is tried too often.

'Do you want to go?'

'To Aleppo? No.' He shook his head. He had thought of it, almost tempted by the safety it would offer and the thrill of the voyage. But he was tired of running away, and life in Aleppo held no attraction. England was his home, his country, and his fate would be decided here amongst these godly people who sought to build a true English Church, the new Jerusalem. And if he must be hated then so be it. It was no more than Christ had endured.

'Are you sure?' Brewster leaned forward with his elbows on the table, fingers clasped before the neat beard, observing Ben with bright, keen eyes. The scrutiny made him uneasy and he shifted in his chair like a child who has been caught out doing wrong.

The ships would be ready soon, he thought, loaded at the dock with their cargos of wool and tin, waiting for the tide. Mentally he stepped aboard. The salt breeze caressed his face before they even left the harbour, the deck shifting gently under his feet. Sails cracked in the wind overhead, ropes creaking with the strain, and a seagull swooped, cawing raucously. He tensed with the fear and excitement of the voyage. It was tempting, a salve for the restlessness of his nature, the freedom and danger of a journey across God's ocean. And freedom too, from the harsh oppression of the English law.

'Are you sure?' Brewster repeated.

Ben drew his thoughts back from the ship and smiled. 'I am sure,' he replied. 'My place is here with you, amongst this fellowship of the faithful. Aleppo is a godless place.'

'We are very glad to have you.' Mistress Brewster smiled, and her husband nodded his agreement.

Ben ate, plainer fare than at the rich merchant's table at Thieving Lane – brawn with mustard, brown maslin bread, boiled green beans fresh from the garden. But its taste was sweeter because of the company.

'Also ...' he began.

The others turned their eyes towards him, something in the tone of his voice that alerted them to danger, senses honed from years of secrecy. He hesitated, uncertain how best to explain.

'Tell us, Ben,' Brewster said. 'If it's bad news we had better hear it.'

'It's nothing certain,' he replied. 'Nothing sure, and I have no wish to alarm you without good cause.'

'It's better that we know,' Mistress Brewster said, laying a gentle hand on his arm. 'Just in case. Don't you think?'

He turned to her with a smile, and wished again his mother were more like her.

'An old friend has resurfaced,' he said. 'Richard Clarke. A clergyman and scholar. A man I once loved like a brother. It was Richard that showed me the way to Christ, when I was young and foolish and still searching. And he was good to me when I was in prison. He visited, he brought me food and drink and clothes, and we argued Scripture, as we always had. It cost him dearly: his loyalties were questioned, he was overlooked for preferment. He gave up his ambitions for my sake. Then when I went to the East we lost touch – his choice, I believed, and I didn't blame him for it, though I regretted it.' He stopped, reluctant to give his suspicions voice and lend them strength.

'And now ...?' Brewster prompted.

'And now he's regained favour in the Church. He is one of the king's translators, one of the First Westminster Company, and he is lodging at my father's house.'

Brewster was silent for a moment, considering. Then, putting words to Ben's fears, he said, 'Do you think he means to betray you?'

He hesitated. Even now he was reluctant to believe it for the love they had once borne each other. 'I cannot say. Many years have passed since we knew each other. He is harder than he used to be, his belief in the English Church more ingrained. And now he moves at the heart of it – he works every day at the Abbey. He dines with the Dean, he preaches at Canterbury. Bancroft can be a persuasive force, and he is ruthless.'

Mistress Brewster shuddered at the name. The Archbishop was feared by them all – his latest vitriol had begun stirring up the people against them, sowing seeds of mistrust. But Ben's fear of him was personal, memories of cruelties inflicted face-to-face.

Clyfton spoke for the first time. 'What does this Richard Clarke know of you now? What information could he give to Bancroft?'

'No more than my father knows. Nothing of import. But he was very eager to persuade me to go to the East again.'

'He would see you safe abroad, then,' Clyfton suggested. 'Which means at least he is reluctant to betray you.'

'Perhaps.' He remembered their last conversation at the bonfire, a steel in Richard's expression he had not seen before. He was uncertain he could trust to the love between them any more: too many years had passed, and Richard had grown weary of the cold.

'Then we must pray for God's protection,' Brewster said.

'And,' his wife added, 'that the translator will remain a true friend to you.'

He was silent. The conversation moved on to some business in the village, two tenant farmers in dispute about grazing rights. With rents on the rise and land in demand, such quarrels were becoming more commonplace. But he was only half listening: his mind was elsewhere, recounting memories of Cambridge, when Richard had been the first among his friends, the two of them thrown together in the tiny room they had to share. Looking back, it occurred to him he had not at first been the kind of friend Richard might have wanted: his reckless sinfulness must have been a trial for Richard to bear. But he had befriended him still, with love and patience and faith that Ben would find his way in the end to know the same joy in God.

They had been so young, boys on the cusp of manhood, but Richard's faith had intrigued him, such inviolable belief wrapped in the core of his being, inseparable from the boy. And even Ben, ensnared in the depths of his own unbelief, could see the joy it brought him.

He had questioned Richard unceasingly, unable to comprehend where such faith could spring from, half-scornful, half-envious of his friend's unswerving conviction, his future path as a man of the cloth already chosen. Unwilling to accept his own life as sinful, and reluctant to ascribe such power to an unknowable God, he hadn't wanted to believe as Richard believed. And though a part of him despised himself for his debauchery, the ecstasy of sex was like a drug he was loath to renounce.

Chapel at college he hated. Rising in the freezing darkness each morning to kneel on cold stone while one old man or another droned some pointless sermon seemed hard discipline to a rich merchant's son who had grown up used to a fireplace in his chamber. Yet Richard went willingly every day, and rose from his knees refreshed and smiling. Ben had watched in wonder, perplexed and curious. For Ben was still searching for he knew not what – something to give his life meaning, and something to define him as a man who was different from his father. But he could not yet believe in Richard's God, so he sought answers instead in the arms of women, and in the dregs of ale amongst boys and men who even then he knew deep down would give him nothing.

'What is it you seek?' Richard had asked him one night when

Ben returned to their room from the brothel, having climbed the college walls, sneaking past the provost. It was a feat he had grown quite skilled in. 'What is it you hope to find?'

'Love,' Ben replied, without thinking. He sat down on the narrow bed they shared in the cold, barren room and dragged off his boots.

'And you hope to find love with women such as those?'

Ben hesitated. It was not a question he ever allowed himself to ask. Driven by his instinct and the reckless impulse of his youth, he had refused to consider beyond the satiation of his lust, the temporary fulfilment of desire.

He shrugged. 'Perhaps not love,' he conceded. 'But acceptance, perhaps? Fulfilment?' He stopped. The next word on his lips had been *pleasure*, but he swallowed it down with a sudden awareness of the truth of its meaning, the void inherent within it. He looked up at Richard, who sat down beside him, blue eyes bright with concern and with love, the pale, chubby face cherubic with innocence. It was a face Ben had come to know better than any other – every dimple, every furrow, the way his eyebrows came together when he was thinking. But now for the first time Ben saw a knowledge behind the innocence. Not knowledge such as he, Ben, possessed, of women and ale, not even the scholarly learning he knew his friend to be master of, but something deeper, something more eternal. Unnamed and undefinable, it was a knowledge that he wanted for himself.

'Ben,' Richard said gently, 'you will not find love by seeking pleasure. It can only distract you from what you search for, and offer you a fleeting respite from your restlessness. Only in God's love can you find all you need, all that you search for.'

Ben was silent with reluctant recognition: it was true that the brothels and the alehouse had begun to lose their allure, the excitement of the pleasure waning with familiarity and the growing realisation it was as Richard said: the pleasure was ephemeral, the fulfilment fleeting, and afterward the emptiness within him still remained.

'Take my Bible,' Richard offered. 'Read it. It will guide you and give you comfort.'

Ben shook his head. 'It is yours and you'd be lost without it. I could never take such a precious thing from you.'

'Most of it I know by heart. And it would be a far more precious thing indeed if it could bring you close to God. I would gladly give it up to save you.'

So Ben had taken it, holding it gently, reverently, slightly afraid. The leather cover had been worn and soft with use, and the pages seemed fragile when he flicked through them lightly with his fingers. He had known then – he still knew all these years later – how much the book had meant to Richard, the immensity of the gift. And for a long while, both of them thought it had been wasted, Ben still passing his life in sin, without faith. But in time it became the Bible he carried with him always, Richard's name still inscribed across the first page. It was the Bible that had sustained him in prison and nurtured his soul in Aleppo. He pictured it now, lying by his bed, his rock and his comfort, the most precious thing he owned. It had been the greatest gift one man could give another, and for that he would love Richard always.

~

THE NEXT DAY, crossing the yard at the mediaeval hall at Gainsborough, Ben met Sir William on his way out. Bowing a brief greeting, Ben tried to keep moving, seeking the warmth of indoors after his ride, but Sir William stopped at the door, barring the way, so he had no choice but to halt in the bitter cold of the courtyard. He stamped his feet, numbed by the miles from Scrooby, and slapped his hands together to try and coax back the feeling. It made little difference: what he needed was the heat of the hearth that burned inside.

Sir William occupied the threshold step, looking down on Ben a good foot below him, looming large in his riding cloak and furs. Expensive clothes, Ben judged; Sir William had recently been at Court. His father would have known their provenance: though his trade was silk he knew the value of most things that could be bought, and the Kemps were rich because of it.

'Good evening, Master Kemp,' Sir William greeted him. 'In a hurry?'

Ben drew his chilled lips painfully into a smile. 'It's a cold ride from Scrooby.'

'Perhaps you'd have been better to stay home in the warm.'

'Not I.'

'No.' Sir William observed him with shrewd and unfriendly eyes. 'Not you. You've suffered worse than the cold for your faith so I'm told.'

Ben tilted his head and said nothing.

'You prefer not to speak of it?'

'It was a long time ago,' he said. But the wound still bled, the image of Cecily big with child in the doorway of their house, the fear in her eyes as she begged him not to go. He had smiled and told her to hush, then left her standing there with tears in her eyes. He had not even turned back once to see her as he walked away. He had wondered many times since then how long she had stood and watched him. Her last sight of him, striding away to a separate fate. He should have stayed with her then as she asked, and if he had she might yet be alive. Cecily had suffered more for his faith than he had – he wanted no credit for his suffering.

'Ah, who can blame you?' Sir William shrugged. 'I met Bancroft at Court.'

He kept his silence and betrayed no feeling.

'You don't like our new Archbishop?'

'If I liked him I would have stayed at Scrooby in the warm,' Ben answered. Instead of traipsing ten miles across country on a freezing night, he thought, to worship secretly against the law.

Sir William laughed. 'Quite so. And between you and me, I didn't much care for him either.' He moved his bulk off the step and their eyelines drew level. 'Be watchful, Master Kemp,' he said. 'The new Bishop of Lincoln has begun asking questions, setting traps, and my hall may not always be so safe.'

'You take a great risk for us,' Ben replied. 'We are grateful.'

Sir William nodded, assessing Ben up and down before he bid him goodnight. Then he turned on his heel towards the stables, his riding cloak billowing out behind him as his form dissolved rapidly into the darkness, his boots silent on the frozen grass. Ben wondered where he was going, if he had business in the town or if he just preferred to place himself elsewhere during their meetings.

'Be watchful,' he had said.

How much longer did they have, Ben asked himself, until the Bishop's traps were sprung? How long could they survive? Rubbing his gloves together and stamping his boots a final time, he stepped through the open door and into the warmth of the dining chamber, where the others were already waiting.

CHAPTER 7

B eware of false prophets which come to you in sheepes clothing, but inwardly they are rauening wolves. Yee shall knowe them by their fruits: Doe men gather grapes of thornes, or figges of thistles? Euen so, euery good tree bringeth forth good fruit: but a corrupt tree bringeth forth euill fruit. A good tree cannot bring forth euil fruit, neither can a corrupt tree bring forth good fruit. Euery tree that bringeth not forth good fruit, is hewen downe, and cast into the fire.

Wherefore by their fruits ye shall know them.

(Matthew 7:15–20)

EARLY MORNING and the weak winter sun had not yet risen high enough to disperse a morning mist that curled catlike through the city. Crossing the open expanse of Broad Sanctuary on his way back to Thieving Lane for breakfast after matins, Richard shivered and pulled the fur-lined collar of his cloak closer to his throat.

Broad Sanctuary was bustling. Traders' voices sang out as they hawked their wares: fishwives bawled from behind their panniers, butchers' boys held strings of sausages aloft, calling out their quality, and a sweet scent of baked apples pervaded the air. A group of beggar children was fighting over a loaf of bread, a small dog barking as it watched, anxious, and everywhere people loitered, watching, laughing, arguing. It seemed all the city was abroad and lively before the Abbey doors, and Richard strode amongst them, eager for food and the warmth of a hearth, chilled from the early hours of stillness at study and at prayer. The cold seemed to bury itself deeper inside him these days, he reflected, and lingered for longer in his bones. He could feel the stiffness in his joints and closed his mind against the knowledge of the cold winter months ahead.

He had almost reached the corner of King Street when a woman's voice, harsh and jarring, startled him back to the day. Automatically he turned towards her though he had not heard the actual words. A group of wretched-looking women sat round a brazier, a single tattered basket of oranges placed at their feet. The one who had called out looked up when he turned but there was no hope in her eyes.

'Oranges?' she said. 'Fine Spanish oranges?'

'No,' he replied, already regretting he had stopped. 'No.'

He had begun to back away when a male voice at his shoulder spun him round. 'Why not, Doctor Clarke?' the voice said. 'I'll have two.'

Richard watched as the man slipped coins into the woman's hand with a murmured pleasantry that made her laugh, then picked out two oranges from the basket, taking his time, choosing carefully. When he had made his decision, the two men moved a few steps away from the sellers, whose interest in them had died with the purchase.

'Doctor Thomson,' Richard said. 'It's a little early for you, isn't it?'

Thomson laughed, exuding the sour stench of wine on his

breath, and Richard realised the other man had not yet been to bed. 'I've been sampling the local hospitality,' he said, laying a pudgy hand on the vicar's arm to steady himself. 'Westminster has more to offer than you might think.' He gestured to the oranges, held in the splayed fingers of his free hand. 'Want one?'

'No, thank you.' Richard was cold and the warmth of the dining chamber at Thieving Lane was beckoning. 'You're heading to the Abbey?'

Thomson nodded, swaying slightly with the movement. 'I must speak with Dean Andrewes. I'm afraid I'm a little behind with my verses.'

He said nothing, his silence judgemental enough. But inwardly he seethed that a drunkard such as Thomson had been chosen for their task. His inclusion could only fuel the fire of contempt for the Church that burned in men like Ben: his debauchery was a disgrace to the cloth.

Thomson stole his gaze away from Richard's disdain and turned his attention to the orange he was peeling. Aware of the other man's gaze, he began to make a deal of it, dangling the segments above the tilted face before he dropped them one at time into the red wet maw, juice dribbling down his chin and onto his vicar's robes.

'You're wasted in the Church,' Richard said. 'You should be on the London stage.'

Thomson laughed, amused by the insult. 'I know,' he agreed, wiping sticky fingers across his chest, a theatrical gesture. 'It would undoubtedly be a more exciting life. But I fear I've left it too late in life to change now.' He laughed again. 'I must introduce you to some friends of mine ...'

Richard shook his head, appalled.

'Tush, Doctor Clarke. There's no need to be so tedious. There is more to life than biblical scholarship, you know.'

'I am content.' He knew how Thomson saw him – stuffy, prig-gish, dull – but he did not care.

'Dear God!' Thomson was saying. 'You must be the most boring man alive. I could think of nothing worse than the life you lead.'

Because, Richard thought, you would rather soak that brilliant mind in drink and spend your energy on whores. It was a sinful waste of such God-given talent. But he said nothing. There was no point in making the man an enemy.

'But each to his own,' the older man went on. 'Each to his own. It would be a dull world if God had made us all the same.'

He nodded his agreement and thought of the waiting hearth at Thieving Lane. Thomson offered him a segment of the orange, and for something to do to fill the silence he took it. It was cold and sweet and surprising in his mouth, and he wished he had accepted the whole orange when it was offered. Thomson bounced the second one deftly off his wrist and rolled it neatly into the pocket of his gown.

'For later,' Thomson smiled. 'Or perhaps I shall offer it to the Dean.'

Richard found himself returning the smile. There was a strange charm to the roguishness that was hard to resist.

Thomson said, 'By the way, Doctor Clarke, is it true your old friend Ben Kemp has returned to our shores?'

The question took him by surprise and a flush prickled over his skin. He wondered what Thomson had heard, why he was asking.

'It is true,' he replied.

'And you are lodging at his father's house?'

'It is convenient.' He felt the sting of the insinuation, still fresh: he would never learn to wear the slights lightly.

'The connection does you no favours,' Thomson said. 'Accept some advice from a more ... experienced man. Find yourself somewhere different to stay. Sever the tie. People talk, you know. People gossip. And Ben Kemp is trouble – he will come to a bad end eventually. You would be wiser to keep your distance.'

Inside his cloak Richard balled his hands, fingernails biting deep into his palms, containing his anger, his resentment. It was hard to decide whom he hated most at that moment, Thomson, Ben or Bancroft, for putting him back on the outside when he had spent so many years finding his way in. He should have walked away from Ben at the beginning, he thought, when they first began to argue all those years ago, their paths diverging even then. He should have seen where it would lead them, his own devotion to the Church sullied by his friend's recalcitrance. He had been ambitious once, he recalled, aspiring to the Church's heights, hoping his skills as a linguist would ease the way. But his sympathies had let him down. No one would reward a clergyman with a Separatist friend, whatever his talent.

'Thank you for your advice,' he said, voice cold with the effort of self-control. 'I shall consider it carefully.'

'I mean not to offend, but only to offer my counsel. Times have changed and your ... sympathies, your ... charity towards him may not be seen so charitably any more.'

'I must go,' he said. He had stood in the cold long enough and the conversation had taken an unpleasant turn. He had suffered too much already on Ben's account. 'I will see you on Thursday.'

'Thursday?' Thomson looked puzzled.

'The weekly meeting. The Translation.'

'Ah yes!' The older man laughed. 'Of course. The Translation. Thursday.' He turned and walked away towards the Abbey, trading another word with the orange sellers, a laugh with a passer-by. Richard watched him as he wove across Broad Sanctuary, the solid bulk striding with the attentive deliberation of the inveterate drunk.

Let Andrewes deal with him, he thought. It was none of his concern.

～

EACH MAN BROUGHT something unique to the Translator's Company, a different knowledge, a different skill. Doctor Layfield possessed a rare expertise: he had voyaged to the New World as chaplain to the Earl of Cumberland, so he had seen first-hand a lush and distant paradise still barely touched by human hands, unspoiled as the Garden of Eden before the Fall. He knew also of ships and sailing, and the others turned to him for his help with the building of the ark. For a moment Richard thought of Ben – he too knew of ships and sailing, foreign places and voyages to safety. He had sometimes wondered what kind of life Ben had lived in the East, what sights and sounds and thoughts had filled his days. It was impossible for him to imagine a world so different from his own, an unchristian realm, and a part of him envied such knowledge – his own life seemed narrow and dull in comparison. But only a part. He would not want to trade his own life for the vicissitudes of Ben's, no matter how much adventure he enjoyed. The price Ben had paid was too high. He shook his head to clear his mind of any more thoughts of Ben Kemp, and turned his attention back to the Company.

'The Bishops' Bible has the Hebrew *gopher* translated as "pine,"' Andrewes said.

'The Geneva also,' Richard added.

'But we cannot assume such a thing,' Layfield replied. 'Why should we think it is pine more than any other kind of wood?'

'It isn't usual to build ships from pine, is it?' Thomson asked. 'Aren't they usually made from oak?'

Layfield nodded. 'Quite so. And we must remember too that

the word *gopher* may not even refer to the *type* of wood to be used,' he mused. 'It may be a reference to how the wood has been treated. Perhaps it means planed, or covered with pitch. We can only guess at such meanings.'

'Does the word appear elsewhere in the Scriptures?'

'Nowhere,' Andrewes replied with authority. 'I have looked.'

They fell silent, pondering the possibilities, until the Dean spoke again. 'We simply cannot know the right meaning.'

'Then we must leave it untranslated,' Layfield said. 'To change the Word of God on a guess is surely contrary to the truth of our task.'

'But the Bishops' Bible has it so,' Doctor Overall said. 'And we are to follow that translation as close as the truth of the original will permit.'

'And the truth of the original is something different,' Richard said. 'It doesn't permit such a reading. To translate it as "pine" is guesswork merely.'

'I agree with Doctor Clarke,' Layfield said. 'We cannot allow ourselves such laxity. And I think it unlikely that "pine" is correct.'

There was a general murmur of agreement with Doctor Layfield. Doctor Overall glanced around the table in hope, but meeting no answering support in the faces of the others, he dropped his eyes to the papers in front of him and said nothing.

'Then we are agreed to leave it as it stands? As *gopher-wood*?' The Dean's gaze travelled round the table and each man nodded his acceptance. Doctor Overall's assent was given with reluctance.

'Good.' Andrewes smiled. 'So the line will read, *Make thee an Arke of Gopher-wood.*' He took up his quill and wrote the words on the paper before him. The others waited, watching. Then they turned again to Doctor Layfield for his thoughts on the rest of the description of the construction of the ark.

~

BANCROFT SEARCHED out Richard at the Abbey after the meeting. The two men walked in the gardens, the grass strewn with sodden russet leaves, the trees mostly bare above them. Richard would have preferred to talk somewhere warmer but guessed the discomfort was deliberate: no doubt the Archbishop believed a little hardship worked in favour of his questioning, a habit gleaned from all the hours he spent in prison cells grilling reformers and Papists alike. He suppressed a shudder at the thought of it, grateful for his freedom. There would be no kindness in Bancroft's questioning – Ben still bore the scars.

They strolled side by side through the winter afternoon as the daylight began to fail. An automatic sense of guilt for some unknown wrong churned his guts.

'I hear the Translation is beginning very well,' Bancroft said.

'Yes, My Lord. Today's meeting was most successful,' Richard replied. For once, they had been moved by a spirit of concord, a mutual admiration for one another's skill, and agreement over their choice of phrase. Even the ever-fretful Doctor Overall had felt God's hand guiding them, the sacred words safe in their humble hands. The joy had ended abruptly with the sight of the Archbishop but some of the peace remained.

Richard glanced to the man at his side, the grey head level with his shoulder. The king should have given Canterbury to someone else, he thought. Bancroft was not an easy man to like even for the men who shared his views.

'Hebrew is not my forte regrettably,' Bancroft said, 'though my Greek is good. I have much admiration for you Hebraists.'

He smiled an acknowledgement of the flattery and waited for the business that lay behind it.

'Dean Andrewes tells me your mastery of Hebrew is equal to his own.'

'The Dean is very kind.'

'Yes,' the Archbishop agreed. 'He is that.'

They meandered on between flower beds that were bare now, rose bushes boasting only their thorns as adornment, the earth below them dark and moist. Bancroft stopped and turned to Richard.

'You have seen Kemp.'

'Yes, My Lord,' he answered, though it had not been a question. 'He was in London for a few days.'

'On what business?'

'His father asked him to come. He wants Ben to work for the Company again.'

'Doing what?'

'He's asked him to go back to Aleppo. Much of the silk trade comes through there and it is where Ben—'

Bancroft cut him off, impatience in the set of his mouth. 'It is where Kemp went when he was released from prison. I know that much already. What more can you tell me? What answer did he give his father?'

He hesitated, the habit of loyalty hard to break, the love still refusing to die. And Bancroft hardly invited confidence. Perhaps if Andrewes were to ask him he would be more willing: he had always responded more readily to gentleness.

'Well?'

'He refused to go, My Lord,' he said.

'What else?' Bancroft persisted. 'What else do you know of him?'

'He has a position as a tutor to a family in the Midlands, not far from Nottingham.'

'What family?'

'I don't yet know,' he admitted, and as he spoke he realised he was glad, relieved to have nothing useful he could pass on to Bancroft. 'He is ... aware of my position in the Church, My Lord, and of my loyalties.'

'Of course he is,' Bancroft snapped. 'He's no fool. But you were a good friend to him once.'

'Many years ago.'

'You must convince him you are still his friend. Surely you can manage that?'

'As you said, My Lord, he is no fool.'

'Then you will have to try harder. I need to know what he is doing. If he is part of a Separatist conventicle I will know about it. We will root out this canker in the Church.'

He said nothing, thinking only that there would never be peace in the world while men such as Bancroft and Ben existed.

'And if you cannot press him, then press his family. That is why you are lodging there. He has a mother, does he not? A sister? If you can't find out a few facts from a woman, you're of no use to me.'

Rising resentment covered his body with heat, redness touching the pale skin across his neck, inflaming his cheeks. He was glad of the dying light. He said, 'You have no need to doubt me: I will discover what I can.'

'Good,' the Archbishop replied. 'Then we shall talk again.' He bowed a curt farewell before he turned to stride back between the empty flower beds, robes flapping against the short and powerful legs in the breeze that blew off the river.

Richard stood and watched him go, waiting for his pounding heart to quieten. All the peace of the meeting had left him, all the certainties of his faith fading under Bancroft's zeal. The glory of the Church he loved and served seemed tarnished and its beauty dimmed as he gazed across the darkening garden towards the space that the Bishop's retreating back had left. Christ's greatest commandment was to love, and he saw little love in Bancroft. Whom then should he follow? The Archbishop was spokesman for the Church's faith, the guardian of its unity. Who was he, Richard, to question such authority, authority that came from king and God?

Wearied by the conflict, he followed Bancroft's path back towards the Abbey, and made his way to the peace of the chapel of St Faith's. There he knelt, and pleaded with God for an answer.

Dear Lord, guide me. Show me the path I must take. Bancroft frightens me, Lord, so full of hatred, so full of zeal. I do not want to be like him, O Lord. I see hatred in betrayal, a wish to hurt and punish, to avenge imagined wrongs, real wrongs. Does it matter? Such things are not for us to choose, Lord. We need only have faith, You told us. We need only accept Your son as our saviour and He will carry our burdens. But my burden is heavy, O Lord, too heavy. You commanded us to love, to honour friendship. I have only ever loved Ben Kemp, only ever been a friend to him. Why must I deny him now? Why must I betray him? Is that truly Your will? How can you ask such a thing of me who has only ever sought to serve you?

I want no part of this, O Lord. But pride has made me Bancroft's creature. I spent many years outside the Church, O Lord, on the edges looking in, ignored, laughed at, looked down upon for the love I bore Ben Kemp. Bancroft offered me a way back inside the fold. He held out the lure of the Translation and invited me in from the wilderness. Am I right to trust in him, Lord? Is his offer true? I believe in the English Church, have always believed in its goodness, but can its goodness be bought at such a cost?

Ben Kemp is not an evil man, O Lord – he is faithful and true and loves Thee above all other things. And he has suffered for Your sake, suffered more than I have words to say. So how can his betrayal truly serve you? Guide me, Lord. I have lost my way and know not where to turn to find it. Take pity, Lord, as You love me. And as You love Ben Kemp. Take pity on my worthless soul, my prideful, sinful self. Show me what to do ...

'The Archbishop found you?' Lancelot Andrewes stopped him in the cloister as he was leaving the chapel. 'He was most anxious to speak with you.'

'He found me,' Richard answered, hoping the Dean would then just step aside and let him go. His fingers twitched with impatience to be gone and his gaze flicked along the cloister past Andrewes's shoulder towards escape.

'Good, good.' Andrewes smiled, crow's feet crinkling at the edges of his eyes. 'We must keep our Archbishop happy. Now, have you any plans for dinner?'

Richard answered too slowly.

'No? Come dine with me. I believe there is venison.' He placed a bony guiding hand against Richard's elbow and turned him towards the deanery. Richard found he had little will to protest – he was tired suddenly, a weariness that went deeper than his flesh and bones.

'Do you like venison?' Andrewes asked as they walked together. 'It came from the king's own kitchen, killed by the king himself. Or so he said.' He chuckled. The joke was well known, the king an avid hunter who had never yet managed to finish his prey.

Richard smiled politely. The king should take Bancroft along next time, he thought, to let him finish things off: he suspected the Archbishop could slaughter a deer barehanded.

'You can tell me your thoughts over supper,' Andrewes said. 'You seem somewhat troubled.'

'No.' Richard tensed, searching for the strength to resist the tiredness. 'Not troubled,' he said. 'Tired, merely.'

In the deanery they sat at a well-spread table and venison was only one of the meats on offer. He barely ate, no appetite, and he kept his eyes averted from the scrutiny of Andrewes's gaze. He sipped carefully at the cool and fragrant Rhenish, mindful of its strength. It would be very easy to drink it too quickly, and he had never had a head for wine.

'I hear Master Kemp has lately been in London.' The Dean broke the silence.

Richard nodded. So that was the reason he was at the Dean's table: he should have known.

'I told the Archbishop all I know,' he said, and hoped the Dean would read between the lines: he didn't want to talk of it again.

'Which is?' the Dean asked.

He looked up at the gentleness in the older man's tone. It was hard to resist the coaxing voice, the encouraging smile. He admired Andrewes, respected and trusted him, but he knew from Ben that the velvet gloves concealed a hardness and a steel to his belief.

He sighed, silently, and retold what he knew of Ben's whereabouts. 'It has been many years since we were friends,' he finished, 'and it's going to take time to regain his trust.'

'But you are committed to doing so?'

The same mistrust as Bancroft, he thought, only couched in more sympathetic terms.

'I believe in the Church, Mister Dean,' he replied. 'It is a net that gathers the bad fish along with the good. How else should it be? Only God can know the true hearts of His flock.'

'Yet Kemp and his ilk would tear it down, and then where would we be?' Andrewes did not pause for an answer. 'We would be adrift, without order, without authority. And how would men be brought to God amongst so much discord?'

He said nothing, and Andrewes watched him. A servant entered and the draught from the door struck the candle flames and sent them flickering. One of them guttered and went out, and a narrow trail of smoke threaded upwards to disappear in the gloom beyond the candles' reach.

'So you know what must be done,' Andrewes said softly. It was not a question.

'Yes,' he replied mechanically. 'I know what must be done.'

ON THE WAY home it rained, vicious drops that spattered into the mud, drowning out all other sound. He bent his bare head against it and kept his eyes on the road, slippery underfoot. Water seeped through the leather of his boots; within moments the rough wool of his stockings was bunched and squelching underfoot. He ignored it as best he could and kept walking. Lanterns swayed bravely on their hooks but their light made little inroad into the darkness. He was glad it was a familiar path.

At the house in Thieving Lane an argument was in progress. He could hear it from the front door as Alice let him in, Ellyn's voice raised against her father's in the hall. He looked to Alice for some explanation but she gazed back blankly, features carefully set to give nothing away in an expression that was becoming habitual.

'What's happened?' he was forced to ask.

She shrugged, then held out her hand to take his cloak. He swung it off his shoulders and gave it to her, sodden and heavy, before touching fingers to his hair, flicking drops of rain onto the rush mats at his feet. She held the cloak in her arms, apparently oblivious to its wetness against the front of her dress.

'Why are they arguing?' he asked again.

The shouting stopped in the hall and he thought perhaps they had stopped because of him, because they had heard his voice. But rapid footsteps sounded on the hall's wooden floor and the door was slammed open, quivering on its hinges with the force, and

Ellyn ran towards the staircase. If she noticed him she gave no sign, skirts hitched as she took the stairs two at a time.

Alice handed back his cloak and hurried after her cousin. Richard stared after her for a moment, holding the dripping cloak away from his body until more footsteps from the hall drew his gaze that way. Thomas Kemp appeared in the doorway outwardly calm except for the way he clasped his hands before him, knuckles showing white with the tightness of his grip. His gaze lit on Richard.

'Ah, Richard,' he said, forcing a smile. 'My apologies. A family disagreement. My children will be the death of me.'

Richard did not know what to say.

'Come in, come in,' Kemp continued. 'Have some wine and get dry by the fire. It is a filthy night.'

He draped his cloak across the end of the banister and followed his host into the hall, where Emma Kemp sat motionless on a low stool close to the hearth. In her hands was a half-finished piece of embroidery, a shirt perhaps, but her gaze was directed into the flames and the sewing had been forgotten. He wondered if the stoniness was on his account, features schooled to composure.

'Claret?' Thomas Kemp stood by the cupboard, his hand on the jug.

'Yes. Thank you.'

They stood together at the fireside, nursing their wine in the tense silence his presence had caused. Finally Emma Kemp looked up from the fire to her husband.

'You must talk her round,' she said. 'She must marry someone.'

'She's as stubborn as her brother, and twice as unreasonable.'

Richard stared into his wine.

'It's a good match,' Emma Kemp said. 'And she is the right age. She cannot put it off any longer.'

'She has an aversion to the whole idea of it. She remembers Cecily.'

Emma Kemp said, 'We all remember Cecily.'

How could they not? Richard thought. Ellyn had been a young girl then, but the whole household had heard Cecily's cries growing weaker as the night progressed, all of them helpless against her suffering. At least God in His mercy had spared Ben the long, drawn-out sounds of his wife's slow death, facing daemons of his own in gaol.

'It is the fear of all women,' Kemp replied, 'the curse of Eve to bring forth children in sorrow. But life must continue. Women marry and bear children. It is as God ordained and she has been indulged long enough.'

'Let her meet him. She may like him,' Emma Kemp said.

'She will marry him, like him or no. If we wait on her likes any longer she will never be off our hands. I've spoken to his father and it's all but arranged. Now,' he said, turning to Richard, who was still looking into his wine, embarrassed to have heard the conversation. 'Let us talk of other things.'

'Forgive us, Richard,' Emma Kemp said with a smile. 'But you are almost family.'

He forced a smile in return. Her words were meant as a kindness but he felt them as a reproach. It was not just Ben he would hurt, but these good people who trusted him.

'I must go to my bed,' he answered, draining the dregs of the wine. 'It has been a long day.'

He bid them goodnight and climbed to his chamber. Then he kicked off his boots and knelt in the darkness to pray.

CHAPTER 8

NOVEMBER 1604

O LORD *my God, if I haue done this; if there be iniquitie in my hands: If I haue rewarded euill vnto him that was at peace with me: (yea I haue deliuered him that without cause is mine enemie.) Let the enemie persecute my soule, and take it, yea let him tread downe my life vpon the earth, and lay mine honour in the dust. Selah.*

(Psalms 7:3–5)

IT WAS STILL RAINING when Richard woke the next morning, squalls drumming against the windowpanes, a lashing torrent that made him think of the gopher-wood ark. He lay awhile and listened to the spatter on the mud of the road, and a pounding on some piece of metal left out in the street. His head felt heavy and he had no desire to leave the comfort of his bed.

Eventually he found the will to get up, tipping himself reluctantly from the warmth. He stood up and shivered, dressing hurriedly. Then he crossed to the window to see the rain: he could barely see the road below. A pity, he thought. He would have liked to work at the Abbey today, away from the house, where his task oppressed him most. In the peace and solitude of the library he could immerse himself in God's Word, and nothing else existed.

But the rain was a deluge: he would have to be a fool to go out without good reason. He would work in his chamber and train his mind to focus. He took a hurried solitary breakfast downstairs and asked for someone to tend the fire in his room. A churlish boy he hadn't seen before came up a while later and set out the fire with clumsy red hands while Richard stood at the window and waited. Watching the storm, he rubbed his fingers together to keep them warm. The boy was slow at his task and Richard could feel the irritation rising. It would be harder to write once his fingers were cold – they would be stiff for the rest of the morning.

A memory pierced his thoughts: an image of his father on the farm in rain like this, wrestling the sheep in the mud with rough, strong hands, fingers raw from hard labour and the cold. He turned to watch the boy, suddenly grateful for his own warmth and comfort, someone else to tend to his fire. It was a luxury his father had never even dreamed of.

Finally the fire took hold, wood catching and crackling, the first warmth creeping through the room. The sullen boy went away without a word. Richard stood by the fire awhile, warming his hands with a strange reluctance to begin his work. Mostly he was eager to start, but today he had to force himself to the desk, his mind drifting away almost at once.

He rearranged his books and papers, flicked through the pages he had done the day before, trying to ease his mind towards its task. But the words seemed to slip away from him, refusing to be pinned down and offer any meaning. Characters in the story, people he knew as well as friends, confused him – Abram, Sarai, Lot – so that he had to keep checking back to what had come before in order to remember their role in the tale.

The Hebrew made no sense, even after he had checked in the lexicon, often more than once. Sentences failed to cohere into meaning, persisting in their stubborn groups of unrelated words. The work had never been so hard. He felt like his father, searching for lost sheep in deep drifting snow. He persevered through the morning, hoping that in time the meanings would come clear, but the day's verses remained obstinate in Hebrew. When the Abbey bell tolled noon at last, just audible over the dying dregs of the storm, he stopped trying and got up from the desk to stretch the stiffness from his body.

He stood by the fire and held out his hands to it, more a gesture of comfort than a need for more warmth. It was still burning well – the boy had done a good job after all – and the chamber seemed merry in its light. He had never lived in such comfort before. Sliding his eyes from the flames, he looked round the room as if seeing it anew. The painted wall hanging appeared different from what he remembered, the woodland images shimmering, and the curtains around the bed had become darker, thicker, warmer. The bed itself caught his eye and seemed inviting, so he peeled off his jacket, hauled off his boots and climbed beneath the covers.

He drifted.

He was at the farm again, with Ellyn this time, and her lovely hands were red and chapped like his father's. His family was there, all of them wet from the lashing rain and covered in a thick, gelatinous mud that he kept trying to wipe away. His father stood at the farmhouse door, a sheep tightly held in his long, strong arms, fingers twisted in the wool to keep a better grip.

He examined his own hands, holding them out in front of him, turning them this way and that. They were pale and soft – the hands of a woman, his father used to say, useless on a man – and the rims of the nails were black from the ink of his calling.

He remembered the Translation. Figures from Genesis

traipsed out of order across his thoughts – the ark grounded in the Garden of Eden, the serpent around Abraham's neck, Moses interpreting the pharaoh's dream. How was he supposed to understand such a puzzle? And why had such a task been given to him?

He woke up with a start, disorientated and uncertain of the time of day. At the window the rain had calmed to a drizzle, and the house seemed quiet beyond the door. He wanted to get up and get back to work but his head was too heavy to lift from the pillows and his limbs seemed unwilling to move. He experimented, wriggling his pale woman's fingers, but his arms proved too weighty, so he gave up the effort and let himself drift back into his dreams.

The door opened. A man entered and stood at the foot of the bed. Was it Lancelot Andrewes braving a sickroom? Surely not. He must still be dreaming. Or was this reality now? He tried to speak, forming the words with his lips, but no sound came out. The Translation will take longer than we thought, he mouthed. Someone has mixed it up and made a puzzle of it. Andrewes smiled his indulgent smile. *Fear not, Doctor Clarke,* he said. *All will be well. With or without your help we will root out this canker in the Church.* He didn't understand. He thought that they needed him, he thought his work was important.

The figure of Andrewes translated into Ben and abruptly it all became clear. It was Ben who had mixed up the words, a ploy to keep the scholars busy so he could slip past them all unnoticed.

'Ben?' he whispered. A voice answered. Not Ben's. Ellyn? No. Alice? Maybe.

He struggled to focus. The face moved closer and the voice said, *Drink this.* He felt his head being lifted, something cool and wet against his lips and throat. It tasted pleasant, like cool wine on a hot summer's day.

A physician came. He could see him standing next to the bed, peering down and prodding with a hard and bony finger. If he could have moved away from the man's intrusive reach he would have, but his body no longer seemed to be his to command, so he was compelled to stay put and endure it. Finally the man stepped back from the bed and talked to the person who was Ben or Ellyn or Alice.

When he opened his eyes again the physician had gone. He must have slept. Someone lifted his head to give him a draught of a foul-tasting liquid. *Drink this,* the voice ordered. *It will make you feel better.* He drank and the bitterness made him cough so hard he thought his head might burst with the pain of it. But when the coughing fit had passed he thought it might have helped him after all. He closed his eyes and floated once again into sleep.

He was in a prison cell, Ben's prison cell at the Fleet, exactly as he remembered it in his waking thoughts. He could smell the evil river outside the walls, and the rank and foetid stench that originated inside them. Ben was manacled, hanging on the wall, filthy black and naked. There was hatred in his eyes. *This is your doing, Richard Clarke,* he hissed. *And may God forgive you in His mercy because I never will, you false and faithless friend.*

Richard fell to his knees at the feet of his friend. *Forgive me, Ben,* he whispered, over and over. *Forgive me. Forgive me, Lord, forgive me.* But no answer came, and he was drowning, weighted down, Hell opening up to claim him. There would be no more forgiveness and he was damned.

Doctor Clarke? A voice called him back, a hand reaching down to haul him from the depths. A woman's voice, gentle and caressing. Perhaps he would be saved after all. *Doctor Clarke?* He fought to open his eyes, but in the moment he succeeded the light in them was searing, so he let them fall quickly closed. The prison cell had gone and there was only darkness. He wondered if he had met his death.

Richard?

He placed the voice. Alice. Noticed the weight of her hand on his forehead, smooth and cool against the heat of his fever. A human touch. He was still alive. 'Alice?'

'It's going to be all right, Doctor Clarke,' she promised. 'You're going to be all right. The fever has broken now and the worst is behind you.'

He tried to nod and smile to show he understood but instead he tumbled back to sleep. The room spun and twisted and became the vicarage in Kent. It was a pretty house with a well-kept garden. He would like to raise a family there. It would be a good place for a family. Peaceful. Quiet. No prison.

He heard Alice's voice again. 'Try and drink some of this.' Cold liquid touched his lips and in the dream he was kneeling at the stream behind the vicarage, lifting the clear water in his hands to drink. He swallowed gratefully, the fluid soothing the dryness of his mouth.

Sleep took him again but there were no dreams this time, his mind finally quiet and resting until he woke again. Forgetting about the brightness he opened his eyes, but the room was darker now, candlelit, and the light did not hurt him. He blinked, adjusting to a world that seemed unfamiliar.

'Where am I?' he whispered.

Something touched the skin of his forearm, something cool and soft, and he turned his head towards it. A face appeared, small and pale, framed by mousy hair. He puzzled for a moment, trying to place it, trying to remember. A familiar face. Alice.

'You've been very ill,' she said.

He struggled to focus. She was sitting on the edge of the bed, and holding his hand in hers. If he could have found the strength he would have turned his hand to grasp her, to hold flesh and blood, human warmth to keep the nightmares away. But his body still seemed to belong to someone else so instead he tried to speak.

'How long?' he managed to breathe.

'Almost a week,' she answered. 'We thought we were going to lose you.'

'You were here all the time.'

'For all the good I did. There was nothing I could but wipe your brow and pray.'

'You gave me drink.'

'You remember?'

'A little,' he said. But clearer was the memory of Ben against the wall in chains and the hatred in his eyes, his own damnation.

He shifted himself a little in the bed, trying to sit up, and Alice leaned in close to help him, arranging the pillows at his back to prop him up. A scent of lavender breathed around her skin and he remembered the lavender his mother used to grow beside the kitchen, the image vivid and bright.

'I'll fetch you some broth,' she said, standing up. 'Rest now. I won't be long.'

He nodded but he wished she would stay. Her presence was a comfort and her touch a bulwark against the image of Ben that was still clear behind his eyes. He watched her go and when she returned again he had fallen back asleep. She woke him and spooned the warm broth to his lips, and though he could probably have managed by himself he let her do it, finding that he liked the intimacy.

'You talked in your fever,' she said.

He swallowed too fast and almost choked. The spasm wracked his whole frame, pain in every part of him. Alice sat back and waited for the fit to subside and when he could trust himself to speak again, he said, 'What did I say?'

'You talked to Ben, mostly.'

'What did I say to him?' He was almost afraid to hear the answer.

ept begging his forgiveness.'

He closed his eyes and the image sheared again across his thoughts. He steeled himself against it. It was a dream, he told himself. Nothing more. The fevered ramblings of a sickened mind. Alice observed him, peering close with her short-sighted eyes.

'Do you remember?'

'No,' he replied. 'I don't remember that.'

She nodded. Then, getting up from the bed with the half-empty bowl of broth, she said, 'Rest again now. I'll come back in a little while.'

He would have liked her to stay but he said nothing, and by the time the door had closed behind her he was already once more asleep.

It was another week before he was back on his feet and ready to work again. He began working more at the house after his illness: it was easier to rest when he needed, his body still weak, and he found that he could shut out the bustle and distractions after all. He still rose before the dawn, stirring the fire into life himself before he worked in the light of candles in the early-morning peace before matins. He did his best work in those early hours when his mind was fresh. Sometimes he found the answers had come to him in his sleep, his mind waking still in the world of the Holy Land, as yet undisturbed by the more venal world of London that lay just beyond his window.

He worked steadily through the morning. Verses from Genesis and the building of the Tower of Babylon, his mind turning on the fact of different languages, God confounding the people so they would no more overreach themselves, having to find instead their unity in their faith.

The Abbey bell tolled the hour of ten, the chimes rolling in on the breeze. Lifting his gaze from the desk, he let his eyes wander across the fields that stretched away beyond his window. He was glad his room looked out of the back of the house. Sheep dotted the greenery across the river; it was a peaceful scene.

A gentle scent of lavender touched the air, giving away Alice's presence behind him, and he wondered how long she had been there, looking down over his shoulder at the texts she could not understand. But he lowered his eyes once again to his work, pretending not to have noticed so as to draw out the moment longer. He enjoyed her company, an uncomplicated pleasure he knew with no one else. Only when she moved round from behind him and into the corner of his vision did he finally have to admit she was there.

He laid down his quill and turned toward her. 'Alice.'

'I brought you some wine, Doctor Clarke.' She set down a tray on the corner of the desk and he leaned forward to shift his papers, making space.

'Thank you.'

'It's cold in here,' she said. 'And the fire is almost out.'

'Is it?' he replied, turning to look. 'I hadn't noticed.' It was true. Absorbed in the Translation as he was, the world around him receded to the edges of his thoughts: he was in the world of the Israelites, in the heat and sun of the Holy Land, the harsh arid world of Abraham and Sarah, who were real to him, their voices clear and strong, their struggles his own. He inhabited this world more often than the physical world around him. Even walking through the London streets his mind was often there, the rhythms of the Hebrew in time with his footsteps, the images they conjured vivid in his head. He pitied those who knew no Hebrew, who could only ever hear the sacred words in English. For English carried no echoes of the past: it failed to take him there as the Hebrew did, words of holiness that bore him closer to God.

Alice smiled. 'That's no surprise. You get this faraway look in your eyes when you're working as though your soul is in the Bible instead of here. I've been watching you for ages.'

She poured him some of the warm spiced wine and with the heat of it against his fingers he suddenly noticed the chill. He shivered. 'You're right. It is cold in here.'

She moved to the fire and squatted to poke it into new life, throwing on another log. After a minute or two the flames leaped and crackled and in their light her mousy hair glowed golden. He took another mouthful of the wine as she stood up.

'What does it sound like in Hebrew?' she asked, moving closer to the desk, her eyes grazing the pages of script, intrigued. 'Is it like the Latin?'

'No,' he said quickly. 'Not at all. It's nothing like the Latin. It's more ...' He stopped. How could he describe it to her? How could he explain the mystery it held for him? 'It's more beautiful,' he said. 'More ancient. More sacred.'

'Read me some,' she suggested.

He shook his head. 'My spoken Hebrew is poor. How I say it is not how I hear it in my head. It's like hearing a song you like ...'

'... but when you sing it yourself it sounds completely different?' She smiled. 'I know that feeling. My mother had the most beautiful singing voice and as a young girl I would carry her songs around in my head. Then when she died I tried singing them to myself, but I sounded like the woman who hawks fish in the street. It was very disappointing.'

He laughed gently, delighted by her understanding but recognising the sorrow beneath the humour. 'Yes,' he agreed. 'Exactly like that.'

'But could you try?' she persisted. 'Just a little?'

He swallowed, torn between the wish for her to know and the fear that he would spoil it and make the words ugly to her ears.

'Please?'

He took a deep breath and made a decision. 'There's prayer called the Sh'ma, which the Hebrews sing.'

'Like a psalm?'

'Yes. A bit like a psalm. It's from Deuteronomy and you would know the English.'

She was watching him, waiting, and he paused, self-conscious. He began, too softly in an undertone so that his voice cracked and he had to stop. He cleared his throat and began again, a little louder this time.

'Sh'ma Yisrael Adonai Eloheinu Adonai echad ...' He stopped.

She was smiling, looking at him in a way he didn't understand, and the room seemed very warm.

'It's beautiful,' she said. 'What does it mean?'

'Hear, O Israel, the Lord our God is Lord only.'

She nodded. 'Yes. I know that passage. Sing some more.'

He shook his head, colour heating his neck and face.

'Please? It was beautiful.'

Touched and wanting to please her more, he began again. 'V'a-hav'ta eit Adonai Eloheka b'khol l'vav Kha uv'khol naf'shkha uv'khol m'odekka ...'

When he finished there was a moment of silence while she thought about what he had sung. Then she sang the lines softly, perfectly in tune, murmuring the English words, 'And thou shalt love the Lord thy God with all thine heart, and with all thy soul, and with all thy might.'

'It is as beautiful in Hebrew as it is in English,' she said. 'But how do you translate it? How can you tell its meaning?'

'By long hours of study.' He smiled, fingers touching the papers spread out across the desk, eyes sliding over the open pages of his books.

'But how?' she asked. 'How can you know the right meaning?'

He was silent, considering how best to explain. He had never needed to talk of it before; it was so much a part of him, the process instinctive and familiar. It was the greatest of pleasures, serving God in such a way, opening the window on the Scriptures so that all may know their light. He was blessed and humbled to have been given such a gift. After a while he said, 'There are many steps. First I look at the translations that have gone before, into English, into Latin – Tyndale, Coverdale, the Vulgate. I see what other men have made of it, what meanings they have understood. Then I return to the Hebrew and try my own hand at it. See here.' He drew a book towards her that held columns of writing in Hebrew and English. 'This is a lexicon, from the Hebrew to the English. It's a list of translated words. But not everything is there and sometimes the meanings that are there make no sense in the context. So then I have to find other instances of the word in other places in the Scriptures, to see if I can make sense of it that way. Finally, when I have ascribed each word a meaning, I have to try and make it into a sentence in English, and therein lies the skill. Trying to marry the truth of the meaning, the sacred Word of God, into English that reflects the same perfection. Understanding the meaning of the Hebrew is only half of it.'

Nodding to show she had understood, Alice let the tips of her fingers run lightly across the lines of Hebrew in the lexicon, fascinated. 'I can understand that a man might learn Latin,' she said. 'But Hebrew seems to be from a different world. I don't know how you even begin to understand it.'

'It's not so hard once you've studied it awhile,' he said gently. He was touched by her admiration and pleased. 'And it is so very beautiful.'

'You wish you had lived back then, don't you?' she said.

He laughed, surprised. 'Of course not.'

'I can see you there. You would be happy in your ancient world of Hebrew, that prayer on your lips in the desert, a simple love for God, waiting for Christ to come.'

'Well, perhaps,' he admitted. He had never thought of it in such a way, content to inhabit it in his mind. He was silent, observing her, and she dropped her gaze to the floor.

'Forgive me,' she said. 'I meant no offence.'

'I'm not offended,' he answered quietly. 'Just surprised.'

She flicked him a glance and her lips twitched into the beginnings of a smile. Then she moved towards the door and he watched her, wishing she would stay.

'Thank you for bringing the wine,' he said.

Her smile widened. 'It was my pleasure.' Then she squeezed out through the gap without opening the door any wider and disappeared into the passage.

CHAPTER 9

JANUARY 1605

And when they were come into the house, they saw the yong child with Mary his mother, and fell downe, and worshipped him: and when they had opened their treasures, they presented vnto him gifts, gold, and frankincense, and myrrhe.
(*Matthew* 2:11)

AT THE TWELFTH Night revels at Thieving Lane Ben stood with his back to the hearth in the main hall, watching the party unfold. It was still early, the festivities not yet in full swing, and the guests stood in small bands, the women's dresses bright and colourful amongst the merchants' sombre blacks. Drink was flowing freely, spiced wine and Rhenish, claret and ale; extra servants had been brought in to keep the guests' cups full, and others moved carefully through the crowd, holding aloft plates of fashionable delicacies – Greek olives, Italian grapes, plump dates and figs from the East, as well as traditional English pasties and pies. Above the music the hubbub was rising, the wine beginning to have its effect. Women's laughter drifted shrilly across the hall.

Ben sipped at his drink and wished himself in the Midlands. There would be no such revels at Scrooby, no profane celebrations. He stepped forward from the fire a pace, the backs of his legs starting to scald, but he stayed on the outside of the party, a reluctant guest at an ungodly gathering. He was ashamed he had allowed himself to be persuaded.

He scanned the hall. The furniture had been moved against the panelled walls, and the rugs taken up and packed away. Wintergreen ivy and holly hung from every hook, dappled with blood-red berries; mistletoe hung from the ceiling beams, great bunches close above the revellers' heads. As a boy he had gone with his sisters each year to collect the Christmas sprays, climbing to the highest branches to gather the best of the sprigs, throwing them down to Ellyn and Sarah, who had watched him with upturned faces full of pride and concern. He had never fallen, agile as a monkey, though once, larking about and pretending, he had almost tipped and overbalanced. He smiled at the memory, the childish innocence. But he had put away childish things now and the festivities no longer excited him.

A clutch of young women sat at one of the windows, giggling. He recognised Alice among them in a peach silk dress he had once seen on Ellyn. She was laughing and animated, and seemed very different from the timid creature he had talked to in the garden, so that he wondered if it was only in his presence that she became so meek. Beyond the girls, in a corner, a trio of musicians were labouring unappreciated, apparently unnoticed. No one had started dancing yet and in the centre of the floor was a gathering of merchants, their prosperity evident in the rich dark velvets and the cocksure way they held themselves. They were at their ease, cheeks already florid with wine, their laughter loud and confident. He could have been one of them, he reflected, if he'd taken the path his father wanted: comfortable and affluent, his prayers concerned with figures and trade instead of confessions of his sins and hopes for safety to worship. It was hard to imagine such complacency: he had been outside the law for so long, battling against the desires of his flesh and the human instinct for pleasure and security.

A woman he had never seen before approached the group that was giggling at the window. Her hair was red, as Cecily's had been, her shoulders bare and pale against a dress of deep blue silk. For a moment his gaze lingered on the softness of her skin, imagining the texture underneath his fingers, against his lips, lust rising. It was a long time since he had known a woman's touch. Across the room she caught his look and smiled, eyes lowered coyly. He shook his head and turned away, aware of himself once more as a sinner, his weakness as a man before God. Without Christ's love he was nothing. He wished he had stayed at Scrooby, away from such temptations.

A servant passed with a jug of spiced wine and Ben stopped him to refill his cup. Then Richard approached the hearth, just returned to London from his preaching duties at Canterbury. He was rubbing his hands together lightly, gazing at the crowd in slight bewilderment. He looked frozen to the marrow and, reaching the fire, he held out his hands eagerly to the warmth. Though they had not spoken since the bonfire on All Hallows' Eve, they exchanged no word of greeting.

'It's no weather for a journey,' Ben said. He was grateful for the distraction.

'Neither from Kent nor from the Midlands,' Richard answered. 'What brings you south at this time of year?'

'My father requested I come. He still hopes to make of me a merchant.'

Richard smiled, then turned and cast his eyes across the room. 'Who are all these people?'

'Associates of my father, merchants to a man.' He gestured to the group that held the centre of the hall. 'You see the sandy-haired man with no chin and thinning hair?'

The other man nodded.

'That's Hugh Merton, my sister's intended.'

Richard looked more closely, curious. 'He seems ...'

'Dull,' Ben supplied. 'But he's amiable enough, an honest sort of man. I imagine he will make a good husband.'

'She could do worse,' Richard agreed.

In the pause that followed, Ellyn came through the door and all eyes were drawn to her, vivid in silks of holly green with scarlet slashes in the sleeves and the skirt. She crossed the floor towards the women at the window, and if she noticed the attention that followed her she showed no sign. She launched into a story straight away, the other girls rapt, her quick hands describing details in the air.

The two men watched from their distance.

'Look at them,' Ben said. 'Hanging on her every word.' There was a mix of pride and amusement in his tone.

'She looks very pretty,' his friend offered.

Ben's eyes flicked towards him. 'You find her attractive?'

Richard had no answer and a telltale flush reddened his skin. He looked away.

'I'm surprised,' Ben said. 'I would not have thought you'd be drawn to a woman like Ellyn. I'd have thought you'd choose someone more gentle, more studious. Someone more like ... Alice.'

Richard hesitated, the blush still colouring his cheeks. Then he turned his head to face his friend. 'She's very like you,' he said.

Ben was silent, the response unexpected, and he slid his eyes away. He had no idea what he should answer. But perhaps he had misjudged his friend after all, he thought, and the love had not yet died. Perhaps it was just as Richard claimed: a comfortable bed close to the Abbey and a slight hope he might yet win his friend back to the Church. A servant moved close and Richard stopped him.

'Bring me wine,' he said. The servant bowed and moved away to return in moments with a cup.

'To Ellyn's betrothal.' Richard raised his drink.

Ben lifted his cup in silent salute and they drank.

At the window Ellyn reached the end of her story and the girls fell to giggling. Looking out beyond them, she spotted her brother and came towards them, still smiling.

'This looks like a serious conversation,' she mocked. 'Can anyone join in?'

'We were discussing your betrothal,' Ben answered. 'I was just telling Richard what a pleasant young man Hugh Merton is.'

'You're a pig,' she hissed, the merry sparkle turning to fury in an instant. 'How dare you?'

'Calm down, Nell,' he chided. It had always been too easy to bait her. 'I'm only teasing.'

'Well,' she huffed. 'For your information, I have no intention of marrying Merton.'

'Really? So who will you marry instead? How about Richard here?'

She swung to face Richard, cheeks flushed, and looked him up and down in open appraisal. Evidently the thought had not occurred to her before. 'Perhaps I will at that,' she said. 'At least it wouldn't land me in the Fleet.'

Ben's own temper flared, fury she would use such a thing against him, but as he opened his mouth to reply Richard intervened. 'Be at peace,' he warned. 'Your father approaches.'

Brother and sister turned as one, masks in places and smiles for their father, enmity put away. Ben had no wish to antagonise his father any further.

'It is good to have you back, Richard.' Thomas Kemp's pleasure seemed genuine as the two men embraced. 'Have you eaten?'

'I ate a little on the road.'

'Then drink. It's Twelfth Night and we must be merry.'

The men lifted their cups in salutation and drank one another's health before the older man moved away to greet more of his guests. They watched him circulate, cheerful and confident, wearing the fruits of his success with ease. It was not a role Ben could ever picture himself inhabiting, too aware of his own frailties and his unworthiness before God.

The musicians began to play a volta; one of the guests must have asked for it. People drew back and cleared the centre of the floor as a young couple in expensive silks took their places to begin this dance that had once been banned by the Pope. He saw Richard slide a furtive glance his way, and though he tensed against the music's sensuality, the desire embodied in the dance to come, he could not tear his eyes away.

The couple began to circle each other, seductive and enticing, the tambour beating rhythm until the music from the viol brought them close together. The man swung the girl high up in the air in movements that were intimate and graceful, her skirts swirling up and out around her. Ben found himself entranced, heat spilling in his groin. Desire filled him, a memory not of Cecily but of Greta – secret love, forbidden, the sinful pleasures of his flesh. Passion had almost ruined him, lust had led him away from God, and it was Cecily who had paid the price.

The dancers slid their bodies close together in the final steps of the dance as the music came to an end. Applause broke out and the couple laughed, still holding hands, eyes bright with desire for each other. It was hard to look away. The musicians struck up the less seductive notes of a pavane. Other couples moved onto the floor and Ben stepped forward to stand in front of his sister. He bowed.

'Will you dance with me, Nell?' He needed to move, lust in his body as restlessness: if he could not pray, he would dance, and find his innocence again in his sister's presence. She laughed, their hostilities forgotten. Accepting his outstretched hand, she let him lead her into the dance. Within moments he was rapt in the movement, the steps easily recalled from years before when he had partnered Sarah as she practised, Ellyn still a child and watching. Now she was flushed with delight, brother and sister moving as one with the stately beat of the tambour. For the length of the dance his sin was forgotten, joy rising from an earthly pleasure. When the music ended the dancers bowed and left the floor. Ben and Ellyn returned to Richard at the hearth, olive cheeks flushed, lips wide in breathless smiles.

'That wasn't bad dancing for a Bible man,' Richard risked.

Ben made no answer for a heartbeat. He thought of Christ at the wedding at Cana – perhaps there had been dancing at the feast as well as wine. He allowed himself to smile and return the spirit of the joke. 'Oh yes,' he said. 'We Bible men in the Midlands are famous for our dancing. Did you not know?'

'I hadn't heard.'

'Richard is just a poor vicar from Kent. He leads a sheltered life.' Ellyn smiled and flashed her dark eyes at him.

'Not any more he doesn't,' Ben countered, the joke turning dark. He couldn't help himself. 'These days the Reverend Doctor Clarke rubs shoulders with archbishops and deans – he is a man of the world. Before we know it he'll be at court and chaplain to the king.'

Richard said nothing but inclined his head to acknowledge the insult, smile frozen. Ben laughed, then turned away to watch the dancers.

'Ignore him,' Ellyn said loudly. 'He's just a grumpy old Puritan who doesn't like parties.'

Ben did not hear Richard's answer, choosing instead to watch the dancing, eyes following the movements of a quick-paced galliard. The elation of the dance had left him, replaced by awareness of his weakness, his flesh succumbing to desire. All he wanted now was solitude to pray, but he was trapped: his father's quick merchant's gaze would notice his absence in moments. He should have stayed in the Midlands.

To one side of the dancers, Hugh Merton disengaged himself from the knot of merchants and wove through the revellers around the dance floor towards them.

'Mistress Kemp.' Merton bowed. 'You're looking lovely tonight. Very festive.'

Ellyn gave him the most cursory of nods. Merton absorbed the slight but held his ground. Ben stepped in and made the introductions.

'My friend from Cambridge, Doctor Clarke. He is staying in my father's house during his work on the king's Translation of the Bible.'

'Doctor Clarke.' The two men bowed to each other. 'Of course I've heard of your work. It is a great task that you do.'

'It's a wonderful task, and I'm humbled by the honour of it.'

Beside him Ellyn was fidgeting, restless before this man who would soon be her husband.

'How is business?' Richard said, apparently to break a silence growing awkward. 'I understand you're in the spice trade.'

'You're interested in the spice trade?' Merton seemed pleased.

'A little. I like to hear stories of far-off places.'

The merchant laughed. 'Then you'll have to speak with Master Kemp. My place is here, overseeing the imports, the quality, making sure everything is as it should be.'

'How do you tell good from bad?'

Merton straightened up, keen to show his knowledge in front

of Ellyn. 'Take the nutmeg for example. It's simple. A sound nutmeg sinks in water, the unsound ones float and are used for oil.' He smiled at Ellyn, looking for approval. She gazed at him blankly.

'You've no desire to see where it all comes from?'

'Not me,' Merton answered. 'I am sick on a wherry on the Thames. The prospect of months aboard ship is not something that holds much appeal.' He smiled and Ben found he liked the man for his honesty, the confession of a weakness. Ellyn looked bored.

Merton turned to Ben. 'I heard you are planning to go East again yourself, Master Kemp.'

Ben tensed. 'It is yet to be decided.'

'Rather you than me,' the merchant said.

'I have no fear of ships.'

Ellyn laid a hand on her brother's arm. 'Go, and take me with you,' she entreated. 'I would love to go to sea.'

'It's less exciting than you think, little sister.'

'That's easy for you to say, who's done it a hundred times. Perhaps I shall stow away. Or dress up as a cabin boy ...'

'No.' Ben placed his hand over hers and lifted her fingers away from his arm. 'God has other plans for you.' He nodded towards Merton, who smiled, encouraging, hopeful.

She averted her eyes. Then she dropped a small curtsey to no one in particular and strode away towards the door. The three men watched the narrow back as she disappeared through the throng. When they could no longer see her Ben said, 'May God grant you patience, Master Merton. I think you're going to need it.'

The merchant nodded, thoughtful, before taking his leave and threading his way back to the safety of his father and his friends. Ben took another mouthful of wine and the memory of his own courtship trod again across his thoughts. He still writhed inside at the thought of it: the sin of his desire for her that had led him to deceive her. He would carry the stain of that betrayal until the end of his days.

~

ON THE DAY of their betrothal they had walked in the fields outside the city, strolling through orchards of peaches just coming into fruit. The scent had been sweet and heavy in the warm afternoon and they found a spot to sit in the shade of the trees. It was a perfect day, Cecily in rich green velvet that showed off the pallor of her shoulders, her red hair gleaming in the sun as strands lifted and blew in the breeze. His fingers had twitched to reach out and smooth it back in place, his skin burning just to be able to touch her. The memory still stirred his desire and the pain of her loss.

She had kept her eyes lowered away from his, observing her hands and rubbing at the finger that bore no ring, though they had exchanged their vows of betrothal that morning. In three weeks' time when the banns had been called they would be married, and the finger would still be bare. Gently Ben placed a hand over hers, stilling the movement.

'It doesn't mean I love you any less,' he said.

'I know,' she replied, without looking up. 'But still ...'

'You are disappointed.'

She nodded, eyes still cast down. 'A little.'

'But you knew this about me,' he said, softly, to mask the hurt and the fear she might still reject him, and the sorrow that he had hurt her. To see her sad gave him physical pain, an ache inside that even prayer could not ease. 'You knew I don't believe in wedding rings.'

She raised her face to him then, with a small sad smile that almost broke his heart. 'Yes. I knew,' she said. 'Same as I know you would never kneel for the Host or use the prayer book for worship.

But a ring is such a small thing, just a token that tells the world I'm yours. Surely God would not object if you gave me a ring to wear?'

He bit his lip, torn as he had never been between the conviction of his faith and his love for this woman. She watched him, waiting, hopeful. He shook his head and stayed silent.

'Surely even a Puritan may give his wife a ring?' she said. He could hear the puzzlement in her voice, the thought that if he loved her truly, surely he could grant her this one small thing. A part of him was tempted: anything to please her and make her happy, anything to prove his love. But the better part of him refused to compromise, buoyed by his faith.

Swallowing hard, he was aware of the quickness of his heartbeat and the risk in the words he would say to her next: it was time to speak plain truth.

'Cecily,' he said gently. 'You must know that I am more than a Puritan.'

He had made no secret of his beliefs, his desire for reform, his impatience with the Church; he was hoping she already knew enough of him to understand.

She said nothing, waiting for him to go on, her eyes now fixed on his. There was no smile in her eyes to soften the sternness, and he could feel the sweat on his palms.

'What do you mean you are more than a Puritan?' she asked. He could hear the trepidation in her voice and his heart tightened. She did not know.

'I ...' He stopped and looked away along the row of trees. The words were hard to form.

'Tell me,' she said. 'We are betrothed and I have a right to know.'

He hesitated again, afraid that his next words would be the last he ever spoke to her. But she needed to know and understand the kind of life that would be theirs. A life lived for God, the life a true love of Christ demanded, but a life of hiding and danger. Doubt assailed him. Did he have the right to ask so much of her? Finally, he took a deep breath and spoke. 'This is hard for me to say and it will be hard for you to hear.'

She observed him with mistrustful eyes, her chin tilted in challenge.

He went on. 'I believe in all those things that Puritans believe, same as you. We both of us want the same for our church – no bishops, no prayer book, no popish superstition. But I have come to believe the English Church will never be as we wish it, and ... I am a friend to Henry Barrow.'

Instinctively he checked around them to make sure no ears but hers had heard his words. They were alone. In one swift movement she dragged her hand from his and got up, skirts swept aside in a swish of velvet, petals and blades of grass clinging to the hem. She brushed at them with impatient hands and stood over him looking down. He looked up at her with the sun behind her, and her face was a silhouette against the brilliance, her red hair blazing. He shielded his eyes with a hand as he got up to face her, but he was still dazzled by the brightness. He breathed deeply and waited until he could see her face again clearly.

'Henry ... Barrow?' she managed to whisper, her eyes searching the ground for understanding. 'Henry Barrow in the Fleet, Henry Barrow?'

She stepped back from him a pace then turned away, struggling to take in his words. Whatever she had been expecting him to say, this news had come as a shock. He wondered how she had not suspected it – without actually saying the words, he thought he had made it plain.

'The same.' He waited, blood running nervous through his veins, watching her every move.

'Henry Barrow is a Separatist. He's been in prison for how many years?'

'Five.'

Barrow had been foremost among the Separatists. Like Ben he had studied at Cambridge, but his conversion came later in regret for a dissipated youth. Even from his prison cell he still wrote and taught, and still inspired a congregation of the faithful.

Cecily's face remained averted, her expression unknown to him as he waited for her reaction. He struggled to interpret the angle of her head, the movements of her arm, but after a moment or two she turned her back and walked away a few more paces. He watched her, transfixed with fear and indecision. He did not know what to do – he had thought she understood, that she would follow him. Perhaps he shouldn't have told her. But how could he hide such a truth from her when it was the spirit that gave him life?

She swung back to face him. 'You tell me this now?' she breathed. 'After our betrothal? Now we are already contracted? Did you not think I had the right to know beforehand?' She stopped, breathing hard with fury, and her breasts lifted against the square-cut bodice with each breath that she took. Ben's concentration threatened to stray to sinful thoughts, the weakness of his flesh. He dropped his eyes down to the grass at her feet and prayed for forgiveness for his wickedness. Cecily interpreted it as guilt for something else.

'Well might you feel guilty telling me this now. What right have you to do this to me? Why did you not tell me before?'

He lifted his hands in a gesture of helplessness. 'I didn't want to lose you,' he said simply. All the sleepless nights of prayer had made no difference: he had been too afraid to tell the whole truth, the passion of his lust harder than his faith. He had persuaded himself she understood and now he turned his head away, conscious of his sin and ashamed.

'What if I don't agree?' she demanded. 'What if I don't want to live like that? The Church is flawed and imperfect, yes, but it is the Church and I had not thought to leave it.'

'Because you did not think it possible.'

'It is against the law to worship as you do.'

'We ought rather to obey God than men.'

She was silent and he glimpsed a moment of hope.

'You believe the same as me,' he urged. 'You would see a true Church comprised of the faithful, like the early Church of the Apostles. *A glorious Church, not having spot or wrinkle, or any such thing: but that it should be holy and without blame* ... We can have that Church ...'

She cut him off. 'Holland,' she said. 'You went to Holland to a printer. You went to publish writings.' She was striding now, pacing between the trees, her world of happiness cut away from underneath her. 'Barrow's writings.'

'Yes.'

'Barrow is in prison for sedition. God in Heaven, Ben! Do you want to join him there? Father says he'll hang in the end, that there is no way back for him if he doesn't recant. And if you are found with his writings ...' She trailed off, the conclusion too awful to voice.

He said nothing. He had not thought to meet such resistance. He had thought she would come willingly.

'You went to see him at the Fleet?'

'Yes.'

'So they know about you now. They must know. They would be watching to see who came and went. They would have spies. Of course they would.' She lifted her hands from her sides in a gesture of despair and when she spoke again all the anger was gone, her tone low and indifferent. He had never seen her so cold.

'Then it's just a matter of time,' she said. 'It can only be a matter of time.'

He watched her, feeling helpless. The world had never seemed so bleak before. His faith in the truth of his belief and his love for her had blinded him to the reality. How could he marry her if she would not share his faith, and subject her to the hardships that lay in his future?

She said, 'I'll be one of those hopeless wives you see at the gates of the prisons trying to bribe their way in, desperate to see their menfolk, even just a glimpse. I've heard the wardens accept no money from such women, preferring other favours. Is that what you want for me, Ben? To whore myself to some gaoler just for the chance to see you? Or so that we can say farewell before you hang?'

She wiped savagely at her tears with the heel of her hand, and her eyes looked everywhere but at him.

He should have stayed in Holland where he was safe, he thought, and kept himself and his troubles away from this woman he loved. He should have married Greta. Dear God, what had he done?

'Of course that isn't what I want for you,' he said. 'For us. But I thought we were of one mind. I believed you understood, I thought you would be willing ...'

'You have nothing else to say?' The strong voice cracked. She sniffed, swallowing down all the tears that were yet to come, mastering her distress. 'That is all you have to offer in your defence?'

He shook his head, but what other defence could he make? What could he possibly say to make it better? 'I'm a fool,' he whispered. 'A sinful fool. I should have stayed away from you. Forgive me, Cecily. Please say that you forgive me.'

She said nothing, but slumped down to sit on the grass with her skirts around her as though she were sitting in a pool of more luxuriant green. Staring at the ground, she snatched absently at tufts of grass with determined fingers, then scattered them as fast. Ben let himself down gently to sit beside her.

'I love you, Cecily,' he said softly. 'You are my weakness and my strength.'

Some of the tension left her and she gave up her destruction of the grass. But she gave him no answer, her gaze still fixed away from him. For a while they sat in silence and he could think of nothing he might say to win her back to him. Finally she turned her body towards him and laid her hand over his where it lay in the space of grass between them.

'You could come back to the Church,' she said. 'There are many in the Church who think as you do, as I do. There are many who want reform.' She lowered her voice. 'And Queen Elizabeth grows old. It will be a new beginning when she's gone.'

He shook his head. 'The Church will never change. It will never be a true Church. The superstition, the ritual, the hierarchy … they are too entrenched, and too many men with power have too much to lose. It will never change.'

'How can you know that? Who would have thought that Geneva could be Calvinist, that Holland would be reformed? It is still such a short time since England stepped out from under the papal boot. These changes take time, Ben. We must be patient, we must endure.'

His fingers tightened into fists and automatically he drew away from her. She was asking the impossible. 'I cannot go back to the Church,' he whispered. 'I cannot.'

Neither of them spoke, neither knowing how to step across the breach that had opened up between them. Absently, Cecily rubbed at the place on her finger that bore no ring. A group of children, ragged boys up to mischief in the orchard, chased one another through the trees, shouting and laughing. Their voices rang loud in the quiet afternoon. Ben watched them until they had moved out of sight amongst the trees, their childish calls drifting back in snatches. When he turned towards Cecily again she was watching him as though she were trying to read his soul.

She said, 'So what happens now, Ben Kemp? What do we do now?'

Ben shrugged. 'It's your decision. Do you still want to be my wife knowing what you know?'

She looked away with a sigh, gazing out beyond the trees as though following the group of boys in her mind, and he could not even guess at her thoughts. He tensed, preparing himself to lose her. Slowly, agonisingly, she turned again towards him.

'I will still be your wife,' she said. 'Even knowing what I know. And I will join your congregation because you will be my husband and I must follow you.'

'I would release you from your contract if you wish it.'

'Release me now?' She shook her head. 'It's too late for that. We are already betrothed. The banns have begun. To back out now would damage my good name and I would not do that to my father.'

He nodded, relief surging through him that she would marry him after all. But he was aware of the anger behind the calmness of her words, and he understood she would have refused had she known beforehand, if he had given her the choice.

She stood up, wearily it seemed to him, and began to walk towards the city. He caught up with her in two quick strides and they walked in silence side by side all the way back to her father's house near the Strand. At the gate she finally turned towards him, lifting her head to look into his face. Her eyes were stern and there was no smile of love in them any more.

'I wish I knew what to say to you, Ben, but I can't think of anything at all,' she murmured. 'And that makes me sad because until today we could talk with ease all day about any subject under the sun.'

'We are still the same people that we were,' he said. 'Neither one of us has changed.'

'But you have changed for me. You are a different man than I thought you.'

As he had been mistaken in her. 'Forgive me,' he said. 'I will atone.'

She gave him a slight sad smile. 'Perhaps.'

Then she had turned and walked away through the gate and she had not once looked back.

CHAPTER 10

JANUARY 1605

But *they also haue erred through wine, and through strong drinke are out of the way: the priest and the prophet haue erred through strong drinke, they are swallowed vp of wine: they are out of the way through strong drinke, they erre in vision, they stumble in iudgment.*

(*Isaiah 28:7*)

In the morning Richard woke late in a house that was quiet in the aftermath of the revels. Beyond the open curtain the day had turned vicious with sleet and rain, but within, a fire had been lit and the room was warm. He wondered how long since the servant had been in to light it, how he had managed to sleep through. Except for his illness he had always woken before the dawn.

Annoyed with himself for having wasted so much of the day, he swung himself out of bed and dressed quickly. He would work at the Abbey today, he decided, away from Ben, whose presence could only distract him. When he was ready he stood for a moment by the window, looking out at the rain-whipped fields and the river flowing dark and agitated: it was very tempting to remain in the warm and dry. But he wanted peace to work: the morning was already half-gone, and he would find no peace beneath the same roof as Ben. So he gathered up his papers with a sigh and wrapped them carefully in their leather satchel. Then, holding them close to his body beneath his cloak, he hurried down the stairs and outside into the rain.

The streets were quiet – people still sleeping off Twelfth Night, he supposed – and only those with no other choice were out and braving the weather. Twice he nearly slipped, the mud slimy and dangerous underfoot until he reached the cobbles of Broad Sanctuary. He clutched his precious work tighter to his body, fearing to drop it in the dirt.

Reaching the Abbey door with relief, he paused to tip back his hood and raked the water from his hair with his fingers. Inside, the bitter day was forgotten. Torches blazed in sconces on the marble columns, and trees of candles burned brightly, shadows flickering high up onto the vaulted roof. The peace of ages enveloped him despite the hubbub of commerce that echoed, Westminster's populace carrying out its business within the hallowed walls. The Abbey was many things to many people, he reflected, but for him its magnificence was a magnet to draw his soul to Heaven. You could say what you like about the Papists, but they knew how to build a church that could bring a man to God. He smiled at the thought of it, and a sudden memory of the church of his childhood cut across his thoughts. The walls had already been plain when he was a boy, whitewashed in King Henry's time on Thomas Cromwell's orders. But his father had told him that under the white there were hidden the most ornate of paintings, Christ's Passion lovingly depicted in a profusion of colours that plain folk seldom saw. As a child the thought had captivated him, and he had spent long sermons squinting as he tried to see beyond the whitewash to the pictures underneath. And sometimes, when chance had allowed, he had scraped at the walls with a fingernail, itching to find the hidden treasures he knew were waiting. It was a shame, he thought, to take the loveliness and beauty out of worship. For the soul is stirred by such things, and being stirred it opens up to receive the love of God. It was an argument he had fought many times with Ben.

Lowering his eyes, and turning his mind once more to the task in hand, he hurried towards the East Cloister, heading for the library. He saw the Dean as soon as he turned the corner, striding purposefully, apparently deep in thought. Richard slowed and Andrewes pulled up short just in front of him, a broad smile lighting his face at the sight of the other man. Richard looked down and saw his own cloak dripping onto the flagstones and realised the picture he presented.

'It's raining outside,' he said. He gave the Dean a wry smile.

'It is indeed,' Andrewes agreed. 'And what brings you out in such weather?'

'A need for some peace to work. A little solemnity after the revels.'

'Ah yes. The revels.' The Dean nodded. 'I was at Court last night. I understand completely.'

There was a pause.

'How was Court?' he asked.

'The usual masque. Lavish. A little drunken. A little bawdy. It seems the king and his queen are still enjoying the luxuries of the English throne.'

'It's a richer throne than the Scots'.'

'Although less rich than we would wish, so I'm told.'

'It must be a great disappointment to His Majesty.'

'It is. But he is shrewd. And more theologically inclined than our late queen.'

'Then that is a blessing.'

'Perhaps.' The Dean's eyes glittered with mischief. 'But then again, perhaps not.'

'I'm not sure I understand, Mister Dean.' The rain had soaked through his cloak to his clothes and he was starting to feel the cold. He was in no mood for games.

'I have every regard for the king's intellect. He is learned and well read and he likes to debate ...'

Richard sensed a *but*. He was not disappointed.

'But often it is easier for people to agree when some of the details are left a little vague. Too many specifics will make it harder to conform for those who need to compromise.'

'He would have more specifics?'

'Elizabeth was very wise,' Andrewes said by way of reply. 'Perhaps wiser than we knew.'

Richard nodded his agreement. The old queen had steered a careful middle way, the political loyalty of her subjects more important than the finer details of their faith.

'And on the subject of compromise,' the Dean said, 'how fares Master Kemp?'

He smiled at the aptness of the link. 'He is well. He has been in London these past few days at his father's house. His father is still hoping to send him to the East.'

'Let us pray that he does.'

'Last night,' he said, 'at the revels, Master Kemp was dancing.'

'Dancing?' Andrewes chuckled, eyes glinting with good humour. It was hard to imagine him as Ben had described, harsh and unforgiving and no pity in his heart for his prisoner.

The Dean was still chuckling. 'That's a fine piece of news for the Archbishop. It might even put him off his morning ale. A Puritan dancing, eh? What was it? Not a volta, I hope?' He was genuinely amused.

'A pavane.'

'And the lady?'

'His sister.'

'Well,' Andrewes said, mirth subsiding. 'Perhaps he is coming round after all. Perhaps we might yet welcome Master Kemp back into our fold.'

'I make no pretence to know his heart, Mister Dean, but his dancing is very impressive.' He smiled. He had been enthralled as brother and sister moved together in stately unison, hands just touching, feet in perfect harmony, turning in time together as though they practised every day. It had been marvellous to see such grace and lightness, an effortless rapport, and he had been astonished. He had never known Ben to dance in all the years he had known him, but he should hardly be surprised – always his friend had moved with graceful agility.

'I am glad to hear it.' Andrewes smiled. 'We must pray to God to deliver him back to us.'

'Ben is always in my prayers.'

'And mine also.' Andrewes smiled again. 'And now I must leave you to your work, Doctor Clarke. I must away back to Court. The king has called for me. Again.' He lifted his eyebrows. 'I will see you at our meeting on Thursday.'

Richard stood and watched the Dean stride away, long limbs loose in the flowing robe. He sighed. He had only told Andrewes the truth: Ben had indeed been dancing, for reasons known only to himself, but it still felt like a deception. Whatever the reasons for Ben's Twelfth Night levity, it was unthinkable it might herald a change in his faith.

The Dean's figure swept around the corner of the cloister, out of sight. Richard stared at the space he left behind for a moment before he turned away and walked towards the library.

∾

THE BOOK of Ruth had been Richard's mother's favourite: his eldest sister bore the name. He had learned it early, reading the verses to his mother over and over, sitting at the table with the Bible before him and speaking the words as his mother laboured at the endless tasks of a farmer's wife. He had read other passages to her too, he was sure, but none he could remember. Ruth he had learned by heart long before he went away to school.

He had not thought of it in years, those evenings in the kitchen when the whole family gathered in the one room that was warm. His mother had always been toiling as he read to her – he had no memory of ever seeing his mother sit down except to eat or sew. Certainly, she never sat down merely to rest. No wonder then that this woman in the Bible appealed to her, a woman who was loyal and true and hardworking. A woman who followed a hard path that led her to God and redemption. Even now he heard the English in Coverdale's words, the Bible translation he had learned first and best.

He knew of all the books he would find it the hardest to translate. Coverdale's words held the truth for him, and he struggled to render the Hebrew differently. So he worked ahead, giving himself time to find the words he needed, the phrases running through his thoughts in idle moments. But however he rendered the Hebrew in English, none of his words seemed to carry the beauty of Coverdale's, even when he knew they were closer to the truth of the original.

He read the passage again in Coverdale, though he knew it by heart:

And when Boaz had eat & drunk, his heart was merry, & he came and laid him down behind a heap of sheaves. And she came secretly, and took up the covering at his feet, and laid her down.

Now when it was midnight, the man was afraid, and groped about him, and behold, a woman lay at his fete.

And he said: Who art thou? She answered: I am Ruth thy handmaiden, spread your wings over thy handmaiden: for thou art the next kinsman.

Then in the Geneva:

And when Boaz had eaten, and drunken, and cheared his heart, he went to lie down at the end of the heap of corn, & she came softly, and uncovered the place of his feet, & lay down.

And at midnight the man was afraid and caught hold: and le, a woman lay at his feet.

Then he said, Who art thou? And she answered, I am Ruth thine handmaid: spread therefore the wing of thy garment ouer thine handmaid: for thou art the kinsman.

He drew his paper to him and began to write out the words he had been carrying for days in his head:

And when Boaz had eaten & drunk, his heart was merry, & he came and laid him down behind a heap of sheaves. And she came secretly, and took up the covering at his feet, and laid her down.

Now when it was midnight, the man was afraid, and groped about him, and behold, a woman lay at his feet.

And he said: Who art thou? She answered: I am Ruth thy handmaiden, spread thy wings over thy handmaid: for thou art a kinsman.

It would be many months until the Company met to translate

Ruth. But he hoped they would keep Coverdale's *groped about him* as a true translation of the Hebrew. It was such a vivid image of a man's fear in the night; who among us has not experienced such panic in the dark? He feared, though, he would be overruled and that the Company would prefer the Geneva's *caught hold*. In truth he knew it was a more likely rendering, but he could only hope. He hoped too that Boaz might still spread his *wings* over Ruth, with all the connotations of protection inherent in the word.

He thought of his mother again, her years of widowhood and the hardship of the farm. Did she still labour through each day, he wondered, or had age made her frail and infirm? She would be elderly now and approaching her final years, and he was not the good son he should have been – last he had heard she was under the protection of his sister Ruth and her husband, the farm in their hands now. He had no idea what sort of man Ruth had married, if his mother was well cared for, if she was loved and honoured. He rarely even thought of her, he realised with a ripple of shame, the life of his boyhood all but forgotten, her face a blur in his memory. But she would be proud of him now if she knew how far he had come, he consoled himself, a king's translator, a preacher at Canterbury. He would write to his sister, he decided. She could read a little, the words he had taught her as a child, and pass on the news.

He was still pondering his decision when the peace in the library was shattered by the arrival of Thomson, who paused at the top of the stairs to steady himself, his complexion florid, his eyes still red from the excess of the revels. Gaining confidence on his feet on flat ground, the newcomer strode to the table. When he breathed out, Richard blinked and held his breath.

'What news, Doctor Clarke?' Thomson's slur was loud in the hush. But they were alone and there was no one else to be disturbed. 'I didn't think to find anyone else here, though I might have thought you would be.'

'I am keeping well, thank you,' Richard replied. 'Yourself?'

Thomson slumped into a chair across the table, and he had to fight down the urge to shift his own chair back, out of breath's reach.

'As you see me. As always.' He laughed and let out a belch.

'You came here to work?'

'I did indeed.' Thomson let his papers fall to the table. They scattered across the books that Richard had open before him. Richard breathed deeply to counter his growing irritation.

'You would like this section of the table?' he asked.

'It's as good as any other, I think.'

'Then I will move along.' He gathered his papers and books and slid sideways to the far end of the table, rearranging them with care to his liking. It took him a moment to find his place in the text and to train his mind on the phrase in front of him, but the concentration had gone and the words he had formed in his mind before Thomson's arrival had vanished into the air. He laid down his quill.

Thomson leaned on an elbow in his direction. 'Did I disturb you?'

'Yes.'

'Forgive me. I had rather too much Rhenish last night.'

Richard sighed, resigning himself to no more work for the moment. Perhaps at Thieving Lane he could do more, but Ben would be there and today he felt unequal to the argument.

'You look like you could do with a drink yourself,' Thomson said. 'What in Heaven's name is wrong with you?'

'Nothing that a drink will do anything to help,' he replied.

'But at least you'll forget for a while ...'

'I use the Translation for that.'

Thomson blinked and pulled himself straighter. 'Yes. It is absorbing. I agree. And I admire your industry. But regrettably work is no longer enough to make me forget. I find I need the drink as well.'

'What do you need to forget?'

Thomson laughed. 'Don't make the mistake of thinking you're the only one with secrets, Doctor Clarke. Or sorrows. We all of us have some shame somewhere deep inside of us, something that gives us pain, some hidden grief or regret. We are all of us unworthy of our Lord.'

He said nothing.

'And the Lord knows our secrets, knows our griefs. He knows what lies in each man's heart. All of it, he knows. Sometimes I find that less than comforting. Sometimes I think I'd like some things in me to stay hidden. Even from God.' The older man lifted bleary eyes towards Richard. 'I expect you find that shocking. Even heretical.'

'Not at all,' he said. 'You have my sympathy.'

'Between you and me, of course.'

'Of course.'

'You never did pay me that visit.'

'I know.'

'Well, who can blame you, eh? Look at me. I'm hardly good company, am I?'

'That's the Rhenish talking.'

'Perhaps.'

The door opened and there were footsteps on the stairs. Richard turned towards them, attention drawn instinctively. A servant, come to tend the fire. By the time Richard returned his attention to his books, Thomson's head was on the table and he was snoring. Resigned to no more work today, he packed up his things, bundled them carefully in their wrapping under his clothes, and headed back out into the rain.

CHAPTER 11

JANUARY 1605

W iues, submit your selues vnto your own husbands, as vnto the Lord. For the husband is the head of the wife, euen as Christ is the head of the Church: and he is the sauiour of the body. Therefore as the Church is subiect vnto Christ, so let the wiues bee to their owne husbands in euery thing.

(*Ephesians 5:22–24*)

AT THE SUPPER table at Thieving Lane they ate capon with lemon sauce and dates, and the sour-sweet piquancy recalled to Ben's mind the exotic tastes of Aleppo. After three years of prison food and weeks of hard tack at sea, such bright flavours had seemed impossible; now he took the marvels of God's earth for granted, but he could still recall his sense of wonder and surprise. He ate reverently, mindful that such gifts from God were precious. Then he noticed Ellyn's place was empty and recalled he hadn't seen her all day. He said, 'Where's Ellyn?'

There was no immediate reply, his mother's head remaining lowered, his father with a mouthful of meat. He turned to Alice.

'Alice? Where is my sister?'

The girl blushed as he waited for an answer. 'She is in her chamber,' she murmured without lifting her eyes. 'She is feeling a little ... unwell.'

'Unwell how?' He had to bite back the growing impatience, mindful of his cousin's shyness of him. But he was aware that he was missing something, a ripple round the table that had passed him by. 'What am I not being told? Alice?'

She swallowed and finally lifted her face to meet his gaze. There was fear in her eyes and he wondered how she could like him when she seemed scared half to death of him.

'What is wrong with my sister?'

Alice hesitated and flicked a glance to her uncle, hoping for rescue. Thomas Kemp said, 'Leave Alice alone.' Then, 'Your sister was betrothed to Hugh Merton this morning and she is ...'

'Oh,' Ben said, 'I can imagine how she is. Why did no one tell me before?' He looked from his father to his mother, and both of them looked away so that he realised it had been a conscious decision not to inform him. He stopped eating and laid down his knife, resentment taking his appetite. What had they thought he would do?

'Why did you not tell me?' he repeated. 'She is my sister. Am I to be excluded from all family matters now?'

Emma Kemp stood up abruptly, her chair scraping loudly on the boards, and without another word she left the room. After a second's hesitation, Alice got up and followed her. Ben watched them go until the door swung shut behind them.

'Sir?'

'See?' his father said. 'Now you've upset your mother.'

'It was a reasonable question,' he answered. His mouth was tight with anger, holding back the words that threatened to come.

'You've brought enough trouble to this family already.'

'What did you think I would do?'

'One wayward child is enough.'

'Wayward?!'

His father swivelled in his chair to face Ben head-on. 'She needed no encouragement from you in her obstinacy. She has always looked up to you, always craved your approval. Even as a child, her crimes were always down to you.'

Ben was silent. A bright heat pulsated through his body and his fingers worked against the smooth surface of his glass.

'When you were in Aleppo,' his father went on, 'do you know she used to threaten to stow away on one of our ships and go out to find you every time I mentioned the subject of marriage?'

He almost smiled. It would not have surprised him in the least to find her there in the East, her spirit untrammelled by the need to conform. Richard had been right: they were very much alike.

'You misjudge me,' he said. 'I would have told her to marry him. I would have her safe and settled, the same as you.'

'Then it's a pity you won't do the same thing for yourself and give your poor mother some peace.'

Ben acknowledged the rebuke with a tilt of his head. 'I have my reasons,' he said.

His father made no reply but Ben recognised the look of disappointment on his face – he had seen it many times.

'I'll talk to Ellyn,' he said, rising from the table with his supper uneaten. 'Perhaps I can use my influence for good for once.'

'I would be grateful,' Thomas Kemp said, a wry smile beginning at the corners of his lips. 'A betrothal is not yet a marriage.'

Ben nodded. Then he turned and walked away and left his father to finish eating supper alone.

IN HER CHAMBER Ellyn sat at the window staring out at the houses across the street, their curtains drawn against the evening, windowpanes dark and blank. Below them figures hurried in the street with flaring torches. It was a bitter night to be outdoors. The Abbey bell chimed six as he came into the room but she did not turn her head.

She said, 'Do you remember how you used to take me to play at the river? When we used to watch the ships and plan to stow away?'

'I remember.' He sat at the other end of the window seat and observed her. Her face was sad and pinched from crying, the dark eyes clouded and their usual fire extinct. She had been just a small child, and he almost a man. But he had seen himself in her, a kinship between them he never shared with Sarah.

'I should have gone when I could.'

'You would have been disappointed,' he told her. 'It's not as we dreamed.' Then, 'It could be worse, Nell.'

'How?' She turned towards him and he had never seen her look so beaten. Reaching out his hand, he took hold of her small, cold fist.

'He is a good man. He'll look after you. And your home will be just a few streets away so you can still go sit by the river and dream if you want to.'

She kept her eyes lowered, trained on her hand in his. 'I don't even like him.'

'You don't know him. He's not a bad man and he cares for you. I saw it in his face last night. You'll learn to like him in time if you give him a chance.'

Her mouth tightened and she looked away, gazing out once more to the street. It was empty now and the lanterns at the doors glimmered wearily in the drizzle. 'What do you care if I marry happily or not? What is it to you?'

He tightened his hand round hers. 'You are all I have left that I truly love, Nell. I want you to be settled. I would have you be safe and protected.'

'Like you did for Cecily?'

He let go her hand as if it had burned him. Then he stood up and paced across the room to stand at the hearth. The fire was low and he squatted to tend it, throwing on another log and thrusting savagely with the poker to force it to light. He said nothing, and the silent prayer did nothing to ease the pain the truth of her words inflicted. When he turned from the fireplace Ellyn had swung round to face him.

'I'm sorry,' she said. 'That was cruel.'

'What could you know?' he asked. 'You were so young.'

'I was almost a woman. I was old enough to know she loved you.'

'She did not want the life I gave her.'

'But you loved each other.'

'Yes,' he agreed. 'And look where it led us. Where it led her. You're right – I did nothing to protect her, nothing to keep her safe. And I won't let the same thing happen to you.'

'You couldn't have known, Ben. Who but God could have foreseen such a thing?'

He shook his head and kept silent, remembering. They had both of them known where it would lead, and he had given her no choice but to follow him.

'I shouldn't have married her,' he said. 'And perhaps she would still be alive.'

'She was lucky to marry a man she loved and she knew it.'

He stepped away from the hearth and retook his place on the window seat. The chill from the glass made him shiver. 'You will grow to love him,' he said, turning the subject away from his pain onto hers.

'Don't talk nonsense. I'll grow to accept him, that is all.'

'But you will be taken care of, safe.'

'Perhaps.' Her eyes narrowed. 'Why all this sudden interest in making sure I'm looked after, that I'm safe? You never concerned yourself much before.'

'Our parents grow older. If I go ...' He touched his fingers to the glass, unable to finish the sentence.

'Go where?' she demanded. 'You're not going back to Aleppo after all, are you?'

'No. But I may not always be here.' Meaning he might be in prison again, or worse, but he could not say the words. She was safer knowing nothing.

'What do you mean, Ben Kemp? What are you up to? You cannot lie to me.'

'I can and I will,' he said, 'if it will protect you. Marry Hugh Merton, Nell, and be a good wife. Give him sons and be the one child in the family that spares our parents any more grief.'

'I don't want to marry him.'

'Is there someone else you do want to marry?'

She sighed and shook her head.

'You have to marry someone,' he said softly. 'You can't stay here all your life. Our parents grow old, and what will happen to you then?'

'I'll come and live with you.' She gave a wry smile but he knew it was only half a joke.

'Merton is a good man,' he said, and laid his hand on hers. She seemed not to notice, but turned her gaze to the window and stared out into the blackness beyond. 'Father has chosen him well and carefully – no one wants for you to be unhappy.'

'Well, I am,' she snapped back, drawing her hand out from under his, tucking hair behind her ears with restless fingers.

'Unhappy?' he asked. 'Or afraid?'

She swung her head round towards him at that, but her eyes remained lowered, gazing at nothing. 'Why do you say that? Why would I be afraid?'

'Placing your life in another man's care ...' Cecily must have been terrified of her marriage to him, knowing the life he would give her. But the sin of his desire for her had made him blind. 'Of your marriage bed ...'

'No,' she answered quickly. 'Not of that. I am not afraid of that.'

'But you are afraid ...?'

She said nothing, eyes grazing the floor at their feet.

'You remember Cecily, and her labour,' he said, with sudden understanding. 'You were here when she died.'

Her jaw tightened, lips clamped tight, and she nodded once, briefly. Ben lifted a hand to her face and brushed her cheek with the backs of his fingers.

'Oh, Nell,' he murmured. 'It doesn't have to be like that. Cecily ... that was my fault ... if I had been here ... if I hadn't been in prison ...'

Ellyn blinked, trying to hold back the tears, but they came anyway, wet against his fingers. 'It was awful. So long ... it took so long ... I can still hear her cries ... She called for you, near the end when she knew it was hopeless ... She called out your name, over and over and over.'

He tensed against the thought of it and the tears burned behind his eyes. No one had ever told him the details before, but he had imagined it often enough – images of Cecily's death still filled his nightmares. Ellyn had been a young girl on the cusp of her own womanhood; no wonder she was afraid.

'I don't want to die like that,' she breathed. 'Not like she did.'

He drew her to him then and she folded willingly into him to weep against his shoulder. His own tears he blinked back with fierce determination, swallowing down his grief, murmuring silent prayers for strength and for forgiveness. Her body seemed small and frail in his arms, childlike. He remembered holding her the same way when she was little: she had fallen asleep against him many times, safe in her big brother's arms, where nothing could hurt her. It was hard to think she would soon be a wife, a mother – he still thought of her as a girl. He wished he could take her with him as she wanted, but there was danger where he was going and he would never bring her to that.

Slowly her sobs began to ebb, her body trembling lightly against him, her breath coming in uneven gasps. He loosened his hold on her, but still kept her close, protective and comforting. Her breathing slowed, the trembling ceased, and after a while she shifted herself back from his embrace. Looking up into his face she attempted a smile. Ben smiled in return, and moved to wipe the tears from her face with his thumbs. She jerked her head away from his touch and rubbed at her cheeks herself.

'Forgive me,' she whispered, sniffing.

He waited, watching her as she fought to compose herself and still her breathing. When she was calm enough she turned to him again. 'I'm sorry, Ben. I didn't know I was so afraid. I just didn't know.'

He nodded. He knew well what it meant to feel fear and keep it secret. Even from yourself.

'I wish you would take me with you,' she murmured, 'wherever it is you're going. I'm sure I would be happier there with you.'

'Perhaps,' he said. 'But God has willed a different path for you.'

'I have no choice, do I,' she said. It was not a question.

'No,' he replied. 'You have to marry someone sooner or later. It may as well be Merton.'

She gave him a small smile then shifted close to him again, laying her head on his shoulder. He put his arm round her and held the small body close. They sat for a while, his arm still holding her and the cold glass chilling their backs, their faces feeling the warmth of the fire. Finally she turned to look up at him.

'Thank you.'

'What for?'

She shrugged. 'Being my brother.'

He smiled. 'Have faith, Nell,' he said, letting his arm slip from her shoulders. 'Trust in God and all will be well.'

'Perhaps.' She shrugged, moving away from him and smoothing her hair with rapid automatic fingers. She was still sniffing, and her eyes were puffy from weeping. 'But there is little I can do about it either way. Father has decided. It is time for me to put off childish things, time I took my place in the world.' She gave him a small smile, finding her courage, some of her spirit returning. 'Don't fret about me. You've your own cares to think of. I'll be all right. As you say, Hugh's not a bad man. I could do worse.'

'He'll look after you, Nell,' he said. 'And your life will be settled.'

She nodded and ran her hands across her face to wipe clear the last remnants of her tears. Ben waited, giving her time to gather her resolve to leave her girlhood behind her and face her future as a woman and a wife. Whatever happened from now, he had done what he could to see her safe and protected. He could have done no more.

Ellyn gave him another small smile that spoke of dreams unlived and resignation, and his heart turned in pity. Then she took a deep breath and squared her narrow shoulders.

'Are you ready?' he said.

'Yes,' she answered, drawing herself up, and nodding. 'I'm ready.'

'Good girl,' he said. 'Let's go downstairs. You can have some supper and make your peace with Father.' He stood up and held out his hand for her. She hesitated just a fraction of a second before she took it and let him lead her from the chamber towards the head of the stairs. There she paused, breathing deeply, before she stepped forward without another word and hurried down the stairs. Ben followed close behind, careful not to tread on her skirts as they trailed on the steps at his feet. When they were nearly at the bottom, on the second-last stair, she stopped so abruptly he almost ran into her. He grabbed at the banister to stop himself pitching forward.

'He's not here now, is he?' she whispered over her shoulder at him, close behind her. 'Merton, I mean.'

'No,' he replied. 'He isn't here.'

She sighed a deep breath of relief and he stepped down to walk beside her along the passage to the dining chamber. At the door she looked up at him again. 'Be careful, Ben, will you please?' she whispered. 'Stay safe. For my sake.'

He patted the small hand she had laid on his arm.

'Of course I will,' he lied. 'Of course.'

LATER HE SAT before the hearth alone with Richard. The rest of the family had gone to bed, Ellyn reconciled to her parents and sad. Ben had watched her show her brave face through the evening and hoped he had done the right thing. Now the house was quiet. His father's footsteps had ceased across the room above and the only sound was the hollow roar of the fire in the chimney as it fought against the bitter chill of the night. Both men remained close to the hearth, drawn by the light and warmth, cold darkness at their backs. Ben sat on the floor amongst the cushions, smoothing the soft fur of the greyhound with one hand while Richard reclined in his chair, wine glass playing loosely in the fingers of one hand. Ben could feel the eyes of the other man watching him but he did not look up. He was comfortable in the warm and he felt no need to break the silence.

Finally, Richard spoke. 'Are you planning to go?'

'Go where?' he replied, without lifting his head. It had always been easy to needle his friend.

'To Aleppo.' Richard's answer was testy. 'Will you go as your father wishes?'

Ben shook his head. 'I've already told you. And him. No.'

'Why not? It would mean the world to your father.'

'Yes,' Ben agreed, lifting his head at last to regard his friend. 'It would. But I live my life to please God, not my father.'

There was a pause. Richard drained his glass and shifted forward in his chair. 'Surely you realise you cannot go on as you are,' he said.

'I am happy as a tutor.' He was determined not to be drawn into argument.

Richard sucked in a quick breath of irritation. 'Don't play games with me. You know very well what I mean.'

Ben was silent, unsure what to say. The terms of the argument had changed since the old days – his words might be used against him now, and he was no longer sure of his old friend's loyalty. He wished it could be otherwise. He missed the cut and thrust of their debate, and the understanding that all their differences did not spoil the love that bound them: it hurt to believe that Richard might betray him.

'You no longer trust me,' Richard said. He sat back in his chair again, affecting hurt.

Ben tilted his head in assent.

'We are old friends,' Richard said. 'And we have been through much hardship together. Have I not proved myself faithful in the past?' He shifted forward once more, appealing to his friend. 'Why then do you distrust me now?'

Ben considered, watching his fingers against the dog's fur. A memory cut across his thoughts: the first time he had held the greyhound as a puppy, Cecily standing close enough to kiss. He raised his head and met Richard's gaze. The other man was watching him, trying to read his thoughts. Let him try, Ben thought. I will give him nothing. 'Because too many years have passed since then,' he said. 'We are not the men we were.'

'Have we changed that much?'

'You have. You move in different circles now. The Abbey. Andrewes. Bancroft. You're a long way from your precious Cambridge now.'

'Do you think I *like* Bancroft?'

'No one *likes* Bancroft. Even his allies despise him. But he has the Church in his hand, the ear of the king, and you agree with him on almost everything.'

Richard sighed.

'See? You don't even seek to deny it.'

'My views haven't changed, Ben. I have always thought the same, always believed in the inclusiveness of the English Church, traditions unbroken from the days of the Apostles, and yet I was still your friend. Remember how we used to argue? Hour upon hour in that stinking cell, the same disagreements, the same words over and over? We could have the same discussion now and not one thing would be different.'

'One thing would be different,' Ben said. 'You are not a humble Cambridge scholar any more. You are a king's translator at the heart of the English Church—'

'Go back to Aleppo, Ben,' Richard interrupted. 'Or go to Holland. Holland is a Christian place – there are churches already there that follow your way of worship. England is no longer safe for you and your kind ...'

'My kind?' Richard's persistence was beginning to wear down his patience, and in spite of his resolve he could not help but rise to the bait.

'You would rather I spoke plainly?' Richard's voice was raised. 'Should I use the words in this house where your father's servants can hear everything? I would rather not give them cause to hate you.'

'The servants are in bed and you should use the words you mean. Aleppo. Holland. My safety. What do these things matter to you anyway? Why do you still concern yourself?'

'Because I am still your friend. And because ...' He stopped, waiting for Ben to look up again. 'I see the way the wind is blowing in England.'

'Blowing for you or for me?' He leaned forward for the jug of wine that was warming on the hearthstone and refilled his glass. He did not offer it to Richard.

'My safety is not in doubt.'

'Just your loyalty.'

'My loyalty has always been to the Church, though others may have thought different. I only ever sought to bring you back within it.'

'And now?' Ben raised his eyes, searching to meet the other man's gaze. But Richard had turned away, his attention following the flames in the hearth.

'And now,' Richard said, 'I seek to get you gone from here to somewhere you'll be safe.' He set down the glass beside the chair. Then he said, 'Unless you care to recant.'

'I would rather die.'

It was Richard's turn for silence: both of them knew it was not an empty threat. Richard watched him, clear blue eyes intent on Ben's face and in them an expression that Ben could not read. Time was when he could have named every thought in Richard's mind, so clearly could he read him, so close had they been. But the vicar was a different man now and a stranger; older, harder, more worldly-wise. And he was not so patient with his friend as he once had been, his beliefs less tempered by love. Ben marked the change.

'You don't really care what happens to me,' he said. 'You just don't want me on your conscience. I'm your failure and you don't want to be reminded. You'd prefer me far away and out of mind.'

Richard took another swig of wine before he answered, his cheeks rosy from the drink and the fire and his emotion. 'It's nothing to do with my conscience. The law is closing in on you and you know as well as I do what awaits you at the end of that road. God has offered you another path, so why must you be so stubborn?'

'Because,' Ben said, 'I cannot run away all my life. Because there comes a point when you just have to stand firm for your faith and accept whatever God has planned.'

'You would rather go to prison than be safe? What purpose does that serve? What possible good can come of it?'

'You would not understand it if I told you,' Ben replied.

'Try me. I may surprise you.'

Ben lowered his eyes, watching his fingers caress the greyhound's ears. How could he begin to explain to Richard, who had never had to fight for anything? Who had never lost his faith? He thought of the others who had suffered, who had died: his wife, his son, Henry Barrow. Why should he alone be exempt?

'I cannot go,' he said, looking up. Richard was watching him, waiting, still hopeful. Ben shrugged. 'That is all. I cannot go.'

The other man stifled a sigh and turned his eyes towards the hearth. The silence between them deepened above the hollow roar of the fire and, despite the warmth, Ben shivered, disturbed by Richard's fears for him.

They sat a while longer in the quiet until at last Richard got up from his chair, a little unsteady from the wine – it had always been a weakness. He made his way to the door, then turned back to look at Ben.

'I've prayed and prayed you would make a different choice,' he said. 'You will always be in my prayers.'

'Goodnight, Richard,' Ben answered, without looking round. But he heard the sorrow in the other man's voice, and understood the grief that lay behind it. They had lost each other as brothers. In the end their differences were too vast and too political to coexist.

Then he stared into the dying embers of the hearth and made himself remember once again.

He had visited Henry Barrow at the Fleet, unknowing then what lay in his future, that one day he too would be chained and starving. His skin had crawled with the nerves of what he might see, and just in sight of the walls he stopped, gathering his courage and swallowing down the bile. The putrid stench from the river alongside the prison hung heavily over the day and he had wondered if it would be worse inside. He had been so young, so innocent; it was hard to remember that such a time existed. Before Cecily. Before her death.

A group of women hovered outside the gates as they always did, desperation written in their faces. He turned his head away from them as they moved to let him pass. One of them, of a poorer sort, ragged with sickly child in her arms, tugged at his sleeve. 'Alms, sir? For the babe?' He had given her a coin and hurried on to the gatehouse, where the warden took his money and let him through to a bare and wretched parlour that had never seen the sun, with a low ceiling that dripped with damp. Instinctively he shivered, although he knew he had been spared the worst of what the prison held. His imagination filled the gaps. An acrid smell of all the detritus of human misery oozed amongst the stones, blood and shit and piss and vomit, sweat and sickness, fear and death. Instinctively he breathed through his mouth and the taste of it turned his stomach worse than the stench. The wail of a man in pain on another floor drifted on the breeze through the window bars. He shuttered his mind against the thought of it, not daring to imagine the cruelty behind the cry. He was unsure how he would face such a trial.

It seemed ages until Barrow was brought to him, shuffling in through the door, the grime-streaked face lighting up at the sight of his visitor. Evidently he had been expecting someone different.

'Master Johnson sent me,' Ben said.

They embraced uneasily: the prisoner was thin and frail in Ben's arms, barely more than skin across bone. Ben was afraid he would hurt him, and it was hard to overcome a natural aversion to the filth. After a moment they moved apart.

'May God be praised for sending you,' Henry Barrow said. 'I see precious few people these days. The Archbishop pays the wardens well – you must have been generous.'

Ben tilted his head but gave no answer. What did it matter how much he had paid? The sight of Barrow appalled him. He was not an old man, but he was shrunken and gaunt, his teeth black and rotting, his hair turning grey. It was far worse than Ben had prepared himself to see.

'How is the weather?' Barrow asked, moving to one of two stools set either side of a small table, lowering himself stiffly to sit on it.

'The weather?' Ben was surprised by the question, and it took a few seconds to recall the day outside. 'It's an April day,' he said. 'The sun was warm this morning but now there is drizzle in the air. Likely it will rain before the day's end.'

'It is cloudy, then?'

'Yes. Rainclouds. Low and heavy.'

'Thank you.' Barrow's mouth twisted into a smile. 'It's a long time since I saw the sky. It is the greatest torture to be denied sight of God's creation. That, and the company of the congregation. You must forgive me.'

'Of course.' Ben took the other stool and they sat either side of the table. He waited, uncertain what to say. Barrow observed him with eyes that were still clear in the ravaged face, desire for the truth still burning keenly.

'Everyone is well?'

'We are all well. We meet early now, before the dawn. Master Johnson is our leader, and Greenwood is our teacher.'

Barrow smiled. 'It gives me great comfort to know the true Church still thrives, that a faithful people are still gathered by the Word unto Christ.'

'We pray for you.'

'*Cast down, but we perish not.*' Then, 'I have writings for you to take.'

Ben nodded, a rush of fear through his veins. He stifled the impulse to look behind him, to check no one was watching at the door.

'You are aware of the risks, I hope?'

'Of course.' He could end up here like Barrow, his own hair greying and thin, and welts across his wrists from the irons. Or worse. An image of Cecily crossed his thoughts, the auburn hair against her cheek, and he shook it away.

'You've been chained?'

'Often. They hope to break my spirit but I am strong in the

Lord.' He gave a small smile to his visitor and Ben could not tell the thought behind it. How hard would it be to keep faith in here, alone and in chains, in filth? He hoped his own faith would be as strong.

Barrow said, '*Wherefore come out from among them and separate yourselves, saith the Lord.* Ours is the true way, Ben: it is in the Scriptures. They can imprison us, every one, but they do so on their own behalf and not by the will of God.'

'Have you seen Bancroft?'

'Aye. And Andrewes with his false piety.'

Ben tensed with revulsion: the image of self-satisfied clergy on the way up, multiple livings, complacency personified. A poor spokesman for the holiness of the English Church.

'Put away your anger, Master Kemp.'

He breathed deeply to calm himself and the noisome air of the cell filled his lungs. By force of will he held down the urge to retch, and to distract himself he bent to the bundle he had brought and handed it across the table to Barrow.

'There is money and food and blankets. We all of us gave what we could. And paper and ink. I was uncertain what else I should bring.'

'Thank the others for their kindness,' Barrow said, taking the gift in his hands as something infinitely precious. 'I will open it in my cell – it will give me the greatest pleasure.' He looked up, his hands still resting on the bundle, protective. Then, flicking a glance to the door, he passed a slim package behind the bundle's bulk across the table. Ben slid it deftly into his lap. Casually adjusting his shirt, he slipped it inside against his skin.

'To Holland,' Barrow said. 'The same place.'

'I will take it myself.'

'May God protect you. Now go, and don't come here again.

You will be watched from here, your movements noted. Take care to arouse no suspicion.'

Too late for that, Ben thought. Just by being here he had put himself at risk, endangering the whole congregation. They would be watching him now, Bancroft's men, following him, biding their time. But the writings must be published and the teachings must be heard no matter who was taken and imprisoned, no matter who was hanged. The two men stood and this time Ben embraced Barrow warmly, holding him close and gently.

'May God keep you,' he said. Then he had walked across to the door and banged on the ageing wood for the guard to let him out.

CHAPTER 12

I *udge not, and ye shall not bee iudged: condemne not, and ye shall not be condemned: forgiue, and ye shall be forgiuen.*
(*Luke* 6:37)

AT SUPPER in the deanery they ate larks roasted with sage and bacon, and the aroma lingered pleasurably as Richard sipped his claret and pondered the choice of dessert, tossing up between an almond pudding or oranges in jelly. The conversation was in Latin. Like Cambridge, he thought, and immediately he missed it, a simpler, quieter life where study was everything, away from the uncertainties of politics and women. He had loved it from the moment he arrived there as a boy, the promise of his intellect realised by the study, his soul yearning for the knowledge of his masters. Even the austerity and the cold, the rigours of a twelve-hour day that began before the dawn, did not dampen his commitment. He had found his spiritual home, and when Ben arrived to share his room he had known his life would never be so complete again.

After Ben had left he stayed to become first a Master then a Doctor of Divinity, being ordained along the way, never doubting once the calling of the Church. Not then. Not for a long time. And now, amongst these learned men he was for once at home again, his own knowledge equal to or better than theirs, his voice heard and respected, in English and in Latin, his conscience untroubled by doubt. They were talking of the English Papists: another Jesuit priest had just lost his life before the clamorous crowds at Smithfield.

'The king is most irritated by them,' Andrewes said. 'He cannot understand their refusal to be grateful to him. He's left them more or less alone since his accession, but they continue to inflame the situation, smuggling in their priests from Europe, building houses with holes for them to hide in.'

'They had high hopes of James,' Richard said. 'Because of his mother. And because of his wife. They say the queen writes to Rome to beg for help for the community here.'

'Who is saying this?'

'It's the talk on the street,' he replied. The kitchen at Thieving Lane was a fount of information. The cook had a wife, the wife had a sister, the sister had a friend whose boy slaved in the kitchens at Hampton Court. One of the others had a cousin in service at Lambeth Palace. If you wanted to know anything going on in London, you should spend an evening in Thomas Kemp's kitchen and the information would come to you.

'If he can't control even his own wife's religious life then may God help us all.'

'Let's hope she's under better control in other matters,' Thomson slurred, bringing the tone to a baser level. He was already in his cups, but his Latin never faltered. 'Although,' Thomson went on, 'I've heard their interests lie differently these days.'

The table fell silent, shocked: the king's predilections, his penchant for boy favourites, was not something to be openly discussed. Pleased by the reaction he had provoked, Thomson turned to Doctor Overall. 'Speaking of wives under control,' he said, 'how goes your new marriage, sir?'

Relieved by the turn of subject, all eyes shifted to the Dean of St Paul's, who blushed scarlet under the sweep of grey hair. His new marriage was the talk of London. The beautiful Ann Orwell could have married anyone she chose but to everyone's surprise she had picked an elderly scholar and clergyman. Suggestions for her reasons ranged from money to more basic questions of anatomy. Richard found himself trying to imagine it and almost laughed.

'How is your pretty young wife?' Thomson leered in English, a fitter tongue for lewdness. 'And when are you going to bring her to meet us?'

'I wouldn't bring her near you,' Overall flashed back, also in English, a more combative tongue, 'if you were the last man on God's earth.'

Thomson laughed. 'Do you not trust her?'

'It is you I do not trust, sir. Your reputation is of the basest kind. You disgrace us all.'

Thomson shrugged, indifferent to the insult. Andrewes took the conversation back in hand. He said, in Latin, 'Come, let us not argue. I believe we were discussing the question of the Papists.'

'Wives are more interesting ...'

'Only to their husbands,' Andrewes replied gently.

The others chuckled as Thomson regarded the Dean with interest, as though he were deciding whether or not to argue. In the pause Richard said, 'Enough, Thomson. Let us proceed.'

Thomson turned his head from Andrewes to Richard. 'If you say so, Doctor Clarke, I will indeed desist.'

'Good.' Andrewes gave him an indulgent smile. 'Thank you.'

There was a moment of silence, the flow of conversation interrupted by Thomson's baiting.

'They will never give up,' Saravia said. 'A man who is prepared to die in such a way for his faith will never be turned from his path.'

'But why?' Layfield wondered. 'Why do they cling to the old ways with such tenacity? What is the hold the Pope exerts?'

'Tradition?' Richard suggested. 'People like to worship in the faith of their fathers – a sense of continuity, a link back through time and history.'

'There must be more to it than that. Have you seen the way they die? Unmanned, disembowelled, the scaffold slippery with blood and guts ...' Thomson was enjoying the description, the lips of his audience curling in distaste.

'I think we are all aware of the manner of their end,' Andrewes said.

'It is a quicker end than burning,' Richard said. Martyrs' deaths at the stake sometimes lasted hours, winds blowing the flames away and drawing out the agony. He remembered his conversation with Ben at the bonfire on All Hallows' Eve, the same martyr's spirit in his friend as the Papists who had died. His own faith seemed fragile in comparison – he was uncertain it would survive the threat of the fire.

'They are traitors,' Thomson said. 'And they know the penalty for treason. I have no sympathy for them.'

'They are misled,' Andrewes replied. 'And we should pray for them.'

No one answered, the Dean's compassion speaking to them all. Richard took a mouthful of wine. John Overall drained his cup and stood up. 'I must be going.'

Thomson leaned in towards Richard beside him. 'Apparently

the good doctor has more interesting company to go to. He is to be envied.'

Almost forgetting himself, Richard nearly smiled. Overall's departure prompted the others, and the small party began to break up. Richard rose from his seat with reluctance. He was comfortable at the Dean's table, at ease with himself. Servants came forward with hats and cloaks and the scholars tipped out of the deanery and into the yard. There was still light in the sky, the season turning, and the branches of the trees in the grassy square promised buds of green, just starting to spill their colour. The evening was surprisingly warm and the men milled, saying their farewells, all of them strangely reluctant to be on their way and bring an end to the day. Richard found himself crossing Broad Sanctuary alongside Doctor Thomson.

They came to the end of Thieving Lane. A left turn and a short walk would bring him to the Kemps' and the end of the day. Turn right and he would head up into King Street, haunt of taverns and houses of ill repute. Places he had never visited.

'Come take a drink with me, Doctor Clarke,' Thomson invited. 'It is early yet and the tavern is close by.'

He considered a moment, curiosity piqued. 'Why not?' he said on an impulse.

Thomson smiled with genuine pleasure and the two men sauntered along the rutted street, sun glinting off the puddles, unkempt half-timbered houses either side of them, shop signs creaking, the latticed windows crooked and broken. The air was thick with the odour of stale beer and meat, and the heavier stench of the runnels of human waste at their feet. They stepped carefully to avoid them.

The tavern was the Boar's Head, a low doorway leading down an uneven flight of stairs to a cellar where the spring warmth would never reach. At the bottom of the steps he shivered, gazing around, the tavern an unfamiliar world. Rough-hewn tables stood at haphazard angles to one another on a dirt floor strewn with straw. Men of all the lower classes occupied stools or benches, mugs of ale in their hands, the voices made louder by the drink and the lowness of the ceiling. Thomson led him through the crowd to a small table by the wall. A woman in a gown cut improbably low across her bosom approached them.

'Hello, Doctor,' she said to Thomson, with obvious familiarity. 'Who's your lovely friend?'

'He is a gentleman and tonight we are here to drink your finest ale, not to consort with you and your friends.'

She laughed, painted face splitting to reveal broken teeth. 'Well, that'll be a first, Doctor. But as you like.' She winked at Richard, who looked away, embarrassed. When he looked back she had gone, returning a few moments later with a jug and mugs on a tray.

'I'll leave you to your ale,' she said, taking the coins from Thomson and leaving quickly. There was no money to be made by staying.

'You're a regular here?' Richard could not help but ask.

'Do not judge me, Doctor Clarke.' Thomson smiled.

He said nothing and took a sip of the bitter ale.

'You wonder why he puts up with me, don't you?' the older man said. 'You wonder why Andrewes doesn't just slap me down and put me in my place, poor sinner that I am.'

'It has crossed my mind.'

'It's very simple, Doctor Clarke, you know. There is no big secret.'

'So tell me. I'm intrigued.'

'Firstly, I'm brilliant. My translations of Martial are second to none.' The epigrams of the Roman poet, famous mostly for their obscenity. Richard had never read them, in Latin or translated. 'Dean Andrewes knows that.'

'Dear God! You think he's read them?'

Thomson laughed. 'Who knows what the Dean gets up to every morning when he claims to be at prayer?'

Richard was shocked. It had never occurred to him to question the Dean's devotion – the man was almost a saint. He leaned forward. 'Do not,' he whispered, 'accuse the Dean of sharing your filthy mind in my presence. I will not hear it.'

Thomson lifted his hands in a conciliating gesture. 'Perhaps he has, perhaps he hasn't,' he said. 'But my craft as a linguist is not in doubt. It takes great skill to translate such poetry, to retain the meaning and the wit, to do justice to the original. Such skill is useful to him, and to the Company.'

He took a long draught of his ale, placed the mug on the table and refilled it from the jug.

'Secondly, I'm a man of the Church.'

'We are all of us men of the Church.'

Thomson inclined his large head to one side. 'That is true. You are indeed a man of the Church. I don't dispute it. You have a living in Kent. You preach at Canterbury.' He paused. 'But you also have Puritan sympathies. Puritan friends. Separatist friends even. Which I do not. Your loyalty is always going to be in doubt. Andrewes knows my beliefs: they are the same as his and he trusts me.'

Richard took another mouthful of ale before he answered. 'My loyalty to the Church,' he said, 'has never been in doubt. I am no Puritan, nor ever have been.'

'You are lodging with the Kemps.'

'What of it?'

'Ben Kemp is a Separatist.'

'It is many years since Ben Kemp went to prison. A man may surely change in so long a time.'

Thomson shook his head. 'I hope you're not ambitious, Doctor Clarke, because your choice of friends has let you down.'

He said nothing. He had known what would be thought of him if he stayed at Thieving Lane, knew the talk would damage him again. And though the men who mattered knew the truth, the slights still hurt his pride.

'Andrewes will forgive almost anything, you know,' Thomson said. 'He is full of mercy for common sinners like me; he is too aware of his own frailties not to be. But your Separatist friends would see the order of the Church overturned or set themselves apart from it, and that is not so easy to forgive. The order of the Church is the order of society and without it we are lost.' He took a mouthful of ale before going on. 'And they are wrong in their thinking. They would deny man his God-given ability to reason, deny the presence of His grace in the sacraments. Where is the joy in their faith? Are we not capable of pleasure without offending God?'

Richard sipped his ale. It was bitter and unpleasant but it gave him something to do.

'I agree with you,' he said. 'I am no lover of Separatists.'

'They need to be brought to heel and made to conform,' Thomson said.

'It is not so simple a matter,' he replied. He knew. He had spent the best part of many years trying.

'We should fine the Puritans for breaches. Same as the Papists.' The older man put down his mug with a bang. Ale slopped across the table, unnoticed by Thomson. 'And as for Separatists ...'

'What about Separatists?' Richard said, though he knew well enough what was coming.

'Separatists should be hanged.' He let go of his ale and lifted his fingers to his throat in a cutting motion, in case Richard had failed to understand. 'They are a threat to the realm, pure and simple, like a weed that unchecked would choke the life from the crop.'

Richard nodded. An image flashed across his mind, a memory of his dreams: Ben in chains up on the wall. It was easy to speak of Separatists in the abstract, to criticise their thinking, harder to condemn a friend to prison and to death.

'They are few in number,' he said.

'But left unhindered their numbers will grow.'

The ale had left a dirty taste in his mouth. He swallowed to get rid of it but the bitterness still lingered. He ran his fingers up and down the cup as he considered his answer, the cheap glaze rough against his skin. He had no defence for Ben's position: whatever the rights and wrongs of their theology, Separatists were a threat to Church authority, raising doubts about the rightness of the order of the world. The hierarchy of the realm ended with the king. Bring the hierarchy into question and you were starting to talk treason. He knew all the arguments – they were branded on his heart. Ten years ago in the Fleet they had consumed all his conversation, hours upon hours of trying to reason Ben back into the fold.

He looked across at Thomson, the veins across his cheeks and nose fine-threaded, purple, livid. Eyes that were clouded by the haze of drink still managed to track a whore across the room, interest lighting up. All the arguments he knew, but how was the man before him a godlier man than Ben? How should he have the right to judge?

'Do you agree?' Thomson turned his eyes from the whore back to Richard and leaned closer.

Richard stopped breathing and moved back out of range of the other man's breath, wondering if the evil taste from the ale in his mouth had made his own smell the same.

Thomson pressed him. 'Do you not agree that Separatists should be executed?'

'In theory, perhaps.'

'But not in practice? Of course not. You keep company with Separatists.'

'Not so.'

'Ben Kemp is a Separatist. The leopard does not change its spots.'

'He was a Separatist once and he paid dearly for his folly.'

'Three years in the Fleet, I'm told. In chains. Lost his wife, did he not?'

'And his child.'

'Punished by man and God, then. 'Twas no more than he deserved.'

Richard felt hatred surge up from his gut – this self-satisfied sinner, handing out death and judgement to a man whose only crime was to want a more godly life. He was appalled, seeing the Church again through Ben's eyes, its profanity and wickedness apparent in its spokesman getting drunk before him.

Standing up, he knocked against the table in his haste and the half-full mug of ale tipped and spilled, a running blot of beer sliding towards him across the splintered tabletop. He moved away just in time to let the ale run off the edge and onto the floor, where it dropped onto the filthy straw.

'I'll see you next week,' he said.

Thomson lifted his mug in farewell and Richard could feel the shrewd drunken eyes on his back as he headed towards the door and the fresher evening breeze from the street. Outside he stood for a moment, breathing deep to calm himself, heart still racing from the confrontation, the foul taste still in his mouth. The hatred lingered even as his heartbeat slowed, his fists still clenched at Thomson's complacent judgement on his friend. How dare he presume? How dare he claim to understand Ben's heart? Such a man could not even begin to know the pain, the price that Ben had paid for his faith, the doubt his wife's death had lit, the despair. He, Richard, had never thought to see Ben brought so low nor to lose his faith. And he had been the one to take the news. The memory of it still gave him pain – he dared not imagine the agony of Ben's recollection. Richard shook his head, trying to dislodge the remembrance, but it lingered in his thoughts, stirred by Thomson's casual judgement.

HE HAD GONE to the Fleet with a weight of dread in his limbs, laden with the burden of his task. He had eaten nothing all day, guts churning with nerves, terrified of what was before him. Ahead, the great walls of the Fleet crowded out the dull spring light, and the pestilential river that ran alongside threatened to make him retch. But it was not only the prison itself that frightened him, a natural human dread of being witness to suffering, but fear of the man he would find within. It was beyond him to imagine what marks the weeks of imprisonment would have left on his friend, what cruelties he had suffered, and he was afraid of the telling of the awful news he carried, unsure how Ben would bear it. He braced himself for the worst, his steps growing slower, more reluctant, his whole body rebelling against the deed.

At the prison gates a group of women were remonstrating with the gatekeeper. They parted and moved away when they saw him coming – an instinctive respect, he supposed, for his clerical garb. The gatekeeper watched him, waiting, as Richard drew out the precious letter, so hard to obtain, that would give him access to the gaol at last. He passed it carefully across, the coins held in his fingers underneath. The gatekeeper made a show of opening up the page and cast an illiterate eye across the words. But he understood the seal that was beneath them. He folded it back up, pocketed the coins, gave the letter back to Richard and gestured with his head towards the gate. Richard followed him, waiting while the man fumbled with the keys to let him through.

Inside, the stench worsened, and the howls of men drifted in currents on the noisome air. Richard lifted an automatic hand to shield his nose and the gatekeeper laughed with a quick, sharp hacking sound.

'You'll soon get used to it. It gets worse inside.'

He nodded, swallowing down the vomit that heaved in his gut: he would not give this man the pleasure of seeing such weakness. Another gaoler came to meet them with more keys in his hand, blackened teeth in a grimy face. 'Who you here to see?'

'Master Kemp.'

'Oh yes. One of our Separatist friends, is it? If you don't mind me saying so, sir, you don't seem like the kind of man to be having any business with Separatists.'

'Just take me to him.' He wanted to get this over with, appalled.

'All right.' The man scowled. Then he shuffled off back the way he had come, Richard striding after him, fingers gripping tightly the bundle he had brought, the small, precious comforts he could offer to his friend. The atmosphere grew fouler as the gate-keeper had said, no movement of air along the corridors, the stone walls running with mould and damp. He shivered with the cold and thought, How can a man survive in such a low place?

They reached a door where the gaoler stopped and laboriously sorted through his bunch of keys, checking them by touch, the light too dim to tell them apart by sight. It seemed to take an age before he found the one he needed, thrust it hard into the lock and opened the door. Richard brushed past him and went inside.

Ben was standing by the small barred window, staring out, and he did not turn at the opening of the door. He was filthy, his once-white linen streaked with black, his hair matted and dishevelled.

His hands hung at his sides and the chain that connected them fell across his thighs. Straw was scattered thinly across the floor of a room that was bare of furniture, and the stench of human excrement turned Richard's gut again. He felt the heart go out of him, had to fight the urge to leave and flee before Ben turned. Then the door clanged shut behind him, the key scraping in the lock to cut off his escape, so he dug for his courage again and moved across the cell towards the window.

'Ben?'

The gaunt face turned towards him and twisted into the semblance of a smile. 'Richard. I was expecting someone different. I ... am glad it is you.'

'Who did you expect?'

'Bancroft. Or ... others of his kind.'

'You are ... well?'

'I am alive.'

'Your father has promised handsome payments to the warden. You should have better food at least, perhaps better conditions ...' He cast his gaze around the sordid room, and thought he could not survive in such wretchedness, that such a life would drive him mad.

'I've brought blankets and fresh clothes, some bread and honey from Cecily's bees. And your Bible, of course, pen and ink.'

'I am grateful.'

He lowered the bundle to the floor at his feet, the worst of his task still to come.

'Ben ...' he began, and stopped, the words too hard to find, the cruelty of saying them in this foetid place too awful to bear.

'What?' Ben's natural impatience surfaced, his irritation with fools. He turned his body fully to face his visitor, his weight still against the wall. Even in the dim light of the cell Richard could see the weals on his wrists where the manacles had cut into the skin, and the blood that stained the front of his shirt. 'Tell me.'

'Ben,' Richard began again. In the chill he felt the sweat against his skin, the dread of what he had to say. 'I have grave news. Cecily ...'

He stopped. Pain coloured Ben's face, and all the words he had rehearsed fell from his mind. 'Her time came early,' he managed to say. 'It was the worry, the midwives said, and the fear.' He lowered his voice. 'She is with God now, and the boy too.'

Ben closed his eyes and turned himself away from his friend. With his forehead pressed against the window bars, he gripped on to them tightly. He was silent, barely breathing, and Richard watched him with the same helpless uncertainty he had felt at the sounds of Cecily's cries growing weaker through that long, awful night at Thieving Lane. A minute passed, maybe more. Footsteps shuffled past outside the door, keys rattling in a lock further down the passage. At last Ben turned his face from the bars: long streaks from his tears slashed through the dirt on his face.

'I would rather you had been Bancroft after all,' he whispered. 'He could not have hurt me worse than this.'

'I'm so sorry to be the bearer of such news.'

'Don't be. I am glad to have heard it from the lips of a friend.'

Richard stepped forward and lifted a hand to Ben's shoulder. It was all he could think of to offer comfort, and Ben let it rest for a moment before he turned again to the bars, looking out at the foul river below and a narrow glimpse of the early spring sky above it. Richard watched him, seeing the gaunt face in profile and the eyes staring out unseeing.

'What have I done?' Ben murmured. His lips barely moved and the words were so quiet that Richard could not have sworn he heard them.

'It was God's will.'

'Why?' Ben asked, turning. 'Why would He take Cecily and the child? Why did He not take me?'

'It is the woman's lot to bring forth children in sorrow ...'

'If I had not married her she would still be alive.'

'You cannot blame yourself. God takes many women in childbirth.'

'You are kind Richard and I'm grateful you are my friend, but this time you're wrong. She's dead because of me.'

Tears welled and he tipped his head back, trying to force them down. Failing, he turned his head away, gaze resting blindly on some point far beyond the bars. Richard let his hand slip from Ben's shoulder and the grieving man did not notice.

'When we married,' Ben said, without moving his eyes, 'she told me that God had brought us together for a reason, for some purpose of His own we could not know.' He turned then and the look in his eyes was so bleak Richard had to look away. 'What purpose, Richard? What possible purpose?'

'We cannot know His purpose. We just have to trust in Him. *Blessed be the man that trusteth in the Lord.* Have faith, Ben.'

'Why?' Ben spat. 'Why should I have faith? Look at what it has brought me to.' He lifted his manacled hands and gestured round the cell with a tilt of his chin. 'Look at what faith has done to my wife. To my child. My son.'

Richard was silent, nothing he could think of to say in the face of Ben's crisis. He had never thought to see his friend lose his faith.

'You are not yourself,' he said at last.

'I am nothing,' Ben replied, spitting out the words through rigid lips. 'Worse than nothing.'

'You are God's child.'

Ben slid his eyes away. The fire of his anger waned and without it he seemed diminished.

'No,' he whispered. 'There is no God.'

Richard stared. 'You are not yourself,' he repeated. Ben's unbelief frightened him, his own faith threatened by the other man's fall. For all their differences their faith had connected them, their shared love of God, each one sustaining the other on the path, and through their countless arguments his own belief was strengthened and confirmed.

'Pray with me,' he said.

But his words went unheard. Ben's head was pressed once more against the cold metal bars as he wept. A silence filled the cell, broken only by the small sounds of Ben's sobs as he fought against his darkness. Richard faltered, uncertain how to reach his friend and embarrassed by the weeping. He was afraid of what he saw, unable to imagine the horror of losing his faith. God was the centre of his being, the rock on which his life was built: without it his life would be as dust. His mind recoiled from the void, terrified, and long moments passed before he found his strength, God's hand reaching out to him.

'Pray with me,' he said again. It was all he could think of to save his friend and bring him back within God's grace: he could not simply let him fall to his damnation. Raising his hand again, he touched gentle fingers to the other man's shoulder. For a moment it seemed that Ben was unaware of it. Then, awkwardly, because of the shackles, he grasped Richard's hand in his own and lowered his head against it. His chest still vibrated with half-checked sobs as Richard moved to take him in his arms, his body frail in his embrace. The once-lean strength had shrunk to gauntness in the weeks of his imprisonment and Richard held him uneasily, Ben's pain too raw to touch.

He held him for what seemed like an age as Ben wept in silence, face hidden, body trembling against him. He could think of nothing to say, no comfort to offer: all the words of Scripture that came to mind seemed powerless against Ben's darkness. So instead, he prayed in silence, begging God's mercy for his friend, his own face wet with tears as he pleaded. He had never thought to witness such pain, and never felt so helpless. The minutes dragged by, Ben's despair bottomless, fathomless, and for the first time Richard truly understood the meaning of Hell.

He prayed. *Cast him not away from Thy presence, O Lord. Take not the holy spirit away from him. Restore him to the joy of Thy salvation. Have mercy upon him, Lord, have mercy ...*

Finally, he was startled by a rattle at the door that broke the moment. Slowly, painfully, Ben unfolded himself from his friend and turned his gaze back towards the foetid river. The rattle grew louder and the door was shoved open, the misshapen boards catching on the stone.

'Time's up.' The rough voice rasped against his tautened nerves.

'I have to go now, Ben,' he said softly. 'I don't know when they will let me come again.' He waited, wondering if his friend had even heard him, but as he began to back away Ben turned again and grasped at Richard's retreating hand.

'Thank you,' he said, squeezing his fingers. 'Pray for me.'

Richard nodded. 'God keep you,' he said. Then he turned and walked away and the door slammed hard behind him.

CHAPTER 13

SUMMER 1605

And now brethren, I commend you to God, and to the word of his grace, which is able to build you vp, and to giue you an inheritance among all them which are sanctified.
(*Acts* 20:32)

Ellyn's wedding, and she was confident in a new gown of emerald silk with yellow roses in her hair, apparently enjoying the attention. She had not spoken of her fears to Ben again, accepting her fate and trusting, he hoped, in God. But in the days leading up to the wedding she had been fractious and snappy, and the relief that it was done at last was clear on the faces of his parents when she and Hugh Merton were finally joined as man and wife. There was not one person in the household who had not half expected a drama on the day.

Ben had set aside his misgivings to be at the wedding, begging advice from Brewster, and from God. He had agonised about it for weeks, in prayer and reflection, his love for his sister doing battle with his beliefs. Christ had commanded that His followers love Him above their families, that they put their fathers and mothers, their sisters and brothers aside to follow Him. So how could he attend a marriage in a church that was filled with the wicked and profane, built on Romish superstition, to parrot prayers and rituals that had no base in Scripture? It was not a church as Christ commanded – a faithful people gathered by the Word unto Him. He knew what Henry Barrow would have told him – just to set foot inside could endanger his immortal soul. At the very least he would have risked his place in Barrow's church, where there was no room for men whose faith was weak. And if Barrow had been willing to hang for that belief, how could Ben justify going?

Ironically, it was Richard who suggested the solution, Richard who understood his distress.

'Stand at the door,' he had said. 'Watch but don't enter. See your sister married but don't participate.'

'My father ...'

'Your father will be so relieved that Ellyn is doing her duty that he will not give a fig where you stand.'

He allowed himself a rueful smile as he thought of it, waiting now at the churchyard gate for his sister to emerge. Richard had been right, of course; his father had barely noticed him, the older man's attention wholly taken by his daughter. It had been a compromise, and though he would still spend hours begging for forgiveness, confessing the sin of his earthly love for his sister, he was not utterly dejected.

The struggle brought back bittersweet memories of another wedding and a similar agony of conflict, and no compromise that could solve it. Cecily had insisted the marriage take place in the church or it would not take place at all. She would accept all the rest, she had told him, she would partner him willingly in all the hardships of their future, but their marriage must be sanctified by a priest of the English Church. A proper wedding, she had called it, that no man could ever question.

He had begged, he recalled, on his knees before her, the only time he ever knelt, but she had not wavered. Now, when he thought of her, it was that expression he remembered, the stern, still features, a hardness to hide the sadness within. And even though he knew that afterwards she smiled with him often, softening and tender, he had no memory of how she looked when she was happy: he could only picture the pain. He had relented of course, and married her in the church as she wanted, his need for her too great to resist, his desire unquenchable. It had been a test, he knew now, a test that he had failed. Choosing desire before his faith, the love of a woman over love of God: his sinfulness had led them both astray. Now she and the babe lay just behind the church in a grave he could not bring himself to visit, and he spent each day living with the knowledge of his sin and his unworthiness. It was a heavy cross to bear.

Ellyn's marriage celebrations at Thieving Lane lasted late into the evening, music and dancing and feasting, the numbers only starting to dwindle as the end of the long summer twilight lingered in the sky. Night fell slowly, the darkness creeping up unnoticed as the last guests began to find their way into the street, their laughter and chatter still noisy through the open windows as they said their farewells to one another. When the house was quiet at last, Thomas Kemp called his son to him in his study and they sat either side of the great oak desk that occupied the centre of the floor, the hub of everything that Thomas Kemp had built. Around the walls were books and ledgers and the great wooden chests where the Company's documents were stored away, a record of the many years of business. Across the surface of the desk between them papers were arranged in neat piles. Ben cast an appraising merchant's eye across them, the habit of his years in the Company, but nothing caught his interest. As a child, this room had symbolised manhood to Ben, a grown-up world of business and trade. Whenever he thought of his father he saw him at this desk, face stern with concentration, candles blazing late into the night, the room barren of any decoration or comfort.

After the warmth of the hall, the night air in the study was cool in spite of the season. A tree of candles placed on the desk threw light across his father's face, but around him the room was dim, the corners of the room lost in darkness. Laughter from the departing guests rippled through the house, and beyond the windows a man's shout went up from the street. Ben thought of his sister with her new husband now, a few streets away in their new home, and hoped that Merton was using her gently, while his father shuffled the papers on his desk, rearranging their order, tutting with apparent dissatisfaction. One of the servants brought wine and poured it into the best Venetian glasses, kept safe in the study away from the careless hands of the wedding guests. Then he hovered, hoping to stay and learn more of his master's business. But the older Kemp dismissed him with a wave of his hand and the boy left them, closing the door with care behind him so it would not slam.

The two men raised their glasses. 'To Ellyn,' Kemp said.

'To Ellyn.'

They drank. Ben observed his father, waiting, sensing some kind of bad news was coming. He guessed it would be another plea for him to go east, or to Holland, some business his father would claim he needed his son to do. He steeled himself, a tension falling, the lifelong pitting of wills. His father took a deep breath, his ample chest rising under its cover of black velvet. He had grown stout the last few years, the perfect figure of a rich city merchant. But his face was lined, and the hair across his pate was thinning now and grey. Ben thought, We are all of us growing older.

His father took another quick breath, drained his glass and

placed it carefully on the desk before him. Ben watched him. Whatever it was his father had to say, he seemed reluctant to say it. The older man's fingers remained on the stem of the glass, twirling it gently to and fro, watching the shimmering reflection of the candlelight for a while before he let it go and looked up to regard his son with the same expression he might use against a dealer he suspected of trying to fleece him. Finally he spoke.

'Now that your sister is provided for, I have made my will.'

'Indeed?'

'Yes. Indeed.' He paused and in the space Ben understood what was coming. He was going to be disinherited. Merton was going to take his place. He lowered his glass to the desk so that in his agitation he wouldn't snap the stem and give his father one more thing to hold against him.

He said, 'And I am not going to inherit.'

'You will be well provided for. Well provided.'

'But ...?'

Thomas Kemp sighed and made a temple with his fingers before his lips. 'Here's how it stands, Benjamin. You have no desire to take over the business. Agreed?'

But I am still your son, Ben thought, and it is my birthright. I learned the trade as you asked of me. Three years' apprenticeship in Amsterdam, eight years more in the Company to please you, seven of them in the East in an unchristian place a long way from home. The injustice of it rankled bitterly, but he swallowed back the words and said nothing, forcing his breathing to slow.

'You have not the interest to keep the trade going. What do you care for the price of silk? The shipping trade? You've said as much yourself. It bores you and I count myself partly to blame for that. I should have involved you from a younger age instead of sending you off to Cambridge to have your head stuffed full of radical nonsense,' his father went on. 'But what's done is done. You became the man you are and I can do nothing to change it, however much I might wish it. The reality is, Benjamin, that you would destroy everything I've built for this family. You have no wife, no child—'

'I lost my wife and child.' Cecily, and the baby that never lived to see the light of day.

'A man needs a wife, a family. It is as God willed. Ten years have passed and you've shown no inclination to marry again.'

'Because ...'

'Because why?'

Because of my faith, he wanted to say. Because he would not put another woman and child in danger for his faith. He said, 'I can't explain it.'

His father observed him for a moment, shrewd merchant's eyes assessing. Then, 'Well, perhaps it's better I don't know after all.'

Ben nodded.

'I have given you many chances. Holland, Aleppo ...'

'Only to keep me away from these shores.'

'It was to keep you in the Company. And to keep you safe. What man doesn't want these things for his son? To keep him safe and build on what has gone before? Going to the East served its purpose. I would that you had stayed there longer.'

'And now?'

'I would have you go back but you've refused. What am I to do? Do you think I want to give it all to another man's son?'

'And the house?'

'You wish to live in London now?'

'No.'

There was a silence. Two pairs of footsteps thudded along the landing outside the door. They could hear them bounding down the stairs, then raucous laughter cutting through the quiet of the room.

'So the terms of the will are what, exactly?' Let's just get to the details, he thought. We already know all the rest.

His father sighed. Perhaps he had hoped for more understanding from his son, for less hostility. He said, 'Merton gets more or less everything.'

'Even the house?'

'Your mother will keep it for her lifetime. Then yes, it will go to Merton.'

Kemp made a little waving gesture with his hand. 'Of course there are sundry items for the household, bits and pieces here and there. And there will be a sum of money for you – enough, I think, to keep you well. You are, after all, a man of modest wants and you have no family to keep.'

'I am aware of it.'

'Then there is no more to say on the matter.'

Actually, there was plenty more to say, he thought, but it would go unsaid because what would be the point? Instead, he would take his hurt and his resentment back to Scrooby, and the bitterness that his father had made another man his son instead of him. All his life he had borne the knowledge of his father's disappointment, the unspoken wish that Ben had been a different kind of man. They had never seen eye to eye on anything – even as a boy he had sensed the older man's frustration with him. But however hard he tried, he could never be the boy his father wanted, his best efforts always falling short. And he had never been able to fathom what it was he was doing wrong. Not until he found his faith, at least, and his father's dissatisfaction with him found its focus. Even so, he had never thought to be disinherited.

He swallowed, forcing down the hurt so his father would not see it. Then he stood up and flicked his eyes around a room that would never now be his but another man's, a man who at this very moment was probably consummating his claim. He should have taken Ellyn with him when she asked it, instead of working on his father's side towards his own disinheritance.

At the door he turned back. 'Goodnight to you, sir.'

His father softened, fingertips resting lightly on the desk. 'I am sorry, Benjamin. I am truly sorry it has come to this. But what else could I do?'

'You want my approval?'

Kemp dropped his eyes to the desk and began to shuffle his papers once again. 'No,' he murmured. 'No, of course not.'

When he looked up again, his son had already gone.

IN THE MORNING Ben went to his sister's. He found the house easily: a few streets away from Thieving Lane, it was a rambling old building set close to the river, and the front room housed a spice shop behind narrow windows that glimmered in the morning sun. A rusty sign squeaked above the door. He knocked and waited, and from beyond the end of the street he could hear the shouts of the watermen and the splash and thud of oars. In the air hung the faint taint of the sea. Ellyn should like it this close to the water, he thought, she would be able to hear the tide at night.

The door opened on a pungent fragrance of spices: nutmeg, cinnamon and ginger, and the headier breath of frankincense, scents he had come to know well in his trading days in Aleppo. Stepping into the darkness of the entrance hall, he blinked as his eyes struggled to adjust to the gloom. Then he caught another scent beneath the spice, a familiar reek of mustiness and crumbling walls with mice that ran inside them.

He followed the servant up narrow stairs and into a barely lit room overlooking the street. It was hard to picture his sister here in the half-light: her own fire would struggle to stay bright. While he waited he wandered the room, inspecting a Turkey rug that hung on the wall, examining the curiosities displayed on a table. There was a small silver statue of a kind he had seen in the bazaars in the East, some seashells and a brightly coloured feather, from a king-fisher perhaps. He ran his thumb along its edge and then replaced it before he crossed the floor to the window and looked out onto the street below. Footsteps clattered on the stairs from the floor above, running and immodest, and he heard the short halt outside the door as his sister composed herself before she entered.

'Ben.' She greeted him with a voice still breathy from running, and her hair was tied up and hidden under her cap, no longer worn loose as the badge of her maidenhood. He felt a pang of regret.

'Nell.' He went to her and kissed her cheek, taking her hands in his. Surprised by the affection, she stepped back abruptly. 'What's wrong?'

'Forgive me,' he said.

'What for?'

He tilted his head and gestured at the room with a motion of one hand. 'For all of this. For taking my father's part.'

She inclined her head. There were questions in her eyes, puzzled at this change in him.

'Forgive me.'

She shrugged. 'I had to marry someone sooner or later. You were right. It might as well have been Hugh.' She gave him a small smile and took his hand in hers again, leading him back to the window that looked down on the road. Two men were arguing, carters trying to pass each other in the narrow street, both too stubborn to back up. They should have compromised earlier, he thought. They would have the devil's own job to back up such laden carts now.

'Idiots,' Ellyn said.

'How is it?'

She shrugged again.

'Where is he now?'

'At the warehouse. Or at the docks. One of the two.'

There was a silence. The carters had finished abusing each other and returned to their respective carts but neither was making any effort to move.

Ben said, 'Was he gentle?'

She flicked him a sideways glance and nodded, tight-lipped. Ben placed a hand on her shoulder. It was delicate under his palm and he could feel her tension, the latent quivering beneath the skin.

'You'll come to enjoy it, if he's gentle.'

She slipped her shoulder free of his hand. 'Is that all you came to say?'

He smiled. Marriage had not dulled the sharpness of her tongue. 'I came to say goodbye. I leave for the Midlands this morning.'

In truth he had planned to tell her about their father's will, how everything that should be his would go to her husband instead. But she had no need to know, he decided: it would only sow more seeds of resentment and kindle friction with their father. She would find out soon enough and by then who knew what might have happened?

'I wish you'd stay in London longer,' she said.

'No, you don't. You'll be too busy now you're a housewife to have time for your brother. You've a whole house to run, servants to manage, ale to brew, a kitchen to stock, a husband's linen to sew ...' The life of a merchant's wife left no time for idleness.

She smacked his arm hard enough to sting but behind the scowl there was laughter. He drew her to him against her token protest and held her fast in his arms. When he kissed her head she tensed, resisting a moment before she folded into him and let him hold her as he used to when she was just a child. Simpler times, he thought, when problems could be solved with a hug and a cup of warm milk.

She shifted back from him and he loosened his hold, sliding his hands along her arms to take her fingers lightly in his. He was reluctant to let her go, goodbye hard to say this time.

'Go,' she said. 'You have a long ride ahead of you. I'll be fine. You have no need to worry – we're cut from the same cloth, you and I. Tough. And prickly.' She smiled. 'May God keep you.'

He let go of her hands and backed away as far as the door. He still had trouble believing that she was a woman now, a wife with a husband to care for her.

'Write to me,' she said.

'Maybe I will this time,' he replied. 'Maybe I'll surprise you.'

'That would be nice. But I won't hold my breath. Now go. The morning grows old.'

He bowed a final farewell in the doorway then turned and walked away.

CHAPTER 14

SUMMER 1605

A nd the LORD said vnto him, Who hath made mans mouth? or who maketh the dumbe or deafe, or the seeing, or the blind? haue not I the LORD? Now therefore goe, and I will be with thy mouth, and teach thee what thou shalt say. And he said, O my Lord, send, I pray thee, by the hand of him whom thou wilt send.
(*Exodus 4:11–13*)

THEY FINISHED Genesis and moved on to Exodus as spring slowly brightened into summer, cool breezes and showers giving way to long warm days of humidity that hummed in the city streets with a pungency that floated off the river and hung above the open drains.

Sweating in the heat, Richard thought often of the vicarage in Kent, where the apples and plums would be ripening in the orchard, the air lazy with the heavy scent of fruit. In the heat of the summer he was missing its peace and the wholesome air, though when he had gone there first he had hated it, his heart and mind still amongst the books at Cambridge, and filled with resentment.

But Cambridge had given him no choice but to leave. Passed

over twice for promotion because of his conformity to the Church in an academic world that espoused a more Puritan view, he had felt compelled to protest. It had ended badly, as protests often do, descending into personal conflict that almost came to blows. And so, in frustration and fury, he had resigned his fellowship and retreated to his living at Thanet. It had felt like the end of his world – a small rural parish, barely a soul who could even read, and far from everything he loved and valued. For the first few months he was miserable, finding no joy in anything: even his faith had burned less brightly. Slowly though, he had learned to hate it less, a growing awareness of the sin of his pride and his ambition, followed by reluctant acceptance of God's plan for him. Humbled, he studied alone, his triumphs unnoticed by any save the vicarage cat, and finding reward instead in leading his parishioners and guiding them to love the Lord as he did. They accepted him easily, pleased to have a resident vicar at last, and he learned from them too, understanding there was joy to be found in the slowly turning seasons, the abundance of God's earth.

These days, his duties took him there seldom and the care of the parish was entrusted to the curate. But he was called to preach at Canterbury every few weeks, and though he welcomed the break from the London summer with its stink and the threat of the plague, he regretted every day he lost from the work of translation. To make up for it he translated in his head as he rode, the passages of Hebrew perfect in his memory, the English never quite good enough. Sometimes, though, he found great inspiration – lines he had struggled with in the Abbey library suddenly coming clear along the road to Kent. It was strange, he thought, how a man's mind works. To spend all that time at his desk then find the answer he was seeking in a country lane.

At the weekly meeting he sat by Andrewes, choosing a seat a safe distance from the sour breath of Thomson. Though it was cool in the Jerusalem Chamber, a relief from the heat of the day outside, he could feel the dampness on the back of his neck and the runnel of moisture down his spine. A taint of male sweat hung in the room and he sipped at his ale, but it did nothing to refresh him. Waiting for the meeting to begin, his gaze lighted on the vast tapestries of Abraham and Sarah that covered the walls, the same truth in the images of wool and silk that the translators sought to illuminate in words. He loved this room, the peace of ages contained within its mediaeval walls.

The meeting began, talking of Moses's reluctance to do God's bidding: Moses in his humility, asking God to send someone else.

'Ah, but who can blame him, eh?' Thomson said. 'Who could think themselves worthy to lead God's chosen people?'

Richard nodded his agreement but said nothing. Who among us ever thinks himself worthy of God's trust? Or qualified to perform all He asks of us? He thought of his own reluctance in the face of the task the Church had given him and sympathised with Moses pleading to be spared. Though his own burden weighed little compared to Moses's load, he could understand the sense of dismay, his unwillingness, and he took some small comfort from the knowledge that even Moses had suffered doubt. But God at least had spoken directly to Moses – there was no question the task was God's will. He wished God would speak as plainly to him.

'And who would want such a task?' Thomson added.

'God does not call the qualified,' Andrewes replied. 'He qualifies the called.'

Richard turned towards him, struck by the words, listening as Andrewes went on.

'We are none of us capable without God's help,' Andrewes said, 'but when he calls us we must answer. He will give us all we need if we trust in Him, if we obey.'

The men were silent for a moment, weighing the Dean's mean-

and Richard thought, So it comes down to trust. In the end, faith must rest on the trust that all things come from God, and that He will provide. The Church was God's house on earth, the pillar and ground of truth. He could think of nothing more sacred, nothing more divine. Why, then, did he still waver? Why did he fear to have trust? Was it some sin within him, this reluctance to act as the Church demanded? The error of his humanity, too small and frail to understand what God would have him do. He thought of Abraham, trusting enough to give his own beloved son. So why should he hesitate to give up Ben?

The work began, drawing Richard's thoughts back to the text, the problems of his earthly self effaced in the ecstasy of Scripture. They started as always, looking over past translations, comparing each man's attempts against them, searching, sifting, seeking the perfect words to convey God's truth.

Coverdale's version, short and simple, heartfelt:

But Moses said: My LORDE, sende whom thou wilt sende.

It was easy to hear Moses's desperation in the phrase. Please God, send someone else. Richard thought of his own prayers to be spared the task God had set him. Faith was no easy thing.

The Bishops' Bible, closer to the Hebrew word for word:

He said: oh my Lorde, sende I pray thee, by the hande of him whom thou wilt sende.

There was little disagreement amongst the translators: the Bishops' Bible was the most accurate, the truest translation. The Geneva translators had also rendered it the same. Only Coverdale differed.

'So we are agreed? The line will read,

And he said, O my Lord, send, I pray Thee, by the hand of him whom Thou wilt send.'

Andrewes turned his eyes around the table, waiting for each of the translators to give his agreement. Richard nodded in his turn, though a part of him regretted losing Coverdale's simplicity. But their task was to find the closest truth to the original, and so there was nothing for it but to agree.

'Good.' Andrewes bestowed on him the reward of a smile. 'Then let us proceed.'

The translators turned their eyes back to the next verse and the process was begun again.

THEY HAD supper in the oak-panelled dining room at the deanery. By the time Richard arrived the only place left at the long table was the one between Bancroft and Thomson. He paused for an instant, scanning for a way to escape, but there was none so he had no choice but to take the seat. A multitude of candles along the table glimmered, and behind the latticed windows which stood open to the evening air the summer twilight shed its dying light across the city. The conversation did not falter as Richard slid into his place. They were discussing the Translation, giving the Archbishop news to take back to the king.

Richard beckoned to a servant for wine but he ignored the food: the company of Bancroft had dulled his appetite. The servant poured the wine. It was a claret, far too heavy for such a hot day and on an empty stomach. He sipped carefully and wished he had dined at the Kemps'.

'The king grows impatient,' Bancroft was saying. 'He wants to see progress.'

'You may tell him we are progressing,' Andrewes replied. 'Day by day, week by week, little by little, the task is being accomplished.'

'But too slowly.'

'Such work takes time. You must understand, My Lord, and the king must understand, it is a mighty labour that we perform. Surely he would not have us make errors for the sake of saving a little time?'

The Archbishop looked as though he understood nothing of the kind. Mistrustful eyes peered out from deep in the lined face.

'We are all playing our parts, My Lord,' Andrewes continued. 'Each company has made a good beginning and it is still less than a year since we began. The king cannot expect miracles – we are but humble translators of God's Word.'

Bancroft sighed.

Perhaps the Archbishop was feeling the pressure, Richard thought. Maybe it was harder than he had thought at the top, the weight of the realm too heavy a burden. To Richard's mind, Andrewes would have been a better choice, just and clever and humble before God, but perhaps kings look for other qualities in the head of their church. Perhaps Bancroft got the job for his knotted wrestler's muscles and the thick red hands he was not afraid to bloody.

'I shall speak to His Majesty myself,' the Dean said. 'Perhaps I can reassure him.'

Bancroft barely hid a scowl. Despite his closeness to the king, their shared pursuit of nonconformists, it was Andrewes's company the king enjoyed, granting the Dean an easy confidence at Court that was denied to Bancroft.

'The king has asked me to be at Court tomorrow,' Andrewes said. If he was aware of the effect of his words, it was not apparent. 'I can speak to him then. So there is no need for you to fret, My

Lord. All will be well. Now, have some more of the excellent claret, and eat. You have barely tasted a mouthful.' His gaze travelled along the table. 'You too, Doctor Clarke. You must eat also. The veal is especially good. And the capons. I refuse to take no for an answer.' The pale grave face smiled in encouragement.

Richard returned the smile, the Dean's charming persuasion hard to resist. He took a small helping of the veal. It was dressed in some kind of egg sauce with nutmeg, perhaps, and wine. The Dean was right – it was especially good, despite its richness. Next to him and still not eating, the Archbishop took another mouthful of wine before he spoke into the pause.

'We have deprived another Puritan these last few days.' He looked around the table for nods of approval, which he got, with varying degrees of enthusiasm. His gaze ended on Richard sitting beside him. It was like being skewered.

'Who, My Lord?' Richard enquired.

'The rector at Babworth. One Richard Clyfton.'

Thomson leaned forward to look past Richard at Bancroft. 'And where on God's good earth is Babworth?'

'In the Midlands, I believe,' Andrewes supplied. 'Am I right?' He turned to the Archbishop, handing the conversation back to him.

'Yes,' Bancroft confirmed. 'Not far from Nottingham.'

Richard's skin prickled with interest.

'He refused the prayer book and the surplice, wouldn't kneel for the Host. He was given several chances but he refused to submit. They always do.'

'And the living at Babworth?' Andrewes asked.

'It will stay empty until another man can be found, one who will better conform to the teachings of the Church.' Bancroft swung his head towards Richard again. 'You have contacts in that part of the world, I believe, Doctor Clarke. Do you know of this Clyfton?'

'I've not heard of him,' Richard answered. His eye caught the Dean's, unwavering and serious, and the others regarded him with interest, wondering if their long-held suspicions were about to be borne out.

'I would lay odds he is known to Ben Kemp though,' Bancroft said. 'These Puritans mass together like flies on a turd.'

Doctor Overall sniggered. Richard shot him a look of distaste.

'And of course you would not deny that Ben Kemp is known to you?' Bancroft's gaze had not shifted, like a hunter with a quarry in his sight.

'My connection to Kemp is well known. I have never sought to deny it.' What else could he say when it was the Archbishop that had sent him back to the Kemps? He flushed, aware Bancroft was playing with him but unsure of the rules of the game.

'You have news of him?'

'Only that which you already know, My Lord,' he replied. The evening had cooled but he was sweating nonetheless. He took a mouthful of wine. 'And he may well know Clyfton – I believe he lives thereabouts.'

'He is not planning to go back to the East?'

'He prefers to remain in a Christian country.'

Bancroft let out a snort of derision and released Richard from his scrutiny, turning his gaze back to the rest of the Company. 'If he's connected to Clyfton we'll have him soon enough. A whole congregation can't hide for long. Then we'll get the lot of them and stamp out this dissent once and for all.'

Richard said nothing, wondering if Ben was connected to Clyfton, and if Babworth had been the draw that took him to the Midlands. The community there would be frightened now, he guessed, the net closing in on them without the shield of Babworth

Church to protect them, forced back into their own congregations, their own meetings their only place of worship. Their names would be noted now as absent come Sunday services and they would be called upon to explain themselves. As Bancroft said, it could only be a matter of time.

'Tell us more about Clyfton,' Overall said eagerly, second only to Bancroft in his hatred of Puritans. He was almost rubbing his hands with excitement. 'What manner of man is he?' Attention shifted back to the Archbishop. Richard drank more wine.

'From a prominent local family, I'm told. A wife and children.'

And now the man has no living, Richard thought, he and his family exiled to the edges of society, forced to live on others' charity. Frustration simmered. Why could these people not just conform? At least on the outside. Then they would be left alone to worship as they pleased in private, to honour God as they saw most fit. What did it matter if they had to wear a surplice in public? Or kneel for the Host? It was a man's faith that mattered in the end, his love for God.

And yet a part of him could understand the drive for truth, the impulse that propels a man to stand up and say what he believes, to defend his faith against all others. A part of him admired the courage not to compromise, the depth of faith, a sureness of belief that knew no doubt. Men with conviction such as Ben – impossible and maddening, but fired by love of God nonetheless.

Bancroft reached out for more meat and his elbow bumped Richard's arm. Involuntarily he flinched, repelled by the Archbishop's touch. Discreetly he shifted his chair away from Bancroft, closer to Thomson, who was sitting to his right. The older man turned his head and observed him with interest.

'I know what you're thinking,' Thomson said.

'Oh, really?'

'But just because not all of us have the stomach for it doesn't mean it isn't necessary.'

'What's that you say?' Bancroft had caught the tail end of Thomson's words.

Thomson said, 'We were just discussing the need to deprive men such as Clyfton.'

Bancroft's eyes glittered. 'Does Doctor Clarke not approve?'

All eyes turned once again towards him in the hush that fell, but he met the Archbishop's gaze without flinching. He would not allow himself to be humiliated by Thomson: he was playing his part and the Archbishop knew it.

'Doctor Thomson,' he said, 'with his customary wine-led wisdom, claims he can read my mind.'

Thomson laughed. Others at the table began nervous smiles that quickly faded with the Archbishop's stoniness.

'And still you protest,' Thomson said, 'when it is as plain as day that you have a rather large conflict of interest. We are all of us aware of your friendship with Kemp. We all of us know what Ben Kemp believes. Yet even now, after all these years, you insist on lodging with his family.'

No one was smiling now. Behind him one of the servants clattered a large tray of dishes onto the sideboard and the racket reverberated through the silent room. A trickle of sweat tickled against his spine and he was acutely aware of the effects of the claret. He swivelled to face his neighbour.

'Of what exactly are you accusing me?'

Thomson made an expansive gesture with one hand. 'I am accusing you of nothing. I am merely observing that keeping such friends must at times put you in a difficult position.'

'And what of it?'

Thomson briefly slid his gaze past Richard towards the Archbishop. Then he said, 'Am I the only man who thinks it strange that you keep company with a Separatist? Or to question your loyalty because of it? It is not enough to profess no love for Puritans when you choose as friends those men who wish to destroy the Church. Surely I am not the only one to think so?' He flicked a glance around the table and found tacit support in the silence and half nods of the others. There was no one who spoke up in Richard's defence, not even Andrewes.

'My dislike of Puritans is not a matter for debate – it has long been known. Ask any man here. I was passed over twice for promotion at Christ's College for not being Puritan enough and I resigned my fellowship in protest. You were there, as I recall. Perhaps you would remember it if you could stay sober long enough.'

Thomson's eyes drifted away from him, hostility receding, as though he were indeed trying to recall through the fog of his memory. Richard watched him, flushed with awareness of his audience, and remembered anger at the injustice flickered inside him. He had only ever sought to belong, to be accepted for his faith and his intellect, but always he had remained on the outside: in the hotbed of reform that Cambridge had been in those years, his beliefs had been deemed archaic, the last vestiges of the Roman faith that would soon be expunged from the English Church. Then, as now, he had searched his heart to find the truth – hours on his knees in tearful supplication to God, long nights spent arguing with Ben – but his faith had remained unchanged, immutable as eternity. And now, here, amongst these men whose beliefs he shared, he found himself once more excluded from their fellowship – his crime a Christian love for another, a man he only hoped to save. He took another mouthful of claret despite the unclearness already in his head.

'So tell me,' Thomson said, eyes brightening as he turned again towards Richard. 'Why do you continue your friendship with

Kemp when it does you such harm? Why do you keep on risking yourself for such a man?'

'Because,' he said, 'friendship is a gift from God and I have not yet given up hope he will recant.' It was only half a lie and he wished to God it was the truth.

'Doctor Thomson.' The Dean's deep voice drew the drunkard's eyes reluctantly towards him. 'Let us talk of other things now. Doctor Clarke's loyalty is not, and never has been, a matter for doubt.'

Richard looked away. The Dean's words were fine but too late. Thomson had voiced the thoughts of every man at the table.

'If you say so, Mister Dean,' Thomson murmured. But his gaze flicked to the man beside him without much conviction.

'I do say so,' the Dean confirmed, 'and it would become you better to show a little more respect for the others engaged in our task.'

Thomson said nothing, resenting the rebuke, and settled his bulk in his chair. An air of ill will hung across the room.

'Well, gentlemen.' Andrewes interrupted the silence. 'The hour grows late.'

A general murmur of agreement circled the table, the men rising from their places, taking their leave of one another. As they made their way to the door of the chamber not one of them but Andrewes bid goodnight to Richard and he walked out into the yard alone.

～

ONLY ALICE WAS in the hall when Richard returned to Thieving Lane from the meeting, though the Abbey bell had not yet struck the hour of ten and the last dregs of day still touched the western sky. But inside the house it was dark and candles burned brightly near the unlit hearth. Alice sat in the light, peering at her sewing. He wondered she could see enough to sew.

'Where is everyone?' he said, crossing to the cupboard and pouring both of them wine from the jug. It was a Canary, light and sweet and cool. She laid her sewing aside and took the cup with a smile of thanks.

'My uncle is not yet returned from Tilbury and Aunt Emma had a headache. She has gone to bed.'

He sat across the hearth and watched as she resumed her sewing, the needle flickering in the candlelight. 'You weren't lonely?'

'I like the quiet,' she replied. 'And I wanted to finish the shirt.'

'Is it for Ben?'

She shook her head. 'I would hardly dare to sew for him unless he asked me to.'

Her answer took him by surprise. 'What makes you say so? Has he been unkind to you?'

'No. Never,' she answered quickly. 'It is just ...' She stopped, her needle hovering a moment before she placed the linen down across her lap. 'It's just there is something wild about him, something reckless that makes me fear him.'

'You have no need to fear him,' Richard reassured her. 'He has a fiery temper the same as his sister but his heart is kind. He would not hurt you.'

She tidied the sewing away and placed it on top of the basket beside her. Then she said, 'They say in the kitchen that a long time ago Ben went to prison for his faith, that his wife and child died because of it. And they say the grief almost drove him to despair.'

'They speak the truth,' he admitted, though he wondered how the servants knew so much about their master's agony. He had thought that only he had known the truth of it.

'He lost everything, then?'

'Everything he cared about.'

'Except his faith.'

'He lost that too for a little while.' He had remembered it walking home from the Abbey, the memory stirred by Bancroft's baiting. He had recalled every word and shivered in spite of the heat.

She took a sip of wine and thought for a moment. 'Then I am right to fear him,' she said. 'Because a man who has lost everything might indeed be dangerous. He has no reason to be cautious because he has nothing left to lose. A man like that can afford to risk all.'

Richard looked away, unnerved by her perception. He said, 'It was many years ago.'

'Has he changed?'

He hesitated. 'I'm not sure. Perhaps not.'

'Why does he hate the Church so much?'

Richard smiled. 'Now there's a question.'

Alice tensed and turned her head away from the mockery she sensed in the tone. 'You're making fun of me.'

'No,' he said quickly. He hadn't meant it that way. 'No, not at all. But it's a question he and I have fought over for many hours, many years.'

'Then ...?' She lifted her chin, the question still in her eyes.

He smiled again, wondering where he might begin. But he was happy to talk to her, their conversation easy: she had never once made him feel awkward or shy as other women did. He said, 'Ben believes the Church is not reformed enough. He thinks like a Puritan but more so.'

'What more reform would he have?'

'No bishops,' he said, 'no canons, no deans, no king at the head of it all. Each congregation its own community, its officers elected from amongst themselves. And he would have no liturgy, no prayer book, no kneeling for the Host ...'

'But these things have come to us from the Ancient Fathers.'

'He would say they have become corrupted, that they are remnants of popish invention. He would say it is not the Church that our Lord commanded.'

She nodded her understanding but her brow was still creased into a frown. 'But without the Church we are all of us lost,' she said. 'So why would they break it?'

Richard considered for a moment, unsure how to explain any further, how much she would understand. Then, 'Ben believes God is revealed only through the words of the Scripture, that we cannot use our God-given reason, our rational capacities, to keep us safe from sin. So he rejects the validity of tradition, saying it is man-made, and sinful.' He looked across to her to see if she was following.

Alice nodded, an encouragement for him to continue.

'He believes the Church should comprise only the faithful, a gathering of true believers – he sees the English Church as full of sinners and therefore not a true Church as Christ commanded.'

'But then how can people receive God's grace, if they are barred from the Church? It must be all-inclusive, from the lowest beggar to the highest king, or we are no longer a Christian realm.'

'We believe so because for us, the sacraments confer God's grace. For Ben, the sacraments merely confirm God's grace, already given. Do you see?'

She was silent, considering, one hand fingering the sewing on the table beside her. He watched her, wondering what was in her mind, comfortable in her company.

He said, 'They seem to be small things, I know, but they are the foundation stones on which the Church is built.'

She lifted her eyes to him with a smile that chased away the habitual frown. She was pretty when she smiled, he realised. She should smile more often. 'I understand,' she said. 'But I wish he were different. He doesn't know the pain he gives his parents.'

Then, placing the empty wine cup on the floor at her feet, she reached once again for her sewing. He drained his own wine, got up and went to the cupboard for more. She shook her head when he offered it to her. When he had returned to his chair he said, 'So who is the shirt for?'

'For my father,' she said. 'His new wife is no seamstress so I sew his shirts for him now. I know how he likes them.'

'I see.' In two sentences she had told him more about herself than he had learned in all the months he had known her. 'He is lucky to have such a devoted daughter.'

She finished off the seam with a final stitch. 'A more devoted daughter would have learned to like her new mother better I think and would have been permitted to stay.'

'Perhaps,' he replied, though it was hard to imagine how anyone could object to Alice in their household, quiet, willing, kind. But perhaps it was the kindness that rankled, a contest for the master's affection the new wife could not win. Then again, he thought, it might have been her powers of observation that got her sent away. Poor girl, he thought, unwanted by those who should have loved her. No wonder she was so eager to please, so shy. She rarely ventured an opinion on anything much, even to him, who held no power over her. She asked many questions, he realised, but offered little of herself in return. He guessed it was a form of self-defence, so that those on whom she depended would see only her usefulness and find no fault in her otherwise. He felt for her predicament, his heart moved with pity.

'You have brothers?' he asked. 'Sisters?'

'Older brothers. One is a clergyman like you. He was recently made prebendary at Bristol.'

He heard the pride in her voice. 'And of course my father's new family, twin boys and another on the way.'

'Your father writes to you?'

'Yes.' She smiled again. 'And it seems from his letters that his new wife brings him less happiness than he hoped. He says nothing directly of course, but I can tell.' Then, as an afterthought, 'He was devoted to my mother.'

'And you are like her?'

'Very.' The smile flickered again, the knowledge pleasing, and the silence that fell was comfortable. She turned her attention back to her sewing and as the Abbey bell tolled the hour he watched the needle catch the candlelight, flickering in and out of the fabric, nimble and precise.

THE MEMORY of Ben in his darkness remained in Richard's thoughts as he lay down to sleep. For a while he fought it against it, face screwed tight with the pain it evoked, but the images persisted, and in the end he gave up the struggle and let them come.

The second time he had seen Ben at the Fleet he had thought he was better prepared, the memory of the place still sharp in his thoughts. But even so, the stench took his breath away as he stepped inside the gate, and he felt the same sense of hopelessness that oozed from the walls. Inside the cell Ben was still in chains, the place no different from before despite his father's payments to the warden. Richard was appalled at the sight of him: he had aged years in weeks – grey streaks flecked through the matted dark curls, and the gaunt cheeks were sunken. He fought to hide his dismay and the sudden over-whelming conviction that his friend would never leave the cell alive. Ben unfolded from where he sat in the straw with uncharacteristic slowness, standing up stiffly to greet his visitor. The two men embraced.

'I've brought food, clothes, ale, pen and ink.' Automatically he searched for a table before he let the bundle gently down onto the straw at his feet.

'Thank you,' Ben said. 'You are kind to do so.'

'It is your father you should thank. Is there anything else you need?'

Ben shook his head. It was awkward standing together with nowhere but the straw to sit. 'I would offer you a seat but ...' Ben shrugged and moved to the window, leaned his shoulder against the wall beside it, eyes drawn to the narrow view beyond the prison wall. Richard followed but stood a few inches from the stone, reluctant to touch its filthy dampness.

'I spend a lot of time standing here,' Ben said. 'It reminds me that a world exists outside this cell. Though it's a world that holds little light for me now.'

'Time heals, Ben. Time and prayer.'

Ben swung round to face him. 'You have had no wife, no child. What can you know of grief?'

Richard took a breath. 'I make no claim to know,' he said. 'But I know Cecily wouldn't want you to despair.'

His friend's chin lifted to a scornful tilt. 'You would claim to know her mind?'

He looked away. He had not expected to meet such anger, such despondency. 'She would not have wanted you to give up hope,' he said.

Ben turned away and rested a hand on the bars, staring out.

'There is always hope, Ben. *All things are possible to him that believeth.*'

'Have you never doubted?' Ben asked, without turning his gaze from the window. 'Have you never wondered if it is all just a lie we believe in to ease the suffering of life? To give it meaning?'

'No,' he replied, shaking his head. 'Never. I have doubted the Church many times, and questioned the teachings. Arguing with you, how could I not? But we have always agreed on the fundamentals. God's existence is as real as you or I, His presence plain in everything you are, everything you see. I could never doubt the truth of that.'

'Then you are a better man than I am.' Ben's tone was bitter.

Richard could barely believe what he was hearing: he had thought, hoped, that time and prayer would have begun to heal the grief a little, that Ben would have found succour in his faith. But the depth of his friend's despair shocked him, and it seemed his faith had not returned. He said, 'You cannot lose faith now when you have given so much. When Cecily has given so much.'

The other man said nothing, eyes still trained on the putrid river.

'Ben?'

Finally Ben turned, and when he spoke his voice was no more than a whisper. 'I was always so sure,' he said. 'About all of it. Every last detail. Christ's plan for Heaven on earth. It was all so clear to me what needed to be done. All of it written in the Scripture, and if it took my life to see it done, I would have given it, and gladly. But now ...' He shrugged and shook his head. 'Now I don't even know what to reach for any more to save myself.'

Richard's heart welled with pity: he could not begin to imagine the fear in a life without faith. Who would you turn to? In whom could you trust? Without God his life would be meaningless, a void. He stretched out a hand and took hold of Ben's arm. 'You must pray,' he said. 'You must ask for God's help.'

'I cannot pray. My heart is empty.'

'You must try,' Richard insisted. '*Whosoever asketh, receiveth, he that seeketh findeth.* You must not give up hope.'

'All I ask for is my death.' He murmured the words as he turned away, shrugging Richard's hand from his arm and staring once again through the bars.

Richard swallowed down his horror. 'It grieves me to see you like this,' he said to fill the silence and hide his anguish. He could think of no more words of comfort to offer his friend.

'Then do not come again.'

Despite himself Richard's lips twitched. Even in despair, Ben's impatience was undimmed. Perhaps there was hope after all. 'And abandon you to this?'

Ben let go of the bars and looked at his friend. 'Why should you care? It is your Church that put me here.'

'Because I love thee still.' The answer came unbidden and unconsidered, but it came from the heart. It found its mark and Ben dropped his head. Richard could see the muscle twitching in his cheek as he struggled with his emotions. Finally, he turned again towards his friend.

'I don't deserve your love.'

'Perhaps that's true. But love is not conditional. And if I won't forsake you, what makes you think that God would do so?'

Ben was silent, fingers working once more at the cold steel bars, gaze drawn out towards the world beyond his prison.

'You can find your freedom in here, even in the depths of your fear,' Richard said gently, 'if you pray. God will answer you, Ben. It is written; *Jesus said unto them, for verily I say unto you, if ye have faith as much as is a grain of mustard seed, ye shall say unto this mountain, Remove hence to yonder place, and it shall remove: and nothing shall be impossible unto you.* You will find your faith again, if you pray.'

Ben gave no answer, lips pressed tight, eyes unseeing. Richard waited but the other man did not move, his back still turned to the cell, and they stood for a long while, the light growing dim with the fading of the afternoon. Finally, they heard the warden in the passage and the scrape of the keys in the lock.

'I will come again,' Richard said, touching a hand lightly to the other man's shoulder. 'God keep you.'

Then, reluctantly, he had gone out into the clear freedom of the day, leaving his friend to face his darkness alone.

CHAPTER 15

NOVEMBER 1605

The Lord is my light, and my saluation, whome shal I feare?
The Lord is the strength of my life, of whom shall I be afraid?
When the wicked, euen mine enemies and my foes came vpon me to
eat vp my flesh, they stumbled and fell.
(*Psalms 27:1–2*)

In the Abbey library Richard began to pack up his papers, his mind tired and his fingers cold in spite of the fire in the hearth, which could never quite chase the chill that seeped from the thick stone walls. As he left the seclusion of the library, his thoughts still turned on his work, phrases from the Book of Numbers tapping at his brain. Perhaps he would find the answer on the walk home, he thought. Perhaps the crispness of the darkening afternoon would lead him to the words he was seeking.

The Abbey nave was busy with people, humming with voices that were raised in excitement, men of all classes engaged in animated chatter. He paid them scant attention; the Abbey was often crowded and his thoughts were still with the Hebrew as he way to the door. Outside, Broad Sanctuary was lively with unexpected celebration. An impromptu bonfire had been lit before the Abbey doors, flames licking up into the darkness, the air heavy with the scent of smoke. He stopped just beyond the door for a moment, confused, thinking he might have mistaken the day. But All Hallows had been and gone a few days before, the chill of winter settling in with its passing, so there must be some other cause for celebration.

A large crowd had gathered, drinking, talking, laughing. Someone had brought a fiddle, and there were couples dancing to a quick-paced folk tune he did not recognise, the womens' skirts swirling out around their legs as they twirled. He turned his face away from the lewdness of it, but he sensed the tension in the air, an excitement fed by nerves, and drew his cloak more tightly round him, the fur warm against his neck, as he bent his steps towards Thieving Lane where he had no doubt he would find out all he needed to know. In his curiosity the passage from Numbers was all but forgotten.

'It was the Papists, Doctor Clarke,' Alice said, running to the door to greet him. 'Did you hear? They tried to blow up Parliament.'

He said nothing, too shocked by her words to reply. For a moment he thought she was joking until he saw the furrow that brought her eyebrows close together, the pale eyes squinting through the dim evening light to see him better. She took his cloak and hat.

'Doctor Clarke?'

He rubbed his cold hands together, nodding. Then he gestured to the hall. 'Shall we?'

Thomas Kemp stood before the hearth, his wife in her accustomed chair. She held no sewing but sat looking up at her husband, pale hands working together on her lap.

'Have you heard the news?' Kemp turned immediately to Richard as he crossed to the fire to warm his hands. 'They put barrels of gunpowder into the cellars.'

He stared. 'Barrels of gunpowder? How in God's name ...?' He could scarcely credit such a thing was possible.

'One of the devils was taken in the act, no less,' Kemp told him. 'A little longer and it would have been too late. But the one they've caught will talk and no doubt we shall find out more soon enough.'

Richard was silent, still searching to make sense of it. How could such a thing have happened? How could it have come so close to success? The realm under threat, himself, this house, these people, all of them had been within a hair of their deaths. He could think of no words to say. Dazed, he sat on one of the chairs by the hearth and barely noticed when Alice placed a cup of wine in his hand. He sipped at it absently.

They had become complacent, he realised, all of them. So many long years of peace and prosperity had blinded them to the evils of such monsters in their midst. They had thought the Papists vanquished and the threat removed, but the devils had only been biding their time after all, still plotting for power. That men could seek to do such brutish things – it surely was the work of Satan.

'And the Bishop of Rome approved it?' he managed to ask.

'Ah. Who can say?'

'There were bonfires in the streets on my way home.'

'The news has travelled fast. They have set a civil watch on the gates, and closed all the ports.' He was thinking of his trade, Richard guessed, the precious cargos that must now wait to be unloaded.

'Perhaps it was the Spanish,' Alice said, sitting close to Emma Kemp on a stool by her feet, taking the older woman's hand in her own, reassuring. 'I heard there was a mob outside the ambassador's house.'

'Surely not? They would hardly risk war again so soon.'

'What would have happened if they had succeeded?' Alice asked. 'What would have happened if King James and the lords had all died?'

The two men exchanged a look that dared not even contemplate the consequences, the bloodbath that would have ensued. Whatever faults we might find with a king, Richard thought, we cannot return to the days when power could be wrested at the point of a sword. Or at the lighting of gunpowder. It was years since the spectre of a Papist uprising had hovered over England: the execution of Mary Queen of Scots twenty years before had removed the focus for any Catholic claims to power. Instead, they had gone underground, served by an endless influx of Jesuit priests who lived in holes in the walls of their followers' houses and led the Mass in secret darkness. Biding their time and plotting, it seemed.

'It is better not to think of it,' Richard said. 'We must just thank God that the devils were caught in time.'

'I think we would be better to thank the Earl of Salisbury. I understand it was he who discovered the plot.' Kemp winked at Richard, who lifted a hand to his mouth to cover his smile.

'Thomas!' His wife was shocked.

'But yes, my dear,' Kemp placated. 'Richard is right. We should also thank God that they failed.'

'Who can believe it?' Emma Kemp kept saying, her fingers still turning against one another. 'That they would do such a thing?'

'Let's hope they have no more plots afoot.'

'Aye,' Thomas Kemp agreed, with feeling. 'I remember the last go-round with the Papists in power ...' meaning the reign of Bloody Queen Mary, when hundreds of Protestants burned in her bid to drag England back to Rome. Now others had taken up the cause again, men willing to die for the man they called the Pope. Richard wondered at the power the Roman Church held over men, the slavish devotion, men who would risk all to serve it, zealous, fanatical, dangerous. Men with nothing to lose but their faith. Then he remembered what Alice had said about Ben, and wondered how much difference there was between them.

AT THE WEEKLY meeting the talk was all of the gunpowder treason, these men committed to the English Church outraged by the violence the Papists had attempted. Richard was glad of the respite – anger turned against Rome instead of Puritans for a while. It was some months since he had heard anything of Ben, living quietly away in the Midlands, and for a time Richard had hoped to hear no more, allowing himself to half believe that God had relieved him of the burden of his task. But Bancroft had lately begun asking again for news and the months of pleasant self-deception were at an end, conflict and uncertainty bearing in on him again and leaving him exhausted.

'It was meant to be the day of our deaths,' Andrewes said, 'as sheep to the slaughter. We must celebrate God's merciful deliverance from such monsters. That our land should breed such devils.'

'It is but two days,' John Overall said. 'Who can know if they have further plots to destroy us? Westminster Palace is merely a stone's throw from here – we were … we are … all of us at risk.'

They nodded in agreement, aware of the closeness of the danger.

'We would all of us have died,' Overall insisted. 'All of us.'

'But God has spared us,' Andrewes said, 'and we must thank Him for His mercy.'

'And they have caught the conspirators, have they not?' Thomson asked. He raised his eyebrows. 'I wouldn't want to be in their shoes now.'

'One of them,' Andrewes said. 'They have caught one of them. There must have been many.'

Richard was silent. He was as relieved as any that God had delivered them, his blood still thrilling with the shock of it.

'The others have fled,' Andrewes continued, 'but the one who was taken will talk. And in time his companions will join him.'

No one doubted the truth of his words. Richard knew well the deprivations of a prison cell and he had heard the wails of men under torture, but he could not bear to imagine the agony of the rack. It was said no one ever held out against its pain, that many prisoners talked even at the sight of it. The king would surely sanction its use for a crime so heinous.

'We have tolerated dissent for too long,' Thomson said. 'Of all kinds. Papists, Puritans, Separatists.' He flicked a glance to Richard. 'They must all of them be brought to heel.'

'Indeed,' Overall agreed. 'But we cannot prosecute them all. We cannot find them all. They are cunning, and numerous. The Papists with their smuggled priests and hidey-holes, the Separatists with their hidden congregations. How can we find all of them out?'

'We must make examples of the ones we catch,' Thomson answered. 'Send a message that England will not tolerate dissent.'

'But it does no good. These people want to be martyrs – it seems only to serve to bring others to their cause,' Overall argued.

'No one wants to die how these men will die,' Thomson said. 'No matter their faith.'

'So what can be done about them? How can we silence their murmurings, their plottings, before they commit more monstrosities?'

Thomson turned to Richard. 'You're keeping very quiet, Doctor Clarke. Do you have nothing to say on the subject of dissenters?'

He hesitated, aware he was being tested, Thomson's spiteful

needling relentless. Like the bullies of his childhood, he thought, picking on the easy target. He imagined Thomson had been a hateful child. He knew these men distrusted him – they had already excluded him from their fellowship – but he had no wish to confirm their beliefs about his loyalties. He said, 'I am as afraid of Papists as anyone. It seems they've never given up their bid to wrest power from the rightful king. So many years of peace have caused us to forget their treasonous ways and be easy on them, but we must still wage war against them – they have made that plain with this latest outrage.'

'And what of other dissenters such as Separatists?' Thomson lips parted in a smile, and Richard whispered a brief mental prayer for forgiveness for the hurt he would have liked to inflict.

The eyes of every man at the table slid towards him and he chose his next words with great care. 'It is a different battle,' he said, 'but a battle nonetheless, to defend our Church and the conformity that has for so long brought us peace. Dissenters of all kinds must be found out and made to conform – the future of the realm depends upon it.'

'Nicely answered.' Thomson smirked.

Richard tilted his head and smiled in reply, but inwardly he was seething. The other men were still observing him, their doubts about him plain in their faces. He sat upright and still, trailing his eyes around the table at each of them in turn: he refused to be cowed. All except Thomson dropped their gaze as he got to them.

Andrewes said, 'The devils will be found out. By God's marvellous works, the destroyer passed over us, and we shall know more in the coming days.' He cast his gaze around the table. 'But for now we must return to our God-given labour. He would have us finish our task. The Book of Numbers, I believe, chapter eleven?'

There was a murmuring of assent, a rustling of papers as the men turned their minds to the task in hand, Richard's possible crimes paling next to the audacity of the Papists; but a tension remained as an awareness of their danger, an apprehension that there may be other plots to come. All of them were jumpy, focus wandering with each strange noise outside, their thoughts still half-taken by the week's events. But eventually the meeting began their work, comparing the translations that had come before against their own attempts. Within moments they were arguing: as ever, Doctor Overall was defending the phrasing of the Bishops' Bible.

'But *an'an* does not mean *"did wickedly."*' Richard was trying to be patient.

'Neither does it mean *"murmuring,"*' Layfield countered.

'It can only be translated truly as *"complaining,"*' Doctor Thomson said, with a sigh.

'But their complaining is wicked – it angers God. Therefore there is truth in such a translation.'

'Their complaining is such that God hears it but Moses does not. *Murmuring* is surely apt here.' Murmuring is but the outward show of dissent, Richard knew, and rumours and discontent travel quickest in an undertone: the ancient world would have been no different. No wonder it displeased the Lord. He thought of Ben and the rumours of his crimes that Bancroft fed on, murmurings he wanted Richard to confirm with fact.

Saravia said, 'Let us read the lines again so that we can hear them against one another.'

'As you will.' Overall was testy.

Andrewes read them out in turn.

The Bishops' Bible:

'And when the people did wickedly, it was a displeasure in the eares of the Lorde.'

The Geneva:

'When the people became murmurers, it displeased the Lord.'

Then Thomson read his own line:

'And when the people complained, it displeased the Lord.'

There was a silence as each man took time to consider the merits of each possibility. Andrewes rested his fingers on the pages of the Bibles that were open before him and looked up.

'Gentlemen?'

Richard said nothing, though the simplicity of Thomson's phrasing was pleasing. And there was no denying that *complained* was an accurate rendering. They all waited for the Dean to speak again, his judgement in these matters always wise: there was not one of them who would argue against his decisions.

He said, 'I believe that Doctor Thomson has the right of it on this occasion. The line therefore will read,

And when the people complained, it displeased the Lord.'

Andrewes flicked a last glance round the table to invite more comment, but no one spoke and the Translation moved on to the following line.

CHAPTER 16

WINTER 1606

Heare, O Israel, the LORD our God is one LORD. And thou shalt loue the LORD thy God with all thine heart, and with all thy soule, and with all thy might.

And these words which I command thee this day, shall bee in thine heart.

(Deuteronomy 6:4–6)

THE ABBEY BELL tolled the hour. Richard sat back from the desk in the library and stretched out his arms against the stiffness in them, joints cracking loudly. He closed his eyes and rotated his head, searching to ease the soreness in his neck. It made no difference. His mind was tired and his fingers were cold. Opening his eyes, he got up and went to stand by the fire, holding his palms towards its heat. It was burning well, the logs piled high – someone must have come in to tend it while he was working but he had no recollection of it. His thoughts had been elsewhere, absorbed in the greatest commandment, striving to pull the perfect meaning from the Hebrew into English.

He rubbed his hands together gently, warmth returning. It would be dark outside, night coming early on these cold winter days. He should return to Thieving Lane for his supper, and tackle the passage again tomorrow when his mind was fresh, but for some reason he could not let it go. The Hebrew turned again through his thoughts.

Sh'ma Yisra'el, Adonai Eloheinu Adonai echad.

Such a short phrase, so deceptively simple, yet the crux of Christianity contained within it.

Warmer now, he left the fireside and went back to the desk, running his fingers over the pages spread out before him. Older translations, other men who had striven with the same words, and failed to find perfection in their answer. He recalled his attempt to sing the words to Alice, and the fear of failing to render their beauty. The same fear gripped him now, that whatever words he used in English would fall short of God's meaning, the holy message lost in vain translation.

He read the line in the Geneva, the finest of the translations that had gone before, and spoke the words aloud.

'Hear, O Israel, the Lord our God is Lord only.'

His voice was hoarse from disuse the last several hours. He cleared his throat and read it again. The Bishops' Bible had it the same; Coverdale had one word different.

'... the Lorde our God is one Lorde only.'

Neither version seemed quite right to him; neither captured the subtle transcendence of the word *echad*. It was only one word, and the word meant 'one,' but the command was so crucial to what it means to have faith that to render it anything but perfectly could change the very nature of belief. How should he convey the nuances within it?

One God: containing the Trinity – father, son and holy ghost, comprising the One.

One God: to be worshipped above all others;

One God: the only God, creator of all things.

He read the line again in the Hebrew, then cast his eye once more across the translations that had gone before, before turning again to his own efforts to make it perfect.

'The Lord our God is one God.

'The Lord our God is the Lord alone.'

He murmured each possibility in turn, slowly, his fingers tracing the words he had written across the page as the sounds passed his lips.

'The Lord is our God, the Lord is one.

'The Lord our God is one Lord.'

His fingers came to rest on the last of the lines. He whispered it again.

'The Lord our God is one Lord.'

And again. The words shimmered in his mind, left an echo in his heart. His soul filled, lifting him beyond the chilly gloom of the library, and met with an answering love.

There is only one God and to love Him without reservation is the greatest commandment, the greatest truth. The divine love depends on total self-surrender to this truth, and love for our brothers is founded on this first and primal love. For the Jews it must have been a startling revelation – surrounded by other gods, their god was the first to deny the existence of others, to demand total belief in Him alone, total devotion to the one Lord. And now it formed the very core of all faith – Christ as Lord in unity with God, moved by the Holy Spirit. The Trinity forming one Lord. One Lord from whom all things stem.

Richard knelt, joyous and elated, losing himself in the perfection of the Lord, surrendering his heart and soul and mind to Christ, filling himself with the love of God, his own unworthy soul redeemed by Christ's love. He knelt for a long time, unaware of the growing cold of the library or the stiffness in his knees, and when finally his soul formed again within him and he was himself once more, he knew he had found perfection.

Silently, still with joy, he got to his feet, packed up the books and the pages, and headed out of the library towards the waiting supper at Thieving Lane.

~

IN THE CLOISTER he saw Thomson too late to avoid him. His muscles tightened, preparing for defence. The older man smiled as though they were old friends, and Richard had no choice but to stop and greet him. A group of chattering boys from the Abbey school parted like a wave around them and hurried on. He watched the small retreating backs and shivered in the draughty passage. The library had been warm in comparison.

'Did you go?' Thomson enquired, still smiling. 'Did you see them suffer?'

For an instant he was bewildered. His thoughts were still in the world of Deuteronomy, the perfect words of the *Sh'ma* still sounding in his mind.

'The Papists,' Thomson clarified impatiently. 'Did you not go to see them die?'

He remembered. The Papists and their ill-fated gunpowder treason, their failed attempt to blow up king and parliament. He had not wanted to go: he had no desire to witness another man's innards on display when he was not yet dead, nor to see the scaffold slippery with the blood of men still breathing. But persuaded by the suggestion of Bancroft he had done his duty, against his will, to stand with the baying crowd in the Old Palace Yard at Westminster, forcing himself to watch this reminder of the fate that awaited traitors. The violence had sickened him, and the brutal lusts of the crowd had left him horrified. They had not come to see justice served, uninterested in the political need for the deaths of these men or the errors in their faith that required such correction. They were a crowd like the mobs that gather to watch a brawl in the street, drawn by animal instinct and inflamed by a base and carnal passion. He had felt himself to be trapped in the midst of something infinitely wicked, the cries of sinners all around him, corrupted and filled with hate, as though Satan himself were amongst them. Was this how Christ had died, he had wondered, amongst such hatred and lust, ears ringing with the shouts of depravity and evil? No wonder He had thought He was forsaken: it must have seemed as though He were already in Hell. But the men on the scaffold had each died true to their cause, no last-minute recantations, their belief undimmed despite the hellish trial before them. Such strength of faith that could drive a man to martyrdom.

It had seemed to last an age until the last screams faded through the chill morning air, and the obscene, sweet stench of blood and burning guts drifted over the still-baying crowd. When he lifted his head at last to survey the scene in front of him, he saw the body parts of men strewn across the scaffold boards, and other men stooping to pick up the pieces. Sickened again, he turned his face away.

As he was borne away from the scene by the tide of the mob, only half-aware of the chatter all around him and the sweat of lust still across their faces, he had remembered another execution: the death of Henry Barrow years before on the gallows at Tyburn. Barrow, who had helped to inspire Ben's beliefs; Barrow, who had hated the Church as Ben did. Ben had not long been in prison when Barrow died, his ordeal just beginning as the older man's came to its grisly end. His death had been a martyrdom too, less famous than the gunpowder plotters', a smaller audience, but it was martyrdom nonetheless – the giving of his life for his faith. He too had died unrepentant, certain of the rightness of his path.

And Ben was prepared to die the same way, his conviction no less than Barrow's, no less than that of the men who had just been butchered for their loyalty to the pope. If he stayed in England, would he die a martyr too? On a different scaffold from the Papists perhaps, a less brutal death, but death nonetheless: a rope round his neck would end a life just as easily. Ask Barrow. And for what? Had Ben not paid enough already? Had he not suffered for his faith?

God knew that Ben had given more than most, and He was offering him a different path, a way to safety. How many times had Thomas Kemp asked his son to go? Was it God's hand working through him, trying to lead his servant from the wilderness to safety? To Richard it seemed so. Ben could make a good living as a merchant in Aleppo or in Holland. A living in safety. In Holland he could worship how he liked and be in no danger. So why did he still refuse to go? Was it guilt that made him obstinate? Or pure bloody-mindedness?

He must make Ben see it was God's will that he should go. He would talk to him again, he resolved, and make him understand, urge him away from England's shores. He must save Ben Kemp from himself.

Now, in the cloister, Thomson was almost rubbing his hands with relish. 'Did you not think it a fine spectacle?' he said.

Richard drew his mind back from thoughts of Ben to the man before him and said nothing.

'I thought you were a farmer's son.' Thomson clapped him on the back. 'A little blood shouldn't bother you.'

He drew his lips back in a poor pretence at a smile. 'It's

hardly the same, now is it?' He made to walk on and Thomson fell into step beside him, returning the way he had just come. Richard huddled into his cloak and wished the other man would go on his own way and leave him alone. But Thomson was watching him with shrewd narrowed eyes that disappeared into the fleshy face.

'You don't have secret sympathies for Papists as well as Puritans, do you?'

Richard's muscles clenched against the insult, the casual insinuation of his sympathy for traitors.

'No recusant aunts and uncles in that godforsaken place you come from?' Thomson was enjoying himself. 'No priest holes in the farmhouse walls?'

They reached the door and stepped out into the wind. Broad Sanctuary was busy with crowds, voices humming and raised with excitement. It was not hard to guess the topic of their conversation. Another bonfire had been lit in celebration, flames leaping wildly as they were buffeted by the wind.

'Hardly,' Richard answered. 'My forebears had pages of Tyndale under the floors. No secret Papists there.'

Thomson inclined his head as if considering whether or not to believe him. Richard met the look with open hostility: he had given up any semblance of civility. The older man let out a laugh and clapped him again on the shoulder. 'I'm having a joke with you, Doctor Clarke. There's no need to take it all so seriously.'

He tensed under the weight of the other man's hand and turned his face away. His breath was ragged and hard, all the injustice he had suffered on Ben's behalf embodied in this careless baiting. He jerked his shoulder from Thomson's grip.

'How is it a joke to say such things?'

Thomson registered the shift in his tone. 'I meant no offence,' he said. But then, unable to resist, 'But if you will keep company with men like Ben Kemp ...' He shrugged as if to say Richard had made himself fair game.

'Good day,' Richard said. Then he turned and strode away through the throng of people, huddled down inside his cloak and thinking of nothing.

CHAPTER 17

H ow long wilt thou forget mee (O LORD) for euer? how long wilt thou hide thy face from me? How long shall I take counsel in my soule, hauing sorrow in my heart dayly? how long shall mine enemie be exalted ouer me? Consider and heare me, O LORD my God: lighten mine eyes, lest I sleep the sleepe of death. Least mine enemie say, I haue preuailed against him: and those that trouble mee, reioyce, when I am moued.

   (Psalms 13:1–4)

SPRING BLEW in finally late in April with gusts of wind that whipped the petals from the trees so that the air still seemed wintry and filled with snow. In the yard at Scrooby Manor the farm dogs barked at nothing and within the house the wind whipped in the chimneys and rattled the windowpanes.

   '... After John was committed to prison, Jesus came into Galilee, ... pre ... preaching the Gospel of the kingdom of God.'

   The child Love looked up at Ben from the passage triumphantly, then glanced once more to the window where she could see the leaves being swept from the trees by the gusts. He followed her gaze. Such a serious, studious child, yet even her spirits were called away from her books by a windy day.

The children had been skittish at their studies all morning, utterly unable to focus on the passage of Scripture Ben had set them to learn. With infinite patience he had called back their attention again and again from their fidgeting, their eyes drawn to the window and the lure of the wind beyond.

'Go,' he ordered in the end. 'Go outside and run around for half an hour. Perhaps then we can study.'

They needed no second telling. The bench almost tipped as they raced from the room and out of the house, into the yard beyond. He watched them go with a smile, then tidied the books into a pile on the table before he stood up and lifted them across to the shelf in the corner. He could hear the children calling to one another, their voices fading and flowing on the wind. They sounded happy and free: as yet they knew nothing of chains and bars, of cold, dank cells where a man could die for lack of light or air. Dreams of prison still haunted him, fear waking him at night: the pain of despair was not so easily forgotten. He could take himself back there in an instant, memories shivering through him, vivid and close. Lifting his gaze, he looked towards the East, towards Holland, where there existed the possibility of a freedom they would never have in England.

A memory of Amsterdam filled him, the tang of the city the last time he was there, when he took Barrow's writings and risked everything, the sharp salt air and a language only half-understood, the creak and slap of boats at their mooring and the promise of Greta's fish stew. God had offered him a different path that day but he had turned away from it, following instead the sin of his desire for Cecily, and the weakness of his flesh.

~

THE CROSSING to Holland had been rough and frightening, but the risk of it as always had enthralled him. He could understand why men chose to spend their lives at sea – the primaeval struggle with the storm, the sense of God's power of creation, his own humble place in the face of it. But he was unafraid of drowning, dying into Christ to be born again with God. He had stood on deck, gripping on for dear life as the vessel plunged and bucked beneath his feet, wind and spray in his face, and he was awed by its magnificence, God's hand holding the balance of forces. Feeling humbled, he had touched his fingers to the precious packet of writings in his shirt, safe and warm against his skin in its wrapping of leather.

The stone quay in the harbour at Amsterdam felt too still and solid beneath him as he stepped ashore, making him giddy until his legs remembered the ground was not supposed to move after all, and he could stride with ease to the house of his friends. They greeted him with warmth, conversing in a mixture of English, Dutch and Latin, the children grown taller and more serious in his months away, and shy of him now he was no longer so familiar. But the shyness soon passed and the little one with the cheeky smile stood by him with her hand on his leg as she had used to do.

'How is London these days?' Pieter asked him. 'We heard that Henry Barrow is still imprisoned.'

'It's more than four years now. He still writes.'

'Which is why you are here, I assume?'

'And we thought you'd come just to visit.' Pieter's English wife, Anne, chided him playfully. 'We thought you'd come to see our Greta.'

Greta, Pieter's daughter by an earlier wife, kept her head tactfully averted, focusing on the pot she was stirring at the hearth. But the line of her neck was still familiar, the blond hair tucked up under the plain white cap, wisps breaking free to curl against the young pale skin. Like Cecily's, he reflected, heat rippling through him at the thought of her, but he knew the scent of Greta better: his lips had touched that skin. He turned his eyes away from her, prayed for God's forgiveness.

He should have stayed and married her, he thought, and become part of this family with its warmth and laughter, a different world from his own: a father he was incapable of pleasing and his fretful mother. Here there was joy to be found and freedom to worship; he wondered what impulse had sent him back to live in England.

Greta brought the pot to the table and ladled out soup for them all.

'It's lovely to see you again, Ben,' she said, and it was hard to say if there was a reproach in the words or if the pleasure was genuine.

'After we eat,' Pieter said, 'we'll go and see Miller.'

Greta took her seat across from Ben, head lowered away from him.

'Please, Benjamin, say a good English grace for us.'

They bowed their heads as Ben prayed.

'And thank you, Lord,' Greta added, when he had finished, 'for keeping Ben safe and bringing him back to us.'

Ben kept his eyes on his soup and said nothing. He remembered why he had left.

THEY HAD WALKED QUICKLY through the streets of Amsterdam in the cool damp of the spring, slipping slightly on the wet cobblestones. The familiar stink of the city pervaded the air, a different stench from London, more reminiscent of the freedom of the sea. The streets were well known to him and though Pieter often walked in front as though to lead the way, Ben could have found the place alone. He had spent many hours with the printer when he lived here, helping with the transport of books and tracts to England. But in spite of Holland's freedoms there was still need to be wary: the English Church's spies were not confined to England.

Miller greeted them as old friends. Born an Englishman, he had lived in Holland more than thirty years, an exile from Bloody Queen Mary's religious zeal. But he had made his home in Amsterdam and stayed, taken a Dutch wife, and now he made a living printing literature he would have hanged for in England.

It was a lively house filled with children and noise, and the printing press merely added one more facet to the general disorder. There was always a welcome for visitors from England and they sat at the table drinking wine, giving Miller the news from London before they got down to business.

'You have a conventicle now in London?'

'There are fifty of us or more – Francis Johnson was recently made pastor.'

'And you keep safe?'

'We meet before dawn. We move from house to house. There is little else we can do.'

'May God keep you. It is an evil thing when good Christians must skulk about like criminals.' He drained his cup of wine. 'So,' he said, 'show me the tract.'

Ben took the package from his shirt and the printer opened it out, cleared a space on the table and laid out the sheets of writing. The paper was worn and thin from the constant use and need for concealment – it had been folded many times, and in places the edges were ragged.

A TRUE DESCRIPTION OUT OF THE WORD OF GOD, OF THE VISIBLE CHURCH

As there is but one God and father of all, one Lord over all, and one
Spirit: so is there but one truth, one faith, one salvation, one Church,
called in one hope, joined in one profession, guided by one rule, even
the word of the most high.
This Church as it is universally understood, containeth in it all the
elect of God that have been, are, or shall be. But being considered more
particularly, as it is seen in this present world, it consisteth of a
company and fellowship of faithful and holy people gathered together
in the name of Christ Jesus, their only king, priest, and prophet,
worshipping Him aright, being peaceably and quietly governed by His
officers and laws, keep the unity of faith in the bond of peace and love ...

BEN'S EYES flicked over the words, drinking them in, familiar and precious because they were forbidden. To be found with these words in his hands would put him in prison; if it were known he planned to print them, his fate would undoubtedly be worse. Miller ran his gaze across the pages too, seeing them with a professional eye though the message spoke to him also: he nodded his agreement as he read.

'He's still in prison, eh?' the printer said. 'I don't reckon they'll let him go now. He's been there too long and the moment has passed. Whitgift will want to make an example so fools like you can take warning.' He nodded at Ben, who smiled and shook his head. He was used to the printer's teasing. 'Take more than a hanging to make you recant though, eh?'

He smiled but in truth the inside of the Fleet had frightened him, the broken man that Barrow had become. He was unsure he would stay faithful in such conditions, or if fear might make him fall. But there seemed to him to be no choice – he couldn't change what he believed.

'Are you taking them back yourself?' The printer's question cut across his thoughts.

He shook his head, clearing his mind of the doubts. 'Studley's man. The draper. We'll conceal them in the bolts of cloth.'

'That's good.' Miller looked up from the pages. 'If you've seen Barrow they'll be watching you.'

'I know it.'

'You need to be careful, Ben.'

'Yes. I shall be.'

'You need to watch your back.'

Ben caught Pieter's eye and the Dutchman looked away.

'GRETA IS PLEASED to see you again,' Pieter said, walking back in the cool afternoon. 'She's hoping you will stay.'

Ben had forgotten about Greta, his mind distracted by the printer's words. He had spent the afternoon only half-present, on the outskirts of the conversation, his danger bearing in on him. Though he had always known it, the prospect seemed more real now and more likely.

'Benjamin?' Pieter gave him a quizzical smile. 'You were miles away.'

'Sorry,' he said. 'Just tired I think. From the trip. It was a rough crossing.'

'Of course.' Then, 'She has never stopped talking of you. She still thinks you will marry her.'

'I was never going to marry her, Pieter. When her husband died I was there, that is all.'

'Her husband was not as good to her as you were. You were gentle and kind and she took it for love.'

Ben shook his head. Though he had made her no promises, he still prayed for her each day, confessing his sin, aware of his weakness as a man. 'It was never love – I should have let her be.'

'Why don't you marry her? You can stay here, safe, and pray unhindered. No one cares here how you worship. We are a civilised country. No more hiding and risk. No more danger. So much fear is no good for a man's constitution; it wears him down in the end and makes him old before his time.'

He thought of Henry Barrow, grey-haired, black-toothed.

'She would make a good wife for you, a good mother for your children. You should have a wife, Ben, and a family. Every man should have a wife and family and the freedom to worship as he will.'

'I know.' An image of Cecily stole across his thoughts, the sunlight from the window lighting up her auburn hair.

'Then why not?'

'Because ...' Why not? What reason did he have not to marry Greta as Pieter said, not to live in Holland? It would be the wisest course: he could work here, enough of his father's trade in the city to keep him busy, to make a home with Greta. He could live, as the Dutchman said, in safety and in peace. No more worshipping in secret, illegally. No more having to watch his back. It could be a good life, honest, simple, godly. But in London there was Cecily ...

'Because,' he said, 'I am needed in England. Because I have work to do there, to make it like here so that men like me and you and Miller can worship in safety in England. Because God needs men who refuse to hide from the dangers of following the truth. I cannot walk away from Barrow, from the others. It is in the Scripture: *And ye shall be hated of all men for my Name: but he that endureth to the end, he shall be saved.*'

His friend smiled. *'And when they persecute you in this city, flee into another.'*

Ben returned the smile. 'Ah, Pieter, perhaps I should stay here, but my heart calls me always to England.'

Pieter stopped, and two paces on Ben stopped too and turned back to hear him. 'You have the spirit of a martyr, Ben. Time was when you would have burned.'

Ben bit his lip, considering Pieter's words. He had no wish to be a martyr: the thought of such a fate filled him with fear. 'I am what I am,' he said at last. 'And I cannot change.'

'You are a good man,' Pieter said. 'Greta could do worse than marry you.'

He shook his head. 'There is a part of me that wishes I could, that I were a different man who could settle here and be happy as a husband to Greta and live a quiet life. But God has other plans for me and I am blessed to His bidding.'

They slowed their walk. Above them, over to the west beyond the high roofs of the houses, the clouds parted slightly and a sliver of palest blue sky peeped through.

'God has found a true servant in you, Ben,' Pieter said. 'But He would wish for your happiness also.'

'I will find my happiness doing God's work. You cannot know the corruption of the English Church: a false and anti-Christian ministry, profane and wicked congregations, the bishops using the Church for their own advancement. They care nothing for the souls of the people they are called to serve, blinding them with ritual and living handsomely on the proceeds. They are no better than the Papists. No better at all.

'We must found a true Church in England, a fellowship of the faithful separate from the unbelievers, a Church that gathers in the name of Christ, their only king, priest and prophet.' He stopped, breathing hard on the tide of his emotion. Swallowing, he stemmed the flow, then turned again towards his friend. When he spoke again his voice was once more soft and calm, his passions once more under his control.

'Forgive me, Pieter. I meant not to preach.'

The older man smiled and dropped a friendly hand onto Ben's shoulder. 'You must do as God wills you and we will find another husband for Greta. Do not fret over her.'

'I am sorry for what happened, for giving her false hope. I am unworthy of such kindness.'

'Your path lies another way, my friend. God has willed it so and He will forgive you. Now come, the afternoon draws on and I am growing hungry for my daughter's fish soup.'

Ben had smiled as the men walked on, grateful for his friend's understanding, his belief in God's forgiveness for his sins. But it was not so easy to forgive himself, and the knowledge of the weakness of his flesh had never left him.

Now, outside in the yard, a door slammed, caught in a gust of wind, and the noise drew his gaze to the window and the present world around him. He could hear the children's shouts in snatches on the wind as they played.

He should have stayed as Pieter had wanted, he thought for the thousandth time. He should have married Greta and turned away from Cecily, done God's work in Holland. But instead he had followed his lust and his desire, though he had called it love. The memory still shamed him, shadowing his every prayer. He sighed and shook his head to clear it of the memory. Then, turning from the window, he followed the children out of the door and along the passage to the bakehouse at the back of the building.

'Stopped for dinner already?' Mistress Clyfton looked up from the dough she was kneading.

'Not yet. They've got the wind up them so I sent them outside to play for a while. We were getting nowhere.'

'Children and cats,' she said. 'They both go scatty in the wind. We used to have a cat at Babworth ...' She trailed off and he saw the mental effort she made to ignore the pain of the memory, to finish the thought. '... and he used to go quite mad when it was like this. Up and down the apple trees, round and round the garden. Like the Devil himself was riding him.' She smiled, remembering. Then, 'I wonder what happened to him. He was nowhere to be found when we had to leave.'

When Bancroft forced her husband from his living and they found themselves homeless, she meant, for preaching God's true word. Absently he rubbed at the scar on his wrist, aware of Bancroft's malice edging closer. Mistress Clyfton caught the movement and slid her eyes away.

'Horses play up in the wind as well,' he said, shifting the topic away from her memories. 'Bessie's spirited at best of times but with the wind behind her even I can hardly hold her.'

She dabbed at her forehead with the back of a doughy hand and made no sign she had heard him.

'Do you need anything doing?' he asked.

She shook her head. 'No. You just sit. I'll leave this to prove and then I'll fetch some dinner for us all.'

He sat and watched her working as she covered the bowl with a towel and placed it just so in a spot close to the hearth. She had made herself a role in the household, an able brewer and baker, so that Mistress Brewster had more time to spend in her beloved garden tending her vegetables and preserving its fruits. But there was a fretfulness about her, an agitation that always put him on edge. He could think of nothing more to say and so they kept company in silence until the awkwardness was broken by the two

Williams trudging in from outside. Their faces were whipped red by the wind and they stood at the fire, warming their hands.

'Any news in town?' Ben asked.

'Aye,' Brewster answered. 'And not good for us either.'

'What news?' He sat up and turned on the bench to face them, giving them his full attention.

'The new Archbishop of York ...' He trailed off, shaking his head. The younger William finished for him.

'He has Bancroft's zeal.'

'Have they taken anyone yet?'

'Some have been fined at Lincoln for non-attendance at church. But it's only the beginning.'

Ben was silent. He had hoped they were safer in the Midlands, so far from Bancroft's reach, but with the new appointment it seemed the Archbishop had cast his shadow wider: there was nowhere that was safe for them now.

The younger William said, 'He is already preaching against us to stir up hatred and mistrust. It is that more than anything that will betray us, if the people turn against us.'

Ben looked up at Brewster. 'What can we do?'

'There is nothing we can do but put our trust in God.'

The memory of a cold cell and manacles prickled across his skin.

Mistress Clyfton said nothing, standing motionless at the table, staring down where she had kneaded the bread. Her hands gripped the edge of the board, bone showing white at the knuckles. Brewster caught Ben's glance towards her.

'God will protect us,' he said. 'We are safe enough here for the while.'

Ben nodded his agreement but Mistress Clyfton did not lift her eyes from the floured board. As William had said, it was only the beginning.

CHAPTER 18

SUMMER 1606

Not forsaking the assembling of our selues together, as the manner of some is: but exhorting one another, and so much the more, as ye see the day approching.
(Hebrews 10:25)

THE DAYS LENGTHENED and spring's fresh coolness gave way to the warmer breezes of summer. Around Scrooby the hay had been harvested, and the cattle grew fat on lush grass. But every week brought fresh news to the manor house of others of their number taken before the Archbishop to be questioned and fined. More Puritan ministers lost their livings and were forced on the charity of like-minded others who risked much in helping them.

Bancroft was a fool, Ben thought. What were such men to do when they were deprived of their ministry within the Church but take up a new one outside it? With each new case he felt the net shrinking round them and the time growing short. The fear of prison began to taint every waking thought, and in the solitude of the predawn grey he spent hours alone in prayer, begging forgiveness for his weakness, for his sins, and courage for the trials and suffering yet to come.

Beyond the window the sky began to lighten, bands of paler grey chasing off the darkness. Ben reached out for the Bible he kept by his bed, the same Bible that Richard had given him their first year at Cambridge, when God had begun to call to him and he was thirsty for His Word, a gift given in love. The leather of the cover was worn and smooth in his hand, comforting, and he wondered if Richard remembered it too, the love that had bound them once, the bond his friend now thought to dishonour.

Ben flicked through the pages, and Cecily's letter fell from its place between them to the floor, her last words to him before she died. He kept it there always, a constant reminder of his sin and his weakness, but he hadn't reread it in many years, the memory too painful. Reaching down, he took the precious page between his fingers, turning it over and remembering when it came to him, hidden in the Bible Richard brought to him in prison, when he had been in darkness. He could still bring to mind the sense of hopelessness, nowhere to turn for help. Without his faith he had been adrift, and for the first time in his life he had truly felt afraid. Not for his body as he feared now, the stings and whips of prison and death, but for his soul – the terrifying emptiness that had taken the place of his faith.

For the first time in years he unfolded the page, fingers trembling, remembering the first time he had held it, his skin grimy black against its purity and the sense that his filth was a desecration. He had been expecting her judgement, he recalled, for what he had brought them to, and it had taken all his courage to read what she had written. Now he scanned his eyes once more across the lines, though he knew every word by heart, and his fingers brushed the words on the page, the strokes that she had made, the last physical connection. The letters were tall and strong, as she had been, no sign of the fear that had shadowed their life together.

> My love,
>
> I do not know what I should write to you. I have no words that can cross the distance that now lies between us. But one day soon Richard will be allowed to visit and I must write something for him to take so that you know I am still your Cecily and that I love you.
>
> I make no pretence to know the horrors you face in prison: I cannot bear even to think of it. But I know that you must stay true to yourself, Ben, and to your faith. I would not have you otherwise – it is the Spirit in you that I love.
>
> You are strong, my love, and I am weak, and it was only ever my fear that made me want to change you. You have faith that can move the mountain and nothing shall be impossible for you.
>
> Your heart is firm, my beloved husband, and you have no need to be afraid,
>
> Your loving wife,
>
> Cecily x

The tears fell as he read and he let them come, but his jaw was set tight against the pain. Then, folding it quickly, he slipped the letter back into its place beside the first psalm, where Cecily had hidden it first. She had chosen well as a hiding place: it was a page he turned to often and the words he had found there had helped him begin the slow journey back towards his faith.

An image of her smile cut across his thoughts, a rare and precious image he seldom recalled: mostly when he thought of her, her look was coloured by his pain and his sadness, but he remembered now that she had smiled often, the stern face softening, the love they shared a joy to both of them. Youthful love, youthful passion, the excitement of a life beginning together. Lying in the big feather bed at the end of the day, sharing thoughts and hopes and laughter. He had almost forgotten how she could make him laugh, teasing him out of his seriousness, mocking him gently, unsettling him with that look of challenge in her eyes he had loved so well. No other woman had ever stirred him as she had, her self-possession enchanting and infuriating, unknowable. And he had loved her for it, her company all he had ever desired.

These days, he realised, he laughed very rarely. It would have made her sad to know that, he thought, and allowed himself a rueful smile that was intended for her.

Then he put the Bible back on the table by the bed, Cecily's laughter still in his thoughts, and went out to start the new day.

AFTER SUPPER WILLIAM BREWSTER searched him out in the yard behind the house. He liked to sit out in the long warm twilight and watch the stars appear above the wide expanse of fields, marvelling at the beauty of God's creation and his humbleness before it. Ben loved this land, the low-lying fields and the fish-rich river, the soft light that filled a vast and open sky, and the flatness of the landscape, the horizon so far away it was almost lost to view. There was a wildness here too, the untameability of a land of frequent floods. It was God's good earth, and every day he prayed his thanks.

This evening a light sweep of cloud brushed in threads across the surface of the sky, but the stars still lit up bright and clear in the deepening darkness as the familiar constellations formed one by one. Above the stream that marked the border of the manor, a kestrel hovered, making the most of the last of the daylight. It was the sight of the sky he had missed the most in the Fleet, the disconnection from the turning day and the wheel of the seasons, each day the same confined in cold grey stone. The knowledge it might soon come again to that brought him outdoors as often as he could.

'It is indeed a marvellous sight.' Brewster lowered himself to sit on the wall beside him. 'I brought you some ale.'

Ben took the proffered cup with a smile, and drank. One of the farm dogs slunk across the yard to lie at his master's feet, and Brewster touched its head with his fingertips. Ben thought of the greyhound in her new home with Ellyn and wondered if she ever got to run any more.

'You must not lose your courage, Ben,' the older man said. 'Christ was hated also.'

'I know.' He took another mouthful of ale. 'But I have bitter memories.' Instinctively he felt for the scars on his wrist, symbols of his faith and his sin, the lasting marks that tied him to Cecily's death.

'You have suffered much.' Brewster's gaze was fixed on the heavens but his nearness lent Ben a strength: at least he was not alone. 'Grief, imprisonment, exile,' Brewster said. 'No man could do more.'

'My wife gave her life. My child too.'

'And they are with God, at peace. You must learn to forgive yourself and let Christ bear the burden of your sorrows.'

He nodded, and though he accepted the wisdom of the words with his head, his heart would always remain tight with the pain of it.

'God will find a way for us,' Brewster said. 'He has brought us this far and He will not abandon us now. We must keep our faith and not be afraid.'

'My faith is strong,' Ben answered, and the older man turned from his contemplation of the stars to look at him. 'But I can no longer see hope for us on these shores, only more suffering and death.'

His companion observed him carefully, weighing his thoughts before he spoke. Ben waited, used to Brewster's painstaking consideration of his words.

'I have been thinking so also,' he said at last. 'Perhaps the time has come when we must go into another place.'

'*When they persecute you in this city, flee into another,*' Ben said.

'Exactly so. Perhaps the time has come at last. I will think on it,' Brewster said, 'and pray for guidance. But now ...' He heaved himself to his feet. 'I will leave you to your thoughts out here beneath God's stars.'

'Thank you,' Ben replied. Then he watched the older man trudge back to the house with the weight of the community on his shoulders. It was a heavy burden for one man to carry.

WORSHIP LASTED LATE into the evening, all of them hungry for God's Word, all of them straining under the weight of their fear. The service had already begun when Ben arrived, and he slipped in silently to stand just inside the door, the preacher's voice clear and soft across the hush in the crowded room.

The passage was from Ecclesiastes:

Two are better ... for if they fall, the one will lift up his fellow: but woe unto him that is alone: for he falleth, and there is not a second to lift him up ... And if one overcome him, two shall stand against him: and a threefold cord is not easily broken.

It was a call for fellowship, a standing together against the forces that assailed them, a buttress against the weariness that fear engendered. Their numbers had fallen in the months since the new Archbishop's appointment, faith shrivelling in the face of harsher persecution. But those who remained were true, and the words of Scripture gave them hope. They listened as one, the Word of God being spoken through the gentle tones of the preacher, their faith being bound in brotherhood. By the end of the evening not one among them doubted the rightness of their path.

Ben was one of the last to go, reluctant to leave this place of peace and strength, wandering out into the last of the darkening twilight. The others had already dispersed, hurrying through the night to the safety of their homes. All of them would be watchful, all of them aware of their danger. He could see their torches bobbing along the road that led from the hall. Looking up, he surveyed the sky. A bright moon, three-quarters full, lit the night behind scudding clouds and he was glad of its light. It was a long ride home to Scrooby, and the way was dark.

Beyond the borders of the town he slowed the mare to a walk. The last remnants of the daylight had died away, the sky a velvet black above. But the intermittent moon gave him enough light to guide his way: it was a path he knew well and his thoughts remained on the evening's worship, the words of the psalm running in rhythm in his mind.

When I was afraid, I trusted in Thee. I will rejoice in God, because of His word, I trust in God, and will not fear what flesh can do unto me ...

Thou hast counted my wanderings: put my tears into Thy bottle: are they not in Thy register? When I cry, then mine enemies shall turn back: this I know, for God is with me. I will rejoice in God because of His word: in the Lord will I rejoice because of His word.

In God do I trust.

He thought of Henry Barrow all those years ago at the Fleet when this life had just begun for him, remembering the fire of God's love in Barrow, the Spirit strong within the frail and damaged body. The same teachings he had heard tonight, the same call to be true to God's Word. It was the path Christ had commanded, a path the English Church had turned from long ago with its ritual and riches, its hierarchy under the king. So he would walk with Christ on that path with joy and with love for there could be no other way to walk. He smiled to himself, content with his choice, his fear at bay in the knowledge of his rightness and his oneness with God. Henry Barrow had died for that choice and if need be he would do the same. He would suffer all the griefs that God asked of him and his heart would be glad.

He paid scant attention to the road. It was dry and firm beneath the horse's hooves and a pleasant night for riding. An owl hooted beyond the hedgerow and the mare skittered lightly sideways until he reassured her and she trotted on. Up ahead, the forms of two riders emerged from the darkness, one of them carrying a lantern that swung gently with the gait of the horse. Travellers, he assumed, on the way to spend a night in Gainsborough. But he was wary, senses prickling: the road at night was an unsafe place and it was rare to meet others on this stretch of track. Hedgerows bordered each side and the path was narrow. Ben tensed and kept the mare gathered ready beneath him.

The riders drew closer, faces hidden behind the brightness of the lantern. They were riding abreast, taking up the width of the lane, and he wondered if they had not yet seen him through the dark. He didn't have to wait long to find out. They halted right in front of him, reining in their horses and blocking the way, so he had no choice but to stop. One of them held up the lantern and in the swaying light that it cast, Ben saw the crossed-keys symbol stitched onto their livery. His heartbeat quickened, sweat oozed down his spine, and the mare sidled underneath him, sensing her master's unease. They were the Archbishop's men, and the meeting was no accident.

'Benjamin Kemp?'

It crossed his mind to say no. 'Who wants to know?'

'Just answer the question.'

One of the men nudged his horse alongside Bessie, placed a hand on the rein near the bridle. The mare tossed her head and tried to dance sideways, but the man's grip was firm and there was little room for manoeuvre.

'You can tell us now. Or you can tell us at Lincoln gaol. It's all one to us.'

The other man came closer, his horse's flank touching Bessie's shoulder. He reached the lantern forward and peered into his captive's face, his own features shifting in the changing light so that it was hard to see what kind of man he was.

'So, I'll ask you again,' he said. 'Are you Kemp or not?'

'I am Ben Kemp,' he answered.

'Then you are under arrest.'

'For what crime?' he demanded. The mare stood trembling, unnerved by the buffeting of the other two horses. He murmured to her and rubbed a hand along her neck. She settled slightly but he could feel her nervousness, her whole frame vibrating with energy. One touch of his heels and she would break free from these men. She could easily outrun them: the men's horses were poor and ill-kept nags, no match for a fine horse like Bessie, a fit mount for a rich merchant's son. It was tempting, fear in his blood and the instinct to run.

'You know what crime,' the man with the lantern sneered. 'You and your troublemaking sort. We know all about you.'

'I demand to know my crime.' It took all his strength to hold the horse to her place.

'Where you been tonight, eh? Praying? Giving yourself the Host, not going to church like you should? Do you think it doesn't get noticed when you don't go?' The younger man's horse swung round to bump against the mare. 'I suppose you think God's going to protect you. Well, I don't think so. God doesn't like men like you. Men who think you're too good for the English Church.'

The other man laughed. 'And more importantly,' he sneered, 'the king doesn't like men like you either. He doesn't like men who want to split his Church. So it doesn't really matter one way or the other what God thinks about it, because the king is in charge in England. And what the king says goes. You're coming with us.'

He lunged forward to grasp the other side of the bridle. Bessie snorted and jerked back from his reach, rearing her front legs from the ground. The younger man's hand was thrown back and in that instant Ben decided. He touched his heels to the horse's sides, loosened the reins and let her go. She was gone in one bound, flying along the lane, her mane in his face as he leaned forward over her neck.

He heard the Archbishop's men shouting after him, but by the time they had stirred their own horses into motion he had rounded the bend in the lane and was out of their sight. He heard nothing else, not even sure if they had tried to follow, but he let the mare run on anyway, eager to open the distance between them.

When, finally, they slowed to a walk, both of them breathing hard, out of instinct he turned in the saddle to look back. But the men were many miles behind him, and he was on the long road to London.

What other choice did he have but to take it?

A LATE-SUMMER HAZE lay over the river when Ben rode through the lanes of Westminster, and the heat hung wearily over the streets. He travelled slowly, both horse and rider spent from the hard days of travel. A carter looked up from his work as they approached and stopped his loading to let them pass, taking the pause to wipe the sweat from his face, his shirt clinging to him wetly. It was no day for hard labour. The air was rank and humid, and underneath the foetid stench there was the heavy sweetness of summer fruit, ripening now in the orchards. The mare's hooves thudded on the hard-baked mud of the road as he turned into the lane that led to his sister's house.

A servant took his horse and another led him inside, barely hiding his distaste for the road-soiled stranger as he showed him the way up a narrow staircase. It was cool in the gloom after the heat of the day outside, and a scent of oriental spice lingered in the warmth; the fragrance took him back to Aleppo and another dark staircase, to the room of a woman whose name he could no longer recall. But he remembered the scent of her and the touch of her hands, the sinful darkness of her arms that had helped teach him to live once again in the world of the living.

The servant rapped on a door and showed him into the narrow sitting room at the front of the house above the shop. His sister sat in the alcove of the window, looking out onto the street below. She turned without interest at the sound of the door, but leaped to her feet when she saw who it was and threw herself into his arms. Out of old habit he swung her round as he once used to do when she was a child.

'I didn't see you arrive!' She laughed. 'And I was watching the road. You have to watch the carters when they unload, or they steal things.' She nodded towards the window. 'But he doesn't know I'm watching and so far he's been honest.'

She stepped back from him, his hands still in hers, to look at him better. 'What are you doing here?' she said. 'It's been ages. You haven't even seen the baby.'

'How is she?' It was hard to imagine his little sister as a mother now, older than Cecily had been when she died.

'She is *gorgeous!*' Ellyn said. 'Another little Sarah and not just in name. She has the sweetest, most placid temper.'

'She must take after her father.'

His sister laughed. 'When she wakes I'll bring her to you. I've told her all about her uncle Ben.' She stopped, a moment of worry that he would prefer not to see the child, her baby too painful a reminder of his own. 'If you like, that is. If you would like to see her.'

'I would like to see her very much.' He smiled, Ellyn's happiness in her child hard to resist.

'We thought about naming her Cecily,' she said.

'You can call the next one Cecily.'

'The next one is going to be a boy.'

'Then you may name him Ben.'

'Perhaps we shall.' She led him towards the window and they sat on the cushions on the window seat, looking down on the busy street below. The carter had finished unloading and gone on his way. Ellyn's fingers still held his, small and light and delicate. 'And when you finally take another wife, Ben,' she said, 'you may call your daughter Ellyn.'

He turned his eyes from the window and gave a wry shake of his head. 'I shan't be taking another wife.'

'You should,' she replied. 'A man should have a wife, a family. It's the way God meant things to be.'

He observed her for a moment, remembering her reluctance. There was a new roundness to her cheeks, a contentment he had never seen in her before, the sharp edges softened by it. 'You've changed.'

She shrugged. 'I've grown up, is all. But you ...' She squeezed his fingers. 'You haven't changed a bit. I doubt you ever will.'

'Is that good or bad?'

She took her hand from his to smooth back a stray hair from her cheek, and regarded him thoughtfully, a glint of the old cynicism in her eyes.

'It depends,' she said, after a moment.

He turned his gaze back to the road and said nothing.

'Why are you here?' Ellyn asked then, the levity falling from her tone. She reached out to take his hand again. 'Why have you come here like this, unannounced?'

He sighed and turned towards her but he kept his eyes lowered to where she held his fingers. His whole body ached from the ride and now that he was about to explain it, his flight seemed the action of a fool.

'Can you keep a secret?' he said.

'Of course.'

He met her look, observed her, considering. Perhaps it would be safer for her not to know. Perhaps he should have taken his troubles elsewhere: he wanted no one else to suffer on his account.

'Do we need to cut our thumbs and swear in blood?' She was growing impatient. 'I'm willing if you are.'

He smiled at the memory of their childhood pacts, and the fact she had changed less than he thought. 'No,' he said. 'We don't need to swear in blood. Your word is good enough.'

'Well?'

He swallowed and shifted on the seat to sit up straighter, facing her. He said, 'Three days ago two men of the Archbishop of York tried to arrest me.'

She lifted her hands to her face. 'Dear God, Ben, will it never end? What happened? What do you mean, tried?'

'They were incompetent. I took the chance and ran.' He shook his head. 'I know it was foolish but it was the instinct of the moment. I know what prison is ...'

'Oh, Ben!' She touched her fingers to his forearm and they were cool against the heat of his skin. He looked up at her, saw the and fear in her eyes. He should not have come here, he thought, bringing danger to her door.

'I should go,' he said.

'Where will you go?'

He shrugged. There was nowhere that was safe for him. No one else in London he could trust, the community long since scattered and broken.

'Then you must stay,' she said. 'At least for the night. You are exhausted. Please.'

He tilted his head in acquiescence, too weary to argue, and they sat for a moment, her fingers still resting lightly on his arm.

'Did they tell you the charges?' she asked.

'I was on my way home from worship. The new Archbishop, he's clamping down on ...' He stopped and made a vague circle in the air with one hand in place of the word he was reluctant to use in his sister's house.

'On people like you?' she supplied, with a half-smile.

'Yes.' He nodded. 'People like me. Separatists, nonconformists, Barrowists ... whichever term they prefer to use of us.'

'You have a congregation.'

'There are two. Until recently it was safer there than here. Now nowhere is safe.'

She said, 'Why don't you go back to Aleppo? Or even to Amsterdam. Father would send you. He would love for you to work with him again in the Company. It gives him such pain that you don't.'

'He has said so?'

'It's in his face every time your name is mentioned.'

He was silent, wondering if he should tell her he had been disinherited, his legacy willed to her husband now, that their father loved him less than she supposed. But then he thought, What good would it do?

'Why don't you leave? Why don't you leave these shores and be safe? You don't have to work for Father. There are other ways you could go.'

'Because ...' He shrugged. Why did he not go? Why did he stay and choose to put himself in danger? So he could put himself in harm's way and die as Cecily had died? Perhaps. He said, 'Because I've stayed away long enough avoiding things. I cannot run away all my life.'

'But England does not want you and you will never be free here. You are a thorn in the side of the Church and you're going to end up back in prison eventually. Or worse.'

'England is my home.'

'Then come back to the Church.'

'No.' He rubbed at his scars, dropped his voice. 'No.'

'Why do you do this to yourself?' Her voice was growing shrill with desperation. 'Why can you not just accept things as they are?'

'Because I know better,' he answered, shaking his head. 'Because the Bible tells us otherwise. I will not put my soul in danger so my body may be safe. Christ died for us, so why should I be afraid?'

'Is that what you want for yourself?' She stepped away, then wheeled to face him, eyes savage. 'To die like He did? To be a martyr? Is that the end you're seeking?'

'No one wants to be a martyr.'

'You have a choice, Ben.'

'No,' he said softly. 'I don't. I don't have a choice. Do you think I haven't questioned myself? That I never feel fear or doubt?'

'You? Doubt?' She snorted.

He swallowed, half tempted to explain himself: his loss of faith in prison, the fear he still wrestled every day. His guilt for Cecily, his sin, his unworthiness in front of God. But where would he begin? And how could she understand?

He said, 'You know me less well than you think.'

'Then tell me,' she replied, and he saw from her face that his words had hurt her.

'It's beyond the power of words to explain, and it is my burden to bear. I would not trouble you with my sorrows.'

'But you are troubling me. You are here in my house on the run from the law. How much more trouble could you bring me?'

He smiled. He had no other answer to give her. Then, 'I am weary, Nell. Give me food and ale, some clean linen, and I'll be gone. No one need know I was here.'

'Except the servants, of course. Probably half of Westminster knows already. So you may as well stay. The damage is done.' She sat once again beside him on the window seat, took his fingers in her own. 'What happens now? Will they come for you here? Will they be looking?'

He turned his eyes away from her towards the window, but saw little of what was there, his mind turning on what he had done, the danger he was in. 'I don't know,' he said. 'Perhaps. I should not have come here. I've put you in danger too.'

'You are welcome here always, Ben. You are my brother, whatever you have done.' Then she said, 'Will you visit our parents?'

He drew in a breath, still undecided. 'I would prefer Richard not to know what has happened,' he said, though he had no doubt Richard would hear of it soon enough, from Bancroft or from Andrewes, or from one of the others who spent time at Court. 'It would be better if he doesn't know I'm here.'

'You don't trust him?' Surprise flickered across her features. 'But he's your oldest friend.'

'He was my friend, Nell, many years ago. Things have changed since then. We have changed since then.'

She said, 'You were like brothers once.'

'It was a long time ago.' But still, he had believed he could always count Richard a friend, their love undimmed despite the hardships and their differences. To distrust him now felt unworthy somehow, and it saddened him, but his instinct left him no choice.

She nodded, thoughtful, unconvinced, but she said no more about it. Instead she said, 'You look exhausted. And filthy. You have no linen?'

He looked down at his road-blackened clothes and could smell the sourness of his sweat. 'I left in a hurry,' he replied. 'Remember?'

'I'll find you clean things. Hugh's shirts will fit you and you can wash in my chamber. Come, I'll show you the way.'

She stood before him, fingers still in his. Then she turned and led him from the room, along the spice-filled corridor and up another flight of stairs. There she left him to cleanse himself with a jug of water that was cool and pure.

CHAPTER 19

To him that is afflicted, pitie should be shewed from his friend;
But he forsaketh the feare of the Almighty.
(Job 6:14)

AFTER SUPPER RICHARD sat in the garden in the shade of an apple tree, the branches sagging with fruit above his head, and he was thinking more or less of nothing, allowing his mind to wander in the warm summer evening. Between the trees, the sky above him was striated with high wisps of cloud that were slowly turning pink, edges gold-rimmed as the sun began to leave the sky. It was a pretty sight and he was still and peaceful with contentment.

Alice's approach did nothing to mar the tranquillity. He liked her company: the unassuming manner belied a sharp mind and curiosity. She asked him often about his work, which he explained as best he could. She seemed to understand his stumbling explanations, and asked more questions, which showed at least he did not bore her.

'It's a beautiful evening.' She smiled, seating herself on the other end of the bench, a small distance between them.

'Indeed it is,' he agreed. 'God's Heaven in all its wonder.'

'I'm not interrupting you?'

'Not at all. I was merely enjoying the view. I've finished translating for the day, even in here.' He tapped at his temple.

She laughed. 'But I thought you never finished.'

He smiled, pleased by her laughter but made unsure by her teasing. He had always lacked Ben's ease with women, in spite of all the sisters on the farm. He was silent, uncertain what to say.

Alice smoothed her skirts across her thighs then lifted her eyes to the sunset. After a moment she turned her face towards him, took a breath as though to speak, then changed her mind and looked away, once more smoothing her skirts with nervous hands.

'Alice?'

She raised her head and gave him a quick smile but did not meet the question in his eyes.

'What's wrong, Alice? What is it you would say?' He was curious now, wondering what could make her nervous of him when they were usually so easy with each other.

'I heard something today,' she said, without looking up from her hands. 'In the kitchen.'

'I gather the kitchen is a great source of news ...'

She flicked him a small smile but did not go on.

'What is it you heard?' he prompted, gently.

'Ben is at his sister's house,' she replied, lifting her face and turning towards him. Above them the last of the sunlight flared behind the clouds, trimming them with a pink-gold brilliance before withdrawing and leaving the sky to the oncoming dark. 'And his parents do not know. Do you not think it strange?'

Richard said nothing, wondering. Ben would not have travelled so far with no good reason – it did indeed seem strange his parents did not know. But perhaps he wanted time alone with his sister first. Perhaps he would come to Thieving Lane in time.

'Doctor Clarke?' Alice was peering at him with curious eyes. 'Do you not think it is strange?'

'A little,' he conceded. 'But I'm sure he has his reasons.' Reasons he also had no doubt that Bancroft would be keen to know.

'Will you go and see him?' Alice asked.

He sighed. He would rather not face Ben's contempt and mistrust. He would rather have no knowledge he might report back to his masters.

'We are no longer friends,' he said. 'I doubt he would be pleased to see me.'

'You were like brothers once though.'

'It was many years ago and our ways parted a long time since.'

'Still ...'

He observed her for a moment, wondering. He said, 'Did the servants have any suggestions as to the cause of his arrival?'

She shook her head, but did not meet his eyes.

'Alice?'

She sighed, lifted her face briefly towards him, then shook her head again. Whatever the servants were saying, he realised, she was reluctant to pass on to him. Was she trying to protect Ben in some way? Or was it him, Richard, she was hoping to shield?

'Do you not trust me?' he coaxed.

'Of course I trust you,' she answered quickly, looking him in the face, hurt by the suggestion. 'But it is only gossip after all, and not worth repeating.'

'They think he is in trouble?'

'Yes,' she conceded, sliding her gaze away. 'That's what they think. They say he has run from the law. And I thought perhaps if you went to him you might be able to help ...'

He said nothing for a moment, touched by her faith in him, so far from deserved. Lifting his eyes to the sky above the trees, he saw the dying moments of the day, dark clouds edged and flaring with brilliance.

'I think he is beyond any help I can give him,' he said gently. If Ben was truly an outlaw now, there was little to be done to save him.

'But surely you can try?' she persisted.

He was silent, considering. He had made a promise to himself, he recalled, a promise to God that day at the scaffold when he had watched the Papist martyrs die. He had vowed to make Ben see sense and to save him from himself. So now he could not simply turn away. He must go to Ellyn's, he realised, as Alice wanted, and do all he could to send Ben to safety across the sea, to Holland, to Aleppo. Somewhere, anywhere, out of Bancroft's reach. Somewhere far, far away where betrayal by a friend could not hurt him.

EVEN SO LATE IN the day the sweat broke out along his spine as he walked, the humidity still unbroken. Richard cast his eyes skyward in vague hope of seeing the beginnings of a storm, but the clouds were high and thin and there was no promise of an end to the heat. He wiped a hand across the back of his neck and kept walking, looking about him and unsure of the road. The house was close to the river; the shouts of the boatmen lifted and fell above the slapping of the tide against mud and shingle.

He found the street: a row of merchants' houses, all much the same, narrow brick and timber with an upper storey that reached out above his head. At the level of the street many served as shops, but they were closed now for the evening and there were few people about. He stopped at Merton's house, remembering Alice's description, a bright blue door, and the sign above it that announced the spice shop within. A lantern had been hung from the hook, its light just beginning to make itself felt against the encroaching night, and a fragrant scent of spice surprised him. He lifted a hand to knock then lowered it again, hesitating. He knew he had scant chance of success in his task – Ben was the most stubborn man he had ever met – and his instinct was to walk away. But his fate was tied to his friend's: God had given him this friendship for some purpose he could not know, so he resisted the urge to turn and leave and raised his fist again to bring his knuckles against the wood, rapping loudly. He took a deep breath as he waited, heartbeat quickening, sweat along his spine. Deep inside the house a dog barked and a woman's voice was raised. Footsteps clattered along a passage and the door was hauled open. A servant greeted him politely.

'Is your mistress at home?' Richard asked.

'It is late,' the servant returned. 'Who shall I say is asking?'

'Richard Clarke.'

'Wait here.'

The servant closed the door and Richard heard the footsteps briefly retreating into the house. Then the door opened again and Ellyn was there, backing away to admit him into the narrow hall.

'Richard.' There was surprise in her voice. 'What brings you here at this hour?'

'I heard Ben was here,' he replied.

'Ben? Why would Ben be here?'

He glanced behind her, lifting his eyes to the top of the stairs. She stood like a sentinel before them, innocence in her smile, but he was not persuaded.

'I know that he's here, Ellyn,' he said.

'Why would I lie?'

'I'm sure you have your reasons.'

A footstep at the top of the stairs drew their attention. Ben's voice sounded out of the gloom as his form descended into view. 'Let him in, Nell.'

Ellyn turned abruptly and trotted up the stairs with Richard following on behind her. He found himself in a sitting room that was hot and airless, and instinctively his fingers reached to loosen his collar. Ben sat near the empty hearth and the greyhound rested her chin on his knee. With one hand, her master absently fondled her ears. Across from him sat Merton, nursing a cup of wine. He gave the visitor a cursory nod of greeting but said nothing. No one offered him a drink or asked him to sit and the hostility in the room was stifling. Richard drew a chair near to the hearth and sat down. There was a silence until he spoke into the tension. 'What brings you to London, Ben?'

'I wanted to visit my sister. I had not seen the child.' Ben leaned over and picked up his cup from the hearthstone, nodding to Ellyn, who came with the jug to refill it. 'She is a delightful baby. Have you seen her?'

'No,' Richard replied. 'I haven't. Perhaps another time.' He gave a quick smile in Ellyn's direction. She was standing now behind her brother's chair, hands gripping the back of it, in profile to where Richard was sitting. She turned her face away from him.

'It was a sudden decision?'

'It was.'

'But you didn't think to tell your parents?'

'I have argued with my father.' Finally Ben turned his head towards his visitor and fixed him with his eyes. There was no trace of friendship in their light.

'I am sorry to hear that. He has mentioned nothing of it to me.' Then, because it seemed too late for the normal courtesies, he said, 'What have you argued about?'

Ben tilted his head. 'He still wants me to go to the East. I would rather avoid another argument about it. That, and ... other matters, which would be of no interest to you.'

Richard looked again towards Ellyn, still standing at her brother's back, hoping to find some softening, but her gaze remained trained towards the hearth. The ill feeling in the room was palpable, and though he understood their reasons, their distrust hurt. He had not yet earned such hatred; he still hoped to save Ben and not betray him.

'Ben?' he ventured. 'What has happened, Ben?'

'Nothing. Nothing has happened.'

Ben drained his cup, pushed the dog's head from his leg and stood up, crossing the room to the sideboard that stood behind Richard. He poured himself more wine then remained at the cupboard, leaning his hips against it, putting distance between them and forcing Richard to turn awkwardly in his chair to look at him.

'Why have you come here?' Ben asked.

'Are you in some kind of trouble?'

Ben smiled at that. 'You haven't heard? News must travel less quickly to your masters than I thought.'

'What news?'

'No doubt you will hear soon enough.'

He did not know what to say in the face of Ben's contempt for him. How could he persuade him to leave England now? How could he even broach it?

'You want me to trust you? To confess?' Ben said.

'Do you have something you ought to confess?' Richard got up from his chair and turned it round towards the other man. Then he sat, balanced on the arm of it, facing Ben, waiting.

'I hope you pray hard at night,' Ben said.

'I pray for you always, Ben,' Richard answered. 'And I pray

that you will leave these shores and be safe. I have only ever wished that for you. That you might be safe.'

'And far away from you.'

Richard said nothing, reluctant to admit the truth of it.

'I am right, am I not?' Ben said. 'If I stay you will have to make a choice. Whether to remain a friend to me or be loyal to your Church. Because the time has long passed when you can fool yourself I might one day recant.'

'Why do you refuse to go? There can be only danger for you here.'

'I don't have to explain myself to you.'

'You will end up on the scaffold like the Papist traitors. Or like Henry Barrow. Is that what you want?'

'You will never understand.'

'Then explain it to me.'

Ben regarded him with interest, head tilted, eyes appraising, judging. Richard met the scrutiny without flinching: he would not allow Ben to rattle him. He wished they had offered him wine. After a moment Ben said, 'I owe you nothing.'

'Ben?' Ellyn's voice drew both men's attention from each other. 'Please.' There was a silence as she went to her brother and placed her hand on his arm, looking up into his face. Richard could not read the look that passed between them, but he saw Ben twitch the corners of his mouth into an attempt at reassurance before he lifted his head once again.

'You should go,' Ben said softly, gesturing to his sister and her husband with slight movements of his head. 'I would like to spend some time with my sister and her family. So go and do whatever it is that you have to do.'

Richard held his gaze. 'Tell me what's happened at least.'

'Why? What difference would it make? You have chosen your side ...' He shrugged.

'You think it's that simple?' Richard's voice grew harsh. He was almost quivering with emotion. How could he make Ben see how hard this was for him? 'You think it is that black and white?'

'Yes. It has to be. The Church accepts no dissent, no separation. You are loyal to the Church. What other choice do you have? In the end you will come to it.'

'I have always been loyal to the Church,' he said.

'That is true,' Ben agreed. 'But you used to have hopes you could bring me back to it.' Ellyn's hand was still on his arm and he covered her fingers with his, patting them gently, but his attention never wavered from Richard.

'You didn't visit me all those times in prison because you enjoyed my company. You came because you thought you could save me and take me back inside your fold. But now things are different. You know that's never going to happen. You know there's no hope I will ever go back. I will never return to your Church. Never.'

The cruelty of the accusation almost took his breath away. 'I visited you because you were a brother to me.'

'And in brotherhood you thought to win me back.'

'Yes, but it was not only for that I came. I thought ... I hoped ... my visits brought you ... comfort, pleasure even. Did they mean nothing to you?'

Ben hesitated. Then he said, 'Yes, they did. And I was grateful. But now I think my comfort is no longer of much concern to you. You have bigger fish to fry.'

'I wish you only well, Ben. I would have you go somewhere safe away from all of this, where you can worship as you will, unhindered, free.'

'And if I don't you will betray me. In the end you will betray me.' It was not a question.

'You cannot stay here. You will never be safe.'

'Because of men like you?'

'Because of the law. Because the king demands conformity. You would disobey your king?'

'Yes. If he puts himself above the Law of God.' He pushed himself away from the sideboard, the muscle twitching in his jaw, his chin in that combative tilt Richard had seen so many times before.

Richard said, *'Let every soul be subject unto the higher powers: for there is no power but of God ...'*

Ben's response was quick. *'We ought rather to obey God than men.'*

'Stop it!' Ellyn pleaded. 'No good can come of this. You can argue Scripture all night and what good will it do?'

Ben turned his face away. 'Forgive me, Nell,' he murmured. 'I should not have come here. And you ...' He flung the words at Richard. 'You have no right to come here like this, to my sister's house, to her husband's house. How dare you come here with your false friendship, your offers of help. No one is fooled by you, Richard. We all know why you came. So go. And let's have no more of this pretence at friendship.'

Richard lowered his eyes so as not to see the hatred in the other man's face, and to hide the tears that prickled behind them. It was a hard test that God had set him, this choice between love for a brother and love for the Church.

'Please go,' Ellyn said, stepping forward towards him. She stood before him, waiting for him to lift his face. Their eyes met for a moment, long enough to see each other's pain. 'Please go now, Richard. There is no more to say.'

He nodded and got to his feet. Then he bowed a brief farewell and crossed to the door. There, for an instant, he paused, wishing there was something else he could say, something that would make Ben understand, but there was nothing, and so he stepped out into the cool gloom of the passage and hurried down the stairs and away.

∽

He had failed. He had known it was a slender hope when he set out – Ben's mind was not easily turned from its course. But now the future was set out before him and the day would come when he must make his choice. And all the while a memory of his dream flickered at the corners of his mind, Ben in chains and Richard on his knees, pleading for forgiveness. The image had lingered in the months since his illness, catching him at unexpected moments, vivid and unwelcome. He shuddered at the choice that lay ahead and wondered if his faith was strong enough to bring his friend to that. He walked slowly through the sultry roads, sweat in his back and under his hair. A cat, sleeping on a doorstep, lifted its head at his passing, eyes glinting in the lantern light. It watched him for a moment, then turned its gaze away, without interest. London's stench hung poisonously in the humid air and by the time Richard got home he felt sick with it.

At the window of the Kemps' house Alice's face was dimly lit by the glow of the candles in the room behind her. She jumped up as soon as she saw him approach and disappeared from view. A moment later the door opened wide to let him in.

'You shouldn't have waited up,' he said. 'It's late.' He had wanted to be alone with his thoughts, in peace to pray for guidance.

'I wasn't tired,' she replied.

He followed her into the hall and after she had straightened the curtains to hide the room from the view of the outside world, she poured him wine and they sat before the unlit fire, the hearth the centre of the room that drew them to it regardless of the season.

The great stone fireplace stared back at them, cold and grey and empty. He stretched out in the chair, rolling the tension from his neck, the cup held loosely in in his fingers.

'What happened?' she said. 'Did you speak with him?'

'Yes.' He nodded, straightening himself in the chair, resigned to the conversation. 'I spoke to him. He told me he was here to see his new niece and that he had argued with his father.'

Disappointed, she lowered her eyes, searching across the pattern of the rug that lay on the boards between them. He watched her, remembering the way her eyes had used to follow Ben, her feelings for him plain across her features. He wondered if she still felt the same, or if time and lack of hope had killed such pointless longings.

Becoming aware of his scrutiny, she lifted her face towards him, the groove between her eyebrows darkening as she struggled to see him through the gloom. 'Do you think it's the truth?'

He took a mouthful of wine before he answered. 'I think ...' he began, then stopped for a moment, undecided how much to tell her. 'I think he might be in some kind of trouble but I do not know for sure.'

There was a silence as she considered his words. Men's voices raised in laughter drifted in from the road outside. He drank more of his wine and felt a tiredness seeping through him, emotion draining.

'So you cannot help him?' she asked.

No, he thought, I cannot help him. But he said nothing. If Ben had chosen to stay, then he, Richard, must also make a choice. His friendship or his Church. Love or faith. What then should he do?

HE SPENT the night on his knees. He prayed for many things, but most of all he prayed for an end to the conflict inside him. His faith wavering, he was tossed by the wind, and he begged for certainty to anchor him. Andrewes, Ben – opposed but never doubting, prepared to suffer for their faith, never fearful of the rightness of their path. Why did God withhold the same conviction from him? Why must he always walk in fear he was mistaken?

But no answer came, and when the Abbey bell tolled six and he got off his knees, he was still filled with uncertainty, his faith in his Church still torn by his love for his friend. Stiffly, with painful knees, he got to his feet and crossed to the window, looking out through the dark blank panes to the street below. He was getting too old for so many hours at prayer. Perhaps there was something to be said for Ben's Church, refusing to kneel. He gave himself a wry smile. Beyond the window, lanterns burned at the doors of the houses but the street was already astir, the sun almost up.

If only Ben had stayed in Aleppo. If only he would leave again. He must know where staying in England would lead him, so why had he chosen to remain? That he might pay for his faith? As Barrow had. And Cecily. A memory of Ben's grief cut across his thoughts, his friend's body gaunt and childlike on the prison cell floor, huddled in pain.

Cecily. He guessed the answer lay with Cecily: Ben's refusal to seek safety was an expiation for her death, his guilt and grief a cross he would always carry. He had wanted to die all those years ago in the Fleet, all faith lost in the blackness of his desolation. He had found his faith again, in time, but perhaps the desire for death remained, the only way he could atone.

Weary now, and still grieving for his friend, he lay down on the narrow bed and gave himself willingly to the oblivion of sleep.

CHAPTER 20

SUMMER 1606

I*f the world hate you, yee know that it hated me before it hated you.*
(*John 15:18*)

BEN LEFT London before the dawn. He took his time on the northward road: he was in no hurry to face what awaited him at his journey's end. But it was better to hand himself in than give either Richard or Bancroft the satisfaction of betrayal. He no longer doubted that Richard would betray him – the conviction of the translator's faith demanded nothing else. But he had seen the struggle, the conflict within, and he regretted it.

He broke his fast at a roadside inn, unhurried, both horse and rider still spent from the southward flight. He sat at a bench in the yard in the still cool morning, the heat of the day yet to come, and picked at the bread and mutton before him. Weariness had taken his appetite and he thought of the soft bed he had left at his sister's with a vague sense of longing. Ellyn would be about her household tasks by now, a busy housewife, but her dark eyes would be dimmed today from the sleepless night and the tears she had wept for him.

They had fought in the early hours, Ellyn sensing a turning point, using his fears to try and tip the balance. He had been almost tempted to relent.

'What good is served by your imprisonment?' she had questioned. 'How can it help your Church for you to be in prison?'

'We must be steadfast in our faith,' he had replied. 'Christ was hated also.'

'But you can be steadfast somewhere else. It doesn't have to be here. You could go to Holland and be safe. Do you not want to be safe? To worship unhindered, without hiding, looking over your shoulder all the time?'

'Of course I want to be safe.'

She pressed on, standing close. 'There would be no Bancroft in Holland. No one threatening irons or the noose, no danger of being betrayed by friends.'

'I know.'

'So why do you still refuse to go?'

'Because I can't run away all my life. Because we are a congregation, a community, and we must stand together. I cannot just leave the others to save my own skin.'

'And if Cecily were still alive?'

'Cecily is dead!' He spat out the words, furious she would try to use Cecily against him, opening wounds that had never fully healed.

His sister was undeterred. 'And if she weren't? What would you do then? What would Cecily want you to do?'

'What difference does it make?' He turned away from her and crossed to the fireplace, standing with his back to the room, putting distance between them. She followed, slowly, and stood beside him again. When she spoke her voice was gentle, coaxing.

'She would want you to be safe. That's all she ever wanted for you. For both of you.'

'You know nothing about it,' he hissed, without turning to look at her. 'You were barely more than a child.'

'I know that she loved you.'

'Yes. She did,' he agreed, 'and she understood me better than you. She would not have told me to go.'

'Then she would have been as big a fool as you are.'

Ben swung towards her at that, the muscles working in his cheek, fists balling and flexing as he fought to control his rage. The pain of her words almost took his breath away – it was he who had been the fool, and Cecily had followed him, reluctant and with little other choice. His foolishness had cost her her life, and her memory was sacrosanct: he would defend it to the last breath in his body. When, finally, he could speak, the words came as a whisper, forced through lips drawn tight with fury. Ellyn shrank back, afraid of his anger.

'Don't you ever speak like that about her. Never! You can say what you want about me, but you can never say those things about her. Do you understand?'

She nodded, her head lowered against the reproach, and her chest heaved in great breaths as she struggled not to cry. 'I'm sorry,' she whispered. 'But you are my brother and I don't want to lose you. Not to a prison cell. Not to the gallows.'

He softened, rage ebbing as quickly as it had come. 'That isn't going to happen.'

'Can you promise?' Dark eyes lifted to him, tear-filled, pleading as she used to as a child: a secret told, an offered treat.

He swallowed. He could make no such promise. He took her hand and the skin was cool and dry even in the summer heat. His own palm was moist.

'I cannot promise.'

She blinked hard against the gathering tears then stepped in close to him. He held her, his cheek against the sleek, smooth hair, the scent of her familiar as his childhood. Then abruptly she pulled back from him.

'You're going back to face them, aren't you?' she said.

'I shouldn't have run.'

'What will happen to you?'

He shrugged. 'A fine, probably.'

'Even though you ran?'

'I don't know,' he lied, preferring not to speak of what he knew was coming.

'Well,' she said, with a small attempt at a smile. 'I hope God appreciates your efforts.'

He said, *'Blessed are they which suffer persecution for righteousness' sake, for theirs is the kingdom of Heaven.'*

'Then you are indeed blessed.'

'I do only as I must. I can do no other.'

Then he kissed her head and strode from the room, footsteps thudding on the narrow dark stairs as he had taken them two at a time. He had wanted to be away, back at Scrooby with his people, even though his punishment was waiting. Because there at least he was sure of the rightness of his path and no one had the power to make him doubt.

THEY CAUGHT up with him not far from Nottingham, four men in the crossed-keys livery of the Archbishop of York. He had been waiting, fearing every hoofbeat at his back, but still when they came he felt the instinctive fear of the hunted, the same impulse to run.

So Richard had betrayed him after all and the pain of his

treachery hurt worse than Ben had imagined: in his heart, he had not thought it would come to this, believing, hoping, that their God-given love would spare him. But in the end, he supposed, Richard had little choice: he had sold himself to the English Church, and Ben's head was the price for his place as translator.

Would Bancroft give Richard the news of the arrest himself? he wondered. A smile on the ruddy face, knotted hands rubbing in pleasure? And how would his old friend react? With delight at a job well done? His loyalty proven at last, welcomed back into the fold of the English Church? He doubted it; he knew his friend too well. Richard had tried to make him to leave, hoping to be spared the betrayal. Even now he could not picture his friend taking pleasure in it. But still the knowledge of Richard's falseness turned heavily inside him, the bitterness of loss welling up with tears that stung behind his eyes. There could be no way back for them now: Richard had damned himself, and all they had once meant to each other was as dust.

He drew Bessie to a halt, and prayed for deliverance as the riders wheeled their horses across the lane in front of him, blocking his way.

'Are you Ben Kemp?' one of them said.

'I am,' he replied.

'And where do you think you're going?'

'I am on my way back.'

'Back where?' the same man sneered. 'To see your godless friends?'

'To see the Archbishop.' He kept himself calm with effort, instinct quickening his heartbeat, heat across his skin. The mare sidled under him and he fought to hold her to her place though his senses urged him otherwise.

'The Archbishop, eh?' One of the other men laughed. 'Well, that's right, that's where you're going now, whether you want to or no.' He reached out and caught at Bessie's reins, holding her steady while one of the others nudged alongside, a rope outstretched in his hands.

Ben swallowed, fighting down the impulse to run again, grief and fear turning to hatred. He struggled with the waves of his emotion, forcing them down by the strength of his will. '*But I say unto you which hear,*' he murmured to himself, lips moving in silent prayer. '*Love your enemies: do well to them which hate you.*'

'Praying's not going to help you now, Kemp,' one of the men said. 'It's praying that's got you here in the first place.'

He said nothing. He had lived only as Christ commanded and God would deliver him. For it was written, *Whosoever he be of you, that forsaketh not all that he hath, he cannot be my disciple.* He could have done nothing different.

'Give us your hands.'

Stretching out his wrists for the rope took all his strength, and the man wound it tight, tying it hard with cruel enjoyment. The jute was rough and chafed painfully against the scars. He laid his bound hands on the pommel of the saddle as one of the men lifted the horse's reins over her head and tried to lead her onwards. She plunged, unused to being led and reluctant. Ben touched fingers to her neck and spoke to her, soothing. She steadied a little with his voice and the man had sense enough not to drag her on, riding alongside instead, coaxing her forward.

Helpless, bound, Ben was in the hands of God. With a silent prayer on his lips, he gave himself up to their control and let them lead him to his punishment.

～

IN PRISON he sat in the stinking straw, his back against a heavy stone wall that was wet with the damp of centuries. In the light it would have been mottled green and black with mould and filth, but the light rarely penetrated the small barred opening, so he sat in the gloom and recited Scripture in his head.

We give no occasion of offence in any thing, that our ministry should not be reprehended.

But in all things we approve our selves as the ministers of God, in much patience, in afflictions, in necessities, in distresses. In stripes, in prisons, in tumults, in labours, By watchings, by fastings, by purity, by knowledge, by long suffering, by kindness, by the holy Ghost, by love unfained ...

The words were his rock and his comfort, the surety of the rightness of his path as they had been for Barrow and countless others before him. He tipped back his head against the wall, feeling the wetness through his hair. His beard had begun to itch, dirty, and his limbs ached from stillness; he tensed the muscles of his outstretched legs just to feel them move and remind himself that he still existed as a body.

With the movement he remembered he was hungry: it was many years since he had known the gnawing pain of hunger, his belly starting to contract in upon itself. Starvation would be an agonising death, he thought, and he had eaten only mouldy bread the last few days. He was beginning to lose count, the cycles of the sun blurred in the dull monotony of the gloom. There had been one sunny morning, he remembered, a day or two after he arrived when for an hour there had been a bright patch of sunlight on the straw, a beam across the room where the dust motes floated, and he had lain in its path warming himself, following its rapid journey towards the wall until it was gone. It had been cloudy since and there had been no more brightness in the cell. In the stone-cold chill it was hard to recall that outside it was summer.

But he was in God's hands. The fear of prison that had made him run had slipped away as soon as the door was bolted fast behind him. A cell was a familiar world to him – he had lived through its deprivation for three long years and survived. And it was still less than the price Cecily had paid. So he had stood in the centre of the foetid room, eyes closed, reaching inside to inure himself to the cold and the stench and the solitude, calling on the Spirit that governed him.

The Lord is my strength, and praise, and He is become my salvation. He is my God, and I will prepare him a tabernacle: He is my father's God, and I will exalt him.

Then he had chosen for himself a spot against the wall where he could see both door and window, settled himself in the flea-ridden straw, and busied his mind in prayer.

CHAPTER 21

AUTUMN 1606

*A*nd *it came to passe when hee made an ende of speaking vnto
Saul, that the soule of Ionathan was knit with the soule of
Dauid, and Ionathan loued him as his owne soule.*
(*1 Samuel 18:1*)

THE LATE-SUMMER HEAT broke with storms that wracked the
realm for days on end, roads flooded and impassable, trees
uprooted and causing chaos. The sky hung low, slate grey above
rooftops that were barely visible through the rain, and the surface
of the river was whipped into points. It was a lean time for the
boatmen on the Thames.

Richard made the short walk to the Abbey to work, papers
clutched to his chest, leaning into the storm, his cloak billowing out
behind him. Broad Sanctuary was busy in spite of the rain: workers
still hurried back and forth on their way: the city's trade didn't stop
for the weather. Around his feet a flock of geese had scattered,
their owners scuttling to and fro trying to shepherd them back

together, and two merchants dressed in black velvet stood in the lea of the Abbey wall to watch, laughing.

He paid them no heed, his thoughts already turning on the words of Scripture. Treading quickly through the marketplace that occupied the Abbey nave, he headed for the sanctuary of the library, seeking its peace, eager to begin. Though he often worked in his room at Thieving Lane, he liked the atmosphere of the library and the large desk to spread out his books. The shelves around him held a treasury of knowledge, and many of the translations that had gone before. He was humbled and inspired by so many words, each volume shedding more light on the Scriptures, each of them building on the stones painstakingly laid by others.

When the books were arranged to his liking and he was settled, he ran a finger across the words in the Bishops' Bible until he found the verse he wanted.

And when he had made an end of speaking unto Saul, the soul of Jonathan was knit with the soul of David, and Jonathan loved him as his owne soule.

He read the verse out loud, his voice disturbing the hush of the library. Then he turned to the Hebrew, whispering the words, aware of his inability to render them truly aloud. He let the phrase hang in the air, testing the meaning as he heard it in his mind. Next, he read the English again. It was a good translation: the Geneva had it exactly the same. There was no truer phrasing he could find, no improvement he could make: it seemed the bishops' choice of words was perfect. His fingertips rested on the page, tarrying, as his mind turned over the verse one final time. He had to be sure the words were right and true, a perfect expression of the love that bound the two men together. A friendship given by God.

When he was satisfied, he sat back with a sigh, and Ben stepped unbidden across his thoughts. Not for the first time he wondered why God had given such a friend to him. Time was when he had thanked God every day for the love between them, his own soul blessed by their fellowship. Ben had found his faith through the love they shared as brothers, and Richard never doubted it came from God, a gracious gift, as Jonathan had been to David, their souls knit in the sacred bond of friendship. For many years Richard believed it was given to him to save Ben, to bring him back within the Church's fold and keep him from a path of sin and error, to see him safe.

But now? Now he no longer knew how to honour that gift. Ben would never return to the Church, of that he was certain, no matter the love that existed between them. So what would God have him do now? He had prayed constantly for an answer but understanding still eluded him. All the teachings of the Church he loved and served would have him dishonour the bond, for the Separatists sought to break the Church, denying its truth and authority under God. So why did he, Richard, still waver? Why the reluctance to denounce his friend to protect the Church he loved?

Because they had walked together as fellows in their love for Christ, their souls knit as one, as the souls of David and Jonathan had been bound in their love for God.

Because love was Christ's first and highest commandment.

How then should he betray such a love?

The conflict wearied him, and he lifted a hand to rub at his temples, seeking to ease the tightness. But it made no difference and the threat of a headache lingered, dull pain tracing a path around his skull as he recalled the contempt in Ben's eyes the last time they met at Merton's house, when he had tried one last time to make Ben go. He had seen no trace then of love in Ben's heart for him any more, the bond of friendship spurned, and the knowledge twisted painfully inside. For all that had happened between them, for all the anger and heartbreak and frustration, his own heart had stayed true: whatever the course he took, the love would always remain. Their bond was a gift from God, immutable, only now it felt like a burden and he no longer thanked God for it in his prayers.

ON HIS WAY home the storm had begun to clear, rays of sunlight stabbing through gaps in the stream of clouds and lighting the puddles in the mud. Richard trod carefully, the way slick and treacherous. But he was in no hurry to reach Thieving Lane. His feet felt heavy, and there was no joy in his heart. He had seen Andrewes at the Abbey: Ben had been taken by the Archbishop's men.

When he got to the Kemps' the house was in turmoil. He stood just inside the door for a moment, bewildered. The servants ignored him, striding with purpose from room to room carrying bundles of linen or basins of water. Alice trotted down the stairs, watching her feet, and stopped short when finally she lifted her eyes from the ground and saw him. She was flushed and harried and wisps of hair had escaped the white linen cap. 'You startled me!' she said, an automatic hand clutching at her breast.

'What in Heaven's name is going on?' he asked.

She glanced around her, as if only now noticing all the activity. 'My uncle has taken ill,' she said. 'There is a physician with him now.'

'Is it serious?'

She nodded. Then, with a sigh, she said, 'He keeps asking for Ben.'

He said nothing, thinking Thomas Kemp would have been better to fall ill a week ago, when his son was free and at his sister's.

'We have sent a letter to Scrooby,' Alice said.

'It will take more than a letter,' he murmured, so that the servant passing behind them with more candles for the sickroom would not hear. 'I have just been at the Abbey. Ben is in prison.'

Alice was silent, slanting her eyes away from him. He could only guess at her thoughts.

'Is Ellyn here?'

'Upstairs, with her father. But perhaps you should speak with my aunt,' she suggested. 'Shall I fetch her?'

He nodded with a sigh, dreading the telling, more strain on Mistress Kemp's already fragile nerves. Alice turned and hurried up the stairs and he wandered into the hall to wait. It was deserted now, the household's attention taken by their master's illness: the sick-chamber had become the new centre of the house. He hovered near the hearth, idly pacing, rehearsing the news in his mind. It seemed a long time before Mistress Kemp's footsteps sounded on the stairs, light and rapid, and she appeared at the door with Alice at her shoulder. He was glad of Alice's presence, a woman for support.

'Richard.' Emma Kemp greeted him with a fleeting absent smile, her thoughts still upstairs. 'Alice says you have news I must hear?' She flicked a glance across him but her focus was distracted, anxious only to get back to her husband.

Richard looked to Alice for aid, a way to break the news less painfully. The younger woman understood and ushered her aunt towards the chairs by the unlit fire, settling her carefully with cushions around her. Emma Kemp allowed herself to be arranged, then looked up at Richard expectantly. He drew a stool close, and Alice remained beside her.

'I am sorry to bring you this news at such a time,' he began. 'I know your husband is gravely ill, but I'm afraid this cannot wait.'

She gasped with sudden understanding. 'My son?' she whispered.

He nodded. 'Ben has been arrested. He was taken a few days ago. He is at Gainsborough Prison now.'

'You are sure of this?'

'I just came from the Abbey. The Dean told me himself.' Andrewes had come across him by chance in the cloister, and had given him the news almost as an afterthought.

She slid her eyes away from him, searching the empty hearth, her hands twisting helplessly in her lap. 'How long?' she breathed. 'For how long?' She turned her head to see him again, but there was no hope in her eyes for an answer.

'I don't know,' he replied, though he guessed Ben would not be released any time soon. 'It's for the Archbishop of York to decide.'

'You must go to him,' she said.

'I cannot. Forgive me, but I cannot.'

She reached for his hand, grasped it in her own cold fingers. 'But you must,' she pleaded. 'You must take him food and his Bible. You must counsel him and bring him home. Why can you not?'

'It is impossible, madam. I cannot.' What could he say? He flicked a desperate glance to Alice.

'But why?' she persisted. 'You are his friend. His oldest friend. You cannot turn your back. He needs you ...'

Alice laid a gentle hand on her aunt's shoulder and Emma Kemp's head swung round to her, surprised by her presence. 'Come, Aunt,' Alice said. 'You are distraught. Perhaps you should rest now. It's been a difficult day.'

Emma Kemp nodded, overcome by the griefs of her family, and biddable. Kindly, Alice helped her to her feet and guided her away towards the door. Richard watched them go with relief and only half returned the smile that Alice gave him before the door closed behind her and she disappeared from view.

He gave them a moment, waiting till he could no longer hear them on the stairs, Alice's reassuring tones fading into silence. Then he followed them out, climbing to his own room quickly, wanting to be alone to pray.

He had barely begun when the door slammed open behind him. He spun round, startled by the crash. Ellyn was in the doorway, closing the door behind her. She was with child, he realised, her belly growing large. He wondered he had not noticed it before.

She was breathing hard, and not only from the effort of the stairs: her face was hard with anger, the same set he had seen so many times on Ben, mouth clamped shut, eyes both black and bright. Obviously Alice had told her the news. He got up from his knees and turned himself to face her.

'You Judas!' she spat. 'What are you doing here? How dare you show your face after what you've done.'

'I have done nothing,' he breathed. Her fury quickened his heartbeat, and the injustice of the insult caused the blood to pound in his head. He reached a hand to the desk to steady himself.

'You lie.' She took two strides forward and when she spoke her voice was low. 'How can you live with yourself?' she breathed. 'For two years you've taken my family's hospitality, pretended to be a friend. I am almost glad my father is too ill to know the truth. He would be heartbroken. He thought of you like a son.'

'I know what you think, Ellyn. You think I betrayed him. But I didn't. As God is my witness, I love him still and it tears me in two. But I did not betray him.'

'I don't believe you,' she said. 'And neither would Ben.'

'It grieves me to know that.' He bit back the tears – it seemed a cruel irony. And still he did not know if he had done right, the conflict still raging in his thoughts and heart, absorbing all his prayers. Either way, he thought bitterly, it seemed he was to be punished.

She folded her arms and tilted her chin, the same contempt in her face he had seen in Ben. 'I think you should leave this house,' she said. 'You are not welcome here any more, and my mother cannot bear any more heartbreak.'

He swallowed. He could think of no more words to defend himself. They faced each other across the small room and she waited, no softening of her stance, no glimmer of understanding.

'I will go,' he murmured finally, with a shrug. What other choice did he have? He let his gaze travel the room with regret – he had never lived anywhere so comfortable, and he had no idea where else he would go. 'If that is your wish, I will go.'

'It is my wish,' she replied. 'And the sooner the better.'

'I am sorry you think so ill of me.'

'Why did you come here in the first place, if not for this?' She lifted her chin as though to look down on him. 'Why did you not just stay away from him? Why come here at all if you did not mean to betray him?'

For a moment he thought about telling her the truth and trying to explain himself, to make her understand, but the scorn in her eyes was set and unchangeable: no words of his would ever alter her belief that he had only ever planned to betray her brother. Then he said, 'It is a comfortable house. And very convenient for the Abbey.'

She let out a half breath of derision and set her lips in a line that was ugly with contempt. She said, 'I will leave you to your packing, Doctor Clarke. Don't bother to say goodbye.'

He watched her as she turned away to snatch open the door and heard the rapid footsteps in the passage, down the stairs as she returned to her father's bedside. The house subsided once more into quiet anxiety with the servants' voices hushed and the usual clatter muted. He had better stay at an inn tonight, he decided, and search for new lodgings on the morrow.

With a deep breath he shook off the weariness and forced himself to think about packing his few belongings.

CHAPTER 22

WINTER 1606

*F or which cause we faint not, but though our outward man
perish, yet the inward man is renewed day by day.*

*For our light affliction, which is but for a moment, worketh for
vs a farre more exceeding and eternall waight of glory,*

*While we looke not at the things which are seene, but at the
things which are not seene: for the things which are seene, are
temporall, but the things which are not seene, are eternall.*

(2 Corinthians 4:16–18)

BEN WAS RELEASED as the country blazed with bonfires to celebrate a year since the gunpowder treason. William Brewster came
to get him and they rode away from the prison in silence under the
watchful eyes of the guards. Outside the town and across the river,
Ben drew rein and turned to his companion.

'Did you bring food?'

Brewster smiled. 'Of course.' He reached behind him for a
bundle and passed it across to Ben, who took it with trembling
hands. His time in gaol had weakened him and the winter cold bit

into his bones. He had not felt warmth in many weeks. But it was good to see the sky above him, however grey and menacing, to feel the damp air fresh against his skin, clean in his nostrils. He fumbled with the knot on the bundle, untying it with difficulty, and his hands were black against the whiteness of the linen cloth. In prison he had become immune to his own filth and the stench of his body, but outside he was suddenly aware of it, and filled with shame. He could hardly bear to hold the food in his fingers.

'Eat a little bread and cheese,' Brewster said. 'It will give you strength for the journey. Then let's get you home to a warm hearth, hot water, and some soup.'

Ben stuffed bread and cheese into his mouth, the first fresh food to pass his lips in weeks. He knew he must seem like an animal to Brewster but hunger drove him, and desperation for the strength the food would give him. His shrunken stomach churned but held the meal down, and slowly the trembling in his limbs began to ebb, energy returning to his muscles. When he had eaten all he could, his belly filling fast, he tied up what was left and gave the bundle back to Brewster, who fastened it behind his saddle. Then, as the first drops of rain began to fall, he drew his cloak tighter round him, and they set their horses along the road to Scrooby.

By the time they arrived at the manor house they were sodden and chilled and Ben could barely keep on his feet as he slid from the mare. Brewster took Ben's arm across his shoulders and half carried him inside, leaving the horses for someone else to tend.

The women of the house came running.

'Dear God! What have they done to him?' There was terror in Mistress Clyfton's voice.

'Get him dry clothes and blankets,' Brewster ordered as he set Ben down on a chair at the hearth. 'And some broth.'

Brewster's wife fled to the stove but Mistress Clyfton did not move, frozen to the spot with horror.

'He needs dry clothes,' Brewster repeated.

She stared for a moment, uncomprehending until he gave the instruction again. Then she turned, and they heard her heavy tread on the stairs as she hurried in search of clean linen.

Ben was only vaguely aware of the activity around him. The hearth blazed hot as Brewster squatted before it, throwing on more wood, but even before its heat Ben was cold, the shivering deep in his bones and uncontrolled. He sank his head gratefully against a cushion that someone placed at his shoulder.

Mistress Brewster bent towards him – he was aware of the closeness of her face but the details of it eluded him. A faint scent of sage lingered round her: she must have been preparing supper when he arrived.

'We need to get you out of these wet clothes,' she said, and it felt like being a child again, his mother helping him undress after a long day that had left him half-asleep on his feet; but she was gentler than his mother had been, more patient, and his pride gave way before his weakness. He let her move his body as she needed to, submitting to her care as she sponged the worst of the filth from his skin. Then she rubbed him dry and put a clean shirt over his head.

'You'll do,' she said, with a smile. 'Not perfect, but for now you'll do.' Then she turned to her husband. 'He should be in bed.'

Brewster nodded his agreement, and sent the younger William to make up a fire in Ben's chamber. When it was done, together the two Williams shouldered Ben's weight and half carried, half dragged him to his bed.

Afterward, he would have no memory of any of it.

HE WOKE WITH THE DAYBREAK, the cockerel declaring the morning in the yard outside. For a moment he was startled, unfamiliar sounds and sunlight bright at the window. He thought he must still be in his dreams. Then he remembered: he was no longer in prison. The bed was clean and soft beneath him – he was free.

He turned his head on the pillow and saw Mistress Brewster just waking from her vigil in the chair beside the bed. Seeing him awake, she smiled.

'Good morning, Ben. How are you feeling?'

He hesitated, uncertain. 'Weak, I think. And in need of a bath.' He could smell his own sour scent, see the dirt ingrained in his skin.

'All in good time,' she said, placing a hand on his arm. 'You need to rest for a while and gather your strength.'

'You know me better than that,' he replied, and she smiled. They both knew he would be up as soon as his limbs could bear him, that taking rest went against his nature. 'God gave us the day to use. I plan not to spend it in idleness.'

'It is not idleness to recover your strength.'

He said nothing but struggled to sit himself up in the bed. She watched him, shaking her head with a sigh, before she gathered the pillows and arranged them behind him so that he was comfortable.

'I'll go and fetch you some broth,' she said. 'And then we'll see how you are.'

He nodded, but already he was weary, and when William Brewster returned with the broth he had fallen back into fitful sleep.

The older man woke him gently and set the tray so that Ben could feed himself. Then he sat in the chair where his wife had spent the night and watched Ben eat in silence. The broth was flavourful and nourishing and Ben had to force himself to take it slowly. He felt his strength returning with every mouthful he swallowed, muscles itching towards activity. But after less than half the bowl he could eat no more and all he wanted was to sleep again.

Brewster took the tray and placed it on the dresser. Then he sat back in the chair, hands clasped neatly on his lap before him, his face drawn and serious. Even through his torpor Ben sensed there was unwelcome news to come.

'What is it?' he said. 'What news do you have for me?'

'I have had news from your family, Ben,' he replied gently. 'Your father is gravely ill.'

Ben forced himself to sit straighter, concern cutting through the weakness. 'How long?'

'Since soon after you were taken.'

'And he is ... still alive?'

'So far as we know.'

'Then I must go to him.' He moved to push himself out of bed but was stayed by Brewster's hand against his arm.

'You are in no fit state to ride to London.'

'My father is dying,' he said. 'I must go.' The harsh words of their last parting flickered in his thoughts, barely visited in the weeks of his imprisonment: his disinheritance, his father's disappointment, his own resentment. But there was still time to put things right, if he could leave right away. There was still a chance to be reconciled. He shrugged off the older man's touch. 'I must go.'

Brewster complied, withdrawing his hand, stepping back as Ben struggled to raise himself up and swing his legs to the floor. The movement left him breathless and lightheaded and he was forced to stop, sitting on the edge of the bed, swaying, the room spinning round him. 'I have to go,' he whispered. 'I have to.'

Gathering all his strength, he managed to stand but only for a moment before his legs buckled under him, and Brewster was beside him, breaking his fall, easing him back onto the bed.

'How far do you think you'd get?' the older man said. 'You can barely get yourself out of bed.'

Ben shook his head with frustration. So much time had already passed, his father's days growing short. 'I have to go.'

'Give yourself time,' Brewster said. 'You will ride quicker for it and you may actually arrive.'

He bit his lips, fists clenching round the sheets as he fought against his weakness. Brewster was right of course. He would be lucky to make it to the gate in his condition; London was an impossible task. He had no choice but to wait. Furious, he turned his face to the window, squinting in the brightness of the low winter sun.

'Rest now,' Brewster said gently. 'Get strong. And I will see about arranging a bath for you this morning.'

Ben nodded, reminded that his skin still carried the taint of prison, his fingernails black, his hair and beard matted and overgrown. But already he was exhausted by the morning's exertions, and before Brewster had even closed the door he had fallen back into sleep.

CHAPTER 23

WINTER 1606

How are the mightie fallen in the midst of the battell! O Ionathan, thou wast slaine in thine high places. I am distressed for thee, my brother Ionathan, very pleasant hast thou beene vnto me: thy loue to mee was wonderfull, passing the loue of women.

(*2 Samuel 1:25–26*)

THE YEAR HAD TURNED to winter with bitter winds and rain, and Richard's new lodgings were cold. The widow who owned the house did the best she could, but the building was close to the water and no matter how bright the fires blazed in the hearths there was a chill that never shifted. He spent as little time there as he could, working at the Abbey until the hour was late, absorbing himself in Scripture.

The Company met in the Abbey library now, since Andrewes was no longer Dean and no longer resident at the deanery. He had been given the bishopric at Chichester, rich reward for his loyalty to the king. Richard regretted the change: he missed the solemnity of the Jerusalem Chamber with its tapestries of Abraham and Sarah to inspire him.

They took their places and began work at once, the routine familiar from their long months of labour. They were testing the merits of the words *overthrown* and *fallen*. In Andrewes's mellifluous voice it was hard to choose between them.

'*How are the mightie fallen* against *How are the mightie overthrown.*'

'But we are to follow the Bishops' Bible, as little altered as the truth of the original permits.' The always-worried John Overall, fretting. His young and gorgeous wife was giving him trouble, Richard had heard, her attention straying to younger, more interesting men – no wonder he was fretful.

'Yet *fallen* is closer to the Hebrew.' Richard looked around the table and there was a general murmur of agreement. 'I think we are agreed on that.'

'But *fallen* is the Geneva's translation ...'

'Yes,' he said, testily, 'and it is truer to the original than *overthrown.*'

Overall sighed as though he were being hard done by, and Andrewes took up the silence. 'I think we understand that this particular passage has its own difficulties.'

Dealing as it does, thought Richard, with issues of rightful kingship. The obedience God expects from a king. The rejection of a monarch who took upon himself the role of priest. He should have brought Ben to this meeting, he thought drily, to hear his views on the matter. He could imagine the argument now: Scripture seeming to validate the Puritan claim that the duties of a priest do not belong to a king.

No one spoke, all of them aware of the need to tread gently.

'The Geneva's notes here offer nothing to offend,' Andrewes said then. 'Even the king could surely find no fault.'

'And *fallen*,' Richard could not resist saying, 'is more nuanced, less ... political, shall we say?'

Thomson laughed. 'God forbid we should produce a political Bible after all.'

Andrewes smiled indulgently. Then he said, 'We must aim only for the truth.'

'So, *fallen* it is?'

'*Fallen* it is.'

Andrewes read over the line once more.

'How are the mighty fallen in the midst of battle!'

The translators listened in silence, still striving to judge the rightness of the words, if their humble efforts had brought light and true meaning. All of them were aware of the weight of their task, God's Word in their trust.

'We are content, gentlemen?' Andrewes enquired. There was the silence of assent. 'Then we shall continue.' He dropped his eyes to the papers before him, found his place in the narrow lines of writing with a bony finger and began to read again.

ALICE CAME to find him sometimes on his way from the Abbey. She knew his habits, the hours he kept and when she could find him crossing Broad Sanctuary on his way to his lodgings for dinner. He was grateful for her visits. Each time he passed the end of Thieving Lane he couldn't help but cast his glance that way, wondering if Thomas Kemp had yet breathed his last, if Ben had been released in time to see him before he died.

This morning he caught sight of her before she saw him. She was standing just inside the doorway of the Abbey, taking shelter from an easterly wind that whipped in from the river, a shawl clasped tight about her shoulders. She was moving in rhythm from side to side, lifting one foot then the other in a bid to keep warm, and the chill had brought a flush to her cheeks. He came quite close before she noticed him, frowning in his direction as his blurred form moved finally into focus.

'Alice.'

'Doctor Clarke.'

'Shall we get out of this infernal wind?'

She nodded and he led her back the way he had come through the Abbey to find a quiet spot close to the quire. Trees of blazing candles lent the place an illusion of warmth and, in the quire, the choristers were practising for Advent. The boys' young voices carried high and sweet above the hubbub of activity. Both of them stopped for a moment to listen, their souls drawn by the music's beauty until the choirmaster, hearing some imperfection, brought the singers abruptly to silence with an impatient reprimand.

'It sounded good enough to me.' Richard smiled.

'To me too,' she agreed.

There was a silence. The boys of the choir began again their 'Veni, Emmanuel.' This time their master seemed better pleased and let them continue.

'How are your new lodgings now the weather has turned?' she asked.

'They suffice,' he replied. 'Though I must confess I miss the comforts of Thieving Lane. And the company of course.'

She smiled. 'Of course. We miss your company too. It's a very quiet house now.'

There was a pause and he realised his words had given her pleasure, the smile still playing round her lips. Apparently she had got over her liking for Ben and transferred her affections. The awareness brought an unexpected heat across his skin and he swallowed, surprised by his reaction.

'How is your uncle?' he said, automatically, his emotions still confused.

'He is the same. Sometimes his mind is with us, sometimes he is elsewhere. But still he asks for his son.' She shook her head in pity. 'And he is in great pain. God would be merciful to take him soon.'

'There is nothing the physicians can do?'

'They have done plenty,' she said. 'Purges, bleeding, draughts of this or that. But nothing has helped. Nothing at all.'

'Then we can only pray that God will be merciful.'

'Yes.' She turned her head away, listening to the voices, and the light from the candles behind her caught tendrils of the mousy hair and made them golden. The smile still touched her lips and there was a dreaminess in her gaze. Heat passed across his skin a second time, and flared inside his loins. He wrenched his eyes away and stared towards the choir, self-conscious of his sin.

She said, 'Your work here must be nearly done.'

'Almost.'

'And then the new Bible will be printed?'

'Not for a while. The work of each company will go before a committee for a final check.'

'It is a long process.'

'It is indeed.'

'And you? What will you do then?' She turned to him again.

'I shall return to my parish in Kent. I have been away too long.' He pictured it, the pretty garden, the quiet lanes, simple folk, their worlds turning with the seasons, lives unchanged through generations. It was a long way from the worldliness he inhabited now.

The music ended. 'I shall miss you when you're gone,' she said.

Then, quickly, 'I should get back before my aunt wonders where I am.'

'It was good of you to come.'

They walked together along the aisle towards the door where she had waited. As he reached out his hand towards it, the wind snatched it away from him, slamming it open. A gust of chill air rushed in and both of them shivered. Then, with a brace of their shoulders, they left the Abbey's shelter and set out side by side across the Sanctuary. It was too cold to talk but the silence was friendly, and when they reached the end of Thieving Lane they parted with a smile to go their separate ways through the winter afternoon.

Only later, listening to the widow's prattle over supper at his lodgings, did it cross his mind to realise that he would miss her too.

CHAPTER 24

WINTER 1606

B *lessed are they that mourne: for they shall be comforted.*
(*Matthew 5:4*)

THOMAS KEMP LINGERED INTO WINTER, the light of his life dimming slowly with the year, his body wracked with pain no medicine could alleviate. As the child within Ellyn grew and quickened, so Thomas Kemp shrank towards his death. He was never alone, the vigil shared by his wife, his daughter and his niece. But he kept on asking for his son and they would nod and look away and say nothing.

Ben finally arrived almost too weak to stand, frozen to the bone and trembling. His mother met him at the door and her hands flew to her face at the sight of him. 'God in Heaven! We shall be burying you both. Come to the hearth. Get warm.' She reached uncertain hands towards him, seeking to guide him into the hall, towards heat and rest, but he waved her attentions away.

'How is he?' he said.

'He's dying,' she replied. 'Slowly. Day by day.'

'Then I am not too late.' Relief surged through him. 'I'll go to him.'

'He would like that. He keeps asking for you.'

Ben nodded and put a foot on the bottom stair, pausing a moment to find the strength to climb the rest. He heard his mother call for spiced wine to be brought as he set his will forward and started upwards, resting often against the banister and finally sliding with relief into the chair that was set at his father's bedside. It was many years since he had been inside this room; memories of secret games here as a child glimmered at the corners of his thoughts. The bed had seemed vast to him then. He had been caught just the once, using the bedcovers to make some kind of den, and he remembered the sting of his father's belt.

Now the old man lay motionless, his breathing ragged and uneven, skin stretched tight and grey across the angular bones of his face. There was no sign of the plump and prosperous merchant he had been, and Ben took the claw-like hand in his own cold fingers. He was appalled at the change so short a time had wrought, and the recollection of their last exchange remained a bitter memory. He was here to ask forgiveness.

'Father?'

The old man made no sign that he had heard. Ben looked up at Alice, sitting across the bed, watching with her habitual frown.

'Does he know I'm here?'

'It's hard to say,' she replied. 'He seems to go in and out. Sometimes he's quite lucid, others he is as you see him. But he is more peaceful like this – his illness gives him great pain.'

'Father?' Ben bent closer to the old man. 'It's Ben. I've come back to see you.'

His father's fingers tightened on Ben's. Ben glanced up again at Alice with a small smile of relief. His father knew he was there at least, and he had not tried to take his hand away.

Thomas Kemp's lips started to move, struggling to make the shapes of the words he needed to say. 'Ben?' he managed to rasp.

'I am here, sir.'

Thomas Kemp turned his head towards the voice and his eyelids flickered as he fought to force them open. Eventually his gaze settled on his son.

'I am glad you came,' he breathed. 'Perhaps now I'm dying you will listen to me.' He paused as his body tensed against a sudden spasm, his breath quickening. The grip on his son's fingers closed like a vice: Ben was astonished at the strength that was still in the emaciated hand.

The spasm passed and the grasp loosened, but his breathing came now in great heaving rasps. His eyes fixed once again on his son. 'I have left you enough to go,' he whispered. 'To Holland.'

Ben nodded, and flicked a quick glance of concern towards Alice. She pretended not to be listening, eyes lowered to the shirt she was sewing in the candlelight. He returned his eyes to meet his father's.

'You've been in prison again,' Thomas Kemp said.

Alice started in her chair, a small jump of shock, and pricked her finger. Lifting it to her lips to suck at the blood, she got up from her chair, using the movement as an excuse to leave them.

'They think I don't know. But they talk when they think I am sleeping ...' He pulled back his lips in an attempt at a smile.

His son smiled in return. 'I am free now.'

'Aah. I am glad to see you. But you must use your freedom and go. Go to Holland. Promise me.'

'I cannot promise.'

'Promise me.' Even through the rasping breath and the whispers, there was something of the old determination to have his way. His fingers grasped tightly again, another spasm wracking his frame. He tensed and closed his eyes, shuddering until it had passed. Then he slowly turned his head once more towards his son.

'Promise me you will go,' he breathed. 'Swear.'

Ben swallowed and turned his face away from the searching eyes, as shrewd now in the cadaverous death mask as they had ever been.

'I want to know you're safe before I go,' the old man said. 'So that I may go to God in peace. Now swear.'

Ben struggled, his own weakness threatening to claim him. He tensed to stop himself from swaying, eyes still averted.

'Swear,' his father repeated. 'And let me die in peace.'

What choice did he have? he thought. In the end he would have to go. They would all have to go, Bancroft's web all around them, all of them watched, harassed, taken, fined, imprisoned. What was the point when God was offering a place of freedom across the sea?

He turned his eyes back to his father and returned the pressure of the old man's grip. 'I swear,' he said. 'I will go and be safe as you wish.'

'Aaahh,' the old man sighed and the tension left his face, the skin softening across the bones, eyes closing in relief. 'Aaahh. Thank you, Ben,' he said. 'Thank you.'

They were the last words he said.

IT WAS ALMOST Christmastide before he died. Though he spoke no more, he often held on to Ben's hand, grasping, so that they knew his mind was still with them, even if his eyes remained closed and his lips could do nothing more than move in the formation of words that would never be heard.

It was painful to watch, the slow demise of the body, weakened and incapable. But the hold on life was tenacious, and he still accepted the small spoonfuls of broth that they gave him. Even though he had gained his promise from his son, Thomas Kemp still refused to yield quietly. Ben barely left his side. Across from him his mother, his sister and his cousin took their turns at the bedside: they had long since given up urging him to rest.

Alice watched him as he got up from the chair to stretch, limbs aching, strength returning. It would be good to be active again, he thought, his muscles crying out for movement. For something to do he crossed to the fire and squatted before it, tossing on a new log. It was burning low and drawing well, a good warmth against the bitter cold of the December night. Rattling the grate with the poker, he let the ash fall through. The new log caught with the sudden pull of air, crackling loudly in the silent room, and he poked at it more, arranging it to his liking until it was burning evenly and well. Finally satisfied, he stood up, knees cracking, rubbed the dirt from his hands and returned to his place at the bedside.

'You should go to bed,' he said to Alice. 'There is no need for us both to be here all night.'

'I'm fine,' she replied. 'It's warm and comfortable and I don't like to leave him. It is you who should be in bed. You've barely rested since you got here.'

'I've slept in worse places.'

She frowned, focusing her gaze more closely on his face. Then, in a voice that barely lifted above the crackle of the flames, she said, 'Will you go to Holland, Ben, as he bid you?'

'Do you think I should go?' He wondered how much she knew and who had told her, if she had Richard's confidence.

She slid her eyes away. 'I think you should come back to the Church.'

He was silent, aware that perhaps he had mistaken her shyness for meekness.

'But if not,' she said, 'then yes, I think you should go to Holland.'

'You are afraid for me?'

She hesitated. 'A little,' she said. Then, 'And I would have you honour your father's wishes.'

He gave an equivocal tilt of his head, surprised that she cared: he had thought she despised him for the grief he caused his family. 'I made a promise.'

'You've been there before, haven't you?'

'A long time ago.' Another lifetime it seemed to him now, before Cecily, before prison. He had been a different man then, barely more than a boy, with big hopes and dreams for a new Church in England. Now he knew it was impossible: the Church would never reform and those who hoped for it would always be hunted and oppressed. What choice did they have in the end but to leave?

'Did you miss England?' she asked. 'I think I would miss it very much.'

'Sometimes,' he said. 'But I was young and the world was full of adventure.'

She smiled. 'Tell me.'

'It was exciting. I was learning the world of trade and meeting men from all parts of the globe. Men with strange-coloured skin, men who spoke many different tongues. Arabs, Turks, Chinamen, Christians, heathens ... Amsterdam was ... is ... a melting pot. And there are many godly and gracious people there.'

Greta stepped unbidden across his thoughts and filled him with the fragrance of the nape of her neck. Strange how after all these years her scent was still familiar. Cecily's perfume was harder to recall.

'And now you are older?'

'I am here.'

She nodded and both of them turned their attention once again to the pale man that lay between them, still just connected to his life by the thin and hard-fought breaths that rasped unevenly. Ben took his father's hand but there was no response.

'How much longer, do you think?' Alice whispered.

'He is in God's hands now,' Ben answered. 'He will take him when he's ready.'

'Should we pray?'

He smiled. 'We should always pray.'

She lowered her eyes to cover her embarrassment. She had never lost her nervousness around him – it was better hidden now, but there just the same. Ben began to murmur a prayer. Alice half rose from her chair as if to kneel on the floor, but Ben merely bowed his head and so she sat back instead and closed her eyes.

The time of our life is threescore years and ten, and if they be of strength, fourscore years: yet their strength is but labour and sorrow: for it is cut off quickly, and we flee away.

Who knoweth the power of Thy wrath? for according to Thy fear is Thine anger.

Teach us so to number our days, that we may apply our hearts unto wisdom.

Return (O Lord, how long?) and be pacified toward Thy servants.

Fill us with Thy mercy in the morning: so shall we rejoice and be glad all our days.

Comfort us according to the days that Thou hast afflicted us, and according to the years that we have seen evil.

Let Thy work be seen toward Thy servants, and Thy glory upon their children.

And let the beauty of the Lord our God be upon us, and direct

Thou the work of our hands upon us, even direct the work of our hands.

❧

LATER HE DOZED. Half his mind remained at the deathbed in front of him, aware of his cousin's watchful gaze, but the rest fell into dreams of imprisonment, a ship leaving harbour without him. As the vessel slid from view across the sea, he fought against the chains that held him and woke up with a start, rubbing hard at his scars. Alice was still watching him.

'You were dreaming,' she said. 'I wasn't sure if I should wake you.'

He said nothing. Her constant presence was starting to oppress him and he wished she would go to bed and leave him alone with his father.

'Was it a nightmare?' she asked. 'You seemed ... distressed.'

'Just a bad dream.'

They settled back into silence. The room was warm against the winter night beyond the curtained window and the house creaked and groaned in the quiet, the familiar sounds of childhood nights when sleep had failed to come. But the noises now would hold a different memory.

His father stirred, the slow rasping breath breaking rhythm. He moved his lips as though he would speak, and his fingers twitched in search of human touch. Ben reached out and took his hand between both of his, sitting forward to be closer.

'I'm here,' he said. 'And all is well.'

A long voiced breath escaped his father's lips, a last drawn-out sigh that signified his passing. There were no more breaths to come. Ben bowed his head above his father's hand and prayed a silent prayer.

~

AT THE GRAVESIDE, Ben stood tense as the minister recited his stinted prayers, a ceremony that still smacked of popish ritual; it grieved him to be part of it. Heartfelt prayers by those who knew his father best would have been more fitting, but his mother's grief could bear no more heartache and for her sake he had kept his peace.

Beside him, her shoulder almost brushing his arm, Emma Kemp trembled as her husband was lowered into the ground. She was going to be lost without him, Ben thought: with no strong hand to guide and to comfort her she had already begun to falter. A small sob escaped her lips, and with a slight movement of his hand Ben grasped her fingers in his own and squeezed. She stiffened at the unexpected affection, but then she turned a small and grateful smile his way. She was a good woman and he was sorry for all the distress he had caused her. The minister's voice droned on:

'Forasmuch as it hath pleased Almighty God of His great mercy to take unto Himself the soul of our dear brother here departed, we therefore commit his body to the ground; earth to earth, ashes to ashes, dust to dust; in sure and certain hope of the Resurrection to eternal life through our Lord Jesus Christ ...'

Ben stopped listening, and let his eyes travel over the mourners on the other side of the grave. A lot of people had come – his father had been well loved and respected. They were merchants mostly, a few with their wives, all of them huddled into their cloaks against the biting cold. A cold metallic sun lit behind the clouds but the day was bitter.

Most of them he barely knew, their faces only vaguely familiar from the Twelfth Night revels or from years ago when he had worked with his father for the few brief months between Amsterdam and prison.

Then behind them he noticed Richard Clarke, standing well back from the graveside, his eyes resolutely lowered. Rage flooded him that Richard would dare to intrude with his counterfeit grief for a man whose trust he had so willingly betrayed. Sweat covered him beneath the layers of clothing. He wrenched his gaze away, lowered his eyes once more to the open grave.

The priest fell silent.

Ellyn squatted down briefly and dropped a sprig of rosemary into the grave. His mother let slip a spray of purple heather, but the stalks caught on the dirt at the lip of the opening and Ben stooped quickly to retrieve it, passing it back to her. She stretched out a shaking hand and took it, then stepped closer and let it fall again before she quickly turned away and took her daughter's arm.

Away from the grave, the mourners approached her. 'We should get her home,' Ellyn murmured.

He nodded his agreement and with gentle pressure against her mother's elbow, Ellyn turned her mother along the path to lead the procession quietly out of the churchyard and back to Thieving Lane for the wake.

The mourners milled in his father's hall, cups of fine wine in their hands while their eyes appraised the quality of the furnishings, the silks that hung at the windows, the rugs that adorned the walls. Merton would need to be careful with his father's trade – these men were no respecters of inheritance, whatever their feelings for Thomas Kemp had been.

They spoke to Ben one by one.

'Your father was a good man, an honest man ...'

'He will be sorely missed ...'

'God knows there are few enough like him in trade ...'

'If there is anything we can do for your mother ...'

'Thank you, you've been very kind.' He murmured the expected responses.

Ellyn barely left her mother's side through the gathering, and Ben saw through the smile to the weariness behind it. She was close to her time. She should be resting, he thought, preparing herself for what lay ahead. Her husband hovered as close as he could but it seemed it was already known that the Company had come to him: snippets of shop talk peppered the condolences. Then Richard emerged from the group and came towards him. Instinctively Ben braced, pulse quickening. He was appalled that Richard saw fit to show his face.

'I'm sorry for your loss,' Richard said. 'He was a good man. He was always kind to me.'

'Yes,' Ben agreed. 'That he was.'

There was a pause. Richard turned his eyes away from the hostility and clasped his hands together in front of him, working the fingers together tightly. Ben waited, enjoying the other man's unease until finally Richard looked back to him with nervous hesitation. 'Can we talk?' he said.

'I have nothing to say to you.' Though if he had not been at his father's wake and constrained, he would have had words aplenty.

The other man nodded. 'I understand,' he said. 'But it is not about that. This is a different matter entirely. And it is important or I would not ask.'

Ben tilted his head, considering. It was tempting to say no and give the man nothing, but his curiosity was piqued. 'Come to my father's study.'

'Thank you.'

They went out of the hall and up the stairs to the room that now belonged to Merton. It was unchanged since the days before his father's death, except for the great ledger which had gone from the desk when Merton took over through the long weeks of illness. Ben stood by his father's chair, one hand on the smooth wood back of it, but he could not bring himself to sit down. It was his father's chair, his father's place, and it was not God's will that he should ever fill it. The two men stood and faced each other across the neat piles of documents that covered the desk.

'What have you to say to me?' Ben demanded.

Richard gave a half-smile, hesitating, and smoothed a hand across his hair. Ben observed him, wondering what might be about to come. He could make no guess, and this coy sheepishness was something new. He said, 'Well?'

'Always so impatient.'

'I have a house full of guests.'

'Of course,' Richard said quickly. 'Forgive me. I will get to the point.' He smoothed a hand across his hair again. 'I ... wish to marry Alice.'

Ben stared. Of all the things he had imagined Richard might ask for, this was perhaps the most unexpected. He was almost tempted to laugh. 'You wish to marry Alice?'

'I think she will be agreeable.' Richard's tone suggested he was offended by Ben's incredulity.

'And as you are now head of the household it falls to you to approach her father.'

Ben smiled, shaking his head in disbelief. Richard and Alice, husband and wife. It was hard to imagine it. He had come to think that Richard would never marry now, his passions dried out by too many years at study. He recalled him as a young man at Cambridge: they had been different people then, loyal to God and to each other, their friendship ardent and intense. But perhaps a woman would be good for Richard. Perhaps a wife could tease back his humanity. And Alice would suit him: he could imagine them shy and reserved with each other, unendingly polite. She would make a good country vicar's wife, working hard and uncomplaining, grateful for what God had given her. But it was hard to think there might be passion.

'I'm not sure why you smile,' Richard said. His lips were tight with offence. 'I thought we would wed when the Translation is completed, and Alice can return with me to Kent.'

Ben was silent. He did not know what to say.

Richard continued. 'I think we will be very well suited.'

'Yes,' Ben agreed. 'I'm sure you will.'

'I am not asking for your permission. She is of age and we have no need of your permission to marry. We can do it without you if needs be, but I like to do things properly ...'

Ben's lips twitched into the beginnings of another smile.

'... so I would be much obliged if you would speak to her father.'

The smile faded. He was in half a mind to say no to this man who was his enemy, a defender of an idolatrous church, a betrayer. But then he thought of Alice. She was not so young any more and she had little to recommend her as a bride: a plain face, a small dowry. Richard might be her only chance and it was a match Thomas Kemp would have approved. For once Ben could do something for his father, something that would please him. He only wished he could have done so before his father died.

He said, 'I will speak to her father.'

'Thank you.' Richard's words were clipped, as though it cost him dear to say them. 'I will take up no more of your time. I bid you good day.' He dropped his head in the briefest of bows and took a step to leave before he halted and looked back at Ben, as though there were more he wished to say. He hesitated, undecided.

Curious, Ben waited. The moment lingered. The murmurs of the voices at the wake downstairs rumbled through the floor.

'What is it you would say?' Ben asked finally, but without impatience.

Richard lifted his eyes, ran his tongue across his lips, still hesitant.

'Tell me.'

The other man took a breath. 'It was not me that betrayed you,' he said.

Ben said nothing. He wanted to believe him, unsure if he should.

'As God is my witness I did not betray you. You must believe me.'

'Then I am glad,' Ben replied. He met his friend's gaze briefly, saw the pain in his eyes and looked away. How had they come to this? he wondered. Such mistrust, such sorrow. The narrow gate was so difficult to find, the demands of faith a hard burden to bear. For both of them. For a moment, he wondered if such sacrifice was worth it, so much pain. But then he remembered the darkness after Cecily's death, the godless Hell he had inhabited, and knew that his faith was everything. Without it he was damned.

The two men stood silent, neither knowing what else to say. He was moved by his friend's assertion, relieved that the love remained after all, but the breach between them was still impassable, a void they could no longer reach across.

At last Richard spoke. 'I will wait to hear from Alice.'

'Yes,' Ben replied, nodding. He could think of no other answer.

Richard waited, apparently expecting the other man to say more. Then, realising there was no more to be said, he dipped his head. 'I bid you good day.' Then he turned, and his shoes rang loud on the boards to the door.

Ben made no bow in return but stared after him, watching the door long after it had closed behind the retreating back.

HE ROSE BEFORE THE DAWN. The house was not yet astir, its creaks in the darkness still the groans of night-time, and beyond the curtains at the window, the stars were still lit above the city. He dressed hurriedly, hoping to slip out unseen before the servants were up to ask questions and report back to his mother. His stockinged feet were noiseless on the stairs, a silence learned in childhood, and beyond the front door he stopped, squatting to pull on his boots and to button up his doublet against the chill morning air.

Thieving Lane was already awake in the light of lanterns burning low, flickering at the doors of the houses. A young man stumbled past, labouring under the weight of a sack across his shoulders and, beyond him, a dog raised its hackles and barked. Above the roofs the sky began to lose its blackened depth, day creeping slowly in and extinguishing the stars.

He stepped out into the street and, striding with purpose, made his way along Thieving Lane toward Broad Sanctuary, where he headed for the church at St Margaret's. Ahead of him the Abbey loomed up darkly out of the dawn, and he turned his face away.

His footsteps slowed, reluctant, as he approached the church. He lifted his head and cast his eyes across the white towers high above him, remembering the bells ringing out for his marriage. A different lifetime it seemed, but the memory still raised a flush of shame. Finally he came to a halt and stood a moment with his hand on the worn, crumbling wood of the gate.

With a prayer on his lips he found the courage to lift the latch, and stepped through into the churchyard. His heart was racing but it was not from the exercise. It was many years since his feet had trodden this path towards the graves that lay behind the church: the wound had been fresher then, but though the years had dulled the edge a little the cut was still keen enough to hurt him.

Picking his way through the mounds in the half-light of early morning, he found the grave he was seeking easily, sheltered under the west wall, the wooden cross lopsided now and rotting with neglect. In a few more years, he thought, there would be no sign to show that they had ever been here, Cecily and the child that never lived to draw breath. They would exist only in his memory, no one else that would remember them, no one else who cared.

'Forgive me,' he whispered.

Painfully, he let himself down to kneel at the graveside, and the familiar sickness rose in his gut, the sense of unworthiness before her that no amount of prayer would ever ease. Leaning forward, he fought to straighten up the cross, hands scrabbling in the black earth at its foot, dirt getting caught under his fingernails, but he could not get it to stay upright, so in the end he left it at the tilt and sank back on his heels.

'I don't know what I'm doing here, Cess,' he murmured. 'I don't know why I came. You're not here, after all. You're up there with God, looking down on me, poor foolish sinner that I am. But I never got to say goodbye to you before. Not properly. And this time it's for good. I won't come back again.

'I'm leaving England. I made a promise to my father to go from here, to be safe. I pray we are all of us going, the whole congregation, to settle in Holland and build a new English Church. A Church of the true and the faithful as Christ commanded. I should have gone years ago when I could have taken you with me. You and little Ben. Others went, but I was too proud and too stubborn and I thought with God's help we could change things in England. I thought we could build a true Church here.' He shook his head at the folly of his youth. 'But I've grown wiser in the years since then, and I know now that things here will never change. You were right. Too many are against us. Too many walk in sin. I should have listened to you, my love. I should have understood.'

Pausing, he dragged a dandelion out of the earth on the edge of the grave, then settled the earth neatly again with his fingertips.

'We buried my father yesterday, just over there.' He lifted his gaze and gestured with his head towards the new dug grave, the cross still upright and sturdy. A solitary seagull stood on the mound, probing the fresh dirt for worms. 'He bid me leave these shores before he died and made me promise I would go. So I will go. All of us will go. And you'll be with me in my heart, Cecily, always, to remind me of my pride and my sin and my foolishness.'

He sniffed and wiped a savage palm across his cheek. He would not permit himself the luxury of tears: he did not deserve them. Then slowly he got to his feet, like an old man aged with grief and regret. For a moment he remained beside the grave. 'May God forgive me for what I did to you,' he whispered.

Then, without another backward glance, he turned and strode across the churchyard, head down, jaw clamped tight, fists clenched inside his cloak. The walk back to Thieving Lane was too short, his emotions still roiling when he reached the door, but he swallowed them down, put on his mask, then went inside to meet the rest of the day.

CHAPTER 25

JANUARY 1607

*U*nto the woman he said, I will greatly multiply they sorowe and thy conception. In sorow thou shalt bring forth children: and thy desire shall be to thy husband, and hee shall rule ouer thee. (Genesis 3:16)

It was a relief to leave London at last, to set his face towards the future and leave the past behind. It had been a sombre season at Thieving Lane, with no Christmastide celebrations, and his mother's every look had carried a reproach that he would soon be leaving. But she had Ellyn and Merton to take care of her, and God had willed a different road for him.

The weather had turned in the last few days, the hard, dry cold giving way to winter rain. The road was bogged and slippery, Bessie's hooves sliding in the mud, and the going was slow. He met few other travellers, most preferring to wait for less miserable conditions. He should have left earlier, he reflected, when the sun was still shining and the road still hard underfoot. Drawing his cloak tighter round him, he sat hunched in the saddle, and by the end of each day's travelling he was shrammed and shivering and eager for a warm hearth and dry bed.

He had stayed in London for Ellyn's confinement, which came hard on the heels of the funeral, giving his sister no time to rest or prepare herself. He had sat with Merton through the sleepless night of her labour, his mother and Alice and the midwife in the chamber above, their footsteps sounding busily overhead. Above the hollow roar of the fire they could just hear Ellyn's groans, his sister strong in her childbed as in everything else, and he wondered if Cecily had been as quiet or if she had screamed out in the pain of her slow death as he sometimes dreamed. The hours passed with agonising slowness.

The Abbey bell had not long tolled six when Alice finally appeared at the door. Both men swung towards her. Her hair had come loose from her cap and her face was flushed as she wiped her hands on an apron that was stained with blood. They could no longer hear Ellyn's cries.

'She is delivered?' Merton managed to ask.

Alice nodded.

'And?'

She hesitated.

'For the love of God!' Ben cried. 'Tell us, woman.'

'Ellyn is well ... but the child ... the boy ... did not live. I am sorry.'

'Thank you, Alice,' Merton said, lips tight, eyes flicking across the floor in front of him. 'May I go to her?'

She nodded and stepped aside to let him pass. They heard his heavy footfalls on the stairs, two steps at a time, then the murmur of his voice in the room upstairs. Alice let out a sigh.

'Come sit down,' Ben said. 'Have some wine.'

She stared at him blankly, eyes clouding with tiredness and tears. She looked as though she might collapse at any moment.

Gently, he took her hand and guided her to one of the chairs by the fire, then poured her some wine.

'Drink it,' he coaxed. 'It'll help.'

She managed a smile and sipped at the wine.

'How is she?'

She lifted her shoulders in a shrug. 'Weary,' she said. 'And sad.'

'But she is ... well?'

She looked up at him then, caught by the fear in his tone. 'The midwife says so, and that she can bear again.'

'God be praised.' To lose his little sister as he had lost Cecily would be a grief too great to bear.

They sat in silence a while until Merton's boots sounded on the stairs again, thudding down hard and quickly. The door swung open.

'Ben. She's asking for you.'

Surprised, he drained his wine and made his way up the stairs. At the door he paused: he had never attended a childbed before – he was uncertain of what he might see, if imagined memories would overwhelm him. He swallowed, knocked and pushed open the door.

The room was dark, the dancing glow from the hearth the only light, and the air was stifling; he felt the sweat break out along his back. His sister was propped up in bed and his mother sat in a chair close by, but her gaze was far away and weary. He could not tell what her thoughts might be. In the corner of the room, the midwife was busy clearing up bundles of blood-soaked linen and she made no pause in her work as he entered, as if she were unaware of his presence. He wondered what she had done with the body of the boy.

'Ben?' Ellyn's voice was weak, her face pale and unwholesome-looking, like uncooked dough. Strands of hair lay slick across her cheek. He hesitated, unsure for a moment until he mastered his fear and went to sit beside her on the bed. Reaching out, his fingers brushed the hair away from her face. She tossed her head back from his touch with surprising vigour, and in spite of himself he smiled.

'The boy ...' she breathed, nodding towards the midwife. 'He is unbaptised ... he was already dead when he ... and it was too late for the midwife to say the words ...' She clutched at his arm, small fingers digging into the muscle. 'Will he be saved, Ben? Will he be saved?'

Ben laid his hand over hers. 'Baptism is the symbol of God's grace only. A confirmation. Nothing more. So don't fret, Nell. The boy is safe with God now.'

'You'll see him buried? Properly?' she whispered.

'I'll see it done.'

She nodded, tearful and exhausted, overcome by the rigours of her labour and her grief, sinking back into the pillows, weariness overtaking her. He held her hand a while longer, watching as her breathing deepened, soft and regular, her face turned towards him. When he guessed that she was finally asleep he leaned across to kiss her forehead. She did not stir and gently, he let go of her hand, sliding the cool thin fingers from his own. Then he turned to his mother. She had not moved, her eyes watching the movements of the midwife without interest, expression blank. She was weary too, overcome by the trials of her family and no will left to fight against it. She seemed very old suddenly, and frail, and he regretted all the pain he had ever caused her. He should have left England long ago, he thought again, when he was young and Holland beckoned, offering him a different path. A safer path. It was not just Cecily who would have been spared.

He said, 'You should go and rest now too, Mother. It has been a long night.'

She turned to him as though surprised by his presence, taking a moment to come to herself. Then she nodded and gave him a small smile before she got up and slipped quietly from the room, the door closing noiselessly behind her. He watched her go, and all the sadness of so much loss threatened to rise inside him. He breathed deeply and closed his eyes a moment, a silent prayer for strength:

Be merciful unto me, O Lord: for I cry upon Thee continually.

When he opened his eyes again, the midwife was before him, standing with a bloodstained bundle in her hands. Without a word she held it out for him to take. He stood up, nerves and muscles tense with reluctance as she placed the tiny body in his arms. Tears prickled at the edges of his eyes, grief for his own lost son reawakening, the child he never saw.

The midwife said, 'May God have mercy upon you.'

Ben nodded, no voice to speak. Then he bowed his head, the precious child held tight in his arms, and allowed the tears to come. He did not notice the midwife leave.

HE ARRIVED at Scrooby Manor as the light was just beginning to leave the sky and the downpour was easing to a drizzle. He was exhausted and drenched. The last miles through the flooded lanes had taken much of his strength, the going slow and dangerous, the mare unwilling. At the manor house the curtains were drawn across the windows, but a bright warm light peeped through a chink between them and a lantern blazed on a hook by the door. It was a most welcome sight. He settled the horse in the stables, his presence unnoticed by the family within, then stumbled in through the door, his feet numb with cold and the log fire beckoning.

William Brewster turned from the pages he was reading at the fireside and smiled with pleasure. 'Welcome back, Benjamin.' He stood to embrace the younger man, in spite of the sodden cloak.

'Come by the fire, get warm.' He turned to his wife. 'Get him spiced wine – he is half-frozen to the core.'

Ben needed no second telling. He shrugged off his cloak and settled himself in the hard-backed chair at the hearth. Childish footsteps clattered along the passage and stopped abruptly at the threshold, and when the door opened, the children showed no signs of their haste, waiting politely to be invited in. Ben beckoned to them with a tilt of his head and they ran to him. He put his arms around them and they leaned in close against him, their little bodies warm against his.

Mistress Brewster came with the wine and shooed them away from him. 'Get away, he doesn't want you hanging off him the second he gets home. And look at your clothes ... soaking wet already ...'

They hung their heads beneath the scolding and retreated to the table to sit and watch from a distance. Ben took the wine their mother had brought. It was good and warming, a different spice from what he had become used to in London. More cinnamon, perhaps? His father would have known. And Merton too, he guessed.

Brewster took the chair across the hearth and sat down.

'We are sorry for your loss,' he said. 'It was good of you to write. And it is very good to see you safely returned to us.'

'It's very good to be here.'

'And the rest of your family is well?'

He hesitated, thinking not to burden Brewster with any more cares, but Brewster caught the indecision.

'Your sister?'

Ben nodded. 'She lost her child. It has been a sad season.'

'But she is recovered?'

'Yes,' he replied. But she had still been tearful and weak when he at last took his leave of her, and it had wrenched his heart to go.

He was uncertain if he would see her again, or if the farewell had been their last.

There was a silence. Mistress Brewster set the children to a task at the table, clearing away the papers and books in readiness for supper. They worked silently, listening to the adults talk around them.

'What is the news?' Ben asked. Their letters to him in London had risked no information, and he had no idea of the situation now. It had been many weeks since he left.

'The same as when you left us,' Brewster answered. 'Gainsborough is ever a wicked place, filled with drunkenness and bawdiness, and a clutch of base-born children. Scrooby is quieter but we have our share, and there is much unrest. Rents have got higher and food is short. Such conditions breed ungodliness.'

'And the community?'

Brewster allowed himself a small sigh. 'Things are growing worse for us. The new Archbishop ...' He shrugged. There was no need to explain the Archbishop's role: Ben knew it well enough. 'We are beset and hated on all sides. They watch us constantly and many have been fined for non-attendance. For some it's too heavy a burden and they've left us because of it. The fear of prison is ever present. It's a sorry realm when godly people are afraid to worship.'

'I'm sad to hear of it,' he said, though he had expected nothing different. It was a sinful world they lived in, vice and wickedness all around and the faithful punished for their love of God.

Brewster said, 'I think we can no longer go on as we are.'

Ben shifted forward in his chair. He was warmed now from the fire and the wine, his shirt steaming slightly in the heat. He had been tired before but Brewster's words sparked a new liveliness.

'Have you made plans?'

Brewster nodded. 'We have begun, but it's no small undertaking to find safe passage for so many.'

'God will find us a way,' he said, and smiled. His heart lightened, joy rippling through it – he could honour his promise to his father in good faith. 'Surely God will find us a way.'

Brewster answered the smile.

It was good to be home.

Behold, *I stand at the doore, and knocke: if any man heare my voyce, and open the doore, I will come in to him, and will sup with him, and he with me. To him that ouercommeth, will I graunt to sit with mee in my throne, euen as I also ouercame, and am set downe with my Father in his throne. Hee that hath an eare, let him heare what the Spirit saith vnto the Churches.*

(Revelation 3:20–22)

THOMSON WAYLAID him as Richard strolled across Broad Sanctuary on his way towards the Abbey. It was a glorious day, early spring teasing with a promise of the warmth to come, the last dregs of winter losing their hold on the season. Windblown wisps of cloud brushed across a turquoise sky, and the mid-morning sun blazed in all her glory, striking the puddles with a blinding light. Absorbed in the beauty of God's day, Richard failed to see Thomson approaching until it was too late.

'Doctor Clarke.' Thomson's greeting was effusive as he waddled his bulk across Richard's path, forcing him to stop. The pleasure of the morning slipped away and a hard-edged coldness took its place; the pretence at civility sickened him.

'Doctor Thomson.'

'You are on your way to the library?'

He nodded. There was no point in lying: he was carrying his books and papers.

'As am I.' Thomson smiled.

He stifled a sigh, all his will to work lost in an instant.

'We shall walk together.' Thomson stepped to one side then fell in beside him, and they made their way to the Abbey. Two harlots passed them arm in arm, giggling, and one of them blew a kiss their way.

'Friends of yours?' Richard couldn't help asking.

The older man laughed, apparently untroubled by the slur. 'Well, I doubt very much it was you they recognised.'

'I should think not.' He lifted his gaze to follow them as they passed, the painted faces, their breasts pushed up, ankles on display beneath the gaudy skirts. It should not have surprised him that they were familiar with Thomson – he had no illusions about the other man's character. But his brazenness never failed to appal him, that a man of the Church and a king's translator could have sunk so far into sin and be so unrepentant.

Thomson acknowledged the women with a wave of his hand and they moved on, satisfied.

'Not your type?' Thomson turned to Richard, still smiling. 'Ah yes, that's right. I remember. You are spoken for now, are you not? A prior claim on your virginity. You are to be congratulated. I didn't think you had it in you, to be honest.'

Richard stopped in his tracks, breathing hard. His fingers tightened their hold on the books he carried, and he was uncomfortably aware of the quickness of his heartbeat. The casual disparagement of his virtue by a man so wicked enraged him. 'You disgust me,' he spat, with all the venom he could muster, and all the force of the months of resentment. 'You are unfit for the task we do. Unfit to belong to the Church. God's Word is defiled in your mouth.'

Thomson stared, shocked, and for once at a loss for words.

'When I look at you,' Richard went on, the tide of his anger still flowing, 'I see all the corruptions of the Church that men like Ben Kemp despise, and yet you would sit in judgement on others for their way of faith. The wages of sin is death and I have yet to meet anyone more sinful than you.'

Thomson was still silent, tilting his head to one side and considering, as though pondering the truth of the other man's words.

'I have lost my appetite to work in the library,' Richard said. 'The company has spoilt it.' Then he turned on his heel and strode swiftly away, leaving Thomson to stare after him in surprise. Only when Westminster was far behind him did he slow his pace, anger waning finally and leaving in its place a tired and disappointed lethargy. He sat down on the grassy bank and watched the river flowing past him out to sea, bearing away the detritus of London. On the south bank and a little way upstream he could see the palace at Lambeth, home to the head of the Church for more than five hundred years. With a sigh he turned his face away from it, staring instead downriver, towards the freedom of the sea.

His outburst had probably been foolish and he suspected he would pay for it later, his loyalties in doubt once more, murmurs circulating. But Thomson's wickedness sickened him – it was not enough that a man should be loyal to the Church when his soul was so steeped in sin. And part of him was proud of himself for speaking up; Thomson's depravity had gone unchallenged for far too long.

He sat for a long while in the morning sun, still too riled and too tired to think about work. It was pleasant on the grass, the spring breeze still warm and the trees coming into leaf all around him, new and vivid green. The river flowed by unchanging, oblivious to the vicissitudes of men, and boats of all sizes and shapes rowed past carrying their cargos to the ships docked at Tilbury that would bear them east or south, to Europe or the Middle East, the Holy Land. Places Ben had been to. Richard followed the voyage in his mind, trying to imagine the weeks and months at sea, the bright and sacred land at the journey's end.

A bank of dark clouds edged towards him from across the river, chasing the sun, and he shivered in the sudden chill. Reluctantly, and scanning the sky for signs of coming rain, he gathered up his books and papers and got to his feet. Perhaps Thomson would have left the library by now, he thought. Perhaps he could do some work after all. With that thought in mind and his books tucked under one arm, he set off along the riverbank and retraced his steps towards the Abbey.

AT THE MEETING Richard sat as far away from Thomson as he could, but he was on the outside of all of the Company. In spite of his skill with Hebrew he knew his presence was barely tolerated, and without Andrewes he doubted the others would have admitted him at all. Not one man among them spoke to him; not one would meet his eye. He was silent, watching as the others settled themselves in readiness, chatting amongst themselves, and he remembered his delight when Bancroft had offered him the post at Canterbury, the short flicker of hope that his days on the outside were over. He should have stayed in Kent, he reflected, away from the corridors of power, away from Ben Kemp, and kept on with his simple life. But his pride in his Hebrew, his ambition, had led him from the narrow path; his own sin had brought him here, and all he prayed for now was forgiveness.

Then the day's work began and such regrets were forgotten, his passion for the words effacing all the hardship: all that mattered was the sacred Word of Scripture. He hoped he was still worthy for such work, that his sinful soul would not defile it.

Bishop Andrewes read out the line from the Bishops' Bible.

'And after the earthquake came fire, but the Lorde was not in the fire:

And after the fire, came a small still voice.'

No one spoke for a moment, each man considering the words. Then Thomson broke the silence. 'It is a good translation, but yet ...'

The others waited. In spite of Thomson's drunkenness, the others had respect for his skill with Hebrew. Thomson's weaknesses were borne with a good grace that still infuriated Richard, as though a man's intelligence could compensate for a sinful life. He recalled again what he had said to Thomson outside the Abbey a few days since; though anger bubbled at the recollection, he still felt a slight sense of pride in his response. For once, he had told the truth as he saw it and Thomson had had no answer to his words.

'*Qol* does not have to mean "*voice*,"' Thomson was saying now. 'It can also mean "*sound*," and if I recall correctly, we have also translated it as "*thunder*."'

'Where did we do so?' Overall asked.

'Exodus 19:16.'

There was a silence. Then Richard said, 'But *d'mamah* means "*still*" and *daqqah* means "*gentle*," so how can we then translate *qol* as "*thunder*"?'

Thomson opened his hands in a conciliatory gesture. 'I'm not saying that *voice* is wrong. I'm just pointing out that there are other readings that are possible.'

'It is true,' Andrewes said, 'that *qol* has many readings. But I think Doctor Clarke has the right of it. The context surely indicates it is a quiet sound. God speaks through the gentleness of His son, not through the terrors of earthquake and fire. It is the quiet call of the Gospel that calls men to do His will, against the thunder of the law.'

Richard was silent: the still, small voice was hard to hear sometimes − too still, too small, the call to his soul unclear. He had prayed and listened over and over in the past few months, begging for answers, but still no voice had come. Glancing round, he wondered if the other translators ever doubted as he did, if God's voice sometimes eluded them too. Then he thought of Ben, always so sure of God's wishes, and envied him his certainty.

The other men were nodding, satisfied with the Bishop's explanation. Andrewes's glance circled the table, inviting comment, and Richard signalled his agreement.

'So are we agreed, gentlemen, that we shall translate *qol* as "*voice*"?' When no one answered, the Bishop asked each man to read out in turn his own interpretation. Apart from Thomson's, all of them were similar, and barely different from the best of the Bibles that had gone before. Finally they married the best of all their contributions, and Doctor Layfield, who was scribe for the day, wrote down the line:

And after the earthquake, a fire, but the Lord was not in the fire: and after the fire, a still small voice.

They waited as he wrote, the quill scratching in the silent room, and when he was finished they went on again to the next line.

∼

AFTERWARDS HE LEFT QUICKLY, so the others would have no opportunity to shun him further. Wistfully, he recalled the sumptuous suppers in the deanery before Andrewes's elevation to Bishop, when he, Richard, was still hopeful for his future.

In a dream, he walked blindly and his feet automatically traced the path towards Thieving Lane, instinct choosing the well-known road. He was almost at the Kemps' before he realised where he was and he pulled up short, wheeling on the spot to walk back the way he had come. He had only gone a little way back up the lane when Alice appeared at his side, breathless from her haste to catch up with him. He slowed his steps, anger bending into pleasure at her presence. Thomson and his insults were almost forgotten.

'Doctor Clarke,' Alice breathed, her cheeks flushed from running. 'What brings you here?'

He stopped and turned to face her, drawing back into the lea of the house behind him, out of the road. A loaded cart trundled past, a sway-backed horse sweating with the weight of it. Alice moved with him, their bodies almost touching.

'I've told you before, Alice.' He smiled. 'You must call me Richard.'

She laughed and dropped her eyes. 'Forgive me. Richard. But you have been Doctor Clarke for such a long time ...'

'And old habits die hard?'

'They do indeed.'

He smiled and offered her his arm, and they strolled back along the lane towards the Abbey, their bodies close and touching with each step.

'So what brought you to Thieving Lane?' she asked again.

'I ...' He stopped, sensing the truth would sound idiotic but unable to think of a lie that sounded better. He said, 'I was in a dream. I had no thought for where I was going.'

'And yet you came to me,' she replied. 'I am flattered.'

He was silent but he was touched by her delight.

'And I'm very glad you did. I hoped to find you later at the Abbey – there is something I have to tell you.'

'What news?' They had reached Broad Sanctuary. Small groups of people stood in knots before the Abbey, talking, trading, arguing. They stopped close by the Abbey door and stood with the sun on their faces. After the long winter chill the heat felt like a luxury. The harlots were nowhere to be seen. 'What news do you have for me?'

He touched the tips of his fingers to hers and felt the frisson of her shiver. She was looking up at him, her brow furrowed with concentration, and if they had been somewhere less public he might have kissed her. Thomson's insult rankled again at the back of his thoughts. He should marry her here and now, he thought, and take Samantha to their marriage bed right away. But the Translation was not yet done and married life was sadly many weeks away.

'I have news of Ben,' she said.

He let go of her hand, stepped back, all desire for her consumed in a mix of dread and irritation. Damn Ben Kemp, he thought. Must he always ruin everything?

'What now?' he asked. 'What is it now?'

'He is leaving for Holland,' she murmured.

'God be praised.' Finally it was over. He was free at last and Ben would no more be in danger. He could have wept with relief. He lifted his eyes towards Heaven and the beginnings of a prayer of thanks touched his lips.

But Alice had not finished speaking. 'Not as a merchant with papers,' she whispered, looking around, making sure no one but Richard could hear her words. 'Not as his father wished it.' She squeezed his fingers, brought his gaze back to her face. 'The whole congregation is fleeing, Richard. The whole congregation.'

Relief slid into dismay. Why had Alice brought him this news? Why? 'How do you know this?' he asked, hoping that maybe she was mistaken, that perhaps it was not true.

She dropped her gaze away. 'I heard Ellyn and her husband talking. A message came.'

An unwelcome image of Alice at a doorway, eavesdropping, spilled across his thoughts. He suppressed a shudder.

'I didn't mean to listen in ... I just happened to be there, to overhear.'

'It was a letter from Ben?'

She nodded.

'And you're sure of it?'

'Yes. I'm sure. They plan to be gone by summer's end.'

He looked down at the small woman at his side, her face gazing up at him, serious and questioning, and wished she had not told him.

'I thought you would want to know,' she said.

He nodded. 'Yes. Thank you.' It was all he had ever wanted, for Ben to be far away. Seven years in Aleppo had seemed like a gift. But not like this. Not like this, illegally, as a criminal. Why did he not go when his father bid him, as a merchant with papers? Why must he choose to go now when it was forbidden?

'But they are not allowed to go,' Alice said. He saw the confusion in her eyes, and bewilderment.

He was silent, gaze resting in the distance beyond her shoulder, seeing nothing but the visions of his nightmare – Ben naked and in chains, his own begging for forgiveness and Hell at his back.

'He is your kinsman, Alice.' He forced the images to the corner of his mind, brought his attention back to her. 'And you have never been inside a gaol.' Perhaps she would be less eager if she knew the of a prison cell, if she truly knew what she was asking. But she was right, of course. They were not allowed to go. Ben's congregation had no case in law for fleeing England's shores. It was an act against their king, against the realm, against the Church. The Church that Richard served. He could not just turn away.

'I did not mean that you should ...' She trailed off, uncertain. 'I only meant ... can you not stop him from going? Make him see sense?'

He almost smiled at her innocence. 'Oh, Alice. Alice, my dear. You have no idea what you are asking, what ill news you have brought me.'

He swallowed down a rising sense of dread, the decision to be made. It was a test, he knew. A test of his faith. The love that Christ commanded for a brother, or obedience to God's Church. Indecision crippled him. He did not know which way to fall, which path would lead to his salvation, which path would lead to Hell. Panic thrilled inside him, his eternal soul at stake.

'I will pray for guidance,' he said. 'Then I will do as I must.'

She smiled, still uncertain, and a single cloud passed across the sun, slipping them into shadow. Without its heat the day turned cold. He shivered.

'We will speak again,' he said. 'Soon.'

She stepped away from him with another smile and a nod of farewell, and he watched her quick, short stride back the way they had come until her narrow form disappeared out of sight. Then he turned and made his way towards St Margaret's, where he hoped to find peace to pray. There, on his knees, and the world around him forgotten, he pleaded with God for an answer.

I worship Thee and humble myself under Thy mighty hand. Have mercy upon me, O Lord, and bring me out of my trouble. Lighten my eyes that I walk not in darkness, wretched sinner that I am.

I have lost my way, O Lord, and I know not which way to turn. All my certainties I have come to doubt.

I only want to serve you, Lord. Show me the way, and teach me the path. Lead me forth in Thy truth and teach me, for Thou art the God of my salvation.

Thou knowest my foolishness and my weakness. Thou knowest too my love for Thee, my love for Ben. But what must I do to serve Thee? I am so afraid to fail Thee, Lord, afraid that in my foolishness I will mistake the path, and fall from Thee. I am just a poor sinner, and I cannot find the way. Thy Church demands a betrayal but my heart rebels against it.

Why have You given me this burden? Why have You given me this choice? Help me, Lord, I beg of You. Grant me strength and wisdom to take the path of righteousness ...

He prayed for hours, weeping, baring his soul before Christ, begging for some understanding, for a sign to guide him. Finally, when the bright coloured glass of the windows began to darken with the failing day and lose its lustre, he climbed once again to his feet, stumbling, his knees grown stiff from kneeling. He felt old and weary, and the prayer had brought him no joy. Candles had been lighted along the nave and on the altar, flames bobbing lightly in the draught as though they were dancing in rhythm. He shivered, noticing the cold with surprise. Then, with a last glance towards the darkening image of Christ in his Passion with the spear tip close to his side, the colours of the glass dull and greying, he turned from his prayers and went out into the bustle of the Westminster evening.

CHAPTER 27

SUMMER 1607

*A*nd the Lord spake vnto Moses, Goe vnto Pharaoh, and say vnto him; Thus sayeth the Lord, Let my people goe, that they may serue me.

(*Exodus* 8:1)

'WE HAVE FOUND a ship that will take us,' Brewster said. At Scrooby Manor they were sitting at the table in the hall, the women clearing up the supper around them. With Brewster's words they stopped their work and turned their attention towards him. The silence weighed heavy: this was news they had waited a long time to hear. Mistress Clyfton twisted the cloth between her hands but she was not the only one who was afraid. It was a terrible risk for all of them, the greatest test of their faith they had faced.

'God be praised,' Mistress Brewster breathed, reaching a hand to steady Mistress Clyfton's writhing fingers. The other woman jumped, startled by the touch, and Ben heard her sharp intake of breath behind him.

'What ship?' His voice sounded loud in the hush.

'It belongs to a cousin to one of the brethren at Gainsborough. He is captain of his own ship. I am told he plies the route to Holland often and knows the waters well.'

'You've met him?' Mistress Brewster still held Mistress Clyfton's hand, keeping her steady.

'Aye. Briefly.'

'Can we trust him?' Ben asked.

Brewster was a shrewd judge of character: years spent in the turbulent world of politics in London and his post as a bailiff had sharpened his judgement and made it keen. He tilted his head, considering before he spoke. 'He seemed to me like a man who might be trusted for the right price.'

'Then we must pray that no one offers him a better one,' Ben replied. He kept his tone light but the fear behind it was real enough. The next few weeks would be dangerous, their every movement risky. It would take only one man to suspect them and they would be lost.

Brewster gave a wry smile. 'Indeed we must.'

Silence fell, all thoughts on the dangers that lay ahead of them. He thought of Ellyn and his mother, tempted to ride south to say farewell. But he dare not take the risk. He would send a message.

'Where will we go?' he asked.

They had talked of it often, Ben and Brewster, and the younger William and Richard Clyfton, running through the possibilities, counting the Englishmen already there, the Dutchmen who might give them aid, trying to decide who best to turn to first. It was no small thing to shift a whole community to a foreign land, to house and feed and provide for so many, and they would need help to begin.

The women resumed their toil in silence, the hush interrupted only by the clatter of pots and water splashing. Love and Mary were summoned to help. Jonathan remained at the table with the men. He was the same age Ben's son would have been had he lived: he was almost a man. Ben turned the cup of ale between his fingers on the table and tried not to think of it.

'To Amsterdam,' Brewster answered. 'We can join with Johnson's Ancient Church. They will give us succour and help us find our way.' He turned to Ben. 'You have friends there too. Will they help us?'

He nodded, and left off his turning of the cup. 'It was many years ago. But they were godly people and I have no doubt they would aid us.' Greta, he thought, and wondered if he would see her again.

'How will we go?' Jonathan asked. 'How will so many travel to a harbour unnoticed?'

'We will travel to the coast in several groups and meet at the place during darkness. The where and the when have yet to be decided and we will have to trust to our captain for that. But with God's grace we will be gone by summer's end.'

'So soon?' Mistress Clyfton had returned to the table, the same cloth still wringing in her hands.

'We will leave in fair weather,' her husband replied. 'And the crossing will be smoother for it.'

Ben looked up. He had made the crossing more than once and knew the season was no guarantee against rough seas, but he kept his silence.

'There is much to do before then,' Brewster continued, 'and we must begin to make ourselves ready.'

'Then the others must be told.'

'At the meeting tomorrow I will give out the news.'

One of the candles on the table guttered and died with a flicker. Ben turned his eyes towards it and watched the thin twist of smoke as it rose from the stub and disappeared into the air above them.

~

AT THE MEETING there were many who were absent. In the light summer evenings the way was more dangerous, and for the farmers among them there was work to be done while the light lasted. But enough had come that the word could be passed to the others, and at the appointed time Brewster began the worship with a prayer.

Ben lowered his head to listen, his soul growing light with God's tenderness. The room seemed filled with His presence, a warmth and joy that suffused him, a growing completeness within him as the words touched him with their call to God.

Brewster finished the prayer and moved on to a passage from the Holy Scripture.

'*Therefore I say unto you,*' Brewster read, '*be not careful for your life, what ye shall eat, or what ye shall drink: nor yet for your body, what ye shall put on. Is not the life more worth than meat? and the body than raiment?*'

Ben raised his head and cast his eyes across the hall, saw the worshippers all about him standing rapt, held in the palm of God's hand. He knew each of them, their struggles and fears, the hardships of their daily lives and all of it forgotten in their devotion to God. They came from all walks of life – servants and artisans, tenant farmers and labourers, merchants, drapers, blacksmiths. They were his family now, a community of brothers and sisters in God; he trusted each and every one of them.

One of the girls caught his glance and smiled shyly: the blacksmith's daughter, lately become a woman. He half smiled in return then slid his eyes away – she was young enough to be his daughter. But she would grow to womanhood in safety now, and her life would not be blighted by fear and danger.

'*Behold the fowls of the heaven: for they sow not, neither reap, nor carry into the barns, yet your heavenly Father feedeth them. Are ye not much better then they?*

'*Learn how the lilies of the field do grow: they are not wearied, neither spin:*

'*Yet I say unto you, that even Solomon in all his glory was not arrayed like one of these.*

'*Wherefore if God so clothe the grass of the field which is today, and tomorrow is cast into the oven, shall he not do much more unto you, O ye of little faith?*

'*Therefore take no thought, saying, What shall we eat? or what shall we drink? or wherewith shall we be clothed?*

'*For your heavenly Father knoweth that ye have need of all these things.*

'*But seek ye first the kingdom of God, and his righteousness, and all these things shall be ministered unto you.*'

In Holland they would be free. God would care for them on the journey as he had cared for the Israelites on their search for the Promised Land. They would face adversity and danger, but they had one another and their faith was strong, their lives dedicated to Christ. They would trust themselves to God and He would be their strength and shield.

After worship was finished Brewster addressed them again. 'We have found a ship,' he said.

The effect was immediate. Everyone began to talk at once, expressions ranging from delighted to eager to scared. Ben stood on the outside and watched, guessing that some there that night would prove too fearful to leave, the terror of uncertainty greater than their faith. In his prayers he would ask God to lend them strength in their weakness. The blacksmith's daughter sought him out again with her eyes – he could see the excitement and the fear, cheeks flushed at the prospect of a new life, a new beginning in a promised land where they would be free. The voices died away as Brewster lifted a hand to call for quiet.

'We have found a ship that will take us to Amsterdam before the summer's end,' he said. 'Do nothing yet, but pass the word to the others to prepare themselves. I will speak with each of you in the coming days to make our plans.'

'What is the ship?' someone asked.

'An experienced man,' Brewster answered. 'A cousin to one of the brethren at Gainsborough.'

'Can we trust him?' another man asked. The same question Ben had asked, the question all of them feared most.

'We are in God's hands.'

The hubbub began again, doubts voiced amid the excitement. A woman big with her first child began to wail. 'How will I go? I cannot, I cannot, not now, not till after, the danger is too great ...'

Brewster threw a glance to his wife, who went to the woman with a reassuring hand on her arm, a soothing voice. The wailing quieted to sobs but her cries had kindled the fears in the others.

'It is too soon,' another man said, one of the tenant farmers in their midst. 'How can we sell off our livestock in time without notice? How will we live unless we do?'

Brewster raised his hands again, appealing once more for calm.

'Have faith,' he said softly. 'Take heed of the Scripture and God will provide for us. God will provide and protect us.' He took a deep breath, but his words had served to reassure and quiet them. 'But for now,' he went on, 'the hour is late and it is time we sought our beds. Go with God, all of you, and we will talk again soon. Pass the word to our brothers.'

In small groups the worshippers drifted out of the hall and into the dying moments of the twilight. Ben followed them into the yard and stood beyond the reach of the torches to watch the stars slowly light up the heavens. One by one they glimmered through the fabric of the darkening sky: the same stars that Christ had looked upon, unchanging, constant.

It was a wondrous sight. Joy in God's creation filled him, the blessed ecstasy of the love of Christ, a oneness with God he would willingly die for.

The soft voices of the others drifted back to him in snatches as they turned along the lane towards the village. He waited till the last voice faded into silence before he turned back inside the welcoming light of the hall.

Soon they would be free.

CHAPTER 28

SUMMER 1607

Y*ea mine owne familiar friend, in whom I trusted, which did eate of my bread, hath lifted vp his heele against me.*
(*Psalms* 41:9)

LATE IN THE afternoon when the promise of summer had reverted once more to spring and a cold wind whistled across Broad Sanctuary, Richard made his way to find Lancelot Andrewes at the palace at Whitehall. He walked slowly, with trepidation, and his knees were sore from the hours he had spent on them. But no sign had come to him, no word from God to help him, and he had stumbled to his feet in the end just as torn inside.

At the palace his clerical garb gained him admittance. He barely knew the way to Andrewes's rooms: he had been there only once, and he had to ask a passing liveried servant for directions. The young man looked him up and down and sighed, but then led him back along the way he had just come. Richard looked about him as they walked, no longer fretting about finding his way.

Whitehall had been the residence of kings for centuries; fine artworks covered the walls, and cabinets held treasures from all parts of the globe. Everything here was fine, grand, kingly, and for the first time he truly understood the smallness of his role in England's life. He felt unworthy in his vicar's robes and he was acutely aware of the ink on his hands, like a schoolboy who had made a mess of his work.

Following his guide up a staircase, he came to a gallery that looked out over the tilt yard. Though it was empty now, it was easy to imagine the knights on fine horses, and ladies bejewelled and dazzling handing out their favours. The ceiling was of gold, and a huge portrait of Moses gazed down on them as they hurried along on their earthly business. This was the home of God's anointed king. No wonder Andrewes felt himself as humble, sinful, unworthy, when he moved among such reminders of God's magnificence every day.

Richard rotated his head, his neck stiff from looking up at all the wonders. Long ago he had aspired to reach these heights, to advance in the church like Andrewes, to be a bishop one day and welcome in these walls, loved here and respected. As a young man at Cambridge it had all seemed possible – he had possessed the skills and the ambition, his tutors had seen his promise. But his choice of friends had let him down. It was not only Ben's wife and child that had paid for Ben's faith.

They turned along another corridor. Two women in bright silks cut low across their bosoms hurried past them, giggling. He turned to watch them disappear and almost bumped into the servant, who had stopped before a door to knock. He stood back to let Richard approach. 'In there,' he said. 'That is where you'll find him.'

He took a deep breath, recalled his scattered thoughts to focus and stepped through the door. Inside was a north-facing chamber, small and ill-lit: no sun ever penetrated here. But a good fire blazed in the hearth and the room was pleasant. Fine tapestries hung on the walls, Turkey rugs covered the floor and Andrewes sat at a massive oak desk that was neatly strewn with books and papers. There was no ink on the Bishop's fingers and Richard felt slightly ashamed.

'Doctor Clarke.' The Bishop motioned to a chair by the desk, but the nerves of his errand made Richard too restless to sit so he stood beside it, one hand working round the warm timber of its back.

'I received your message,' Andrewes said, pouring Rhenish for them both. 'You said it was a matter of some importance?'

'Yes,' Richard agreed. He stepped forward to take the glass then stepped back to his place by the chair.

Andrewes's shrewd eyes levelled for a moment, considering. Then he said, 'What can I help you with?'

'I have spent many hours in prayer today, My Lord, asking for God's help,' he said. 'But He has chosen not to answer me, and so I have come to you.'

The Bishop gave a rueful smile. 'Over the years,' he said, 'I have found that when God seems not to answer my prayers that He usually has a good reason. Most often, I have realised, it is because I already know the answer, but it is an answer I do not want. So I keep praying in the hope that God will allow me to take an easier path.'

Richard nodded, recognising the truth of the words. It was exactly as Andrewes said.

'It is no easy thing to be a Christian, Doctor Clarke. The way is narrow and few there are that find it.' He put down his glass on the desk and made a steeple of his fingers before his lips, regarding his ith wise, clear eyes. 'May I venture to ask what is troubling you?'

He sighed. He had known the conversation could only go one way but still he was reluctant. The narrow gate, he reminded himself, is not easy to find. He lowered himself into the chair, watching the wine swish in the fragile glass in his hand, searching his heart one last time before it was too late.

'Doctor Clarke?'

'Ben Kemp, My Lord.' Lifting his eyes to meet the Bishop's, he met pity, and he looked away, embarrassed.

'You have information?' Andrewes asked.

He tilted his head in assent but said nothing.

The Bishop said, 'Come, Doctor Clarke, you have made your decision or you would not be here. So now you must tell me what it is you know.'

And so he came to it at last, the moment of betrayal – giving up Ben to prove his faith. He hoped he was passing the test, that serving God's Church in England demanded nothing less, and he could do no other. He swallowed, his mouth dry, heart racing.

'He is planning to leave England, My Lord,' he said, softly. 'The whole congregation at Scrooby is planning to leave for Holland by summer's end. They are searching for a ship that will take them.'

It was done. At last it was done, but he felt no relief, only a sadness unlike any he had ever known, a loss that felt like a part of him. He would have given anything but his soul to spare his friend. Weary with masked emotion, he sat back in the chair and drank off the sweet, strong wine. He had eaten nothing since morning and he felt his head go light. 'Would it not be a mercy just to let them go, My Lord,' he asked, 'and be free of them?'

Andrewes raised his eyebrows and gave an equivocal tilt of his head. 'That is not for us to decide. The law is the law.'

'Of course, My Lord,' he replied. 'I didn't mean to suggest otherwise.'

'I understand. And ...' The Bishop opened his hands, making circular gestures with his long white fingers. 'I can see the merit in what you say, but we are commanded to be obedient to our masters. The king is after all ordained by God. It is a teaching our dissident friends would do well to heed. For all their insistence on *sola Scriptura* they do seem to pick and choose which teachings to obey.'

'I have thought the same thing, My Lord.'

'And you have spent more time arguing the point than most I would guess.'

'Indeed.'

'So I can understand you would like to see him gone across the narrow sea. He has brought no little trouble to your door.'

'He was my friend.'

'And your diligence in serving him is to be commended. But sometimes we best serve our friends in ways that seem harsh. Like the discipline of a child to make a better man of him. Saint Augustine warns us that desire to please a friend can lead us into sin. After all, it was Adam's wish to make Eve happy that made him take the apple.' The long face crinkled into a smile. 'But I understand it is not easy to do.'

Richard's fingers worked around the stem of the wine glass gently. He still felt no sense of relief, still the same dread he had erred. Even here in the company of Andrewes, whose piety he had never doubted. He waited for the Bishop to continue.

'You had no choice but to tell me,' Andrewes said. 'The Separatists have set themselves apart from everything the king holds dear, and everything the English Church believes. They question the king's authority, the authority of the Church, and they encourage others to step outside the fold with their writings and their preaching. So how can we allow them to flaunt the law and get away with it? How can we let such things go unpunished?'

Andrewes paused and leaned forward, resting his forearms on the table, clasping his hands. The amethyst in his bishop's ring caught the light of the candle and glinted.

'The congregations must be broken up. It must be known that England will not tolerate nonconformity.' He sighed. 'Holland is not so very far away after all. We know from experience that exiled dissenters have a way of returning to our shores to preach their falsehoods, to spread their malcontent. And we also know that they use Dutch freedoms to publish their heresies and spread them to the people here in England. We cannot risk such things.'

Richard nodded again. His duty done, he wanted to be gone. The justifications he had heard before. He knew them to be true – they were the reasons that had brought him here – but he was too sad and tired to discuss them now.

'Master Kemp has chosen his own path, Doctor Clarke, and he knows the risks as well as any. You must not hold yourself responsible for his fate. You have done more for him than any man has a right to expect.'

He said nothing. The praise seemed hollow to him now and his skin felt tainted. Draining the last drops of his wine, he stood up to go. In the distance he heard the Abbey bell strike the hour, the chimes drifting on the wind in their direction.

'Supper time,' Andrewes said, rising from his chair with an alacrity that was always startling in a man of his age, moving briskly around the edge of the desk. 'Come, dine with me. I would welcome the company.'

Richard started to shake his head to demur but the Bishop refused to take no for an answer, laying a pale hand on Richard's arm. 'You may tell me your thoughts on the Second Book of Kings over another glass or two of Rhenish,' he insisted. 'And I believe there is trout.'

'As you wish, My Lord,' Richard acquiesced. Then, with an aching heart that craved the solitude of prayer, doubt still circling that he had made the right decision, he allowed the Bishop to steer him through a door by the fireplace that led to a dining chamber beyond.

CHAPTER 29

SUMMER 1607

*A*nd *Iacob vowed a vow, saying, If God will be with me, and
will keepe me in this way that I goe, and will giue me bread
to eate, and raiment to put on, so that I come againe to my fathers
house in peace: then shall the LORD be my God.*
(*Genesis* 28:20–21)

THE DAYS PASSED QUICKLY, the cycle of life unchanged as the
congregation prepared in secret for their journey. But it was harder
to set to the usual tasks of summer. Though they brought in the hay
as always, the vegetable garden was barely tended: there was no
pickling and preserving, no cheese- nor butter-making, no planning
for the months beyond summer's end. Each day took them closer to
their promised land, every moment loaded with God's promise of
deliverance. They had waited many years in the wilderness,
praying for the new Jerusalem in England, but God had set their
path a different way.

July turned to August and the children helped with the winter
oats, excused from their lessons, every hand needed for the harvest.

Ben relished the work, using to the full the body God gave him, muscles aching at the end of each day, a good sleep each night earned by his labour. But a part of him grieved, as he guessed all of them grieved, to leave their homes and all that was loved and familiar. Many had never even left the Midlands before, their lives bound by the village of their birth, and they were fearful of a strange land, strange customs, an unknown tongue. He had no fear of what was to come, Holland a familiar world to him, but he knew the pain of exile and the longing for England's shores that would never leave them.

'We will find our peace in God,' he told them. 'In the company of a true and faithful people, gathered in His name. We are coming home at last to be with God, free and safe, our exile almost done. Trust in the Lord, and He will be our strength and shield. Do not fear, but have faith and believe.'

All of them knew the truth of it but it was hard to keep faith, so much uncertainty ahead of them, so much unknown, and they asked him many questions about his time in Amsterdam: what sort of city was it? What sort of people? He reassured them as best as he could.

'The people are not so different from us, the same fears, the same dreams. And Holland is a godly place.' His memories of Amsterdam were mostly happy, Greta treading through his thoughts, and pleasure mingled with repentance for youthful sins. He had been so full of hope, his faith still new and untested, and Holland was a haven of freedom. He had never been inside a prison cell, never known the fear of torture. With the prideful self-belief of youth, it had seemed that everything was possible then, and though he had struggled often with the weakness of his lust he had known true joy also, God's love vibrating through him, the joy of longing and desire that was the ecstasy of faith.

Greta. He wondered if he would see her again, and if she

would still rouse the same sinful desires. She would be married now with children of her own, he guessed, and they would be similar in years to the age his son would have been, had he lived. He shook his head against the thought of it: such musings did no good.

As the summer drew on and the day drew nearer, details were arranged, dates and times and places. Some of their number backed away, the leap of faith too great to make, their trust in God too unsure. The blacksmith was one of them, and Ben saw the disappointment in his daughter's face as he, Ben, tried in vain to talk her father round.

'We have a good life here,' the blacksmith argued. 'God provides for us well.'

'You must have faith.'

'I can have faith here. In safety. Not for myself but for them ...' He lifted his chin towards the house, his wife and daughters.

'I will pray for you,' Ben told the girl as he left the forge for the final time. 'Have faith and do not give up hope.'

She gave him no answer, but only turned her eyes away.

THE BREWSTER FAMILY group was among the last to set out on a warm August morning. To all of them it seemed a good sign, God blessing their flight with the sun and an easy road. But it was still a hard way to leave, with most of their goods abandoned. Though some had managed to sell their chattels, doing so carried the risk of drawing attention, and Brewster had sold off little more than the livestock. They would face new hardships at their journey's end, reliant on others for aid.

Love cried as they left the manor house behind, aware of the gravity of the journey and all that she was leaving, but riding in front of Ben on the great black mare, safe between his arms, was a rare treat and a distraction from her tears. He made the journey an adventure, telling her for the first time about his voyage to the East, about the life in Amsterdam they would have. Then together they recalled the journey of the Hebrews out of Egypt and the hardships they endured before they reached the Promised Land.

'We are God's chosen people too, aren't we?' She turned her head to look up at him with serious eyes. 'On the way to a promised land.'

He smiled down at her. 'That's right,' he replied. 'Holland is our promised land. And in Holland we will be free.'

Mistress Brewster, riding alongside, caught the words and smiled.

It was a long journey, and their hope and trust in the Lord was tempered by fear of what was to come. They travelled slowly, making the best of the long summer days as their road snaked across the flat green pastures of the Midlands, ancient hedgerows of hawthorn and holly alongside the lanes, and wild blackberries ripe and tempting. Love was enthralled as Ben rode Bessie close to the hedge so she could reach out from her place in front of him and pick the berries as they passed, plucking the best ones that had always been out of reach before.

'Like manna from Heaven,' she told him. 'God providing for us on our journey.'

But mostly they rode in silence, thoughts turning on their danger, and their loss. For all of them grieved to go, to leave everything they had ever known and loved. Holland was a foreign place, with a different language, different customs, and they, arriving there with nothing but their faith to sustain them. Truly, being Christian was no easy thing. But they had done as Christ commanded: they had forsaken themselves and taken up their crosses to follow Him. They were in His hands and, if they trusted, He would provide.

As they rode, Ben thought often of his sister and her child, the children yet to come that he would never see. He thanked God she had found some happiness – a good husband, a comfortable life. She was well provided for and he had no need for worry on her account. He was glad he had helped her to marry even though he lost his inheritance because of it. Resentment had been pointless, he knew now, merely sinful yearning after earthly wealth that meant nothing beside the riches of God.

Love spotted more berries and he drew the mare close to the hedgerow. He held the girl's waist as she leaned across to pick out the best and the juiciest, offering some to him with a smile. He took a couple, and blinked at the tartness as they burst in his mouth. They would have been better, he thought, in a pie with some sugar.

'Do they have blackberries in Holland?' the girl asked.

'Yes, they do. And mulberries too.'

'I'm glad,' she murmured, her mouth still full, her fingers stained purple by the juice. 'They're very good. I'd be sad if we couldn't have them any more.'

He smiled and they rode on, catching up easily to the others.

THEY SOLD their horses in Lincoln. Ben got a good price for Bessie but he was sad to see her go. She had served him well and faithfully, and he hoped she would be well cared for. The rest of the way they made on foot, slower and more wearisome, their meagre baggage weighing heavy on their shoulders. On the second day of walking they spotted the great church tower at Boston beckoning them in across the flat country of the Fens. It would still be many hours before they reached it but they took it as a sign, a symbol of the new church they would build in Amsterdam, the new Jerusalem.

They arrived in the late afternoon, weary and footsore. The children were silent and unsmiling; the adventure had become an ordeal. The adults were in a sombre mood too – the moment of reckoning was almost upon them, the most dangerous hours of their journey just ahead. They took supper in a roadside inn a little way outside the town, a simple meal of bread and cheese, cold pork and ale, but Ben had no appetite, his belly tight with nerves, and he picked at the food without interest. It was the last time he would break bread on England's shores, and the knowledge saddened him. They would never now forge a true Church in England; the realm was lost.

His thoughts turned to Richard, serving masters such as Bancroft and Andrewes, his love of God subsumed by worldly ends, the truth eclipsed by his ambition, his desire for earthly gains. Their argument was over now and their friendship all but dead, but it gladdened him to know that Richard had not betrayed him after all.

After supper they rested, waiting for the beginnings of the twilight that would cloak the last miles of their journey. The time passed cruelly slowly, and though Ben tried to pray, his mind wandered often. His heart was heavy with nerves, and the enforced inactivity was difficult to bear.

Finally, slowly, outside the tiny latticed window the light began to fade. Brewster settled the bill with the landlord and the little party made its way out to the street, bending their footsteps towards the shore for the last stage of their overland journey. Ben held Love's hand as they walked, shortening his stride to keep pace with her quick, determined steps.

Others had reached the beach before them, sitting silently on the windblown grass at its border, the water lapping gently further out, grey and foreboding, a metallic sheen across its surface that reflected the dying sun. Few words were spoken. Even Love's surprise at the sight of the sea was silently expressed: a delighted smile as she turned to Ben, her little hand quivering in his. They walked down to the water together to see the waves' ebb and flow, and they watched in silence for a long while, marvelling together at the wonder of God's creation. Then as the twilight dwindled, stars lighting up overhead in a darkening sky, they left the water's edge and went to sit and wait with the others higher up on the beach. Love curled her small body up against his, fighting the desire for sleep.

Through the passing hours of the night they waited, and at their backs the flat marshlands of the Wash stretched towards the town. Bit by bit the last small groups of the faithful picked their careful way along the narrow path that cut across the marshes to the shore.

A new moon, a slivered crescent, hung behind the travelling clouds and reflected now and then on the water before them, shimmering silver. The women and children huddled on the shingle with their bags by their feet, all their worldly belongings in bundles they could shoulder. The breeze was cold enough to chill despite the season, and some of the children, growing weary, were beginning to cry. Their mothers tried to comfort them with prayers and murmured songs, hiding their own fear and weariness.

There was no sign yet of the ship, nor the small boats that would ferry them to its safety, and Ben could sense the growing impatience, the fear the waiting engendered. He lifted his eyes to watch the moon, the telltale sign of the passing hours. The night was growing old; the boats should have come by now. Standing up, he lifted the sleepy child back to her mother. The heavy sense of apprehension that had been chafing hardened into something more urgent. If they did not go soon it would be too late. He went to stand with Brewster at the water's edge, torch held aloft signalling fruitlessly out to sea. Along the horizon, a narrow band of sky seemed to pale and the stars above began to lose their vivid lustre. It was almost dawn and they needed to be gone.

'Perhaps they have been delayed,' a voice said in the darkness. 'Perhaps a storm turned them from their course.'

'It is possible,' someone else replied.

Ben's eyes flicked to Brewster's face, gaunt above the beard, shadowed and grim in the flames of the torch. Whatever the cause, they would be not be leaving tonight. 'We cannot risk staying any longer,' he said. 'We must get everyone off the beach before daylight.'

The older man nodded his agreement. Ben turned and scanned the groups of silent shadows that were huddled, waiting.

'And we must be quick.'

He set off across the shingle, head down, urgency driving his movements. It would take time for so many to wend their way back from the shore, to find the narrow path, and by then the town would be awake. He dared not let himself think beyond the need to clear the beach.

A sudden cry from one of the women, a shriek of panic, startled him from his thoughts, and he lifted his head to look. A row of torches bobbed in floating columns above the flatlands, moving towards them across the marsh, and the raised voices of men called to one another over the rush of surf against the shingle.

'We are betrayed!' someone shouted.

Richard, he thought, instinctively. But how? Then there was no time to think anything more. The women turned en masse and backed down the beach towards the water, clasping their children to them, crying out in fear. A few of the younger men darted away into the darkness, hoping to find a hidden way across the wetlands towards the relative safety of the town. But the most part remained, trapped between the Bishop's men and the sea. Ben watched them advance, torches flaring brighter as the men closed in, no way to get past them. But he would not have run even if he could in spite of his fear: they were God's people, all of them, and they would stand together.

The torches reached the beach, too many to count, flames dancing wildly in the wind that had begun to blow from the sea. The men that bore them remained in flickering shadow as the congregation waited. Behind him Ben heard a child start to cry.

A single commanding voice boomed along the shore. 'There will be no ship for you tonight, you godless bunch of traitors. You are under arrest on the Bishop of Lincoln's orders.'

One of the women wailed.

'And you had better come quietly or so much the worse for you!'

The men began to advance towards them. There was nowhere for them to run. A scuffle broke out as one of the men fought back against the rough hand that tried to waylay him. His wife ran to help, struggling to drag the Bishop's man from her husband, pulling at his arm, begging. 'For the love of God!'

A backhand across her face sent her spinning to the beach. A scream was raised, her child crouching over her. 'Mama! Mama!' Screaming louder as a brutal hand yanked the boy from his mother and thrust him away across the pebbles.

Heat flaring through him at such violence, Ben sprinted across the shingle.

'He is just a child!'

The man was bent over the woman now, rough hands searching through her clothes for hidden money. She was crying out and struggling to break free, a hand stretched out towards her boy, who stood watching his mother's violation in helpless fear. Ben shoved the man away with all the strength of his rage.

The man sprawled across the pebbles on his back, still spitting hatred.

'Child! Woman! You're all the same. Godless traitors, a threat to the king.'

The child ran to his mother, who held him in her arms, sobbing.

Ben stood over the Bishop's man, fists clenched, forcing down the urge to hurt. 'Where is your pity?' he demanded.

The man sneered, and got to his feet. 'You people deserve no pity.'

A woman's shriek nearby turned them both to look. Some of the Bishop's men had begun to rifle the bags, tipping out the few precious belongings across the beach. A petticoat caught in the breeze and blew along the shore to the sound of laughter.

Ben launched into a run towards them, fury pounding in his blood, stumbling on the pebbles, the Bishop's man close behind him. Then another man came at him unseen from the side, bringing him down with force. Pain seared through his arm, and a fist smashed into his face over and over, grinding his head against the stones. He struggled for a moment, tried to protect his face with his hands, but the other man was stronger.

Before he passed out Ben tasted the blood in his mouth and felt it run warm across his face, and the last thought that coloured his mind before it turned dark was of Cecily, peaceful and waiting, a child in her arms and a smile of welcome.

HE WOKE on the floor of a prison cell, surrounded by the close warmth of others – men, women and children all packed together in a low airless room that already stank with fear and mess. He opened his eyes slowly, painfully, blinking them into focus in the gloom. Mistress Brewster was kneeling beside him.

'God be praised, you're alive.'

He nodded carefully, pain shifting in his head with the movement before he turned to spit the blood from his mouth into the straw behind him. Lifting tentative fingers to his face, he found clotting blood, a swollen nose and a right eye that was too tender to touch. Wincing, he lowered his hand and tried to sit up, but the pain in his head was too great to lift it from the balled-up cloak someone had placed as a pillow, and he sank back, exhausted by the effort.

'Rest now, Ben,' Mistress Brewster murmured. 'There is nothing else you can do. And we will need all our strength for whatever trials God has placed before us.'

'Where are we?' he managed to whisper.

'Don't speak now. You need to rest.'

He took a deep breath through his mouth, his nose broken and still clogged with blood. 'Where are we?' he said again. 'What prison is this?'

'Boston. We are still at Boston.'

'I'm thirsty.' His throat was parched and sore and the taste of dried blood was sickening. He needed to drink and he could think of nothing beyond that need. 'Thirsty,' he whispered.

William Brewster floated into view above him. 'He says he's thirsty,' his wife relayed.

'There is nothing to drink,' Brewster told him, squatting down and laying a strong hand on his shoulder. 'And we are all of us thirsty. But we have been praying and God in His mercy will deliver us. Rest now. You will need your strength.'

Ben closed his eyes and let himself drift back into the darkness.

CHAPTER 30

SUMMER 1607

G oe yee, enquire of the Lord for me, and for the people, and for all Iudah, concerning the wordes of this booke that is found: for great is the wrath of the Lord that is kindled against vs, because our fathers have not hearkened vnto the woordes of this booke, to doe according vnto all that which is written concerning vs.

(2 Kings 22:13)

RICHARD WORKED ALONE in the library on the last few chapters of the Second Book of Kings. Two or three more meetings to go and then his part in the Translation would be finished. He would return to Kent with his wife, a humble vicar once again, and his brief flirtation with politics and power would be over. Though he was grateful and honoured by his role – the words of Scripture in his hands for future generations – he regretted the price he had paid. And still, he was unsure if he had walked the righteous path. He would be glad to go and put this all behind him. Flexing his fingers in readiness, he picked up the quill and turned his eyes to the pages before him.

ng Josiah, finder of the forgotten book of the Law, reforming all things according to the Word and returning his lost people to their Father. Richard's fingers found the words in the Geneva translation that lay open on the desk.

For great is the wrath of the Lord that is kindled against us, because our fathers have not obeyed the words of this book, to do according unto all that which is written therein for us.

He read the words aloud, testing them for truth and rightness. Then again, silently. But it was not his own voice he heard in his head this time but Ben's, in a sudden memory of an argument from years before. He searched his mind to place it, sifting the memories until he found himself in the filthy straw on the floor of a cold cell at the Fleet, debating Scripture. The memory was vivid: the chill in the cell and their breath in puffs of vapour before them as they argued, the stench of fear that pervaded the prison, and the grimy blackness of Ben's skin and clothes. But all of it was forgotten in the fervour of their argument – the rightness of their faith at stake, the safety of their souls.

Ben had turned to this passage again and again, a proof of the primacy of the Word, the need for Scripture to be the centre of all worship, of all faith. Without the Word, he had said, there is nothing. All the rest is idolatry and God will take His punishment. Josiah was loved by God. The Scripture tells us so. His people were lost, they had forgotten the Word, and Josiah tried to save them by bringing them back to the Book. He tried to reform things, Ben had said, as the Puritans try to reform things now. The English Church is not ruled by the Word, he had said over and over, nor governed by Scripture: like the Judah of Josiah, it is ruled by the laws of men. And that is an abomination to God.

Richard sat back from the page, remembering. Ben's zeal was

clear in his mind, every word he had said perfectly recalled. He remembered too the heat in his own denial of what Ben claimed, his spirited defence of the Church. They had argued this passage many times, but for the life of him he could not recollect what he had said, what words he had used in response. He scoured the memory, baffled and searching, but his recollection gave him no answers, and the spirit of Ben's words rang in his head. His hand rested on the page, middle finger marking the verse while his mind lingered on the memory.

One of the candles flickered and went out, and he started, thoughts shifting back reluctantly to the library and the present world around him. But he could still hear Ben's voice in his head, and the words of Josiah.

For great is the wrath of the Lord that is kindled against us, because our fathers have not obeyed the words of this book.

A dull sense of dread trickled from his gut, a shadow of foreboding. He thought of Ben as he was now, an outlaw, a wanted man because of his faithfulness to the Word, his belief in the primacy of Scripture. And he thought of the English Church – the king, the bishops, Andrewes, Bancroft, all of them beholden to the laws of men. King Josiah had been a reformer and iconoclast, sweeping away superstition and impurity, restoring God's Law to his people. All these things Ben also sought to do. A pure Church, bereft of the man-made trappings of Rome, a true Church of the faithful. It was all here in the Scripture as Ben had said, clear as winter sunlight, and he was baffled why it had taken so long for him to understand.

He swallowed, sliding his hand away from the page and onto his lap.

'Dear God, what have I done?'

He was trembling, fear and regret sliding through him. The image of Ben from his dreams, manacled and naked, shuttered out all other thoughts. *May God forgive you,* the image spat, *because I never will.*

Richard shoved back the chair with a clatter and fell to his knees on the cold stone floor, hands clasped in supplication, whether to God or to Ben he could not have said. The prayers tumbled from his lips in rapid whispered murmurings.

'*Forgive me,*' he wept over and over. '*It was a test, O Lord, and I failed. Forgive me. I did not hear Your voice, crying out to me. Forgive me, wretched sinner that I am. Forgive me, Lord, Forgive me.*'

He was still on his knees when the door scraped open with a jolt, startling him from his prayers. Scrambling to his feet, he had time just to stand up and turn his face away as the servant's head appeared at the top of the stairs. Relieved it was only a servant after all, he kept his head averted, wiping the tears from his cheeks with his fingertips as the man worked silently around him to replace the candles that were spent. But his breath still came in sobs and so he moved away towards the bookshelf against the wall, fighting to calm himself and slow his breathing.

By the time the man had finished and gone, Richard had mastered his outward emotions, but inside him was desolation. He needed peace to pray. Slowly, with limbs that seemed to have lost their strength, he gathered up the papers and books and made his way down the steps, through the low wooden door and out into the cloister.

'Doctor Clarke!'

He had not gone far when he heard his name being called. Inwardly he cursed: he was in no mood to talk to anyone, his emotions raw and painful. He wanted to be alone to pray, aware-ness of his wretchedness and sin burning through him. But he stopped nonetheless and turned towards the voice that had hailed him. As he had thought, it was Lancelot Andrewes, striding towards him, smiling. Taking a deep breath and consciously composing his features, he braced himself for the meeting.

'A word, Doctor Clarke?' Andrewes said, gesturing towards the library. 'Somewhere less busy perhaps?' The cloister was indeed crowded, he noticed abruptly. Men and women and children from all walks of life, all chattering, or hurrying past. Briefly, he wondered where they had come from, where they were going.

'Of course.'

He let the Bishop lead the way back up the stairs. The room had grown cool with the late afternoon despite the warmth of the summer outside. The Bishop sat down and took a moment to make himself comfortable, arranging his robes, straightening his sleeves, before he clasped his white fingers neatly in front of him and observed the other man with searching eyes. Richard remained standing and waited, suspecting what was to come; he could feel the thrill of his heartbeat quickening with anticipation.

'I have news of Ben Kemp,' the Bishop began.

'Yes, My Lord?' He swallowed, wishing Andrewes would just come out with it, resentful at being made to wait.

'He has been arrested.'

He said nothing. The same image of Ben flickered at the corners of his thoughts and he fought to close his mind against it.

'The whole congregation was taken,' Andrewes said. 'Men, women, children. They were on the beach preparing to board a ship for Holland.'

He nodded, not trusting himself to speak. Andrewes was waiting, expecting him to ask for more of the details, but he didn't want to know: he could imagine it well enough, the early hope of freedom, then the fear and pain of disappointment, the rough treatment at the hands of the Bishop's men. It grieved him to know he had sentenced women and children to prison – he had thought of only Ben till now. He had been hoping all along, he realised, to hear that all of them had got away. The silence grew awkward. The Bishop was still observing him, assessing, waiting.

'What happened?' Richard forced himself to say.

'Once we knew they were planning to leave we tracked down their choice of captain. And in the end he proved to be a loyal subject.'

For the right price, Richard assumed. 'What will happen to them now?'

Andrewes inclined his head. 'They will be fined and released in dribs and drabs, the women and the children first. No doubt some of them will decide the risks are too great to continue such a life and we will welcome them back to the Church. The others ...' He lifted his palms in a gesture of exasperation. 'The others will return to their old way of life until the same thing happens again. Others of their stripe have already fled: a number of their sister congregation at Gainsborough took flight a few weeks ago. I assume they would be in Holland by now.'

They should have just let all of them go, he thought. They would get there in the end, regardless, and all this would have been for nothing. So much hardship, so much suffering: what purpose did it serve? He should have just let them go.

There was a silence. The Bishop waited for him to speak, observing him, but he could find no words to say. The image of his dream still hung across his thoughts, and the same sense of remorse that had filled him then swelled inside him.

'May God forgive me,' he murmured.

'For what?' Andrewes asked.

'Ben was ... is ... my friend,' he replied. As Judas had been the friend of Jesus.

The Bishop said nothing, his long fingers straightening the silk cuffs of his sleeves, waiting. Richard swallowed down the rising tide of his emotions, and set the mask back in place. 'Which prison was he taken to?' he asked mechanically. 'So I might inform his family.'

Andrewes finished arranging his sleeves and looked up. 'He is in Lincoln gaol, awaiting trial with the others.'

'Thank you, My Lord.' He got up quickly and gathered his belongings. He had no inclination to stay longer. 'Thank you for letting me know.'

'You are very welcome. Good day, Doctor Clarke.'

Richard bowed. Then he turned and hurried from the library into the warm and busy cloister beyond the door.

HE PRAYED. In the tiny chapel of St Faith's he poured out his heart to God, oblivious of all around him. He had betrayed his friend and now that it was done, at last he understood. At last God spoke to him. '*Too late, O Lord*,' he wept. '*Too late*.'

In his error he had condemned Ben once more to punishment and prison. For what? Ben was no sinner. Misguided perhaps, the path of Separation unwise, but his faith was strong and his love for Christ was the light that gave him life. Why should he be condemned? For the first time he truly understood the darkness that could take a man's soul. He remembered Ben at the Fleet losing faith, the despair that the knowledge of his sin had begot. Ben would willingly have died to take back his actions, the desire and lust that had driven his pursuit of Cecily, anything to rid himself of the corruption in his soul.

And now Richard understood: his soul was just as tainted. He had wandered from the path, led by pride and his ambition. He had denied his love for his friend and the betrayal was a blackness inside of him, not the work of God after all but the work of Bancroft and Andrewes and the king. Worldly authorities with great power to wield and protect, the Devil working through them to shore up their earthly gains. It was not the Word of God they sought to defend against the Separatists, he realised, but the strength of the English Church. He had been deceived, his belief in the Church's goodness mistaken, his faith in its authority misplaced. He had betrayed the love of his friend for the promise of the Translation, his thirty pieces of silver.

He wept as he knelt, begging God's forgiveness, his heart filled with repentance.

I only sought to serve Thee, Lord, but I lost my way. I could not hear Thy voice, I could not find Thy path. I was blinded by the work of the Translation, seeking worldly recognition for my skill, approval of my loyalty. I believed in the Church, O Lord, and I did not see the truth. I did not love as Thou commanded. Take pity on a wretched sinner, Lord. Forgive me, Lord, forgive me ...

He could not have said how long he stayed on his knees, but his tears had dried out and his voice was hoarse with prayer by the time he heaved himself back onto his feet and stumbled out of the chapel.

He was dreading telling Ellyn but what choice did he have? It would be some kind of atonement, the beginnings of his redemption. A flush of nerves burned through him at the thought of it and he walked with dragging feet. Outside, the afternoon had begun to cool, soft clouds drifting in across the face of the sun as he wound his way from the busy precincts of the Abbey towards the quieter lanes near the Merton house.

At the door of the house he stopped, running his eyes across the face of it, tall brick and timber looming over him. It was tempting to walk away. He took a deep breath and lifted his fist to the door then lowered it again. Turning to look along the street, he saw two drunken workers staggering home. Then, finding his resolution, he lifted his hand again and banged hard on the door. Ellyn opened the door herself, clearly expecting someone different to be there. For a moment she stared, shocked, before her features slipped into hard hostility.

'You?' she demanded. 'What are you doing here?'

He dropped his gaze, avoiding the fury in hers. 'Forgive me, Ellyn,' he said. 'But I bring news of your brother.'

She drew in a deep breath, her hand still on the door, apparently in half a mind to slam it in his face. He tensed in preparation. Then she said, 'You had better come in.'

Turning, she led him up the narrow stairs to the same parlour he had been to before, the window overlooking the long-shadowed street. The early evening sun struggled in flashes through the cloud, lighting the windows of the house across the road in bursts of blinding brilliance. She stood at the window and did not offer him a seat. He had expected nothing else.

'What news?' she said.

He drew in a deep breath and slid a hand across his hair. 'Ben is in prison again.'

She said nothing, turning her head away, eyes flitting unseeing across the floor that lay between them. She seemed unsurprised to hear it.

'It isn't just Ben this time. The whole congregation was taken. They are awaiting trial in Lincoln.'

She lifted her face. 'They failed then.'

He nodded. 'They were arrested on the beach.'

'Bancroft told you this?'

'Bishop Andrewes.'

She turned away towards the window, watching the people in the street below. He waited, uncertain. He had not expected her to be silent: he had been braced for her fury, a barrage of accusation.

Now she stood with her back turned towards him and he could think of nothing more to say. A jug of wine stood on a tray on the sideboard and he wished she would offer it. Once he would have felt comfortable enough in her company to ask. It seemed a long time before she finally swung back to face him.

'Was it your doing? Did you betray him again?'

He swallowed, tears rising. 'Forgive me,' he whispered. 'I ...' For once his words failed him, the weight of his act too heavy to carry. He reached for a chair back to steady himself, and Ellyn stared.

'Forgive me,' he breathed again. 'Forgive me.'

'Sit,' she said, and fetched him some wine. He slid gratefully into the chair and held the cup between trembling hands. He could barely hold it still enough to drink and a few drops spilled on his chest. Absently, he wiped them away. Slowly he managed to steady himself, the wine warm inside him, his hands becoming still.

'I will go to him,' he said, searching to find her eyes. She was still staring, not understanding what she saw.

'Why? Why would you go to him now? To gloat?'

He let his eyes slide away unseeing to the floor. 'To atone,' he murmured. 'To beg for his forgiveness.'

She took a step away from him, turned, then turned back again to face him, hands clasped in agitation. 'I don't understand.'

'I was wrong, Ellyn,' he said simply, looking up. 'Forgive me.'

She took a deep breath, still watching him. He could see the uncertainty in her eyes, the desire to believe him against the knowledge of all he had believed. He couldn't blame her for hating him.

'But all this time ...'

'I did not know the truth.'

'All this time you have been Bancroft's creature – why now? What has made you change now?'

He hesitated, unsure how to explain himself. 'I never stopped loving him, Ellyn. Even as I gave him up to Andrewes, I loved him. But I believed in the Church, in its goodness, its rightness ...'

She nodded then tilted her chin, still challenging. 'So what changed?'

He shook his head – he was still unsure of his own transformation, the light the Scripture had lit for him. He gave her a small smile of apology. 'I cannot rightly say. Josiah, in the Book of Kings ... I was translating ... I heard it in Ben's voice ...' He trailed off, aware he was barely making sense. But it made no difference: God had shown him the way at last.

She observed him a while, still unsure, and he sipped at the wine, the cup still trembling gently in his fingers. Then she said, 'How will you go to Lincoln?' she asked. 'It is a long ride.'

He shrugged. He had not yet considered the practicalities – horses, provisions, money.

'But you are decided?'

'I must.'

She turned her face away, considering. Outside in the street a dog started barking and a man's voice was raised in anger. A string of curses drifted in the open window. She swung back to face him, her decision made.

'You can hire horses,' she told him. 'We will give you what you need: food for him, ale, clean linen. And money. If all of them are taken there is no one left on the outside to pay the fines.'

There was a moment's pause.

'Thank you,' he replied. 'At first light tomorrow I will go. Thank you.'

She gave him a half-smile that didn't reach her eyes, mistrust still behind them. He lowered his gaze away, ashamed. Then he bowed a quick farewell and hurried out into the street, back to St Margaret's to pray.

~

WITH MERTON'S money he hired a fresh horse each day and rode hard, sliding from the saddle every evening with sore legs and an aching back. He was getting too old for such a journey, his soft scholar's muscles unused to such rigours: Kent seemed an easy two-day jaunt in comparison. Now he was almost at his journey's end, a warm morning sun on his back and the massive towers of the cathedral guiding him into Lincoln. But it was early afternoon by the time he was allowed to see the Dean, and weariness and hunger had made him irritable.

The Dean was an elderly man with a harassed air who bid him sit in a room warmed by great shafts of sunlight that fell in blocks across the floor. In spite of his irritation, the beauty of it made Richard smile and the Dean responded in kind.

'It is lovely, isn't it?' the old man said. 'God's work in all its glory. Now what may I do for you, Doctor ...?'

'Clarke. Richard Clarke. At your service, sir.'

'What brings you to Lincoln, Doctor Clarke?'

'A sensitive errand, Mister Dean,' he replied, then hesitated, still uncertain how best to broach it, aware he needed to tread carefully. It was by no means certain the Dean would grant him access. He went on. 'I was informed by the Bishop of Chichester that you have in your gaol a number of Separatists. I understand they were brought here from Boston a few days since.'

The Dean's countenance hardened. 'The Bishop told you this himself?'

'Yes. I am a member of the First Westminster Company for the Translation of the Bible. I meet with the Bishop on a regular basis.'

'Indeed?' From the change in the old man's expression he was suitably impressed. 'One of the Bible translators, eh? And what is your interest in our Separatists?'

'Well,' he began. This was the most delicate part of the negotiation and he had rehearsed it carefully during the many hours of his journey. 'I have a particular interest in one man, a Master Benjamin Kemp. His family are well known to me: they are respectable people, merchants, and they have asked me to do what I can to secure his release, or at least to make his time in prison more comfortable.'

'The Bishop is aware of this?'

'The Bishop is well aware of my connection to this man, Dean. I believe that is why he told me of Kemp's imprisonment.' It was only half a lie and the Dean seemed to believe it.

'I see,' the old man said, leaning back against the high wooden back of the ornate chair, fingers smoothing the carved ends of the armrests. 'Well. I'm afraid there is no question of him being released at present. He must stand trial with the others. The Archbishop has, in his mercy, just this morning allowed some of the women and children to return to their homes. But the others ...' He lifted his hands, palms facing Richard. There was no need for him to finish the sentence.

'I understand. I thought as much. But may I be permitted to see him?'

The Dean observed his visitor carefully. 'Have you been inside a prison before, Doctor Clarke?'

'Many times. Too many times.' He smiled. 'I am well aware of what to expect.'

The Dean returned the smile. 'They pay a high price for their dissent.'

'Indeed.'

'Puritans and Papists alike.'

'May God forgive them,' Richard said.

The Dean nodded his agreement, then reached for a sheet of

paper. 'Bear with me a moment, Doctor Clarke, and I will prepare the necessary papers.'

'Thank you.' He sat back and waited. A cloud shifted across the window, dimming the shafts of sun, and the room fell at once into gloom. It took a moment for Richard's eyes to adjust, everything dark for a time, but the Dean made no pause in his writing. When he had finished he very neatly rolled the paper and pressed his seal to the join. Then he held it out for Richard to take.

'Thank you.'

'Tell me, Doctor Clarke,' the Dean said as Richard rose to leave. 'How did you come to be so close to the family of such a man?'

Richard took a step towards the door before he turned back to answer. 'We were at Cambridge together, he and I,' he said, 'and for many years we disagreed on almost everything. But it is not given to us to decide who we love ...'

The Dean smiled, eyes crinkling. 'Friendship is a precious gift from God. Use it wisely, Doctor Clarke.'

'I shall,' Richard promised him. Then he bowed and left the room.

He went to the market for provisions. Ellyn had given him clean linen and a Bible, but it was fresh food and drink that Ben would need most. He bought bread and cheese, cheaper here than in London, and summer fruit – blackberries and apricots. He also bought ale and, thus loaded, he made his way up the hill towards the great Norman castle that stood over the town.

He was sweating by the time he arrived though the afternoon had cooled, and his heart hammered as he stood before the high stone archway of the east gate. The prison itself held no fear for him. He had spent too many hours in the deprivations of the Fleet, and the horrors of its walls were well known. He doubted Lincoln gaol would be much different. But he was afraid of seeing Ben, the sin of his betrayal beyond him to atone for. Now at last he understood Ben's despair at Cecily's death, and the enormity of error that had caused it. For while God might forgive his penitent heart, it was harder to forgive himself. The image of Ben from his dream had haunted him on his journey, his own begging for forgiveness and the refusal on Ben's lips.

The papers from the Dean secured his entry, and he followed a guard through the gate. Walking in the shadow of the high walls, Richard shivered, his guts tightening with nerves. Then they were heading down a stairwell that never felt the warmth of day. Torches flickered now and then in sconces on the wall, and he walked carefully, afraid to miss his step on the steeply cut stone. A chill seeped up to meet them as they descended, and a familiar stench warned him when they had almost arrived. But still, when the door to the cell was thrust open the odour that billowed out almost brought him to his knees. It was worse than anything he had known at the Fleet and he had to fight to catch his breath. With an effort of will, he stepped inside, an instinctive hand to his face, but as he stood in the doorway and felt all eyes turn to observe him he was ashamed and lowered his hand.

It was a narrow cell, strewn with filthy straw, and there was no light save for one flickering torch in the passage outside the door. Even after the gloom of the stairs it took his eyes a moment to adjust, and then he realised that the cell was warm with a press of bodies. He sensed the tension ripple through them with his appearance, a deeper silence as they waited.

'My name is Richard Clarke,' he said. 'Is Ben Kemp here?'

'What do you want with him?' a young voice demanded.

'Hush, Jonathan,' an older man counselled. 'Keep your peace.'

Rising from his place against the far wall, he approached the visitor. His hair was white, his beard neat, even here. 'Master Kemp is over here,' he said, gesturing back towards where he had been sitting. 'But he is poorly.'

'Poorly?' He had never thought to find Ben ill. Unease pulsed through him as he stepped across the cell towards a form lying close beside the wall.

'Ben?' He knelt down in the dirty straw and Ben turned his face towards him, slowly, painfully. He was barely recognisable, a broken nose, a split lip, a swollen eye that was starting to fester, blood still matted in his hair. One arm was bandaged in a piece of blood-soiled linen that had been torn from a shirt or a petticoat. 'Dear God. What happened to you?'

'Richard?' Ben murmured. The good eye struggled to focus and even in the gloom it held the unnatural brightness of fever. 'I didn't expect to see you here. Have you come to gloat?'

'No.' He shook his head, blinking back tears. 'I've brought food, ale, linen, a Bible ... as I used to do ...' He turned his head to look up at the older man, still hovering at his shoulder. Reassured that Richard meant no harm to Ben, he took the bundle with a nod of thanks and retreated to leave them in peace.

'What happened?' Richard asked again. He was becoming accustomed to the stench: his heartbeat was beginning to slow and his breathing was less ragged. But fear and pity flooded through him, and the weight of his betrayal almost broke him.

'I didn't come quietly,' Ben said.

'As ever.' Richard forced a smile. But the horror of what he saw appalled him and the image from his dreams hovered in his mind once again, almost now in truth before him. He had brought his friend to this.

'Like old times,' Ben said.

'Almost.'

'Shall we argue Scripture?'

'Maybe next time.'

Ben's mouth twisted in an effort to smile. 'How is Ellyn? Sarah?'

'They are all well, Ben. Your mother too.'

'We were leaving. There was a ship ...' Ben said. 'We were betrayed ...' He tried to lift his head to see Richard better, grimacing with the effort, and Richard slid his eyes away from the scrutiny.

'I know,' he replied, bracing ready for the accusation. It was what he wanted, to be accused, to admit his guilt, to beg forgiveness. But Ben said nothing about it.

Instead he asked, 'How goes the great Translation?'

'It is almost done.'

'God's Word in your hands for generations to come. You are truly blessed.'

'I am humbled by it. And unworthy.'

Ben nodded, carefully, painfully, every movement measured and hard. He lifted his hand to search for Richard's and when he found it he grasped it, strength still in the bony fingers. Through the dim light, his gaze locked on to his friend's.

'Bury me with Cecily,' he breathed.

'What talk is this?'

'And no liturgy. No stinted prayers. A prayer that comes from the heart. Please?'

'You're not going to die. Not here. Not yet. I'll get you out and take you somewhere you can be cared for properly.' It was a miserable place to die, foetid and reeking, black with filth.

Ben shook his head and gasped with the pain. When he could speak again he said, 'It is too late for that. Too late. And this is where I belong. Among these godly people. I will die here among these good folk, in peace.'

'Ben ...' He blinked but could not stop the tears from coming.

'My burial ... promise me ...'

'I promise,' he said. 'I promise.'

'Thank you.' Ben's grasp on Richard's hand loosened. His gaze drifted away. 'It was good of you to come.'

'No ... I ...' The confession was almost on his lips, the need for Ben's forgiveness, but it was hard to find the words to tell his friend the truth. He groped in his mind, searching for some way to give voice to all he needed to say. 'Forgive me, Ben,' he murmured finally. 'I have done a terrible thing and I've not been a true friend to you. Forgive me. Forgive me for the wrongs I have done you. I love thee still, Ben, but I was led astray ... My pride, my ambition, made me blind to God's truth. I did not see. I did not understand and I took the wrong path. Forgive me. Forgive me.'

'We are all of us sinners,' Ben whispered. 'And only God may judge.'

'Thank you,' he breathed. 'Thank you.' But Ben's words did nothing to ease the pain in his soul. Then, swallowing his tears, 'You are confessed?'

'I am ready. I am afraid, but I am ready.'

'You have no cause to be afraid. If you are not saved then what hope is there for the rest of us?' He had never once doubted that Ben was one of the saved: the depth of his faith and his love for Christ was boundless.

Ben was murmuring. 'But in my pride and my anger, my desire ... it was my desire that killed her ... my lust ...'

'Hush, Ben.' Richard squeezed his hand. 'God's mercy is great to those that fear Him.'

But Ben's eyes had flickered shut as he slid back into the relief of semi-consciousness. Richard turned his face away, his fingers still in Ben's. He let the tears fall and remembered the boys they had been at Cambridge when all had been before them: the love, the hope, the passion for life.

'Forgive me, Ben,' he breathed again, over and over. 'Forgive me.'

He could not have said how long he wept there at his friend's side, their fingers still entwined, but Brewster's gentle hand on his shoulder startled him from his grief and he jumped, shocked to find there was someone other than the two of them.

'Do not mourn, son,' the older man said. 'He will soon be at peace.'

Richard nodded but he could not bring himself to move away until finally the rattle of keys at the door and the squeal of the door scraping open on the flagstones drew him back to himself at last. The visit was over. The final visit. There would be no more. He sniffed and dragged the back of a hand across his eyes to clear them. Then, leaning over his friend one final time, he kissed the bloodstained forehead.

'Forgive me, Ben,' he whispered again. 'And may God speed you to your rest.'

Then, with creaking knees, he got to his feet and followed the guard out of the cell, up the steps, and into the bright summer's day outside.

BIBLE QUOTATIONS

Translation it is that openeth the window, to let in the light; that breaketh the shell, that we may eat the kernel; that putteth aside the curtain, that we may look into the most Holy place; that removeth the cover of the well, that we may come by the water.

From the Translators' Preface to the Reader
King James Bible, 1611.

Chapter One

And then shall many be offended, and
shall betray one another, and shall hate
one another. (*Matthew 24:10*) KJV

The Lord is my strength and my shield.
Mine heart trusted in Him, and I was helped.
(*Psalms 28:6-8*) *Geneva Bible*

Chapter Two

> For it was not an enemie that reproached
> me, then I could haue borne it,
> neither was it hee that hated me, that
> did magnifie himselfe against me,
> then I would haue hid my selfe from
> him. But it was thou, a man, mine
> equal, my guide, and mine
> acquaintance.
> Wee tooke sweet counsell together, and
> walked vnto the house of God in
> companie. *(Psalms 55:12-14) KJV*

> Notwithstanding blessed are ye, if ye suffer for
> righteousness' sake. Yea, fear not their
> fear, neither be troubled. *(1 Peter 3:14)*
> *Geneva Bible*

Chapter Three

> A friend loueth at all times, and a brother
> is borne for aduersitie. *(Proverbs
> 17:17) KJV*

> Judge me O God, and defend my cause
> against unmerciful people: deliver me
> from the deceitful and wicked man.
> For Thou art the God of my strength:
> why hast Thou put me away? Why go
> I so mourning, when the enemy

oppresseth me? (*Psalms 43:1-3*)
Geneva Bible

Let your conversation be without
covetousness, and be content with
those things that ye have, for He hath
said, I will not fail thee, neither forsake
thee: (*Hebrews 13:4-6*) *Geneva Bible*

Chapter Four

Obey them that haue the rule ouer you,
and submit your selues: for they watch
for your soules, as they that must giue
account, that they may doe it with ioy,
and not with griefe: for that is
vnprofitable for you. (*Hebrews
13:17*) *KJV*

Chapter Five

Thinke not that I am come to send peace
on earth: I came not to send peace, but
a sword.
For I am come to set a man at variance
against his father, & the daughter
against her mother, and the daughter in
law against her mother in law. And a
mans foes shalbe they of his owne
household.
He that loueth father or mother more then
me, is not worthy of me: and he that

loueth sonne or daughter more then
me, is not worthy of me. And he that
taketh not his crosse, and followeth
after me, is not worthy of me.
(*Matthew* 10:34-38) *KJV*

A soft answer putteth away wrath: but
grievous words stir up anger. (*Proverbs*
15:1) *Geneva Bible*

And the woman said unto the serpent, We
may eat of the fruit of the trees in the
garden. But of the fruit of the tree
which is in the midst of the garden,
God hath said, Ye shall not eat of it,
neither shall ye touch it, lest ye die.
And the serpent said unto the woman,
Ye shall not surely die (*Genesis*
3:1-4) *KJV*

Chapter Six

Beloued, let vs loue one another; for loue
is of God: and euery one that loueth,
is borne of God and knoweth God.
Hee that loueth not, knoweth not
God: for God is loue. (1 *John*
4:7-8) *KJV*

Chapter Seven

Beware of false prophets which come to

you in sheepes clothing, but inwardly
they are rauening wolues.

Yee shall knowe them by their fruits: Doe
men gather grapes of thornes, or figges
of thistles?

Euen so, euery good tree bringeth forth
good fruit: but a corrupt tree bringeth
forth euill fruit.

A good tree cannot bring forth euil fruit,
neither can a corrupt tree bring forth
good fruit.

Euery tree that bringeth not forth good
fruit, is hewen downe, and cast into
the fire.

Wherefore by their fruits ye shall know
them. (*Matthew 7:15–20*) KJV

Make thee an Arke of Gopher-wood.
(*Genesis 6:14*) KJV

Chapter Eight

O Lord my God, if I haue done this; if
there be iniquitie in my hands:

If I haue rewarded euill vnto him that was
at peace with me: (yea I haue deliuered
him that without cause is mine
enemie.) Let the enemie persecute my
soule, and take it, yea let him tread
downe my life vpon the earth, and lay
mine honour in the dust. Selah.
(*Psalms 7:3-5*) KJV

Hear, O Israel, the Lord our God is Lord only. (*Deuteronomy 6:4*) *Geneva Bible*

Chapter Nine

And when they were come into the house, they saw the yong child with Mary his mother, and fell downe, and worshipped him: and when they had opened their treasures, they presented vnto him gifts, gold, and frankincense, and myrrhe. (*Matthew 2:11*) *KJV*

That he might make it unto himself a glorious Church, not having spot or wrinkle, or any such thing: but that it should be holy and without blame. (*Ephesians 5:27*) *Geneva Bible*

Chapter Ten

But they also haue erred through wine, and through strong drinke are out of the way: the priest and the prophet haue erred through strong drinke, they are swallowed vp of wine: they are out of the way through strong drinke, they erre in vision, they stumble in iudgement. (*Isaiah 28:7*) *KJV*

And when Boaz had eaten, and drunken, and cheared his heart, he went to lie

down at the end of the heap of corn, &
she came softly, and uncovered the
place of his feet, & lay down.

And at midnight the man was afraid and
caught hold: and le, a woman lay at
his feet.

Then he said, Who art thou? And she
answered, I am Ruth thine handmaid:
spread therefore the wing of thy
garment ouer thine handmaid: for thou
art the kinsman. (*Ruth* 3: 7- 9)

Chapter Eleven

Wiues, submit your selues vnto your own
husbands, as vnto the Lord.

For the husband is the head of the wife,
euen as Christ is the head of the
Church: and he is the sauiour of the
body. Therefore as the Church is
subiect vnto Christ, so let the wiues
bee to their owne husbands in euery
thing. (*Ephesians* 5:22-24) *KJV*

We are persecuted but not forsaken: cast
down, but we perish not. (2
Corinthians 4:9) *Geneva Bible*

Wherefore come out from among them,
and separate yourselves, saith the Lord.
(2 *Corinthians* 6:17) *Geneva Bible*

Chapter Twelve

Iudge not, and ye shall not bee iudged:
condemne not, and ye shall not be
condemned: forgiue, and ye shall be
forgiuen. (*Luke* 6:37) *KJV*

Blessed be the man that trusteth
in the Lord, and whose
hope the Lord is. (*Jeremiah* 17:7)
Geneva Bible

Chapter Thirteen

And now brethren, I commend you to
God, and to the word of his grace,
which is able to build you vp, and to
giue you an inheritance among all
them which are sanctified. (*Acts*
20:32) *KJV*

Chapter Fourteen

And the Lord said vnto him, Who hath
made mans mouth? or who maketh the
dumbe or deafe, or the seeing, or
þe blind? haue not I the Lord? Now
therefore goe, and I will be with thy
mouth, and teach thee what thou shalt
say. And he said, O my Lord, send, I
pray thee, by the hand of him whom
thou wilt send. (*Exodus* 4:11-13) *KJV*

And Jesus said unto him, If thou canst
believe it, all things are possible to him
that believeth.
(*Mark 9:23*) *Geneva Bible*

For whosoever asketh, receiveth:
and he that seeketh, findeth.
(*Matthew 7:8*) *Geneva Bible*

And Jesus said unto them, Because of your
unbelief: for verily I say unto you, if ye
have faith as much as is a grain of
mustardseed, ye shall say unto this
mountain, Remove hence to yonder
place, and it shall remove: and nothing
shall be impossible unto you.
(*Matthew 17:20*) *Geneva Bible*

Chapter Fifteen

The Lord is my light, and my saluation,
whome shal I feare? the Lord is the
strength of my life, of whom shall I be
afraid? When the wicked, euen mine
enemies and my foes came vpon me to
eat vp my flesh, they stumbled and fell.
(*Psalms 27:1-2*) *KJV*

'And when the people complained, it
displeased the Lord.' (*Numbers 11:1*)

Chapter Sixteen

> Heare, O Israel, the Lord our God is one
> Lord. And thou shalt loue the Lord thy
> God with all thine heart, and with all
> thy soule, and with all thy might. And
> these words which I command thee
> this day, shall bee in thine heart.
> (*Deuteronomy* 6:4-6) KJV

Chapter Seventeen

> How long wilt thou forget mee (O Lord)
> for euer? how long wilt thou hide thy
> face from me?
> How long shall I take counsel in my soule,
> hauing sorrow in my heart dayly? how
> long shall mine enemie be exalted ouer
> me? Consider and heare me, O Lord
> my God: lighten mine eyes, lest I sleep
> the sleepe of death. Least mine enimie
> say, I haue preuailed against him: and
> those that trouble mee, reioyce, when I
> am moued. (*Psalm* 13:1-4) KJV

> Now after that John was committed to
> prison, Jesus came into Galilee,
> preaching the Gospel of the kingdom
> of God. (*Mark* 1:14) *Geneva Bible*

And ye shall be hated of all men for my
Name: but he that endureth to the end,
he shall be saved. And when they
persecute you in this city, flee into
another: (*Matthew 10:22-23*) *Geneva
Bible*

Chapter Eighteen

Not forsaking the assembling of our selues
together, as the manner of some is: but
exhorting one another, and so much
the more, as ye see the day approching.
(*Hebrews 10:25*) *KJV*

Two are better wages for their labor. For if
they fall, the one will lift up his fellow:
but woe unto himthat is alone: for he
falleth, and there is not a second to lift
him up ... And if one overcome him,
two shall stand against him: and a
threefold cord is not easily broken.
(*Ecclesiastes 4: 9-12*) *Geneva Bible*

When I was afraid, I trusted in thee. I will
rejoice in God, because of his word, I
trust in God,andwill not fear what
flesh can do unto me. Thou hast
counted my wanderings; put my tears
into thy bottle; are they not in thy
register?

When I cry, then mine enemies shall turn
back; this I know, for God is with me.

I will rejoice in God because of his word;
in the Lord will I rejoice because of
his word.

In God do I trust (*Psalm 56:4-11*) *Geneva
Bible*

Chapter Nineteen

To him that is afflicted, pitie should be
shewed from his friend; But he
forsaketh the feare of the Almighty.
(*Job 6:14*) *KJV*

Let every soul be subject unto the higher
powers: for there is no power but of
God: and the powers that be, are
ordained of God. (*Romans 13:1*)
Geneva Bible

Then Peter and the Apostles answered,
and said, We ought rather to obey God
than men. (*Acts 5:29*) *Geneva Bible*

Chapter Twenty

If the world hate you, yee know that it
hated me before it hated you. (*John
15:18*) *KJV*

Blessed are they which suffer persecution

for righteousness' sake; for theirs is the
kingdom of heaven. (*Matthew 5:10*)
Geneva Bible

But I say unto you which hear, Love your
enemies: do well to them which hate
you. (*Luke 6:27*) *Geneva Bible*

So likewise,whosoever he be of you, that
forsaketh not all that he hath, he
cannot be my disciple. (*Luke 14:33*)
Geneva Bible

We give no occasion of offence in any
thing, that our ministry should not be
reprehended. But in all things we
approve ourselves as the ministers of
God, in much patience, in afflictions, in
necessities, in distresses. In stripes, in
prisons, in tumults, in labors,
By watchings, by fastings, by purity, by
knowledge, by long suffering, by
kindness, by the holy Ghost, by love
unfeigned, By the word of truth, by the
power of God, by the armor of
righteousness on the right hand, and on
the left, By honor, and dishonor, by evil
report, and good report, as deceivers,
and yet true:
As unknown, and yet known: as dying, and
behold, we live, as chastened, and yet
not killed:

As sorrowing, and yet always rejoicing: as poor, and yet making many rich: as having nothing, and yet possessing all things.
(*2 Corinthians 6:3-10*) *Geneva Bible*

The Lord is my strength, and praise, and he is become my salvation. He is my God, and I will prepare him a tabernacle: he is my father's God, and I will exalt him. (*Exodus 15:2*) *Geneva Bible*

Chapter Twenty One

And it came to passe when hee made an ende of speaking vnto Saul, that the soule of Ionathan was knit with the soule of Dauid, and Ionathan loued him as his owne soule. (*1 Samuel 18:1-3*) *KJV*

Chapter Twenty Two

For which cause we faint not, but though our outward man perish, yet the inward man is renewed day by day. For our light affliction, which is but for a moment, worketh for vs a farre more exceeding and eternall waight of glory, While we looke not at the things which are seene, but at the things which are

not seene: for the things which are
seene, are temporall, but the things
which are not seene, are eternall. (2
Corinthians 4: 16-18) KJV

Chapter Twenty Three

How are the mightie fallen in the midst of
the battell! O Ionathan, thou wast
slaine in thine high places.
I am distressed for thee, my brother
Ionathan, very pleasant hast thou
beene vnto mee: thy loue to mee was
wonderfull, passing the loue of women.
(2 *Samuel 1:25-26) KJV*

Chapter Twenty Four

Blessed are they that mourne: for they shall
be comforted. (*Matthew 5:4) KJV*

The time of our life is threescore years and
ten, and if they be of strength,
fourscore years: yet their strength is but
labor and sorrow: for it is cut off
quickly, and we flee away.
Who knoweth the power of thy wrath? for
according to thy fear is thine anger.
Teach us so to number our days, that we
may apply our hearts unto wisdom.
Return (O Lord,how long?) and be pacified
toward thy servants.

Fill us with thy mercy in the morning: so
shall we rejoice and be glad all
our days?

Comfort us according to the days that
thou hast afflicted us, and according
to the years that we have seen evil.
Let thy work be seen toward thy
servants, and thy glory upon their
children.

And let the beauty of the Lord our God be
upon us, and direct thou the work of
our hands upon us, even direct the
work of our hands. (*Psalms 90:10-17*)
Geneva Bible

Chapter Twenty Five

Unto the woman he said, I will greatly
multiply thy sorowe and thy
conception. In sorow thou shalt bring
forth children: and thy desire shall be
to thy husband, and hee shall rule ouer
thee. (*Genesis 3:16*) *KJV*

Be merciful unto me, O Lord: for I cry
upon thee continually. (*Psalms 86:3*)
Geneva Bible

Chapter Twenty Six

Behold, I stand at the doore, and knocke: if
any man heare my voyce, and open the

doore, I will come in to him, and will
sup with him, and he with me.

To him that ouercommeth, will I graunt to
sit with mee in my throne, euen as I
also ouercame, and am set downe with
my Father in his throne.

Hee that hath an eare, let him heare what
the Spirit saith vnto the Churches.
(*Revelation* 3:20-22) *KJV*

And after the earthquake came fire, but the
Lorde was not in the fire: and after the
fire, came a still small voice. (*1 Kings*
19:12) *KJV*

Chapter Twenty Seven

And the Lord spake vnto Moses, Goe vnto
Pharaoh, and say vnto him; Thus
sayeth the Lord, Let my people goe,
that they may serue me. (*Exodus*
8:1) *KJV*

Therefore I say unto you, be not careful for
your life, what ye shall eat, or what ye
shall drink: nor yet for your body, what
ye shall put on. Is not the life more
worth than meat? and the body than
raiment?

Behold the fowls of the heaven: for they
sow not, neither reap, nor carry into
the barns: yet your heavenly Father

feedeth them. Are ye not much better
then they?'
Learn how the lilies of the field do grow:
they are not wearied, neither spin:
Yet I say unto you, that even Solomon in all
his glory was not arrayed like one
of these.
Wherefore if God so clothe the grass of the
field which is today, and tomorrow is
cast into the oven, shall he not do much
more unto you, O ye of little faith?
Therefore take no thought, saying, What
shall we eat? or what shall we drink? or
where with shall we be clothed? For
your heavenly Father knoweth, that ye
have need of all these things.
But seek ye first the kingdom of God, and
his righteousness, and all these things
shall be ministered unto you.'
(*Matthew 6:25-31*) *Geneva Bible*

Come unto me, all ye that are weary and
laden, and I will ease you. Take my
yoke on you, and learn of me that I am
meek and lowly in heart: and ye shall
find rest unto your souls. (*Matthew
11:27-29*) *Geneva Bible*

Chapter Twenty Eight

Yea mine owne familiar friend in whom I
trusted, which did eate of my bread,

hath lift vp his heele against me.
(*Psalms* 41:9) *KJV*

Chapter Twenty Nine

> And Iacob vowed a vow, saying, If God
> will be with me, and will keepe me in
> this way that I goe, and will giue me
> bread to eate, and raiment to put on, So
> that I come againe to my fathers house
> in peace: then shall the LORD be my
> God. (*Genesis* 28:20-21) *KJV*

Chapter Thirty

> Goe yee, enquire of the Lord for me, and
> for the people, and for all Iudah,
> concerning the wordes of this booke
> that is found: for great is the wrath of
> the Lord that is kindled against vs,
> because our fathers haue not
> hearkened vnto the woordes of this
> booke, to doe according vnto all that
> which is written concerning vs. (*II
> Kings* 22:13) *KJV*

ACKNOWLEDGMENTS

Many people helped in the writing of this novel but most of all I would like to thank my husband Steve for his unflagging faith and enthusiasm, Deborah Frith and Robin Wade for their encouragement and feedback, Jessica Gardner for her thoughtful edits, and last but not least, Dr Louise Pryke for her wise and patient advice, and for the sweet counsel of her friendship.

FURTHER READING

I read countless books in the writing of this novel but I have listed below the ones I found most useful.

Bobrick, Benson, *The Making of the English Bible*, London 2001.

Bragg, Melvyn, *The Book of Books – The Radical Impact of the King James Bible 1611-2011*, London 2011.

Brown, John, *The English Puritans*, Cambridge 1910.

Chapman, Mark, *Anglicanism – A Very Short Introduction*, Oxford 2006.

Cheetham, Keith, J., *On the Trail of the Pilgrim Fathers*, London 2001.

Culpepper, Scott, *Francis Johnson and the English Separatist Influence*. Macon 2011.

Evans, G.R., The Language and Logic of the the Bible – The Road to Reformation, Cambridge 1985.

Goldingay, John, Numbers and Deuteronomy for Everyone, Louisville 2010.

Higham, Florence, Lancelot Andrewes. London 1952.

Marsh, Christopher, Popular Religion in Sixteenth Century England, London 1998.

McGrath, Alister, In the Beginning. London, 2001.

New, John, F.H., Anglican and Puritan – The Basis of Their Opposition, 1558-1640, London 1964.

Nicolson, Adam, God's Secretaries – The Making of the King James Bible. London 2003.

Norton, David, The King James Bible – A Short History from Tyndale to Today. Cambridge 2011.

Opfell, Olga. S., The King James Bible Translators. Jefferson, 1982.

Scorgie, Glen, G., Strauss, Mark, L., Voth, Steven, M., The Challenge of Bible Translation. Michigan 2003.

Wilson, Derek, The People's Bible – The Remarkable History of the King James Version, Oxford 2010.

ABOUT THE AUTHOR

Historical fiction author Samantha Grosser has an Honours Degree in English Literature and spent many years teaching English both in Asia and Australia. Now, combining a lifelong love of history with a compulsion to write that dates from childhood, Samantha is bringing her passion for telling compelling stories to the world.

She is the author of wartime dramas ANOTHER TIME AND PLACE and THE OFFICER'S AFFAIR. THE KING JAMES MEN is her third novel.

For news, updates, and special offers, sign up to her newsletter at **samgrosserbooks.com** or follow her on **Goodreads.**

And if you'd like to help spread the word about the King James Men, please leave a review on Amazon. Thanks!

ALSO BY SAMANTHA GROSSER

THE OFFICER'S AFFAIR

England, 1944.

For more than two years, Rachel Lock has waited for her husband to
return from the battlefields of Italy, at last he arrives, yet she is devastated
to find he is a different man, a man she cannot love. Disabled and
embittered, Danny can never resume a normal life, and though Rachel is
determined to restore their marriage, it seems the war has broken their
lives beyond repair.

Then Captain Andrews enters the scene, and despite a deep unease
between Danny and his former commander, for Rachel the attraction is
instant, her heart captured by the officer.

What happened in Italy to make Danny so hostile to an officer he once
trusted and admired? And why has Andrews come to visit him in the face
of it?

As Rachel desperately struggles to shake off the ghosts of the war, she is
torn between her loyalties to an empty marriage and her deepest desires.
Only one can prevail in this heart-wrenching novel, which delves into the
devastation left by the Second World War.

Find out more at:

samgrosserbooks.com